A HIGHLY PLACED SOURCE

A HIGHLY PLACED SOURCE

A NOVEL

MICHELLE DALLY

GHOST ROAD PRESS

Library of Congress Cataloging-in-Publication Data.
A Highly Placed Source
Ghost Road Press
ISBN   (Trade pbk.)
13 digit 978-09789456-9-5
10 digit 0-9789456-9-7
Library of Congress Control Number: 2007921500

This book is a work of the author's imagination. Any resemblance to
persons dead or living is purely coincidental.

Ghost Road Press
Denver, Colorado

ghostroadpress.com

ACKNOWLEDGMENTS

So many people contribute to the writing of a book—whether they know it or not. Some, through life experiences and insight, some through support and love, and finally some through hands-on editing and publishing. I would like to thank them all.

To the those who taught me the craft and responsibility of being a journalist: Paula Bodah, Dan Brogan, Patricia Calhoun, Kristina Lindgren and Fred Brown, my gratitude for your lessons, your dedication, your energy, and your humor.

To all those politicians and political staff people I've had the pleasure of working with over the years—especially Sheila Burke, former Chief of Staff to Bob Dole, who taught me that women could be smart, in charge, and still be great moms too; and Rikki Baum, who always had the answer and was willing to explain it to me, and to Gail Schoettler, who has the class to rub shoulders with queens, but consciously spends her limited time mentoring young and not-so-young women like me.

To those who helped restore me to sanity through the years by giving of their time, their hearts and their recovery—strong, wonderful women like Janelle, Vicki, Mary and Tammy (you know who you are!). And to Pam, who out of nowhere came to be the loyal friend I never had. To the entire gang at BYOG (yes, that's a G!) down at the Cornerstone bookstore. I look forward to Thursdays because of each and everyone of you.

To Diane Kimmell, who has guided me through some of the darkest places in the universe, always holding my hand and making me laugh.

To Jenny Davies-Schley, who has made the past four years a delight by being both my business partner and confidante.

To Diane Dillingham and Chris O'Dell who have razor wit and keen insight and make me laugh my socks off at lunch every month or so.

To Carl Hilliard, who I met with weekly while writing this book, and who has always been a surrogate father to me. To Doug Bell, who graciously agreed to copyedit the first draft of this book, in exchange for some dog sitting. To Mindy Werner and Jody Rein, who carefully guided me through major edits and rewrites. To Robin Vidimos, who lent me books, kept my spirits up, and wouldn't let me quit when the arduous process of trying to get published wore me down. To Michael Balfe Howard, who offered to have a party to celebrate. And, of course, to Sonya Unrein and Matt Davis who for some ungodly reason decided they loved this book and took a chance by publishing it.

Finally, to the most important people in the world: Brian, Tucker, Jordan, Taylor and Nick. How else would I have come up with so many ways to say—well, you know. We don't share last names, but we sure as hell make for one great family. I love you all very, very much. Thank you, thank you, thank you.

To Brian, who always believed...

PROLOGUE

Shock's face filled the small television screen in Father Gil Chavez's kitchen. The popular newscaster was standing in front of a burned-out Packard in the middle of a cornfield, his coattail flapping in the breeze. The bottom of the screen scrolled "Rudell, Iowa." The name of the town struck Father Chavez as vaguely familiar.

"A parent's worse nightmare," Ricardo Shock said. "Time doesn't heal this wound. Even after three years, you can still feel the desolation here—"

Suddenly, Chavez knew what was happening. "Sherry Anderson," he breathed to the empty room around him, "I hope you're a hundred miles from a television set."

"This is a place that cries out for a miracle," the newscaster continued, and Chavez felt his heart sink.

"Anything but this," the priest muttered. "Fish and wine, yes, talk about that to get your ratings—but not *this*."

"This is a place that cries out for a miracle," Shock repeated, methodically increasing his volume so that the statement would end in a near cry. Chavez leaned tiredly against the counter.

"Please, not a resurrection, don't make them expect a resurrection," Chavez whispered.

"But what *will* that miracle be?"

Chavez never heard the answer. Still leaning against the counter, he swept his arm out and with the flat of his hand knocked the TV from its perch. The tube bounced once on the linoleum, Shock's tanned face resting on its side, his voice a jumble of static, and then the screen went blank.

Moving slowly, the priest walked to the Formica dinette set in his kitchen and sank into one of its chairs. There he remained, straight-backed and staring, next to the dead TV. He was praying, silently, and without folding his hands.

There were a number of things Father Chavez prayed for on that night. Some—like the fungus he wished would attack Father Hamilton's long fingernails, to make them curl and darken—are not worth repeating. Others—the good wishes for his congregational members, especially those who were ill or had adolescent children—were part of his regular repertoire. But he asked for two blessings that were unusual for him, which had nothing to do with his impatience with his superiors or his concern for his congregation, prayers that related solely to the miracles now due in two days. Chavez prayed that Sherry Anderson be spared the Ricardo show at the site of her son's suicide, that she not be forced to endure both the painful memory and the empty hope that her son would be brought back to life. Chavez also prayed that he be allowed to witness at least one of the miracles God had in store. "It is not for myself only, my Father," Chavez pleaded. "I am afraid that if I am not there, they might miss it *altogether.*"

One of Chavez's special prayers would be answered.

Part One

The Messenger

CHAPTER ONE

Peter Banks was twelve years, thirty-six days old when he was interviewed on the nightly news for the first time. He had counted his age that way, to the day, every day, for as long as he could remember. It made a difference, he would say, knitting his square brown eyebrows together. "It helps to be precise about things." This was one thing Peter was. It was that precision that made Peter so uncomfortable now. Because, to be precise, he was going to have to say the word "masturbate" on prime-time television. It was not something he was looking forward to.

It had all happened too fast.

Just yesterday he had come across Ms. Blakely's picture in the john. Now here he sat, under the lights and at the business end of a very puffy-looking microphone, waiting to talk about his suspension from Rory Middle School. The newscaster was patting his own hair down, glancing nervously at the camera, and Peter almost jumped as he watched the huge black lens swing their way. "The constitutional booby trap of separation of church and state exploded today right here in Colorado," the newscaster started, biting off his words as if they had stayed too long in his mouth. "And with me I have the boy at the eye of the storm that has followed that explosion."

Peter's head spun with visions of explosions and storms—none of which at all described the scene in the principal's office when the decision was made to suspend Peter.

But the newscaster rolled on. "It had seemed a good idea to administrators at Rory Middle School to make lying to school personnel a suspendable offense," the newscaster continued, a slight smirk on his face. "And for the past five years the rule has been used without controversy to suspend dozens of students who were less than truthful about the contents of their lockers and the authors of their term papers..."

Maybe there's another way to say it, Peter was thinking. He wished he had a dictionary, although he wasn't sure they put words like that in the dictionary. He could barely hear what the news guy was saying.

"But now the school is smack in the middle of a constitutional battle over the suspension of Peter Banks—for, of all things, his insistence that he has talked to God!"

Peter shifted uncomfortably under the lights. The school principal really wasn't a bad sort, and had even gone so far as to not put in the report anything about the locker room john. Mr. Overlay hadn't wanted to talk about that at all. It seemed to embarrass him.

"This is about respect, this is not about needs," Overlay kept saying to Peter after Mr. Lombard brought him down to the office. Peter wondered, if he used the word 'needs' would the newscaster understand what he was saying? But he didn't have much time to think. Because just then the newscaster all but yelled "Peter Banks!" and Peter almost fell out of the prickly chair.

"Peter, have you really talked to God?"

Peter squirmed. "Talked," in the literal sense, was not really what he had done. "He answered a question for me," Peter said softly.

"Speak up, son!" the newscaster barked.

"He answered a question for me," Peter repeated.

"And you told your teacher that you talked to God?" the newscaster asked, oblivious to Peter's choice of words.

"I told Mr. Lombard that God had answered a question for me."

"And he suspended you?"

"No," Peter shook his head. "He sent me to the principal's office."

"And *he* suspended you," the newscaster said, too quickly. Peter looked up and noticed, for the first time, a very thin, frantic-looking woman motioning with her hands, like they were a hamster wheel. Peter knew it was a signal of some sort, but he couldn't imagine for what.

He tried to concentrate on answering the newscaster's question. "Well, not right away," Peter said, trying to be fair to the very slow Mr. Overlay. There was, of course, the issue of popping Chris Paulo in the nose, which had brought the whole thing to the attention of Mr. Lombard in the first place. "We talked a long time, and then he suspended me."

"There you have it!" the newscaster all but shouted. "Suspended for believing in God. Could there be a better case for the ACLU?"

Peter felt his face flush.

"Wait," he moaned slightly, and then, gaining courage, said more loudly, "Wait, there's more, really."

"We'll have up-to-the-minute coverage of this story tomorrow, beginning on our early-bird newscast at six," the newscaster said quickly to the camera, not Peter. And, in case Peter thought about trying to insert himself again in the story, his interviewer moved one of his shiny Ferragamo shoes over about five inches and planted it squarely, and very painfully, down on Peter's right foot.

Peter barely managed to swallow the yelp that rose in his throat, but he got the message. The red light on the camera went off and a fat man in jeans and a vest loaded down with wires came over to take him off stage.

"Um, some kind of important stuff got left out, I think," Peter said cautiously to the man as they neared the studio door.

"This is TV," the man said, pulling Peter none too gently along the narrow hallway to the room where his parents were waiting. "It's our job to leave things out. It's called prioritizing."

Prioritizing was the last thing Peter had been thinking about yesterday in the boy's locker room john. He'd thought he was alone. That it would only take a second and no one would know. He was wrong.

"Look who's washing the bird!" the voice rang out from just over Peter's left shoulder. And his heart sunk. Chris Paulo, his head barely visible over the scraped metal wall that was supposed to provide privacy, was peering down at him. He must be standing on the toilet, Peter thought. A quick look over his right shoulder confirmed what Peter expected the minute he saw Paulo: Billy Frye was ogling the unfortunate scene from his perch on the other side. Between the two of them, they had Peter, still clutching a slightly crumpled picture of their English teacher, Ms. Blakely, dead to rights.

"Working on going blind, Banks?" Billy Frye started in. "If your eyeballs fall out, we'll know why, won't we?" he added, laughing hard. "Maybe we could just give those eyeballs a little help?"

Billy Frye was sort of a wide boy who seemed to have reached maximum density in his shape and would at any moment erupt into the Michelin Man. He wasn't the smartest kid around, and he usually played sidekick to someone else who was smarter and meaner than he was. It was easy for Peter to ignore him.

But Chris Paulo was different. Lanky and blond, Paulo had an edge. He was the kind of kid who would throw rocks at squirrels, with the intention of hitting them. Peter had seen him once empty a birdfeeder a well-meaning teacher had hung outside the school. When the squirrels were huddled around the seeds strewn on the grass, Paulo picked off three of them. There was no doubt about it; Chris Paulo was nasty. He also had the goods on Peter.

"Going to Hell, Banks," Paulo was saying now, laughing and pointing. "Going to burn in Hell," he hissed.

Peter's mind reeled, and he pulled up his pants in a hurry, dropping Ms. Blakeley's picture into the toilet as he did so. Then, he turned to the less threatening of the two.

"Everyone knows, Loser, that jacking off has nothing to do with blindness!" he shot back at Billy Frye. "That's just an old wives' tale."

"Who you calling 'Loser'?" Billy demanded, leaning further over his perch above the stall, balancing his stomach on the very top of the metal cubicle.

Peter was trying to decide if he had the guts to reach up and pull as hard as he could on Billy Frye's shirt when Mr. Lombard, the gym teacher, suddenly appeared and the three of them scrambled to their lockers. That should've been the end right there, but it wasn't.

Because Peter still had a question.

Peter knew that Billy Frye was wrong. They had learned that in Sex Ed last year, that masturbation absolutely did not make your eyeballs fall out. But Hell? That was a new one to Peter, certainly something he had never considered as a consequence of his new favorite pastime.

Suddenly, in that one moment in the gym locker room, Peter felt his first pang of sexual guilt. Could something that felt so terribly good, really be all right? Maybe not. The thought terrified him.

But, who could he ask? His best friend Ben would've been his first choice, except that Ben had moved to Oregon when his parents' divorce was final two months ago. Last year Peter would have at least thought about asking his mom; he used to be able to talk to her about anything. But she'd been acting really weird lately, kinda out of it. And she'd taken to saying stuff that bothered him, but he didn't know why. Stuff like, "At least you love me, Peter." Besides, his *mom*? How can you ask your mom about that?

Peter considered last year's science teacher, Mr. Melser, because that's who had taught the Sex Ed class, but he couldn't think of a good way to catch the teacher alone, much less ask the question.

Of course, there was always his dad. Peter just shook his head at that one. No way. In the end, Peter decided to go to the source, something his father would always recommend. He prayed.

Sitting on top of his bed, surrounded by the rubble of his Gameboy, dirty socks and a stack of *Calvin and Hobbes* comic books, he started.

"Dear God," he began. Then Peter remembered you should really kneel when you asked God a question like this. So now, kneeling under the covers in the dark in his bedroom, he asked, "Hey God, is jerking off—I mean masturbation—is that okay with you? Is that a sin? Do you care if I do that? Can you let me know in a hurry, please? Oh, yeah, this is Peter. Peter Banks."

He also gave his address, just in case. You never know how many Peter Banks there were out there, he figured, and he wouldn't want someone else getting his answer. Or at least he didn't think he did.

The answer was there when Peter woke up the next morning. Right there, in his mind. Later, he would tell adults who asked him—media and church officials alike—that it was as if God had left a short tape behind. And he could make it play; he could listen to the subdued boom of the voice—internally—whenever he liked. There was no possibility that he'd get it wrong or screw it up like a game of telephone. He had the exact words. God had said, precisely, that masturbation was "no big deal." It was like a note in his head.

And Peter couldn't wait to spread the word. "You're wrong Paulo," Peter had sneered as best he could after Geometry let out. "God doesn't care if you jack off."

"How do you know, dickface?" Paulo asked.

Peter didn't hesitate for a second. "I know because I asked, and He said it was all right," Peter shouted at the other boy.

In horror, Peter realized how he had sounded. As if he were some dork who believed in angels and harps and said "Yessir" all the time, like those pansies in the Christmas specials. He stood there, in the hallway of Rory Middle School, feeling his panic rise around him. Chris Paulo, momentarily stunned into silence, simply looked at him, eyebrows headed upward.

And then Peter could just see it: Chris Paulo's brain was beginning to function again. His mouth was opening slowly, and Peter didn't want to hear what it said, so he made his hand a fist and slammed it into the other boy's mouth. Well, that's where he'd aimed. Where Peter's fist landed was Chris Paulo's nose, which immediately erupted into a circle of blood and snot. Peter winced at the sound and feel of the cartilage and bone cracking under his knuckles. Some girl shrieked and Mr. Lombard came out of nowhere, hoisted Peter up by the neck of his shirt, and then shoved him down to the principal's office. That's how Peter ended up telling Mr. Overlay about God's message.

"He said He had more important things to worry about and that I ought to enjoy myself as long as it doesn't hurt others." Peter's voice seemed to hang in the air, along with the smell of glue and old wood.

Martin Overlay was stunned by the boy's insistence. "You had a conversation with God?"

Peter hesitated, because it wasn't technically a conversation. He wanted to describe how God had left the tape behind in his head. But he could tell by the principal's face that he only wanted a yes or no answer. "Yes," Peter said.

Overlay read the long hesitation before the answer as proof of a falsehood. And made up his mind then and there what to do. "I can't have students lie to me because they think it's funny," he told Peter. "And I don't want to even discuss the underlying event that precipitated all this," the principal continued. "This is not about needs. This is about respect."

And that's when he'd done it. Overlay suspended Peter for lying. "Lying is the ultimate form of disrespect," Overlay had told the boy, who was too stunned to respond. "It means you don't think the person you're talking to is worth the truth. Well, I'll tell you something

Peter," Overlay said, his face getting red, in the same sort of slow, lazy way the rest of his body moved. "I'm worth the truth. You can bet on it." All Peter could think of was what his dad was going to do to him when he found out.

At that moment, Edward Banks had all but forgotten he had a son. He was at work, where navigating his way through a half dozen large tort cases and keeping an eye on the constantly shifting terrain of office politics often blocked out all other considerations. But that day was worse than usual. Because Edward Banks felt like crap. It wasn't just the usual off-balance feeling, the vague panic in his groin, the awareness of his own thinning hair that he felt most days. No. This was a wholesale deluge: a sudden assault that made his face and ass burn and the hole in the pit of his stomach deepen. It wasn't anything he could take antacid for, although he usually tried them anyway. Right after which he'd stop and check his ankles to make sure they were covered by his pants' cuff. Memories of his adolescent 'high-waters' were still sharp in his mind, even three decades after the fact.

Today the discomfort had to do with Howard Darcy's passing comment about how some lawyers participated in history, and others merely commerce. It was just after the firm's monthly revenue meeting, and Edward had been feeling quite pleased with himself for the moment, because he had settled a major wrongful death suit against the city (they had failed to warn citizens at a certain intersection that jaywalking was dangerous) and his one-third commission had made him the top producer for the month.

Darcy, who in Edward's view wasted his time and the firm's overhead arguing the vagaries of legislative mandates and whether charitable soliciting should be considered protected speech, had not done so well in terms of cash flow. But Darcy *had* managed to get appointed to the American Bar Association's First Amendment committee, and the accomplishment inspired a lot of backslapping all around.

Edward and Darcy had been walking out of the conference room when Darcy let fly his nasty little comment, making it clear that he thought Banks was nothing but a hack, in it for the money, while Darcy himself was a protector of justice, a Constitutional hero! For the life of him, Banks couldn't think of anything snappy to say in response. He could feel the burn start at his balls and work upward. He kept his eyes on the supple indentation his pants' cuffs made when they swung against his shoelaces. He'd ducked into his office as quickly as possible, groping for his stash of Rolaids.

It was like that for the rest of the day. He just couldn't shake it. Not even the hour and a half he spent as an adjunct law professor—bullying the first year law students to whom he taught Torts—helped. He returned to the firm and spent the rest of the day contemplating both his horrifying school years and whether people would laugh at his funeral.

It was this thought he continued to turn over and over even after he got home and took a seat at the head of the dining room table with his wife and son. For Peter, it couldn't have been worse timing.

His mother, of course, already knew. She'd been called to come pick him up at school; her son had been suspended. Her face was flushed when she came to retrieve him, and her head was shaking even before she laid eyes on him.

"Oh Peter," she said to him—and Peter felt the shame immediately. There was nothing worse than hearing *Oh Peter* from his mother.

"I think this will teach your son a valuable lesson, Mrs. Banks," Overlay said, asking her to sign a paper describing the infraction that had caused the suspension. "Honesty is very important here at Rory."

Vivienne nodded and signed the form without a glance. Peter? Lying? Peter didn't lie. She shook her head, trying to focus. Of course, nothing made sense these days. Not Edward, and now not Peter.

She was tired of trying to figure it out. She looked down at her hands and noticed a chip in her nail polish.

"I am so very sorry about this," she managed, sounding out of breath. She tried to think of what Jackie O would've said in this situation. "It won't happen again," she added.

Peter tried to explain to her while they were buckling up.

"Mom, Overlay thinks I lied—"

Peter had barely started when his mother cut him off.

"Oh no, Peter. We're not talking about this now. We'll discuss it when your father comes home." Vivienne Banks wasn't about to dredge through the sordid details leading up to the suspension (suspension!) of her son. Discipline would have to be Edward's purview. She didn't have the energy. She turned the rearview mirror towards her and grimaced at the sight of her own face.

Still, Vivienne thought, glancing back at the road just in time to avoid hitting the curb, it didn't seem right. She'd never, ever caught Peter in a lie; it wasn't his nature. In fact, he was far too open for his own good. 'I thought you said Mr. Mason wasn't eating dinner with us anymore,' Peter had said once at a buffet party of Edward's partners. 'Because of the way his teeth clicked.' Vivienne had been mortified.

Her head was beginning to hurt. "We'll let your father handle this," she said to Peter.

She made the announcement just after the three of them had sat down to dinner and Edward had taken his first bite of pot roast. "Peter's been suspended," she said, a little sigh as punctuation.

Edward had been lost in his own thoughts, wondering whether Darcy was eating pot roast at that moment. "Peter *what*?" he sputtered, his mouth full of stringy meat.

"I got suspended," Peter said before his mother could answer. He didn't want her bearing the brunt of his father's reaction.

"What the hell did you do?" Edward demanded, wondering if Darcy had a son.

"The charge is lying to school officials," said Peter carefully. "But I didn't," he added quickly, noting his mother's smile. The news was more than Edward could take, after such a day. Now even his son was a liability. Setting his mouth on a grim line, he leaned to his right, toward Peter, then put his face close to his son's. "How could you do this to me?"

Vivienne couldn't stand to hear Edward's voice. Not one more word. So she did something she'd never done. She interrupted her husband. "He said he didn't lie, Edward." Her voice was absolutely even.

Edward blinked a few times, staring into space. Whether it was the sudden interruption by his usually passive wife or the notion that Peter was not a liar, Peter never knew. But it was long enough for Vivienne to forge on with what was quickly turning into his defense. "What exactly do they think you lied about?" she asked, as if the answer could only help him.

There it was. The question he'd dreaded all day. Peter glanced quickly at his father, who was staring right back at him. Masturbation was, of course, the answer. That had God said that masturbation was okay. Peter felt his heart rise up in his throat. He couldn't do it.

"He thinks I lied about talking to God," Peter winced.

Edward, who had opened his mouth in preparation to speak, abruptly closed it. And Vivienne again took advantage.

"You've been talking to God, Peter?" she asked lightly. The question was devoid of judgment or inflection. It was as if Vivienne had merely wanted to know who was on the telephone. She wondered how long she could hold herself steady.

"I prayed," Peter said. It was the truth, but not the whole truth, he reminded himself. This wasn't a court of law, after all, he thought, remembering his father's endless definitions of right and wrong, in and out of the courtroom. Peter hoped he had made it to at least the edge of honesty.

Vivienne sat, confused for a moment, which was long enough for Edward to recover from his shock and re-enter the conversation. Peter expected it; he just couldn't understand why his dad was smiling.

"You were suspended for praying? That's an outrage!" Edward cried. Peter shook his head. He wasn't going to get away with it. He needed to tell them, everything. "I was suspended for saying God said something back," he said quietly, certain that his father would recognize there was more to the story.

But Edward was oblivious. An idea was slowly beginning to form. Surely there was some history to be made here. "It's an abuse of power if I ever saw one!" he said.

Edward Banks chewed for a moment, then made his announcement. "There will be no suspension," he said simply. "They'll never know what hit them. It's the best Constitutional case I've seen in years!"

Confused by his father's sudden change in attitude, the boy sat perfectly still, waiting to see what would come next. Later Peter would wish he'd told his dad about Ms. Blakely's picture, Chris Paulo, everything. Yet by then, it would be too late. People would already be threatening to kill him.

CHAPTER TWO

"Abernathy, got a moment?"

The sound of the managing editor calling her name sent a bolt of panic right through her. *Shit*, Gail thought, *this is it. This is finally it.*

She'd imagined this moment thousands of times since her first date with the Professor. How the summons would sound. She always figured it would be: "Gail, in my office." But "got a moment" worked too. She'd tried to guess who would be in the room when she was told. Whether the word "shame" would be used.

Now she wouldn't have to wonder any longer.

They know, they know, she kept thinking.

"Gail!" This time Fraser wasn't polite about it. "I don't have all day!"

Oh, but I do, Gail thought as she walked into his office. She was surprised to see Fraser alone, sitting at his desk. She'd always imagined he would at least get someone from Human Resources, or maybe even the publisher. It seemed like it would take more than one person to tell her that her career was over. That she was toast. You don't have an affair with a political figure when you cover politics, you just don't. It's cardinal rule number one. And the Professor had represented Colorado State House District 65 for three terms now. So she'd always known it would come to this.

Fraser was talking at this point, but Gail could barely hear him through the din of her own thoughts.

"I need you to cover this Banks thing," he was saying.

Gail shook her head. "I don't know anything about banking," she said dumbly.

"Banks! Banks! Peter Banks," Fraser spat at her. "The kid all over Channel 9 last night—suspended for saying he spoke to God."

Gail blinked. "Channel 9?" *I sound like a retard*, she thought.

Fraser grabbed at the air between them. "Channel 9 News, Gail. Remember the news? That's the kind of work we do here—at least some of us still think so."

He was just getting warmed up. It was early in the day, but he noticed that the reporter standing before him looked like dog shit: eyes red, thin, slouching. Maybe she was sick. Maybe hung over. He didn't have time to think about it longer.

"You want me to cover Peter Banks?" Gail asked, still befuddled. "I don't get it."

Fraser rubbed his balding head, exasperated. "You don't have to get it. Just get down to his damned school," Fraser said, any seed of empathy already long gone.

"The legislature is in session today," Gail said, coming out of her stupor and getting angry now that she was fairly certain she still had a job. "I cover the legislature, remember? Lindsey covers education."

"Yeah, well, right now you cover Peter Banks," Fraser shot back. "Lindsey's working on a Sunday story. Hull can fill in at the legislature."

Abernathy wanted to argue that Hull didn't have a clue about the state legislature, that reporters were not interchangeable cogs in a wheel, but then she was seized with the notion that maybe Fraser did know about the Professor and, instead of firing her immediately, was first pulling her off of legislative duty.

Shit, she thought. *I'm this close.*

"Okay, Peter Banks," she said meekly. Under her breath, she said, "Whatever."

State Representative Darren Preston was already well into his speech on the steps of Rory Middle School before Gail Abernathy had finished lighting her cigarette and fastening her seatbelt in the parking garage at the *Sentinel*. She was praying that her fifteen-year-old Camry would start at her first attempt. It did.

Preston's carefully prepared diatribe covered the outrages of public education, public education bureaucrats, and public education bureaucrats who were union members. The thought of all those demons crowded into one brick building, vulnerable to attack, excited Preston more than he was willing to admit.

Ever since the previous evening when he watched the boy interviewed on the local news, Preston felt a surge of adrenaline like he hadn't felt since his first meeting with William Werthall, the evangelist preacher who had saved his soul and set him on the right track to the Lord and politics. That had been thirteen years ago.

Preston was now a state representative for the God-fearing Colorado District 21, and on his way to holding a leadership seat. He specialized in rounding up what he considered errant and weak Republicans, the ones who thought they could claim the revered capital 'R' next to their names and still vote for the scourge of abortion, gay rights, and union-run classrooms.

When he'd seen the kid's face on television last night, Darren Preston thanked his lucky stars, as well as the Reverend Werthall and the good Lord himself. He had asked for assistance in his long and lonely struggle for what was right and now here it was, Heaven-sent. Because there on the box was the very picture of innocence, the tattered victim of Godlessness and bureaucrats. Darren Preston had known the instant he laid eyes on him. Peter Banks was someone he could use.

Now, standing on the front steps of Rory Middle School in front of two television cameras, Preston was wrapping up his first speech on the subject of Peter Banks, and in his own estimation, it was going quite well. "I talk to God every day. Does that mean I should be suspended, fired, hanged? Denver Public Schools seems to think so." Preston let a dramatic pause fill the air. When he started again, he made sure to make the space in the back of his throat catch, like a choked cry. The effect was stunning. "I love God and my country. I will not allow them to be pitted against one another." Preston was aware of the camera on the left lurching forward, zooming in. He slowly lowered his head and covered his eyes with the flat of his hand. He stayed that way until he felt the cameras back up.

Principal Martin Overlay watched Preston's performance from inside his office, his face plastered at the east window as he looked out over the front steps. It did not take him long to pick up the theme of the legislator's speech. Sighing, Overlay picked up his phone and dialed the same number he had been trying since he first heard from Edward Banks late yesterday evening: Denver City Attorney Charlie Doos. And for the umpteenth time, Overlay listened to the dull drone of Doos' machine.

"I'm either away from my desk or on the other line," Doos drawled. "Please leave a message at the tone."

"Godammit, Doos, where are you when I need you? I'm being sued, and that asshole Darren Preston is here!"

Overlay had barely hung up the receiver when it started to ring and shake—his hand still on it. "What do you want?" the fraying man demanded.

"Overlay. This is Doos. I thought it was *you* who wanted *me*."

"Doos, finally," Overlay couldn't help but breathe out a sigh of relief. "Did you see the news last night? God, where have you been?"

"I saw a tape this morning," Doos said. "What is Preston doing?"

"What do you think? Screaming about God and country to the TV cameras. I'm going to have parents swarming all over me."

"I'm on my way over. Don't talk to anyone." It was an order.

"But what if Banks calls me again?" Overlay wasn't about to wait to ask this one until Doos miraculously showed up in his office.

"The kid? You don't know how to handle a kid?"

"The kid's dad, Edward Banks. He just called me up last night and announced, 'I'm suing you, Overlay,' and then he hung up.

"The boy's father is Edward Banks?" It was the first time Overlay had ever heard the man sound the least bit surprised.

"Yes, yes, Edward Banks. That's Peter's father. He made it real personal. As if it was just so goddamned important for him that his son thinks God told him jacking off was okay."

"Whoa—" Doos, who had been reflecting on the elder Banks' latest travesty of justice, the million-five settlement over jaywalking warnings, felt an electrical surge through his backbone. "What did you say? God told this boy jacking off was okay? That's what the boy thinks he was told?"

"Yes," Overlay said, exasperated. "I can't believe Banks would go through with this."

Doos was hardly listening. "Oh, this is sweet," he finally breathed over the line. "Edward Banks' constitutional issue is based on the dirty deed."

Edward Banks had no idea his Constitutional issue was based on the dirty deed. And Peter Banks was uncomfortably aware of his father's impending embarrassment, and was, as he helped his mother to rearrange the utility closet, trying to figure out a good way to break the news. He couldn't find the words. Everything had gotten totally out of hand.

After his father had pronounced at dinner that he was going to take action and make Peter's suspension a Constitutional case, literally, there didn't seem to be time to talk about anything. Edward had immediately gone to the phone and started dialing. First, there was his assistant, who was unmercifully called away from his evening meal and told to start amassing a portfolio of separation of church and state cases involving religious pronouncements on school property. Then there were calls to Rory Middle School, to Overlay's office, and then his home. These were very short calls, during which Peter held his breath, just waiting to hear his father suddenly stop and then mutter that he was sorry that there had been a mistake. It never happened.

What had happened, to Peter's horror, was that when his father finished with Overlay, he called a friend at Channel 9. Did they want the scoop on a major constitutional case involving religion in schools? Edward was blustery enough, and had enough of a reputation in the legal field to earn Peter a spot on the ten o'clock broadcast. And suddenly, Peter found himself in that prickly seat answering questions far too narrow to permit him to tell the story the way it really happened. After that, the boy merely waited until he had enough nerve to tell his father the underpinnings of the whirlwind he was creating. But nerve was something—in the face of his father—Peter found hard to muster.

And now he was home, a day after the suspension, the morning after the newscast, helping his mother around the house with projects Edward had suggested would be "productive" for the both of them. They were three-quarters of the way through cleaning the utility closet and Peter hadn't felt an ounce of courage stir yet.

His mother seemed to have her own issues with Peter's announcement. Vivienne had been worried about her son, privately, for some time. The boy had been spending too much time alone. She had noticed the door to his room locked on a number of occasions when he had been by himself in there, and she could vaguely hear the sound of the television through the door. Drugs, she had thought briefly, and then dismissed it. There was no sign that Peter was on drugs. His eyes weren't red, his grades weren't lagging. And besides, she thought, Peter knows better than that. So she kept her concerns to herself, noting silently, ticking it off in her head, every time she found the door to her son's room locked.

Now, Vivienne was wondering if that sort of laissez-faire attitude had been a mistake. After all, her son was hearing things, voices, and he had insisted that they were religious. Vivienne shuddered and stopped scrubbing the shelf, feeling the tingling the cleanser made on her fingers.

The Banks' had never been religious sorts of people. Edward thought himself too intellectual, Vivienne, just too tired. Not for a moment had Vivienne believed Peter had actually heard a message from on high. No, she was convinced, turning back to her scrubbing, that the boy was hearing things. *Mental things*, she thought darkly.

And "mental things" were not something she was equipped to deal with. The idea that her son might be psychotic seemed like an unreasonable imposition. Doctor's visits, medication, the causes of it all? And what if someone found out? What would she say? The obligation weighed on her. It wasn't Peter's fault, although she did wonder whether some disciplined thinking on his part wouldn't be of some help. But she was more than a little irritated at her husband. Why Edward had gone public with the thing was beyond her. She hadn't meant for him to start suing people all over God's green acres. She had just wanted him to make sure the suspension didn't hurt Peter, not in any permanent way. But a federal case? It was a bit much.

She watched her son now, squatting next to her, rearranging vacuum cleaner attachments on the bottom shelf. It struck her how unfamiliar he seemed, how she didn't know what was going on inside his head, inside his room. All the doors seemed locked.

Of course, Vivienne might have been relieved to find out what was really going on behind Peter's locked bedroom door. What his mind spent most of its time thinking about. She probably would have been—after her initial shock—delighted to find that it was breasts and thighs occupying the boy's attention, not psychotic thoughts.

But Peter couldn't have guessed that in a million years. He didn't know, at the tender age of twelve years and thirty-seven days, that his mother would prefer to hear that he had been beating off in his room almost daily for six months. They worked in silence, which was punctuated only now and then by Vivienne's attempts to find out just how far gone her boy really was. During the silent moments, she debated the pros and cons of electric shock therapy, something she had read about recently in a magazine while waiting for a dental appointment.

"So when you hear these voices, honey, do you also see something? Is there a person there talking to you?" she ventured after Peter had finished with the vacuum cleaner attachments and moved on to the jumble of mop heads and light bulbs on the next shelf.

"I didn't see anything, Mom," Peter said, his voice muffled by the position of his head under the shelf beneath her. "It was just words," Peter tried to explain, hoping she would ask what those words were, so he could get it over with, get it out, let her know, and thus eventually let his father know about the subject of the blessed message.

"I'm sorry. Did you say you don't see anything when these voices come? Does that mean they're just disembodied voices? They just float around you and say things? Do they scream? Or chant? What does it sound like?" Vivienne tried to keep her voice from rising, but the thoughts of electric shock had set her on edge.

"I only heard it once, Mom, and it was God. It wasn't a lot of voices. And He didn't scream at me. He was just there. Inside me."

"Inside you. Okay honey. I'm not pressing. I'm just curious, you know. It's okay, we'll figure it out." She would've asked him exactly what it was he was hearing inside of him, what the message was, but she looked up at that moment from her scrubbing and caught a glimpse of her son's pale face, a smudge of dirt across the left side of his nose, and decided against more questions. He's about to break, she thought. Any pushing and he could shatter in ten million pieces. "It's okay," she said. "We won't talk any more about it."

Peter, who had been waiting for an exit from the trap of his unholy secret, felt his stomach drop. Both mother and son bent their heads over their respective shelves and worked on restoring order.

Just about the time Vivienne and Peter were finishing with the utility closet, Gail Abernathy stumbled out of her car in the school parking lot and turned to watch Preston's suited back disappear into the blond brick building.

It was a back she knew well. The press table at the legislature was positioned behind the main podium. She had spent most of the day for the past three years watching the backs of state legislators.

"What the fuck is he doing here?" she muttered. The answer was abundantly clear as soon as the question escaped her lips. She could see the long-legged cameras from a distance. In the minutes it took her to gather her purse and notebook, she wondered briefly if this was why Fraser, the managing editor, had wanted her to come. Then she checked herself. Preston wouldn't have called the print media for his little grandstanding, she thought. He was notorious for letting the papers pick up a story only after he had broken it on television. It was his trademark, a smart one at that, since broadcast news wasn't quite as "discriminating" in what they would cover. There was still no good reason for Fraser to have assigned her this story. Which meant it was still a huge possibility that her affair with the Professor had been uncovered and her job was hanging by a thread. "Prick," she said softly as she hustled up the stairs, unsure whether she were referring to Preston or the Professor himself.

By the time Gail found Rory Middle School's administrative office, Preston had already lost his battle with Overlay. "I cannot give you the address of a student, Mr. Preston," Overlay said slowly. It was the same tone, voice, and manner Overlay used with hyperactive students who were brought to his office several times a day. A patient voice that carried with it the message that the big, slug-like man wanted to help, but couldn't. Preston was livid.

"I am a state legislator and therefore an entrusted public servant, and I have every right to know where to find Peter Banks. I must speak with him," Preston was saying. Gail could see he had already developed the twitch he sometimes got on the floor of the House when he made long impassioned speeches. "If only to let him know that there are God-fearing people on his side."

Overlay sighed, long and slow, which made Preston boil more. "I'm sorry Representative Preston. I can't do anything for you. My hands are tied. I am expecting City Attorney Charles Doos any moment now, and you are welcome to talk with him when he arrives. But I'm sure he'll tell you the same thing. Student records, including their addresses, are not for public consumption."

Preston stood for a moment considering his options. It struck Gail how small Preston looked, off the podium, in the real world, facing a man who dealt with egomaniacal bullies on a daily basis. This could be fun, she thought.

Finally, Preston made up his mind. "I will speak to your superiors," he said to Overlay, then turned on his left heel and started back down the hall toward the main entrance and the double steel doors.

It would've been a movie-like exit except that the bell rang and suddenly the tile hallway was filled with the bodies of adolescents in the full bloom of that hormone-ravaged stage. Overlay and Gail watched as the well-dressed legislator, buffeted by the nonplussed students, made an uneven exit through the doors, the back of his neck a radish red. Then Overlay met Gail's eyes. "I can't give you Peter Banks' address either," he said wearily

"That's okay," Gail responded quickly. "I'll find him. I just want to ask you a few questions about the lawsuit and the suspension."

"I can't answer any questions," Overlay told her. "You'll have to speak to the city attorney."

Gail sighed. This was going to be a hard story to write if no one would say anything—and in her experience, city attorneys were the last people to speak on the record.

She felt a wave of desperation. It was going to be one of those days. And she couldn't even have a drink once it was over. The Professor, of course, would be there, but he was anything but effective in his attempts at providing comfort.

Beside her, Martin Overlay was doing what he did best: observing. The woman standing before him wasn't what he expected from a reporter. She certainly wasn't like the little old lady the *Sentinel* usually sent out on education stories. That woman, he thought to himself, was a pushy crone. No, *this* reporter struck Overlay more like one of the thirteen-year-old kids he dealt with every day. The girls with more eyeliner than sense, desperation oozing from every pore. This, Overlay knew at once, was a woman in trouble. And, after twenty-five years of running schools full of girls just like her, Overlay wanted to help.

"I'll tell you what," he said softly, standing in the small pool of silence that had overtaken them both, watching the halls clear as the students disappeared into their next classes and another bell rang. "You should talk to the boy's father, Edward Banks."

Gail came out of her reverie over the Professor and his limp dick just in time. "Edward Banks?" she repeated, jotting the name down on her notebook.

"I'm not supposed to tell you anything, so you didn't get it from me," Overlay said softly. "Edward Banks. He's an attorney in town, and he's the boy's father. He'll tell you his side. But just remember, he doesn't know everything."

"Everything?" Gail stopped. "What do you mean he *doesn't know everything?*"

"You'll see," Overlay told her. And with that, he turned and left Gail in the hallway, alone in the now-empty tiled hallway that smelled like Hostess Twinkies and sour milk. She stood for a moment longer, taking in the scent. Then she remembered that she'd rather be inhaling a cigarette and started making her way out of the school. She was structuring the story in her mind—at least the pieces she had—so she almost missed the hissing of a skinny boy with blond, greasy hair who had signaled to her from his vantage point in a dusty stairwell.

Gail was concentrating on the two pieces she had so far. The father, if he would talk, would tell her he was outraged at the boy's dismissal and he was suing. He might, or might not, let her speak to his son. But he had, she remembered, let his son appear on television, so she had a shot. On the other hand, she also had the virulent Preston, who was no doubt on the warpath—

"Pssst, pssst," she could hear just over her thoughts. Turning, she saw a boy who leaned against the banister, playing with a long chain that was dangling from his belt loop.

Gail approached. "Did you want to talk to me?" she asked, figuring the youth to be about fourteen.

Peter Banks would've been able to tell Gail that Chris Paulo was thirteen and ninety-six days old, but was very immature for his age. Paulo had been held back, flunked, in fourth grade and had been using his larger stature and his older air as a weapon to bully the younger kids ever since. But Gail knew none of this at the time of her encounter with the boy at the top of the stairs. As she got closer, aside from her guesses at his age, the only other thing she noticed was that his nose was swollen and he had a bruise under one eye. "Did you want to talk to me?" she asked again.

The boy—Chris Paulo—hissed. "Not so loud," he said, glancing around. "Are you a reporter?"

Gail smiled. Maybe this was just a youngster who dreamed of becoming Bob Woodward, of breaking the biggest story of the century, of seeing his name in print. "Yes, I'm a reporter, for the *Sentinel*," she answered, more softly.

Chris Paulo had never heard of Bob Woodward and dreamed not of pounding beats and computer keys, but other kids' heads. He hadn't spent more than ten seconds thinking of his future. He was thirteen, after all. No, Chris Paulo had other reasons for asking his question. "You're here about Peter Banks, aren't you?" It sounded more like an accusation than a question.

"Yes."

"I thought so."

"Who are you?" Gail asked, nonchalantly. If the students were going to start talking about it and she could start getting quotes from kids about how they felt about God and messages from Him, the story would be that much better.

"I'm the one who got this from Peter Banks," Paulo said, pointing to his swollen nose. "And I also know what he says he talked to God about."

Gail leaned against the wall next to the kid and breathed slowly. "So says you," she said, looking like she thought the kid was crazy. It was a learned response, one she had developed as the mother of an eight-year-old, one that never failed to make a kid talk more, to make him lose his fear of the ramifications of his statements and just want to prove his case. She had only once consciously used the technique in an interview before, with the House Speaker, who spilled his rather sizable guts instantly.

Chris Paulo was no different. And that's how Gail Abernathy became the first reporter, print or broadcast, to find out exactly what God thought about washing the bird.

CHAPTER THREE

In a two-newspaper town, editors pay great attention to headlines. They're often the reason consumers choose one paper over another. "Scandal Rocks Senate," for instance, sells. "Committee Passes Budget," does not. And on the second day of the Peter Banks story, the first day in which the newspapers even had the opportunity to play, the editors at the *Denver Sentinel* faced one of the biggest challenges of their lives. They had a scoop that was unmentionable.

Lincoln Fraser, the managing editor who had sent Gail out on the story, was well known for his shiny, mostly-bald head in the newsroom, but even he was seen that day pulling at his hair. "The kid asked God about whacking off?" Fraser screamed it across the wide-open space of the newsroom, ignoring the grimaces and cackles that rose around him. "That's what this is about?"

Abernathy, who, for the first time in five days, wasn't thinking about how good it would feel to have a drink, merely nodded. "He asked a question that meant a lot to him," she said, suppressing the smile, "and he got the answer."

Fraser looked at her sideways for a moment and then sighed. "I could've used that answer when I was his age."

From what Gail could see, a lot of men in the newsroom felt the same way. It was the first time she had ever seen other editors, on deadline, offer to help come up with a headline for a story off their beat. Five of them, count 'em, *five* of the *Sentinel's* most feared editors had spent much of the afternoon crowded around the city desk offering support. Buck Olofsson, who knew the difference between a shell and a bullet and was never lax to beat it into a reporter; Joe Random, who once won part of a Pulitzer for reporting on a shady savings and loan deal; Nelson Arb, who made the lifestyle section sing, despite its overabundance of articles on things like aromatherapy; even David Urbach of Business and Mike Carr from Sports crossed the line to the city desk to put in their two cents. The offerings were as varied as they were numerous. Some were straightforward: "God Gives Masturbation Okay." Some took advantage of the device of alliteration: "Self-Satisfaction not Sin." Others, which the five editors gathered and chuckled over, were never meant for the innocent public, but made the rounds in the newsroom in record time. "Oh Cum all Ye Faithful" was a particular favorite.

Gail, for the most part, was too busy to even pretend to join in the overwhelmingly male antics that were taking place around her. She had a story to write, and a tricky one at that. Not only did she have to write a story for a "family paper" about masturbation, but she also was fairly certain no other reporter had the story she did, and she didn't want to press her sources so hard that they panicked and ran to the networks or the *Herald*, the competing paper, to clarify themselves. In short, Gail had figured out that Edward Banks had no idea what he was doing.

It didn't start out that way. Even Chris Paulo, in all of his thirteen-year-old angst, had no idea that he and Overlay were the only people to whom Peter had revealed the message. Unaware of his status as one of the chosen two, Paulo didn't feel particularly blessed or special or enlightened. What he felt was pissed.

Vindictiveness was the order of the day for Chris Paulo when he called the harried-looking woman over to him in the hallway of Rory Middle School. The face of Peter Banks staring out at him from the television screen the night before had galled him. Paulo had spent the afternoon in the emergency room, getting his nose x-rayed (hairline fracture) and trying to explain to his mom that he had nothing to do with the fight Overlay had called her about. Madge Paulo—who knew her son's acid tongue all too well—had not been convinced, and so proceeded to ground him for the next two weeks. Seething and sore, with ropey white cotton still stuffed up his nostrils, Chris had turned on the television set hoping to watch music videos to dull the pain, and instead found himself face-to-face with Peter Banks.

He watched the twerp talk about getting suspended for saying he had a message from God, and it had been too much for the injured boy. "Tell him what your goddamned message was about, you dickhead," Paulo shouted to the oblivious screen, whereupon his mother extended his grounding to three weeks for the outburst.

But Peter hadn't told. There was no mention of beating off whatsoever on the evening news. Nothing. Zip. Chris Paulo had gone to bed that night muttering to himself about the injustice in the world and hoping to God—without really thinking about the entity he was praying to—that revenge would be taken, and taken soon.

He wasn't about to wait for it.

As best as Chris Paulo could figure, Peter Banks had convinced his father that he truly had heard from God about masturbation and his dad wasn't daunted by the subject matter at all. Now Peter's dad was suing the school (something Chris Paulo had always wanted to do) and Peter was a hero on the nightly news while Chris had to sit at home grounded with a slightly fractured nose.

If there was justice to be had, Chris Paulo figured, he would have to find it himself. So when he saw fat old Overlay talking to the woman with the notebook, Chris started forming his plans right away. If Peter's dad thought he could fool the world, sue the school without mentioning that his son beat off, then Chris had news for him.

Gail Abernathy would later think about her discussion with the boy with the swollen nose and wonder how she'd gotten through it without laughing. It wasn't her fault she didn't know what "washing the bird" meant. It certainly hadn't been a euphemism that was bandied about in her childhood. After she had taunted the lanky boy in front of her with the tried and true *so says you*—he ranted about Peter Banks and *washing the bird*.

"What bird?" she had asked, hazily wondering if she wouldn't be better off if Fraser fired her. It would be better than standing in dim stairwells in smelly schools trying to get straight answers from pimply teenagers.

"Washing the bird, you know," Paulo said, trying not to look at the woman's face. "Peter Banks said God told him washing the bird was all right." But she didn't get it. He knew she didn't get it. He stole a look up at her face and could see in her eyes not shock or amusement or any of the expressions he usually saw when a grown-up talked about sex. Instead, she was just staring down at him, looking irritable and impatient, like she hadn't gotten enough sleep, or her stomach hurt. "You know, beating off, jacking it, polishing the pewter,"

Paulo tried to think of all the ways he knew to describe it. In frustration, he thought maybe a visual example would help her, so he grabbed his balls. That did it.

"Oh my." Gail's eyes flew open as soon as the boy in front of her made a move for his crotch. He was talking about masturbation. Peter Banks and masturbation. "Masturbation," she said more loudly than she had meant to, and both of them were trapped for a moment, listening to the word echo up the metal stairs.

"Yeah, masturbation," Paulo said, nodding. He had her now. "Peter Banks told me, right before he gave me this," and here, he pointed at his nose, "that God had told him it was okay to masturbate."

"That's what the message was? That masturbation was okay? Was that all the message was?" Gail asked the boy, suddenly eager to know what else was all right with the Universe. Could it be that having an affair with an almost sixty-year-old, selectively impotent, married legislator was something God thought was okay, too? It couldn't be that easy.

"That's what Peter told me," Paulo said defiantly, satisfied he had passed the message on, that Peter Banks wouldn't get away with his stardom, or with Paulo's broken nose.

Gail stood for a moment in front of Chris Paulo and took a breath. "Does Overlay know about this?" she asked the boy, then watched him shrug inside his oversized T-shirt.

"I don't know what Overlay knows," he told her. "Maybe. He usually knows things."

Gail grimaced. Overlay would never be able to discuss that with her, at least not until it had been become public. She wondered distractedly just how long it would be until Edward Banks filed his suit in court. And even then, would the complaint be detailed enough to list what exactly the religious message in question concerned. *Probably not*, she thought.

Abernathy hadn't stopped to think just why a father would alert the media to the fact that his son was discussing private sex acts with God. If she had thought about it, she probably would've assumed that Peter Banks' father was a model of rationality, tolerant of common— if embarrassing—acts by young boys. After all, she hadn't yet met Edward Banks. But after meeting the man, she'd think again. By that time, she'd also understand that he knew nothing about it. He was fighting to make an impression on someone. But not God.

Before Gail left Chris Paulo, she asked him his name and told him that what he had said to her would be in the paper. "Do you understand that I'm planning to write about this?" she asked the boy, again, trying not to look like she needed his input, that she was desperate for the information.

"Yeah, I know. I don't care. No one I know even reads the damn papers. I just want people to know that Peter Banks isn't some sort of hero, that's all. You tell them that. You tell them that he's just a jerk off who jerks off. You tell them."

Gail nodded. "Oh, I'll let them know what you say," she said carefully, wondering just how she was going to get Fraser to let her write the story without confirmation. Just on the word of a thirteen-year-old boy. No parental release. It would never happen, she figured. It was going to take Edward Banks openly discussing it with her. And that was what she was after when she left the school.

It was fairly easy to find Edward Banks. He was listed in the Denver directory under lawyers, and he belonged to the rather large and staid firm of Holsby & Ashford. She wasn't about to give him the chance to tell her "No comment" over the phone. Gail was in the waiting room of Holsby & Ashford not twenty minutes after she had finished with Chris Paulo.

But as soon as she opened the heavy gilded door to the offices of Holsby & Ashford, Gail knew she was in trouble. Three television cameras, their attendant cameramen, and their attendant television reporters, all busily checking their makeup and holding up white scraps of paper to help the cameramen adjust for the light, were crowded into the usually ample space. And, there, next to the receptionist's desk, stood Jeff Ronald, a reporter for the *Herald*, the *Sentinel's* rival paper.

Gail smiled sadly. How silly to think she'd have a scoop, just because a thirteen-year-old boy deigned to talk to her in the stairwell. She was surrounded by a roomful of reporters, all of whom would ask the question that had struck her the first instant: Just what was the message from God?

Soon the room would be filled with the laughter of television cameramen (generally bored, silent types) and the smirks of their reporters who would try to sum up their stories in twenty seconds or less about the boy who got the go ahead from God to beat off.

But that wasn't the way it happened.

Edward Banks did, of course, allow the interview.

He had been waiting, in fact, for the crowd to assemble, instructing his receptionist to let him know when representatives of all three of local stations had arrived, as well as each of the major newspapers. It was Gail who had kept them all waiting. Not her specifically, of course, but Edward Banks was not going to make an appearance until someone from the *Sentinel* had shown up.

Making history required scribes: eyewitnesses who would record what they saw, what they heard, and why it mattered. He wondered if Darcy took the *Sentinel* or *Herald*.

Gail stood in the corner behind one of the cameras, not wanting to exchange pleasantries with Ronald (she was in no danger of conversation with the television reporters; they didn't usually make it a habit to talk to their print colleagues). But the receptionist spotted her anyway and waved her over. "Are you from the *Sentinel*?" the well-dressed woman asked Gail. The receptionist was slightly out of breath, as if all the activity in the usually serene office had thrown her off. Maybe I should be a receptionist instead of a reporter, Gail thought. It looked like a terribly safe line of work. The large mahogany desk and bank of phones were protection against any element she could think of.

"That's me," Gail answered. The receptionist seemed to be almost gulping air as she punched a button on one of her phones and spoke into the headset that graced her coiffed head.

"Mr. Banks, they're ready for you," she said.

It would take Edward Banks but a few seconds to burst in from the glass door at the far end of the room, striding confidently into the bevy of media. "Now, now, how do you want to do this?" he asked, his voice friendly and accommodating, completely comfortable in front of the cameras. There was some confusion for a few minutes while lighting was adjusted and a chair moved so that Edward Banks would have a well-lit space from which to address the crowd. He was sweating slightly, Gail noticed, and he seemed unusually interested in his pant cuffs. He didn't look at all to her like the type that would be terribly understanding of his son's proclivity to masturbate.

Out of the corner of her eye, Gail saw Jeff Ronald sinking into a seat near the far end, near Edward Banks, but out of the line of the cameras. She could tell he had some questions and wanted to be in a place where Banks could easily recognize him.

I'm toast, Gail thought again.

"I have prepared the preliminaries of a federal case against the Denver Public School system," the elder Banks announced to the room. Gail watched the pens scratch across the surface of reporter notebooks, wondering when she would start to do the same.

"I have done so because I believe a very important Constitutional principle has been violated. And that principle is one I hold very dear. It is what sets us apart from the rest of the world, one that led to the very development of this country, and if allowed to be run roughshod over, will indeed lead to this country's downfall."

Gail rolled her eyes from the safety of her position at the other end of the room. She was sure the Union would continue to exist whether or not Peter Banks had been given the okay from God to beat off.

"That principle, of course, is our long-held and revered belief in the separation of church and state," Edward Banks said, pointing his little finger to make sure the emphasis of the statement got across. Years before, Vivienne had tried to break him of the habit of pointing while he was making what he considered were his most salient points. But the best Vivienne had been able to manage was getting the man to switch from his index finger to his pinky, which now made Edward Banks look even more bizarre than he sounded.

"My son Peter is twelve-years-old," Edward continued. "Yesterday, he informed the principal of his middle school that he had talked with God. An innocent remark from an innocent boy, before an authoritarian figure who is granted his power—and this is most important—from us, the taxpayers in this state."

Gail felt as if she were in a dream. She watched pens scribble hastily, then managed to pull out her notebook and start writing down some of Banks' speech.

"For that, and nothing more than that," Banks continued, his barrel chest puffing out, "my son was suspended from school for lying. For *lying*, ladies and gentlemen." Repetition, Edward Banks had learned in court—after years in front of drowsy judges—was very important. "It's an injustice I intend to right."

Gail held her breath as pens scratched a second longer, and then voices started up from Banks' audience.

"When will the suit be filed?"

"Has your son ever been in trouble before?"

"Is the ACLU joining in?"

The questions bounced off the wall to Edward Banks' right, and he waved at them, as if trying to return them with a squash racquet. "Now, now—" Edward Banks cautioned. "Mr. Doos, the city attorney, has been good enough to agree to discuss the complaint tomorrow in his office. Until then, I can't give you much more detail than I already have." He paused for a moment and added, "For now, let it suffice that my son is a model student. Straight A's, I believe, last semester." Peter Banks would've cringed at this. To be precise, he had received a C in gym and a B in French. But Edward Banks had registered neither grade at the time. He was slightly more accurate on his next response. "As far as the ACLU goes, I have traded voice-mail with their local director for the past couple of hours, so I cannot answer for them. But I assume that once they take a good look at the case, they'll want to file a brief in support of my complaint."

The ACLU director for Colorado was home ill with a bad case of food poisoning. While he may have been cursing the bacterial invasion for the thirteen hours he would alternately vomit and shiver and then drift off into exhausted sleep, later, much later, he would thank his lucky stars.

"Mr. Banks, what did your son talk to God about?" The question, posed by Jeff Ronald, who was ignoring the dirty looks from the television reporters who hated being interrupted, stopped Gail's heart in mid-beat. *Here we go*, she thought.

But Edward Banks looked struck not with irritation, as if someone had asked him a question he didn't want to answer. No, Edward Banks, looked startled, the way a person looks when he has been asked a question which he had never thought of himself. She had been in journalism long enough to recognize the blank stare and raised eyebrows. It was then she knew Edward Banks had no idea what God had talked to his son about. "Jesus Christ," she muttered, loud enough to draw a look of supreme disapproval from the receptionist.

Edward recovered quickly, although the craving for an antacid was overpowering. "I don't presume to question my son about his private spiritual explorations," Edward said quickly, converting the look of surprise on his face to one of disdain. "I respect his desire to make a spiritual connection. We should all have more of that desire."

Gail tried to suppress a smirk. *If Edward Banks only knew,* she thought, *just what sort of desire he were respecting, he might think twice about admonishing others to have more of it.* The television reporters were shouting more questions at the attorney, taking the reins back from Jeff Ronald. Gail didn't wait to hear what they had to say. Only one person had the answer she needed to print the story that was writing itself. That person was Peter Banks.

She left the office just as Banks was giving a recital of his legal background, noting with a certain superiority that he not only practiced law, he taught it to the young minds at Denver University. Gail had only seconds with which to take pity on his students before the elevator doors shut. Then she was on her way down to ground level.

Peter and Vivienne had finished cleaning the utility closet long before Edward had ever started speaking. Convinced her son was going mad or had already arrived there, Vivienne was busy searching the phone book for a decent counselor (she was trying to figure out exactly what would constitute a "decent" counselor and, simultaneously, how that would be evident from a telephone listing, and why she had been the unlucky parent of such a child.) Peter was quietly playing video games in his room, wondering when the shit would hit the fan. He was intent on the game when the doorbell rang, and didn't raise his head until Vivienne called his name.

Gail found Peter Banks easily—too easily, she thought, when she looked up Edward Banks in the phone directory and found a listing for "Edward Banks, Atty." on Sultan Lane. She expected to find a mass of cars stationed outside the house, a defense already arranged within, and the complete denial of her entry. But the reporters— both television and print—who had been assigned to the story were all still at Edward Banks' office, listening to him ramble about the sad state of legal education, the practice of law, and the ridiculousness of allowing judges to be subject to recall.

So she arrived at Peter's house to find the yard deserted, the lilac bushes still intact. She flicked a cigarette butt into one, then stared after it, realizing that it was something the Professor would do. So she bent over and picked it up. Then she crushed the butt on the bottom of her shoe and tossed it in her purse.

When she pressed the doorbell, Gail had her fingers crossed that Mrs. Banks would let her speak with the boy, but she couldn't imagine that happening. Gail herself had long ago given instructions to her son, Dillon, never to talk to a reporter unless she had given him written permission. She knew too well how callous some could be with the misstatements and outbursts of the young, and she already felt that Dillon had been through enough because of her.

But Vivienne hadn't had much practice with the press. And at the time, although she felt her son was in immediate danger from the voices that were stirring inside his head, she couldn't see that the oncoming onslaught would be external. Peter's mother thus answered the doorbell more startled than defensive, and when she saw the woman who was just about her age (actually, about five years younger), she felt a twinge of the loneliness she routinely pushed down threaten to surface.

"Can I help you?" Vivienne asked the stranger who reeked of cigarette smoke.

Gail smiled at the polite greeting. "I'm from the *Sentinel*," she explained, trying not to sound apologetic. "I was wondering if I could have a few words with Peter?"

"The *Sentinel*? The paper?" Vivienne asked, wondering if the woman had seen the *Herald* still lying in the front yard, and if she had taken offense.

"I'm doing a story on the suspension. I believe Peter's already talked to Channel 9 about it?" Gail added quickly. "I wanted to make sure I got it right."

Vivienne's brow furrowed, but she couldn't think of any reason not to let the other woman in. Edward had already exposed the boy to a much slicker looking reporter, that awful man from last night, who had shaken her hand with his cold one and then told them to wait in that despicably dirty green room. "I suppose that would be all right," she answered, holding the door open. Gail moved inside quickly, in case the woman changed her mind. "I'm Vivienne Banks, Peter's mother."

Gail smiled again and took the woman's hand. "I appreciate it, Mrs. Banks," she said carefully. "I'm a mother too," she added. "I won't scare him." It had been the exactly right thing to say. Vivienne moved quickly to close the phone book on the kitchen table. Gail accepted the offer of a cup of coffee and sat down at the immaculate table while Vivienne went to call Peter. When he appeared, it took Gail a few moments to begin. She was so surprised at how young he looked, just a few years older than Dillon, her own son, and with the same sort of little boy shyness.

"Hello Peter. My name is Gail Abernathy. I'm a reporter from the *Sentinel*."

Peter, unlike Chris Paulo, looked at her as if the last thing he wanted to do was talk to a reporter. "Hello," he said simply.

"I wanted to ask you a few questions about your suspension. Is that okay?" Gail asked. Vivienne came back into the kitchen and moved toward the coffee maker, starting to make a fresh pot. Gail felt the boy startle at his mother's entrance. She knew his problem immediately.

"Maybe we should sit in the backyard. Would that make you more comfortable?" she asked, hoping that Vivienne would not object. But Vivienne merely smiled at them weakly, as if it were almost too much for her to navigate a pot of coffee with so much on her mind. Gail followed Peter's lead out the back door, and they began to pace the manicured lawn together, his head at her shoulder. "I talked to Chris Paulo this morning, Peter," Gail said softly after they had rounded an orderly garden of kitchen herbs. "Do you want to tell me about it?"

Peter, who had been holding his breath until he heard the name Chris Paulo, expelled a long stream of air.

"Chris said that you talked to God about masturbation," she said quietly, watching him flinch at the last word.

"I asked Him about masturbation, if it was, you know, okay." Peter tugged at the bottom of his shirt wondering if the woman were going to laugh at him. But when he looked up, she didn't look as though she found anything funny about it.

"You asked Him about masturbation," she repeated, in order to memorize the way he said it. She didn't want to pull out the notebook now. It would put the boy off.

"Yeah, people keep saying I talked to Him like He was standing in front of me and I said it. That isn't the way it happened," Peter told her, desperate to get it right. "I asked Him, I said a prayer," and it was almost as embarrassing for Peter to say "prayer" as it was "masturbation."

"You prayed," Gail repeated.

"Yeah. And then, when I woke up in the morning, I had the answer," Peter said. "This voice in my head. And the voice said God had enough things to worry about and as long as I didn't hurt anyone else, it is fine. Masturbation is fine. He doesn't care." Peter had stopped by an oak and was picking at the bark of the mammoth tree.

Gail nodded. "I see." Her heart sank at the sight of his face. This was one boy who had no desire to be anyone's hero, despite what Chris Paulo had said. What his father had stirred up around him, Gail thought, was a tempest Peter had never dreamed of walking through. "So how did that get you suspended?"

Peter let out another extraordinary sigh, and the words tumbled out. He told her the whole story, even the part about being caught in the stall by Chris Paulo and Billy Frye.

"So Mr. Overlay knows what God said to you?" Gail asked.

"Yes," Peter said solemnly, looking at the ground. "Mr. Overlay knows."

Gail bent down so she could look at his face. "But your dad doesn't know, does he?"

"No," Peter answered, batting his tears with his long eyelashes.

"How about your mom?" Gail asked, in barely a whisper.

Peter shook his head, his mouth clamped shut, suppressing a sob. Gail put her hand on the boy's shoulder. *Good Christ,* she thought, *I don't want to write this story.* There was enough guilt in her life. The old stuff—like divorcing her husband when Dillon was four, the problem with drinking she was trying so hard to deal with—and now the damn Professor. She didn't need anything else.

"You know this is going to come out, don't you?" Gail said, as evenly as she could. Peter nodded again, his hands now covering his eyes.

"I'm sorry, Peter," It was like apologizing before you slapped someone. Later at the office, she would have a long discussion with Fraser about whether it was fair to the boy to run the story, but the bald editor would laugh—literally—in her face. "As soon as Doos and Banks file their papers tomorrow, the world will know, sweetheart," Fraser said. "We'll just have the story a day earlier. That's what this game's all about."

Gail didn't tell Fraser that it wasn't at all a game to her, and that he hadn't looked at the expression on Peter's face and wouldn't have to live with it. It wouldn't have made any difference anyway to Lincoln Fraser. She had the story, and he would run with it. Despite her attempts at discouraging the story, Gail never believed for a second it wouldn't run, or that she wouldn't write it. Even when she was looking at Peter Banks' face as they stood in the expansive backyard and discussed the terrible fate that lay ahead. It would be embarrassing, she knew, and would probably scar the boy, but the story was the result of his father's actions, not hers. Still, she tried to think of some way to soften the blow.

"I think it would be better if you told your mom, Peter," Gail said finally. It was her turn to sigh with relief. That would help, if the family was prepared. Maybe they could stop this thing now.

Of course, every journalism professor in the country would've slapped her hand for that one. You didn't insert yourself into stories, provide advice to people you were interviewing. It was a supreme no-no. If anything, she should've told him not to tell anyone, to preserve the exclusive nature of her story. But she didn't. It had something to do with Dillon and the divorce and all the booze and to some extent, the Professor. Gail felt the urgent need to be on the right side of something. So she told him. "I have a son, Peter, and he's not that much younger than you are. I would want to know, and I would think it was okay. Your mom's going to think so, too."

Peter thought about his mother for a moment. Yes, she would be shocked, but maybe she could figure a way out, a way to avoid embarrassment. She was good at that. Like kicking dropped food under the table, or hiding a stain by rolling up a sleeve. He made up his mind, not with a forceful resolve but like a drop kick in soccer. The ball was there, his foot was swinging, and he might as well aim it.

"Okay," he said. "I will."

"Good boy," Gail said, stroking his hair absentmindedly, forgetting that he wasn't Dillon.

Afterward, when Gail had retreated to her car to drag on a cigarette, Peter would sit down with his mother at the immaculate kitchen table and come clean about the dirty deed. He had been right. After her initial shock, his mother would be an important ally, at least for a while. Vivienne would never tell him that she was actually relieved to hear about the masturbation, relieved that he wasn't hearing voices and losing his mind as she'd thought he was, but simply rationalizing the biological necessity of masturbation. After all, she knew about the biological necessity of masturbation, although she never allowed herself to think about it. For an afternoon at least, she would be relieved that she was the mother of a normal boy, with normal needs and responses, one whose father had gone a step too far. Her relief gave her the courage to call her husband's office immediately, to cut off the spectacle as soon as it was feasible. "Edward, come home now," she had said into the phone in a tone Edward couldn't remember hearing before.

The Banks' gave no more interviews that day, nor the next morning. Edward Banks promised his wife that he would end his assault on the Denver Public School system as soon as he met with Doos the following afternoon at three-thirty. He swore he would make the announcement, the case would be dropped, and they would wait for the fury to die down.

"Not many people read the *Sentinel,*" Vivienne said as encouragingly as she could to Edward, unaware that at the least, the media are intimately familiar with the media, and that as soon as Gail's story hit the streets, the television cameras would bombard Rory Middle School and get enough quotes from Chris Paulo to make a documentary.

CHAPTER FOUR

Bannered across the front page of the *Sentinel* the next morning was the winning entry in the newsroom's contest for best headline: "Solo Satisfaction Sanctioned?" The question mark had been added at the last minute by the paper's publisher, who, while feeling quite magnanimous that he was going to let the story run, didn't want to be seen as being a dupe by publishing messages of a religious nature.

"If we add the question mark, we become objective," Dan Delp told Lincoln Fraser, who always bowed his head just a little when the publisher was in the room. "We must remain objective at all times," Delp insisted. Fraser didn't opt to remind the publisher of the three political and two business stories the man had killed in the last month, citing them as either bad for business, or just against his "instinct."

There was never any question the question mark would run, although Gail hated it and thought it accomplished the exact opposite of objectivity. "It makes us sound like we can't quite believe our own story."

"I don't think that," Fraser said to her, not looking up. "It just adds a bit of, uh, doubt."

"Doubt." Gail rolled her eyes. "Exactly what our readers are looking for." But run the question mark they did, along with the headline and a deck, the sub-headline, which read: "Rory Middle School Student says God Ok's Masturbation."

For Edward Banks, it was like waking up in a bad dream. He didn't anticipate that he'd be as shocked as he was. After all, Vivienne had broken the news to him the previous afternoon, that Peter had finally told her what the message from God was and then why he had prayed and asked in the first place. "Gawd," was all Edward had managed to say then.

Vivienne knew that at least one reporter—the Gail something-or-other she herself had let into the house—had knowledge of the message. Peter had told her that. Just as he had told her, first haltingly and then picking up speed as he went, about the scene in the stall with Ms. Blakely's yearbook picture, the fight with Chris Paulo, and the discussion with Mr. Overlay. So the story was out.

But Edward Banks had found room for hope as the evening played out. The television news was showing clips from his morning press conference, a speech by some ambitious legislator, and a staid, dry statement from Martin Overlay that he could say nothing. Those stations that sent afternoon crews out to see if there were any updates on the story merely had city attorney Charlie Doos repeating Overlay's statement. It was the only variation.

Maybe, Banks had thought, maybe Peter's story about God's real message wasn't going to be believed, or, even if believed, wasn't going to be printed. The whole thing might fade from view.

That thought spurred Edward to make the call to Doos, to leave the message that their meeting might perhaps manage to be one of "reconciliation." Edward, who had eaten three rolls of Rolaids in a little under seven hours, was trying to figure out how to get Doos behind closed doors to negotiate some sort of quiet withdrawal from the case. Perhaps get the city attorney to agree to destroy any and all records he had made of the event. Overlay already knew he had to keep his mouth shut. Edward could see that from his statements on television. Peter would go back to school after the two day suspension and life would get back to normal. Topping Darcy was no longer as much a priority.

The next morning, Edward felt that glimmer of hope surge as he saw the *Herald* with its story written by Jeff Ronald, who seemed to have nothing more than what the television news people had aside from in-depth interviews with Darren Preston (the legislator whom Banks had seen on TV) and the Reverend Werthall of Colorado Springs.

Werthall had gone to town on the school system, taking the opportunity to remind the public that Hitler had made similar moves on the Jews before the Holocaust, ostracizing them for their notions of God and their "different" rituals before resorting to wholesale extermination. What Werthall hadn't included in his analogy, nor had Jeff Ronald, who was vaguely aware of it but didn't have time to check, was the fact that Werthall had already gone on record in the past, in fact repeated it from his pulpit several times a year, that he didn't believe the Holocaust had ever happened. "An ingenious public relations device that has never stopped paying off for Jews," he called it.

Banks, of course, didn't know about Werthall's inconsistency; he'd just read the *Herald's* account of Peter's story with increasing relief and even a twinge of excitement. Ronald had clearly been impressed with Edward Banks' presentation. The reporter had used words like "commanding presence" and "paternal concern." Edward came off like an avenging angel, and would continue to, if the *Sentinel* held firm with the same story. But it was too much to wish for.

He knew it the minute he saw Vivienne's face. She hadn't followed his example of reading the *Herald* first. She went straight for the *Sentinel*, noting grimly that that-Gail-woman's last name was Abernathy, which Vivienne sniffed at, and then started reading.

It was clear from the headline that the reporter intended to lead with the content of Peter's message. Vivienne took a deep breath. Surely this was as bad as the story could be. The story that her tiny, innocent son had received a message from that big bully in the sky telling him to go ahead and do that thing she wished never to discuss. She wasn't prepared for the details. The description of the peeling paint in the stalls in the boys' john in Rory Middle School's gym locker room (Gail had gone back to the school to take a "tour," she'd informed Martin Overlay); the naming of Chris Paulo and Billy Frye (Vivienne felt herself shudder. She had never liked that Billy Frye because she couldn't identify with overweight people). And finally, devastatingly, the part about Ms. Blakely's yearbook picture.

"Peter!" Vivienne couldn't help but protest aloud.

It was at this point when Peter decided it was best to get a jump on the week's chores and take the garbage out to the alley, through the backyard and past the garage to the slim concrete strip that ran between his house and the Davidson's.

"Oh my Lord," Vivienne said, but forced herself to keep reading. She thought she was near the end of the story, that her torture would soon be over, but her heart sank at the reference to the jump to the inside pages. Soon, Vivienne's smooth and celebrated cheeks would turn various shades of gray.

There was a description of Chris Paulo's damaged nose, the result of Peter's fist, and the quotes from Peter about what God had told him, "inside his head," that masturbation was an "okay thing to do, as long as it didn't hurt anybody else."

"God is busy," Peter had said, and Gail had transcribed.

Not busy enough, Vivienne thought. There was more to the article, but now that the details of Peter's action, the real message and the basis for the suspension had been explained, it all seemed ridiculous. There was a description of Edward Banks presenting his federal suit to reporters at his office. Vivienne felt the skin on her neck crawl. "You idiot!" her inner voice screamed.

There, too, was a description of her home, their home. This Gail woman had called it "an impressive house on a quiet and privileged street." *What the hell sort of journalism was that?* She herself was described as well-dressed, immaculately groomed. Vivienne closed her eyes and thanked God and Jackie O for allowing her that bit of dignity. But the rest of the story, that was something else.

That was about the time Vivienne sought the refuge of the living room, away from the churning of the dishwasher and the delighted snorts of her husband as he continued to read the *Herald*.

Vivienne would remain stretched out across the sage damask until three that afternoon, when she'd reluctantly follow Edward, damning him every step of the way, through crowds of reporters flocked outside the "impressive" home, in order to meet with city attorney Charlie Doos. Edward would reassure her that the meeting with Doos would put an end to it all (although, after reading the *Sentinel's* story, his confidence had been thoroughly shaken and he couldn't seem to stop fussing with his cuffs.)

Edward, after he had finished absorbing the article in the *Herald*, would move with some trepidation to the *Sentinel*. He had already heard the outbursts of his wife and watched her take to the sofa in the living room with the look of one who had been hit by the proverbial semi. He wondered vaguely just how many people read the *Sentinel*, or at least, had read the *Sentinel* that morning. Certainly the bulk of the state would get its news from the television stations and the *Herald*, which meant he had a minority of citizens to deal with. That alone, he figured, should mean something.

What Edward Banks didn't know was that the assignment editor at Channel 9 had already dispatched a crew to the Banks' home and was swearing under his breath at the fact that the *Sentinel* had made his own staff look like a bunch of retards.

"Do we have any real reporters here?" he bellowed, watching the offices behind the television studio clear at his approach. "Who the fuck was working on this story?"

Edward had easily turned away a pack of reporters, television and print, from his home the previous afternoon, when they were still polite and felt they were on top of things, and the idea of speaking with Peter had been an afterthought.

"I gave at the office, remember?" he had said, delighted with his own pun. "Nothing more to say today. The boy's resting." And they had all trooped off like the good citizens they were.

But now things would be different. Like hungry dogs they would come and ask and not be dissuaded by polite rebuffs or tight-lipped smiles. Now there was pride at stake, and Edward Banks, who knew a little bit about pride and its motivating factors, would realize that the entire state would have the story by the afternoon, and that what he thought had been his chance at history had suddenly become a ribald joke. He took another bite of fried egg and launched into the *Sentinel* story.

Martin Overlay, at that exact moment, was arriving at Rory Middle School, pissed off at the continuing diatribe reported by the *Herald*, praying that Edward Banks would somehow become one of the few known victims this century of spontaneous human combustion.

As he made his way into his office, Overlay didn't notice the slightly reddened appearance of his assistant, Lucy Crebbs, and even if he had, he would've chalked it up to a mangled attendance report she had been working on. It was still long before any of the reporters would line up outside the school, and the phone hadn't yet started ringing with the startling calls of shocked parents who would be demanding to know "just what kind of school he was running."

No, Martin Overlay was still operating in a sort of bubble of ignorance. And it would last another four seconds before popping with a noiseless spray all over his neatly arranged desk. All it took was a glance at the *Sentinel's* headline for Martin Overlay to know that Edward Banks' jig was up.

There it was, everything (except for the Blakely detail) that Overlay had been praying for. Edward Banks, that overgrown blowhard, looked like the idiot he was. The principal suppressed the desire to laugh out loud and reached out to answer the first of sixteen calls (he would later disconnect the phone) from an outraged parent.

He couldn't have felt better.

Darren Preston, on the other hand, was feeling pretty bad. At his desk in the small statehouse office he shared with two other legislators, he hunched down behind his computer screen and tried not to panic. "Jesus motherfucking Christ," he muttered, staring at the online version of the *Sentinel* story. The chubby that the mere mention of the name Peter Banks had given him yesterday was long gone. The fact that he had aligned himself with an oversexed boy who liked to whack off was a fate he only wished he had had the creativity to inflict on some godless Democrat. Here he was, the author of legislation requiring the Ten Commandments to be posted in schools, a public figure who was a constant harbinger of the collapse of moral values in the state (it happened when all those Californians had moved in) and he was on record as supporting the boy who had received a message from God that whacking off was all right.

The only comfort Preston could see in the whole deal was that he had not been alone in his position supporting the debacle. Werthall himself, if the *Herald* were to be believed, had spoken out on the matter. The evangelist—from whom Preston had taken cues ever since the preacher had saved his marriage by telling Preston that the Lord had nothing against mistresses, just mistresses who were flaunted in public—had aligned himself as tightly with Peter Banks as Preston had.

The Reverend hadn't seen the *Sentinel* story right away. It wasn't the paper he preferred to read. So it wasn't until he had already eaten his soft-boiled egg, smoked a cigarette (only in private), and had a mug or two of coffee that he became aware that there was another version of the story. And only then because one of his deacons was at the front door, holding the offensive rag in his hand. "You should see this," Deacon Todd May said as soon as Werthall let him into the kitchen.

May tossed the paper as if it were scalding hot onto the oilcloth that covered the table, then helped himself to a cup of coffee.

"I thought you should know," he muttered, hoping to score some points with his spiritual leader before the man had read all the way through the gory details.

"Lord have mercy," Werthall breathed after the third paragraph. "Heaven above," he choked after the sixth. "Give me strength," he said grimly as he turned to the jump.

When he was finished, the Reverend sat down and stared at the half-empty mug of his now cold coffee, kneading the flesh just next to his eyes. "I've got more bad news," May said, as if dropping rocks on the stricken man in front of him would've been a good idea. "The gang at Mercy is already organizing a protest. They had a phone vote among the brethren this morning."

Fuckers, Werthall thought. He never allowed himself to say the word aloud, but for now, it was the only one he could think of.

Of course Mercy (his closest competition among the born-again churches in Colorado Springs) would be organizing against him. It was just like them, jumping on the bandwagon, trying to steal his congregation. He had to think fast. "Do the good people at Mercy believe that just because they don't like the message, they can reject what God has said?" Werthall said, listening to his own voice echo out into the kitchen.

May drew a sharp breath. "You're going to stand by this—this—boy, sir?" he asked, looking intently at Werthall, something that would assure him the other man wasn't just agreeing to save face.

Werthall caught the glance and understood its meaning immediately. And he would be damned if he'd be bullied. "What are you telling me, Todd? That you don't take matters into your own hands every once and a while?" he demanded of May.

"No sir, I don't," the deacon answered back, trembling a minute. "No matter what."

"Jesus Christ is testing you, my brother," he said to May. "Do not fail him." May's shocked face was almost too much to bear, and Werthall was poised to go for the kill—ask just what else May never had the guts to even consider when the unfortunate deacon was saved by the insistent ringing of Werthall's home phone.

The Reverend prayed the caller would be a sinner, someone with whom he could deal without feeling the urge to choke. His prayer was answered. Preston was on the line.

"When are you retracting?" the legislator said, not wasting time with pleasantries or identifying himself. Werthall smiled vaguely at the arrogance. There was just too much about Preston that he had control over to reprimand him for his presumptive phone habits.

"What makes you think I'm retracting?" Werthall responded, his eyes still on May. The deacon had let his mind wander, and with it, his hand. It was fiddling with the button flap on his khaki pants. May emerged from his reverie at just that minute and met the Reverend's eyes. Startled, he realized his misdeed and let his hand drop. Werthall suppressed laughter.

"What do you mean you're not retracting?" Preston screeched.

"I mean that when God leaves a message, it is not for us to judge," Werthall said slowly.

Preston let a long breath release into his mouthpiece. That was it! The line he would lead with. There would be no embarrassing retrenching. No humiliating admission that he had no idea what the boy had supposedly talked to God about. If Werthall were holding fast, then he was too. "I just wanted to check," Preston said, now regretting his opening question.

"Representative," Werthall said, "my brother," he continued, feeling Preston melt slightly on his end of the phone. "It is always good to check."

Despite the ribald remarks of his fellow legislators, Darren Preston would thus make it through the day, and the days to come, as a supporter of Peter Banks. His answer in hand, his face saved—or so he thought—Darren Preston hung up the phone and prepared for a day of legislating.

On his end, in the small ranch home nestled in crabgrass, the good Reverend William Werthall hung up as well and faced his deacon with a look he usually reserved for errant Sunday School classes. "You found out very quickly about Mercy's plans, Deacon May," he said, keeping the insinuation light.

"My wife—" May started and then stopped abruptly, not knowing how to continue.

"I see," Werthall said dismissively. "I would hate to lose one of my most stalwart members," he added. "You wouldn't happen to know what time Mercy is planning its little fanfare, would you?"

May nodded dumbly to the Reverend. "Three-thirty today," May told him. "I won't be there," he added.

"Of course you won't," Werthall said.

May left then, and was true to his word about not attending Mercy Church's bible-thumping barrage that afternoon. But his wife, Dara May, demonstrated her headstrong nature not only by going, but also by bearing one of the largest signs seen at the demonstration.

The deacon knew his wife well, which is why he took matters into his own hands in their vinyl-sided home's smallest bathroom, along with a Victoria's Secret catalog and a cold Budweiser.

Deacon May considered it a test he had passed.

CHAPTER FIVE

Gail Abernathy was not thinking about Peter Banks—or his answer from God—when she woke up Thursday morning. She had left the newsroom late the night before, when Lincoln Fraser was still muttering about not winning the headline pool and the publisher was still on the phone, insisting that the question mark be inserted in the headline. But for Gail, the story was over. Or so she thought. She had written too many supposedly controversial stories to be caught up in this one.

Besides, the Professor had called. He'd wanted to see her. He'd missed her, he said. And Gail felt a rush of relief at his words. In them was a promise of a discreet, leisurely dinner, where a state legislator—a former college professor from the extreme north of the state—wouldn't be recognized. Later, they'd retreat to the condo he'd purchased after his second election victory, and listen to jazz or watch the giant screen TV. What would follow would be up to him. She pushed the thought to the back of her head, which was very crowded.

"It's better than going home to an empty house," she'd muttered as she made her way to the parking lot outside the *Sentinel's* brick office building. Her son Dillon would be at his father's house all this week.

As she started the car and drove out of the parking lot, she batted at the insistent thoughts that kept escaping their banishment. It wasn't like she would be with the Professor forever, she kept telling them, taking a swat as they came nearer, threatening to fully form, to become solid. He's a transition man. He's said so himself.

And of course, she hadn't meant to drink that night. Now, in the morning, her headache was almost more than she could bear as she squinted into the obscene morning sun that poured through the window of the Professor's bedroom and bounced nauseatingly off the white and blue striped sheets.

Vivienne Banks was choking on her morning tea about the same time that Gail Abernathy stumbled from the bed to the bathroom, barely making it to the toilet before the inevitable occurred. She consoled herself sullenly that at least she wouldn't gain any weight, watching her stomach acids float around the blue water. But she couldn't stop her heart from sinking. She had made it all of five days.

Last night she'd started with the best of intentions, ordering lemonade at dinner, and then later, while listening to jazz, she had sipped ice water. The Professor had ordered his usual vodka. But it was when they got into bed that the trouble started. The preliminaries went fine: all the touching and kissing. It almost felt good to have the taste of vodka on her tongue again (although she had been a scotch drinker). But then she had felt the familiar pushing, the pressure on her pelvic bone, and then nothing. The Professor sat up in bed, his hand on his penis, jerking it nastily as if it were a key that would not slide into a lock.

"I don't know what it is about you," he said to her, his words slightly slurred. "It works with my wife." That had done it. She was out of bed and in the kitchen, standing there naked under the fluorescent bulbs, not caring who could see her through the windowed wall. She knew where the scotch was, the glasses. She didn't bother with ice. The first gulp burned a bit and then spread out like a welcome dip into a warm bath. It was the only thing that would shut off the screaming in her head. *Maybe it's because you drank a fifth of vodka tonight*, she wanted to scream at him. *Maybe it's because you're nearly sixty. Maybe it's because you're just a fucking impotent prick.* But she said none of it, because she believed none of it.

It worked with his wife, he had said. There was a time in her life that Gail would've seen the comment for what it was, and reamed the commentator for it. But that time had gone, and in its place had come a sense of guilt and faults; a chaos that caused her to internalize the statement instead of reject it.

Back in the bedroom, the Professor continued his hasty jerking motions to no avail. Peter Banks would have told him, had he been present, that the Professor's technique was all wrong. That the motion needed to be constant, the concentration focused. But then,

Peter Banks had never had a problem getting an erection. In fact, if he had a problem, it was quite the opposite.

When Gail had finally returned to bed, bringing the bottle and the glass with her, the Professor had already given up on his dick and was lying against two propped pillows, reading. "You didn't bring me one?" he had asked with a smile. "It's bad to drink alone, you know."

Gail managed to overcome the desire to strangle him and handed him the glass. It was the last thing she remembered the next morning as she stared into the blue water of the toilet. The Professor was gone, attending an early morning committee meeting, and Gail Abernathy was alone, sick to her stomach, and wanting for all the world to die right then and there of some little known disease that took its victims fast during the worst times of their lives. She considered drowning herself in the toilet but decided she didn't have the strength.

Besides, her cell phone was ringing.

Her hands shaking and feeling the scotch sweat from of her pores, Gail wandered through the condo until she found her purse. Fumbling with the phone, she pressed the button that lit its face.

"Fuck," she muttered, recognizing Fraser's number instantly. She pressed the answer key.

"Where the hell are you?" a voice barked. "We got news." It was one of Fraser's favorite sayings. It meant a story was breaking, and promised to be a good one. Gail pressed her left eye hard with the heel of her hand. She was going to have to find some aspirin, and fast.

"Lincoln, I worked late last night, remember? What the hell could be happening this early in the morning?" She was thinking about the possibilities as she asked the question. Maybe the governor had an announcement about his new tax proposal; maybe the feds had finally granted the state the money it needed to repair I-70. She was back into legislative mode now, so Fraser's answer took her by surprise.

"Peter Banks is happening, dearie," he said. "The religious types are up in arms, parents of schoolchildren are screaming, and Charlie Doos himself was on Channel 9 this morning, looking for all the world like the cat who swallowed the canary," Fraser's voice rose with his excitement.

Gail rolled her eyes. "You do have other reporters, Lincoln. I'm going back to the legislature, right?" she pleaded.

"Fuck no," the managing editor told her. "You broke the story, you follow it. That's the rule."

Gail felt her stomach lurch. She didn't have time to debate it with Fraser. "I'll be there in an hour," she mumbled into the phone.

"Make it thirty minutes," Fraser barked. She hung up and reached the toilet bowl just in time.

It was all Charlie Doos could do not to kiss his secretary full on her lips when she handed him a copy of the *Sentinel* that morning and told him that Channel 9 was on the phone asking if he'd make an appearance.

Doos was always in his office at the crack of dawn. His secretary had been specifically assigned to him because of it. She had school-aged kids at home and liked the six-thirty to two-thirty shift. Doos liked it because he never slept past five in the morning. He studied the paper with rising good humor.

Doing the Channel 9 spot was more an act of glee than a job obligation. Doos knew just how far he could take it, just how stupid he could make Edward Banks look without violating the privacy regulations that covered school records. And Doos knew he had done beautifully. He could tell by the newscaster's face that even she thought it was funny, hysterical in fact, and was having a hard time not laughing right there on live TV. When he watched the rest of the newscast, after his part was over, Doos had to cover his mouth on three separate occasions to keep from snickering. There was a live feed from in front of Rory Middle School—where already the Homeschoolers Association had gathered, bearing signs: "Unhand our Kids" and "What are they Learning in There?"

Then there was a cutaway to a previously recorded segment showing Edward Banks addressing a crowd of reporters in his law offices. The attorney was talking about the *values* of the country and the importance of protecting them.

The anchor for the broadcast then took over, filling in viewers on the upcoming meeting to take place in Doos' office that afternoon. "We can only imagine where it will go from here," the anchor concluded. Doos was in heaven. How would he be able to wait until three-thirty, when he would come face-to-face with Edward Banks and watch the other man cower? *I'll tell you where it'll go from here,* Doos thought. *Banks will withdraw so fast you'd think he'd put his John Henry into an ice hole. That's what'll happen.*

And that was more than enough for Doos. He returned to his office, secure in the knowledge that the afternoon would bring no surprises, just the satisfaction of watching Edward Banks cower and beg. Life was good.

For all the energy Doos was expending in his eager anticipation of the meeting, Edward Banks was exerting an opposite force. He knew what he had to do, and the meeting with Doos was the only logical place to do it. But if there was one thing Edward Banks absolutely abhorred, it was eating crow. All day he thought about how he could get out of it.

He liked best the scenarios that involved earthquakes and hurricanes—but even he had to admit that in the middle of Colorado neither seemed likely. Less gratifying but certainly as saving would be if he himself had a heart attack. He was sure that no one would joke about his son and his sexual habits in front of a man with a weak ticker. But Edward had no such luck.

At three that afternoon, Edward, Vivienne, and Peter made their way slowly through the throngs of reporters, photographers, and cameramen who had gathered on the finely-trimmed front lawn, trampling the thirsty Kentucky blue grass and pitting the turf with their collection of tripods and high-heeled shoes.

"Mr. Banks, Mr. Banks," the voices called out as Edward thrust his way forward, scowling at the faces pushing at him.

"I have no comment at this time, I have no comment at this time," Edward Banks repeated in a monotone as they made their way slowly to the brown Volvo.

"Mrs. Banks," the crowd started in.

Vivienne smiled weakly. Edward had instructed her to say nothing. "Keep your trap shut," were his actual words. And she thought it would be easy. She wasn't the one whose lust for the limelight got them into all this trouble in the first place, she thought. But outside, there in the glare of the sun and hearing her name called, Vivienne had to exert great effort to check herself. "This is all my husband's fault," she wanted to scream at them. "Leave my boy alone. He's done nothing wrong." But she didn't. Her tight-lipped expression, her concentration at "keeping her trap shut" would come across in the evening broadcasts and on the front page of the paper the next day as a snarl directed toward the public—not at the man who stood beside her.

Both Edward and Vivienne were too distracted to even notice their son or the fact that he seemed to be in a sort of daze, sleepwalking between them. Peter had finished his chores while both his parents tried to recover from reading the *Sentinel's* story. And then he had disappeared into his messy room, playing video games, blowing the heads off of hideous aliens and Asian-looking intruders while his father had been busy imagining earthquakes saving him from the meeting.

Vivienne had retired to the couch with a wet washcloth across her forehead. She hadn't noticed the lull when the pings and explosions from Peter's room had ceased, nor the pervading quiet that seemed to seep from under her son's door. Even if she had, she would've assumed he was jacking off, now that it was the only image she could muster of her son when she closed her eyes.

It was easy, then, for Peter to ignore the assault from the media that greeted him as soon as he followed his parents out their front door. They weren't really there, those people. Not for him. He walked lightly and the crowd seemed to part for him, as if he were a leper on a pilgrimage.

Gail Abernathy watched the boy move as if in a stupor and suppressed the maternal instinct that rose inside of her. He's in shock, she thought, shifting from one foot to the other as her heels sank into the muddy dirt of the lawn. Her headache had subsided, but she still felt weak and clammy. When the Banks' family approached the area of the crowd in which Gail was engulfed, she noticed that Vivienne Banks' eyes flickered to her. It was but a glance of recognition that both women had met the day before. And Vivienne, for her part, was trying to balance her feelings of anger toward the reporter for the vividness of the story with her feelings of gratitude for encouraging her son to come talk to his mother. Bitch, Vivienne decided, may have been too strong a word. But all Gail could think was, *Oh God, I must reek of scotch.*

In the brown Volvo, which backed rather quickly out of the driveway and only barely missed hitting a slow cameraman, there was silence. Edward Banks was rehearsing his statement and simultaneously praying for his heart attack to descend. Even if he were driving, Banks reasoned, a small heart attack would be a saving grace. Vivienne could grab the steering wheel in time to avoid any serious wreck, and if he had the heart attack in the car on the way to the meeting, it would be seen as a sign of good faith. He had meant to face his opponents, but God had intervened. But it was not to be.

As it turned out, Vivienne was in no shape to be grabbing any wheel, much less dealing with a heart attack victim. She was deep into a reverie of how it must have felt to be Jackie O, and to have again and again faced the mobs so curious about her life. Vivienne loved the late former first lady. She had aspired to be like Jackie all her life. And now, now that she knew what it was like to wear large, dark glasses and try to control her facial expressions, the beautiful Jacqueline had already passed on. Vivienne touched a strand of her hair, remembering Jackie O's permanently coiffed appearance.

"I must look a wreck," Vivienne muttered, the first words to break the silence. She pulled down the visor to check her hair and makeup in its mirror, and that was when she finally noticed her son, sitting in the back seat, in an apparent trance. "Peter, are you all right?" she asked, her voice—this time raised to a more audible level—broke through her husband's cardiac daydreams and caused him to glance into in the rear-view mirror. "Peter. Peter. For God's sake, pay attention, son," Edward barked.

Peter managed to smile softly at his parents, as if he could just barely see them through a thick fog. He said nothing. If Edward Banks had not been in such a hurry to get the whole thing over with, he may have pulled the car over then and there and talked to his son. He may have asked why the boy seemed to be disconnected, unaware of the activity around him. Edward may have even spoken to him softly enough to get the boy to tell him what had happened, again, that morning, while his father was musing over natural catastrophes and his mother was lying on the couch with a washcloth on her head.

But Edward was in a hurry. He was a man who had an unsavory task ahead of him, a drove of television vans behind him, and the offices of the city attorney within three blocks. So he did not stop the car.

Vivienne, being the woman she was, did not demand that he do so, either. She comforted herself by focusing on the role of concerned mother, and thus attempted to reassure her son, who needed no reassurance. She reached over the back of the front seat to grasp his small cold hand in hers, feeling oddly as though she were holding the string of a balloon. When they had paid to park and pulled into a spot, she was almost afraid to let Peter's hand go, however awkward her over-the-seat grasp was. But let go she did, and was relieved to find him still a victim of gravity, seated quietly there on the leather upholstery.

"Peter, let's go," Edward Banks ordered.

The three made their way to the dingy cement office building that bore the city seal. Edward was still desperately praying for his heart attack. "Now, now, you imbecile," he shouted silently to God. It didn't help Banks' rage when Charlie Doos' secretary informed him that their meeting would not take place in the attorney's office, as Banks had assumed, but in the mayoral conference room, in order to accommodate the audience.

"Audience?" Edward Banks bellowed. "What audience?"

Doos' secretary, seeing that she was working overtime because of this big buffoon, was in no mood to explain her boss' decisions. She kept her lips tightly pursed as she showed the family the way down the hall.

"Goddammit!" Edward sputtered. The expletive would change and intensify when he and Vivienne and Peter were led into the conference room. It was a cavernous rectangle about the size of a neighborhood swimming pool, was filled with bodies, cameras, signs, and snaking bits of thick black cord held in place by wide strips of duct tape. Edward recognized a few of the faces in the crowd, those reporters who must have hauled ass from the front lawn of his house to this room in order to witness his entrance. He swore again.

Vivienne, her hand again clamped tightly around Peter's, tried to calm her husband, afraid that she would be reading his barrage in tomorrow's newspaper. "Edward, hush," she hissed through a barely open mouth. Her husband didn't have time to respond. At just that moment, Charlie Doos swooped over to the trio and grabbed Edward's hand. The gesture was meant to capture the attention of the milling cameramen and dozing reporters, and it did.

"Good to see you again, Banks," Doos said.

Edward fought the impulse to check his ankles. "Let's get this over with," he forcefully whispered. "You know what I've come to do."

Doos nodded solemnly. "Of course. Let's have a seat."

Since he had returned from Channel 9's studios, Charlie Doos had been busy orchestrating. It hadn't taken him long to decide to hold the meeting in the echoing mayoral conference room—the bigger the space the better, he thought. He instructed his secretary to stay later than usual, ignored her grimace, and then also told her to tell everyone who had requested access to the meeting that they were welcome. Then, just to make sure the crowd was complete, he had faxed out advisories to the *Sentinel* and the *Herald*, as well as the three local news stations, telling them that he would make the mayoral conference room available at two-thirty—an hour before the meeting started—for them to set up their monstrous gear.

Relaxed and ready, Doos led Edward, Vivienne, and Peter to a long table and chairs, set up at the front of the room on a raised platform, and invited them to take a seat. Vivienne would finally let Peter's hand go as they both slid into the tapestry-covered chairs. But her hand would not remain idle. It instantly went to her hair, checking and rechecking the strands, ensuring that the height remained, the bangs were in place. The ongoing gesture made her look like a fallen angel still checking for the halo that was missing, and the image was not lost on the cameramen and photographers who gathered around the platform to get a shot.

Peter sat between his parents, unaware that his mother had abandoned his hand, also unaware that she had held it in the first place. In his mind, the new message—the one that had come unbidden that day—was playing over and over. It had happened quite suddenly, in the midst of electronic explosions and the carnival music of Alien Apocalypse, his favorite video game. He had been passing the time by blowing the heads off of anything green and foreign-looking when the screen went blank. No matter what he did to the control stick, the image would not reappear onscreen.

And then the voice was in his head, a deep voice full of warmth and familiarity, the one he had heard only once. Slowly it spoke to Peter, first asking him not to be afraid and then describing in detail what he was to do, what he was to say. The boy had panicked when he first heard the names of the Witnesses, not because there was anything scary about them, but because Peter worried he would never be able to remember them, get them right when the time came. But he would be relieved to find that—as with the first message—this second one could be replayed at will, beginning to end. He had been triggering the message over and over.

He liked the way it felt, the continuous replay, each time filling him with a feeling of safety and importance, comfort and energy.

Peter would keep his mind's replay button pushed through the preliminaries of the discussion between his father and Charlie Doos. He couldn't quite hear what they were saying; it was as if they were grown-ups on a Charlie Brown cartoon, squawking at each other in low, distorted sounds. But he'd know when it was time for Peter to speak, and when it came time, he would do a wonderful job.

Unaware of the goings-on in his son's mind, Edward Banks was determined to get the proceedings over with as quickly as possible. He had given up on the idea that an opportune cardiac arrest was going to save him from his fate, and he had moved on to hope that Doos would let him make opening remarks, which for him would also be closing remarks. He was prepared to drop the suit then and there, wishing Doos and the city and its school system luck in their future endeavors.

But Charlie Doos had other plans. He was aware that, given the chance, Edward Banks would turn tail and run as soon as humanly possible, but Doos had some things yet to say. Things, he hoped, that would make Edward Banks pay for embarrassing him in the jaywalking case. Things that would humble this arrogant man. So, as Doos was hosting and thus controlling the meeting, he spoke first.

"Welcome, everyone," the city attorney said into the bouquet of microphones that had been taped to the table where he and the Banks' family sat. "Thank you all for coming. I am hoping that this meeting will clear up a few of the misunderstandings that have been reported for the past day or two. This all is nothing but a misunderstanding, one that has been prematurely, and wrongly, raised to the level of litigation by my colleague here, Edward Banks."

Vivienne watched her husband blanch at the remark and listened to the sea of pens scratch the city attorney's words across paper. Her hand strayed to her hair, checking, checking, as if the perfection of her coiffure would somehow mitigate the embarrassment of the moment. "Looking good," her mother had said to her sometime during Vivienne's high school years, "is half the battle."

"No one is trying to infringe on anyone else's constitutional rights in this case," Doos was watching Banks out of the corner of his eye and directing his comments toward the audience. "The principal at Rory Middle School was only trying to do a job that is too often a hard and thankless one. He certainly did not deserve the legal onslaught brought by Mr. Edward Banks here, and he is due an apology for the uproar that has since followed."

Vivienne wished she were sitting closer to her husband—that Peter wasn't in between them. She wanted to nudge Edward's arm so he'd stop fussing with his pants.

Doos went on at a considerable length, emphasizing words that had a visible effect on Edward Banks. Words like "grandstanding" and "overreacting" and "uninformed." Vivienne watched as scribbling reporters underlined the words, knowing she would read them tomorrow in the newspaper, hear them that very evening on television.

"I can only hope that Edward Banks will do the right thing, the only thing, that can bring this charade to an end," Doos was wrapping up. And then, as if he didn't trust the ever-reddening gentleman who sat beside him to know what that right thing was, Doos concluded by spelling it out.

"Nothing less than an apology, and a full withdrawal of the threat to sue, will suffice." Doos turned his body to face the elder Banks as he completed his speech and held out his hand to indicate it was Edward Banks' turn to step up to the array of microphones.

"Faggot prick," Edward breathed so softly that only Doos and Peter, who sat on his father's other side, could have heard. Doos let the comment roll off, knowing it was a sign that he had triumphed. Peter sat unaware that his father had said anything, listening intently to the comforting words that were replaying in his head.

"I am prepared to do just that," Edward stood and leaned over to the mikes. He was a great lover of semantics and was now hoping that saying he was "prepared" to withdraw and apologize would release him from the actual pain of having to really say he was sorry. "I agree with the esteemed Mr. Doos that the original Constitutional complaint"

—Edward was careful not to take possession of the complaint, to refer to it as if it were an entity in and of itself— "was based on a misunderstanding. For my part, and the part of my family, the matter is over, the suit is withdrawn." Edward had more to say, of course, a summary that would include an explanation of why he felt it was so important to jump to action when the Constitution merely appeared to be threatened, and some chastisement to the press for having blown the story out of proportion. Of course, he wasn't planning to mention his initial phone call to the television station.

But Edward never got a chance to finish his statement. Had it been Doos who had interrupted, Edward Banks would have had no qualms about pushing the man aside. But it was not Doos. And Edward was too astonished, too shocked by the actions of his own son, to do anything about them as they unfolded.

There, in the space it had taken Edward Banks to inhale a long breath before proceeding to save some face, Peter Banks squeaked out just one sentence. "I have something to say," the boy had breathed, just loud and clear enough for the mikes to pick up.

The cameramen and photographers in the front of the room fought for position just under Peter's chair, craning to get the perfect shot of the boy who had been dubbed by the notorious Denver weekly, the *Denver Sun*, as "Peter the Masturbator."

But Peter was unfazed by the ruckus below him. He went on speaking, oblivious to his mother's nails that dug into his right arm, and his father's quickly draining face staring in disbelief. Peter simply spoke, and spoke as if he were demonstrating to a schoolmaster that he had learned a lesson by heart, that he knew exactly what he was supposed to do.

"What I have to say is this," he said, the room suddenly so quiet that even the photographers did not make their usual annoying grunting sounds as they strained to get into position. "I have had another message from God. One week from today at four p.m., there will be three confirmations of His presence. There will be Witnesses to these confirmations. Two of them I can name here: Sherry Setliffe Anderson and Jake Abraham Herron. God told me to tell you to remember that the miraculous is often personal, and always present. That is all."

The boy, with the plain face and an expression of someone who is watching a boring movie and doesn't care to see what comes next, sat back down. The room erupted.

"Peter, Peter," a reporter up front called, "what do you mean by confirmations?" Others, farther back, wanted to know who Sherry Anderson and Jake Herron were, and why they had been named.

"Are you telling us there's going to be a miracle?" shouted Jeff Ronald from his position alongside a cameraman over to the left.

"Just when did all this happen?"

"Why you? Why did He pick you?"

The media seemed to spout the questions like an automatic ball machine, not bothering to alter their behavior once it was clear that no one—especially Peter—was planning to answer their queries.

The room was only made louder, the din greater, by the addition of the Homeschoolers and a small gathering of Pentecostalists who, after they had recovered from their initial shock, started hissing like snakes and then calling out "Liar!" and "Blasphemer!"

Vivienne, who had ceased digging her nails into her son's arm when he had said the words "another message from God" buried her head in her hands and hoped that the part on the top of her head did not show gray roots, or worse, too much scalp.

Doos, blinking slightly from the shock, was the first to recover. He managed to weakly declare, "I think we're finished here," which the crowd didn't hear over the madness.

Edward Banks spoke to his son, turning slightly as if it hurt his neck to move. After staring at Peter for a full minute—the attorney's purple face and bloodshot eyes considered the quiet boy who sat before him—he said, with shaking breath, "Peter, you're grounded."

Part II

The Witnesses

CHAPTER SIX

Sherry Anderson had stopped delivery of the newspaper just after Steven's death and at the behest of a therapist who found Sherry's faithful reading of obituaries "anything but constructive." That was three years ago. Along with the bulky, smearing newsprint went trips to the movies, her interest in literature, plays, and politics. Although it had nothing to do with the newspaper, she no longer worked with beads. The necklaces and earrings that once sprang from fishing line and glass now lay scattered at the bottom of a brown cardboard box, one of many stacked in the recess of her closet.

Sherry Anderson now did what the living dead often do. She worked. In her late forties, a glimmering blonde not yet faded by age, a freckled face that betrayed little of the years—or the experiences—of a nearly five-decade lifetime, Sherry Anderson reminded people who were of an appropriate age of Doris Day. Actually, the truth was that Sherry Anderson looked a great deal more like Debbie Reynolds than Doris Day. But Reynolds' face was not what people remembered about Anderson's blonde, youthful looks. It was Day. Which is why at work, in the corridors of the very modern and self-consciously enlightened Clark Hospital, Sherry Anderson's coworkers sometimes called her "the Doris Day of Death."

Or "Triple D," for short.

"Stillborn in Labor and Delivery Two," they'd mutter to one another. "Call Ms. Doris."

"Cardiac arrest, DNR, in Intensive Care, call Triple D."

Sherry's nickname was shorthand for people who were pummeled by death every day, for those for whom it was more a professional liability, a reminder of the limits of their lives' work. Indeed, the crew at Clark, the other nurses and doctors, had always liked their Triple D. Even before Steven's death. When it happened, they pooled their own closely-guarded vacation time to give Sherry a full six weeks of bereavement leave. It was not animosity that drove the moniker; it was simply an accurate description. When someone died, they called Sherry. It was her job.

Forty-eight-year-old Sherry Anderson was a psychiatric nurse by training, and was now a grief counselor at Clark. She worked primarily with parents of dead children, newly dead children. These parents had suffered what she considered to be the most awful of life's twists, the most painful of losses. She couldn't take grief away. But she could, patiently, explain the avenues the grief would travel, the pavement to expect. In shock and denial, parents would usually stare at her, as if some hallucination had brought back Doris Day in a bad, morbid joke. Many of them would hear warbling strains of *Que Sera, Sera*, and might put their hands to their ears. Then Sherry Anderson would say the words that would make them listen, words that at once would strip the Hollywood stereotype away and shut off the music. "I know what you're feeling. I lost my son, Steven."

The healing could then begin. Not for Sherry, who was beyond healing. She had fenced off the world and padded her walls and rinsed her coffee cup every night listening to the endless drone of the television. But at least for her latest patient, for the wrecked and ruined parents of a stillborn, or a leukemia victim, there on the horizon would be a glimmer of hope. If the nurse could function, could live after such a thing happened to her, why not us, they would think.

So Sherry Anderson went on with her life, or what passed for it, until the day when Peter Banks named her as a witness to—well, no one was really sure what—a week in the future, at a designated time. Then all hell broke loose.

Sherry was on duty the Thursday Peter made his hypnotic announcement. The case she was attending to was unusual for her, a bereaved father, yes, but not because of a deceased infant. There it lay, squalling and unaware in the nursery, its umbilical cord still raw and its head misshapen from delivery. Healthy as an ox. But the infant's mother—who had followed the dictates of prenatal care to the letter, had sworn off alcohol and cigarettes and exercised by taking gentle walks in the park every afternoon—she had suffered a massive coronary during delivery and was gone in seconds, her heart a useless array of burst vessels and collapsed chambers as her son took his first breath.

Sherry had already spent two hours with the stricken husband when Peter made his announcement. She would spend another hour before emerging from the soft blue comfort of the counseling room to news that the hospital's phones were lit up with reporters calling because of something some boy had said about God.

She was confident in her response. "They have the wrong Sherry Anderson," she said, unfettered, her walls as yet unpierced. "It's a common name." With that, she retreated to her small office, its walls adorned with pictures of Steven, a chart of the anatomy of the human body, quotes from Elizabeth Kubler Ross, and she sat down to write up her notes about the unfortunate man who'd become a widower at precisely the same moment he'd become a father.

Her mind kept wandering. "Sherry Anderson" was indeed a common name, and for now that made her safe from some ridiculous frenzy over a boy who thought he had talked to God. But she had once before thought she was safe, when the police had called and told her they had found Steven. Steven Anderson.

"You have the wrong person," she remembered saying into the mouthpiece of the phone. "It's not my son." Although for reasons unknown, she'd known it was. Lying in that Iowa cornfield, surrounded by police cars and flashing lights, she could see the scene although she was hundreds of miles away. "It's a common name," she told them then.

She sat in the cool of her office, pen frozen in midair, remembering the sinking feeling of her heart and the buzzing in her head and the certainty three years ago that the boy with the commonest of names was indeed her son and the police were right. A knock on her office door brought her out of her reverie.

"Sherry. Sherry, I'm sorry to bother you—" said Rachel Baum, one of the hospital's myriad administrators with her own nickname, "The Bomb," which was applied with a good deal more animosity than was Sherry's "Triple D."

Sherry surfaced quickly to open the door, trying to smile at the gaunt woman who had a long sheath of black hair. "These reporters are very insistent. They have your maiden name, or something, and they demand that it is you they want to talk to. Would you be willing to say something, anything, so they'll stop calling? They're tying up the front desk something fierce."

Sherry tried her best to nod at The Bomb, whose nickname

referred to the woman's capacity for rage, her reputation for out-bursts over small infractions like smoking in undesignated areas or uniforms out of compliance with regulation. Brewing under Rachel Baum's surface was an annoyance that could easily expand and erupt. In Baum's mind, Sherry was responsible for the tying up of the all-important front desk's phone bank. There were patients to be con-sidered. An outburst was imminent if Sherry refused to comply. "I'll talk to them," Sherry said, her heart compressing slightly. "Put one through."

The fuse sputtered, and The Bomb graced Sherry with a smile, revealing a horrendous row of uneven, twisted teeth that most of the psychiatric nurses at Clark were sure were the reason for the woman's ungodly temper. "Wonderful. I'll get right on it," Baum answered.

Sherry sat down and stared at her pen, waiting for her phone to ring, half expecting the gravelly, somber voice of an Iowa policeman to come on the line to tell her that her son was dead. But a wom-an's voice interrupted her musing. Nancy Hardy, the woman told her, Channel 9 News. Sherry nodded and then listened to the silence on the line. Finally she managed, "What can I help you with?"

"Ms. Anderson," Nancy Hardy was trying her best to go slow, even though they had all but fourteen minutes to airtime and the top story was still an unfinished mess. "I take it you've heard about Peter Banks extraordinary announcement today?"

Sherry shrugged, but then realized she was speaking to someone who could not see her. "No," she repeated, this time aloud and with-out the body language. "I've been working."

Hardy was taken aback, unused to people who didn't at least have a radio blaring somewhere to keep them up-to-date with the world. Sherry would've been much more prepared for the call if she had been at home, where the television did in fact constantly drone. As it was, a tenth of Colorado's population was already aware of the boy who professed to be a messenger from God, and who had named Witnesses to some mysterious events that were to prove His exis-tence. Sherry was behind.

Hardy tried to fight her rising impatience. "Okay, well, this boy, Peter Banks, the one who said it was all right to masturbate, he had a press conference today—"

Sherry blinked quickly, trying to understand the barrage.

"You mean the little boy, the one who was suspended?" It had, after all, been on the evening news for the past two days.

"That's the one," Hardy felt her heart quicken; at least this woman wasn't totally out of it. "Well, today he made this announcement that God had told him there would be two Witnesses to an event, or events, that will supposedly happen one week from today at four p.m. And those events, again supposedly, will prove God's existence. He named you and Jake Herron."

"Who is Jake Herron?" Sherry asked, stalling for time.

Hardy felt her frustration rise. "We're working on that. What I need to know is why you were named. Do you know Peter Banks?"

Sherry shook her head, and then added, "No, never heard of him, until he was on the news the other day. But I'm sure you have the wrong person. 'Anderson' is such a common name."

Hardy bit her lip to stop a grunt of disgust. "Sherry Setliffe Anderson," Hardy said. "That's you, isn't it?"

Sherry sat for a moment in silence, feeling the receiver tremble in her hand.

"Ms. Anderson," Hardy could barely keep from screeching, "Ms. Anderson, are you religious at all?" It was a question they had asked her after the funeral, all those people who were trying to point her in some direction, any direction, away from the grave.

"Does it matter?" she had asked then, feeling numbness crawl over her, and the padding begin. "Why does it matter?" she had asked.

"Ms. Anderson!"

"I'm sorry," Sherry answered from somewhere deep down under the folds of the past. "I can't help you."

"Ms. Anderson, I need—"

Sherry replaced the receiver quickly, before the woman who had been shouting could continue. Then a feeling crept into her sanctuary, one that was not as comfortable as numbness.

The woman who looked so very much like Doris Day sat alone, breathing short gasping breaths, her body shaking. Sherry Anderson didn't want to witness a miracle, or worse, be witnessed, witnessing a miracle. To Sherry, if God did exist, he could do nothing now, nothing one week from today at four o'clock that would ever make up for his pronounced absence in an Iowa cornfield three years ago.

It had been a bad day already for Jake Herron, legislative aide to U.S. Representative Miranda Davis. He was working in the district office, in Denver. And it was the anniversary of the U.S. Supreme Court's 1973 decision in Roe v. Wade, which meant only one thing. The loonies were out in force.

Roe v. Wade was, of course, the decision by the highest court in the land that abortion was a Constitutional right that could not be denied arbitrarily by the states. It marked not the end, but the beginning, of a contentious, vocal, and often-violent struggle between those who agreed with the court and those who felt that abortion was nothing less than murder and must be stopped.

The latter group—the loonies, as Herron referred to them—used the January 22 anniversary of the decision as a lightning rod for protest. The former group, most notably organizations like Planned Parenthood, NARAL, and NOW, used the date to hold quieter (duller, to the media) celebrations of emancipation.

U.S. Representative Miranda Davis, although a Republican, was a vocal "choice" supporter. So Jake Herron, her most visible staff person, her right-hand man, braced to suffer the wrath of the loonies every year on the decision's anniversary date. Many of the tactics repeated themselves year after year. This year would be no different. First, there would be the requisite bouquet of black roses. For the pro-lifers, as they called themselves, the bouquet was the ultimate symbol of mourning. Herron had come to enjoy the black roses, wondering about their dye process. He kept them in a vase on his otherwise discombobulated desk.

Less enjoyable were the reams of graphic photos that would inevitably be delivered. In plain envelopes, sometimes bearing a return address so mundane as to be completely non-suspect (like the one from "Western Office Supply" or "Government Information Services") the photos spewed forth, horrid scenes of red and pink, dismembered bodies of dead full-term babies—which the pro-lifers tried to pass off as the product of an abortion. It was an unfortunate circumstance that in Miranda Davis' office, as in most other House offices, the mail was usually opened by fresh-faced interns who were panting to be part of the process. These dew-dipped youngsters often lost their cookies, not to mention their political fervor, on Roe v. Wade day. But not one, Herron noted with some satisfaction, had ever become a convert to the pro-life side.

And then there would be the protesters themselves. Almost always older white men and fat younger women, these fervent believers would wave placards and dress up as the Grim Reaper, pointing to members or their staff, screaming "Murderers!" It was never fun, but could be endured. Herron had lived through his share of bad days.

That's what he thought when he awoke at his usual hour, six-thirty, the morning of Peter Banks' announcement. What Jake Herron didn't know—aside from the miracle that Peter Banks had in store for him—was that the director of Colorado's biggest "pro-life" group had been working on some new tactics. "We need to hit home with these unabashed slayers of children," Russell Crenshaw told his followers a full month ago when they'd met in their cramped office quarters. Hitting home is what they did.

It started for Herron when he stepped out of the shower, shaking the water out of his ears. Mentally absorbed in his day's schedule, it took him a moment to register that there was some sort of fracas out in front of his small Denver duplex. And then the noise, at first blurry and unformed, coalesced and focused enough for him to hear the message. It was quite simple, now that he concentrated on it.

"Herron," the group chanted. Must've been a dozen people out there, a dozen with rather large lungs. "Herron and Hitler, mass killers of our time." Swearing, then pulling the towel more tightly around his waist, he'd gone to the front window and carefully peeked out around the vellum shade. They were there all right, the loonies, although he had overestimated the number. Only six people stood outside his house, four men and two women, carrying their gory signs and walking a circle over the square patch of lawn he shared with the owner of the second unit of the duplex.

"Herron and Hitler," they continued chanting. "There's no difference." The sight, even to Herron, who had witnessed hundreds of such protests in front of the U.S. Capitol, Davis' district office, and indeed the representative's own home, was a shock. Those incidents had been part of the job, and elected officials had to understand the implications of their decisions to run for office. This demonstration, on the other hand, was personal.

Jake Herron moved away from the window only as far as the phone, which he picked up, his mouth twisted in anger, and dialed as if the keypad were a picketer's face. "Get me the police," he said when the 911 operator answered. As he waited for Denver's finest, who responded quickly, ever mindful of the increased appropriation that Miranda Davis had eked out of last year's budget bill for inner-city cops, Herron watched the spectacle outside his home, boiling with anger.

Although the announcement of his name as one of God's Witnesses was still hours off, Jake Herron's life had already been affected by Peter Banks. Crenshaw, who at that moment was busy picketing the Governor's Mansion, had planned for a far greater showing at the eighteen picket sites he had carefully selected. But he'd been partially thwarted by the incident at Rory Middle School, with the news that said God thought it was okay to jerk off.

A number of the pro-life groups' most loyal members were home-schoolers, and their attention had been diverted. Hence the half-dozen, as opposed to the twenty or so who were expected to hit each leading staffer's home. And fifty who were to have protested outside elected officials' offices had been reduced to a paltry twenty-five.

"The Devil is working his division today," Crenshaw had told his masses when they huddled to plan their assault in the dawn of the day. "We must make up for it." This is why the six people who now were marching in front of Herron's house were screeching their chants at the top of their lungs. "Herron and Hitler, Herron and Hitler."

Under normal circumstances, with his tousled hair, brown eyes, and beard, Jake Herron closely resembled the Jesus of religious paintings and icons. But under stress, Jake's demeanor, as well as his face, were drastically altered. By the time the first officer appeared on the scene not fifteen minutes after Herron's call, the vein in the young man's forehead, the one that traveled from the top of his hairline down to the inside edge of his eyebrow where it disappeared somewhere in the bridge of his nose, was standing out as if at attention.

The day had gone downhill from there.

When Herron arrived at work, the door to Miranda Davis' district office had been smeared with what was later identified as chum, bloody fish chunks commonly used as bait for large game fish, compliments of the loonies. Inside, Herron was greeted by two nearly-hysterical staff members, both of them young and inexperienced, who had already opened two packets of gory photos and had been petrified by the messy assault on the front door.

As if it weren't enough, dealing with the dicey issue of abortion and the Holocaust before breakfast, Herron had barely caught his breath at his desk when the phone rang and Miranda Davis herself, breathless and with only minutes before a vote on the floor of the House some two thousand miles away, wanted to know, "Just what the hell is an 'LD 50?'" and why she hadn't been briefed that "no less than eighty" animal rights activists "from her district," had come to Washington to make sure she cast the right vote?

Herron, who knew Miranda well enough to know that when she started the old "no less, no less" outcry, it was as close as the usually controlled politician got to completely losing it. He explained quickly about the standard procedure for testing household cleaners and other products. "You give the substance to a bunch of bunnies, little by little, until half of the population dies. Then you know what a lethal dose of the stuff is," he said, speaking rapidly and from rote. The office got hundreds of letters a year on the subject, and they sent out the same form letter to each of them.

"Half the population of bunnies?" Davis' voice was rising on her end of the line, and Herron could hear the roll call being recited in the background.

"Just vote against it, Miranda," Herron snapped, pressing down on the vein that was threatening to leave his forehead and fling itself across the room.

"Against the bill or against the test?" Davis asked, trying to ignore her top aide's obviously inappropriate tone of voice.

"Against the test," Herron answered, trying to control his voice, removing of the sarcasm. It wasn't unusual for members of the U.S. Congress to have no idea what the bill at issue actually was for.

"Where's Stacy?" he asked, hoping that the best of Davis' four other legislative aides was around and knew the content of the bill.

"She's with the group in the lobby, the animal rights people. She's trying to assure them I'm on their side," Davis explained, twitching slightly at the sound of the roll call, the last part of the alphabetical list ticking by.

"Vote the way they're asking you to," Herron instructed her. Davis grunted her acquiescence and hung up just as a piece of bloody meat, stuffed into something pink and lacy, hit the front window of Herron's office. The window cracked, long and threateningly, but did not break. Later, after Herron had called the police for the second time that day, he would hold in his hand the infant's sock, trimmed in delicate Battenberg lace and containing the smaller end of a lamb chop.

Fuckin' fanatics, he thought. *Fuckin' goddammed fanatics.*

About the time Peter was making his announcement to the stunned room around him, Herron was holding a bag of ice on his forehead while he pounded out a speech Miranda would deliver at the NARAL reception that evening. An hour later, after Herron had finished the speech, printed out the following day's schedule for both the Washington and district office, and answered yet another frantic call from Davis who wanted to know how many union laborers there were in her district and if it mattered to them how she voted on some revisions to OSHA standards, he got the first call.

"Hi Jake, this is Jeff Ronald at the *Herald*," the voice said happily.

"Yeah Jeff," Jake answered easily, accustomed to talking to Ronald over the years about Davis's rather perilous position as a moderate to liberal Republican in a city full of Democrats surrounded by a state full of conservative Republicans. Of course Ronald would be calling about the abortion issue.

"Want me to tell you about my lamb chop?" Jake asked, hoping to engage Ronald in a discussion about the increasingly dramatic and fanatical actions of the loonies.

"Uh, not really," Ronald replied, his years at the *Herald* only having served to remove the last vestiges of both curiosity and humor he had ever possessed. "What I really want to know is if the broadcast guys have gotten hold of you yet?"

"You mean about the picket?" Herron asked, hopeful that the media would really give it to these bastards who saw fit to disturb his private residence regardless of his status as a working stiff.

"What picket?" Ronald shot back, and then didn't wait for a response. "No, I mean about Peter Banks."

Herron hesitated. Banks, Banks, it sounded familiar. "The jack-off kid?" he asked when he had put his finger on it. As legislative director, he was responsible for keeping abreast of the news in Davis's district and read both papers religiously, taping the evening news so he wouldn't miss anything in their simultaneous broadcasts. "What about him?" Herron asked.

"Do you know him?" Ronald asked, not bothering to fill in Herron that this was an on-the-record question.

"No," Herron replied, "although, I'll give him credit for having guts."

"Well, you may want to give him credit for more than that in about a week," Donald replied mysteriously.

Herron's vein began to pulse again. "What the fuck are you talking about?" Herron shot back through the agony of his forehead.

"The kid named you today. You and some other lady, some nurse. Said you would be witnesses to a miracle in a week's time."

Herron reached for his ice pack, which sat melting on his desk.

"God damn Russell Crenshaw, God damn him to hell!" Herron almost spat the words out.

"Crenshaw? The pro-lifer guy?" Ronald asked, hoping Herron would keep up with the outburst. "What has this got to do with him?"

"Roe v. Wade," Herron muttered bitterly. "Don't you get it? This is all an anti-abortion hoax. That nurse probably works at Planned Parenthood and in a week we're both going to get a box of dead fetus or something—" he choked on his own fury.

"I don't know," Ronald said, hesitating at the other end of the line. He wasn't at all convinced that Peter Banks, the performance he had seen today, could be tied in with the usual pro-lifer agenda. Especially since he'd already gotten reports from the *Herald's* Colorado Springs reporter about the protest that Mercy Church had staged that afternoon. They were of the Crenshaw ilk, he was certain. "I think that maybe this is—" but Herron wouldn't let him finish. He was shouting, shouting like a madman.

"It's Crenshaw, I tell you, Crenshaw. And you can tell him to shove his miracle up his goddammned ass!" And then he hung up.

Jeff Ronald was trying to convince his editor at the *Herald* to let him lead with Herron's instruction to stuff a miracle up Russell Crenshaw's ass at precisely the same moment Gail Abernathy was standing outside the *Sentinel* building smoking the day's thirty-sixth cigarette and wondering what the hell was wrong with her.

Sure, she had a hangover. A full-fledged temple-thumper. But she had gotten used to those over the years, and they hadn't interfered with her work before. But now, there she stood, watching the buses collect passengers before the pigeons could shit on them. Where she should've been, as she was acutely aware, was on the sixth floor, where the newsroom hummed with the activity of thirty-two full time reporters, all on deadline, writing their stories. And she had a doozie. Peter Banks had let fly an announcement that would grace the front page of the *Sentinel* for days to come. The lawsuit may have been dropped, Edward Banks may have been triumphantly gagged, but Peter Banks' prophecy of miracles complete with live Witnesses was the likes of which Denver had never seen. A miracle in a cow town—it was the kind of stuff television news magazines swoon over. (Gail had no way of knowing it, but Ricardo Shock himself—the star of NBC's popular *Shock Report* was at that moment insisting that his agent book a flight to Denver International Airport so he could insert himself into the holy tumult.)

Despite the great story, the announcement by Peter Banks and the crowd's response when the boy finished—the room had shaken with the reverberations of the Pentacostalists—Gail couldn't get herself to sit down and concentrate.

Jeff Ronald had spoken to Jake Herron; Nancy Hardy had tracked down Sherry Setliffe Anderson, and background research was hastily (and as it turns out, quite inaccurately) being done in newsrooms across the city. But Gail Abernathy couldn't manage to type beyond her byline. Her mind went blank every time she looked at the screen.

"C'mon, c'mon," she urged herself under her breath. "Get with it." Finally she took her own advice, snuffed out her thirty-sixth cigarette, and headed back inside.

It was a simple story, she thought, sitting before the yawning computer terminal, ignoring the mad typing that was going on around her. A meeting that was supposed to be an end, an end to an uproar over a small boy who was trying to justify the experiences common to all small boys, had turned into a prophetic announcement. That was all the lead to the story had to say. For some reason it wouldn't come. Gail glanced at the clock. She had, if her editor ran late, forty-five minutes, tops.

Desperate now, Gail tried another tactic. She turned to the computer that held the databank of *Sentinel* stories for the last ten years. There she entered the names Jake Herron and Sherry Setliffe Anderson and was rewarded with a list of seventy-three articles. All of them were political reports that quoted Jake Herron, Rep. Miranda Davis' legislative director. Gail shook her head in frustration. Of course, she knew that name. She should've known that name. She had talked to Herron herself when Davis' had run for reelection last year and had been trying to portray herself as the perfect mix of fiscal conservatism and social moderation. There was nothing on Sherry Setliffe Anderson.

"What the hell are you doing?" Gail's silent panic was interrupted by the voice of Lincoln Fraser. "You think we've got all day? Delp wants to see this himself."

Gail groaned, louder than she intended. "Give me a moment, Fraser, or forget about the whole thing," she hissed.

"Okay, okay," the balding managing editor took a step backward at her tone. "Don't spaz out."

When the specter of the managing editor had hovered out of range, Gail turned back to the computer. No Sherry Setliffe Anderson. Would most of the reporters she knew write a story about a woman and include her full name? Abernathy grimaced. Not male reporters. Her fingers flew across the keyboard again, typing, "Sherry Anderson." The search took less than a minute.

Two stories. One an obituary. One a business story about Clark Hospital. It was impossible to know if the hospital's grief counseling service that the P.R. guy had bragged about in the business article was directed by the same Sherry Anderson who had lost a son to suicide at a small Iowa college some years back. Frustrated, Gail stamped her foot on the industrial carpeting that lined the newsroom. Then she grabbed the phone.

But no one at Clark hospital would put a call through to Sherry Anderson. "She's left for the day and we're not giving out her home number," the receptionist told Gail. In a last-ditch effort, Abernathy asked to speak to public relations.

"Just a minute please," the receptionist said. After an interminable period that was in reality only twenty seconds, Gail heard a voice on the other end of the line.

"Rachel Baum here." Baum, of course, had nothing to do with P.R., but had insisted the receptionist forward any troublesome media calls to her. Abernathy knew nothing of Baum's nickname, or her propensity to lash out at the slightest provocation, but the greeting, at least the tone it was in, told her this was a force to be reckoned with.

"Gail Abernathy, the *Sentinel*," Gail barked, hoping that her tone would match that of the woman on the other end.

"Ms. Anderson is answering no more questions from the press." Gail smiled. So the Sherry Anderson who was the psychiatric nurse was indeed the Sherry Setliffe Anderson Peter Banks had named. "Actually, I just wanted to check some details about her son's death," Gail responded, taking a risk.

The Bomb lived up to her name. The explosion could be heard down the entire administrative corridor of Clark. On her end of the line, Gail had to hold the receiver several inches from her ear. "You have no business prying into her life!" the Bomb shouted. "Sherry has suffered enough, and we don't need anyone to dredge up all that stuff about Steven all over again," she railed. "I can't believe you people sleep at night, I really can't—"

Gail cut her off. "Thank you," she said quietly, then hung up. As it was, she had gotten more information about Sherry Setliffe Anderson than Nancy Hardy had.

Gail dialed again. But all she got at Miranda Davis' office was the long, strangulated beep of a message machine overloaded. Gail tried flipping through the stories in the *Sentinel* computer library to find an address for Herron, although she doubted his number would be listed even if she found one, which she didn't. But she did find something, a small thing. A single personal note about Herron, which, if she had known about the picket outside of Herron's house earlier in the day, would've guaranteed her outrage at the epithets the protesters had bandied about.

Because the personal note she came across was in a brief article about Rep. Miranda Davis' visit to a local Denver synagogue over the Passover holidays last year, when she was running for re-election. By Davis' side at the event, and answering questions about one of the holiest holidays in the Judaic faith, had been Jake Herron. He was Jewish.

With fifteen minutes to go, Gail Abernathy faced her blank computer screen once again and prayed to no one in particular, prayed that she'd be able to write this story. Just this one, and then she'd go home and dive into bed, or a bottle of scotch, or whatever would make the pounding in her head and the gnawing in her gut go away. Whatever it was that was blocking her, making her freeze at the sight of the screen, her fingers throbbing, lingered. Ten minutes to go.

"Goddamn it," she muttered to herself. "It's a story, okay, it's a story, an easy one at that. Just get it out there, just do it. You can do it." But her thoughts raced and faces flew by, and she realized, finally, as Lindsey Nelson squeaked with alarm across the office, having just opened her Western Office Supplies envelope and poured the bloody pictures across her desk, that she wanted it to be real.

Gail Abernathy wanted to believe in a miracle. Even the tiniest one. And that was what was wrong. Tears formed in the corners of her eyes, and she was oblivious to Nelson's gagging, Fraser's admonitions about "spazzing," and the host of other sounds that made up the din of the newsroom just five minutes before deadline.

Oblivious and relieved, because just after Gail's surrender to the notion that it *did* matter to her what Peter Banks had said, something changed. After the realization that her life, saddled with guilt over a divorce, alcohol, and an impotent (and married) lover, it would be nice to see something positive happen, Gail Abernathy felt a shift.

And so she started typing.

CHAPTER SEVEN

Bishop John Sybrandy was praying for a miracle of a totally different sort as the Denver evening news was threatening to appear on the small television that was all but hidden on the bookshelf in his dusty, cluttered office. The good bishop, responsible ultimately for all that went on in the large diocese that ministered to a heavily Hispanic population and the transplanted Catholic easterners who brought their faith and dreams to the West, had his own worries. Number one among them was money. It never used to be this way.

Twenty-five years ago, when the bishop had come to Denver in the high times of the oil boom, back before he had even been a bishop, money wasn't an issue. First, because the hierarchy entrenched in the New York Diocese, replete with its two hundred year-old woodwork, thought of Denver as nothing more than a cow town and expected little in the way of either membership or collections. "Do what you can, John, with what you have to work with," then-Bishop James Borden had said, patting his shoulder and sending him off with an air of recklessness.

And so Father John Sybrandy had gone west, as Greeley had once admonished young men to do. And that had given rise to the second reason why money never used to be a problem. Because, back in the dawn of the 1980s, Denver had been a heady, booming, and very rich place indeed. The Church's influence was surprisingly large, at least to Sybrandy, who'd been operating under the same assumption as the rest of his East Coast brethren. Membership and collections were already pouring in upon his arrival; it was the reporting to the New York office that had been lagging. Sybrandy, hoping to impress Borden and the rest, merely corrected the reporting procedures little by little, month to month, until it looked like he himself had orchestrated a great gathering of the flock along the Front Range.

And then bells had rung in New York, and Borden himself had

called Sybrandy with the news of promotion—the robe of bishop was soon to grace his deserving shoulders.

There had been problems. Even then. A newcomer, an Anglo, and of course, an easterner, promoted over the heads of the darker skinned, longer-laboring fathers of the region, did not go over well. The fact that Sybrandy had a reputation, even then, only three years after his arrival, as a wafer-munching bean counter, did nothing to increase his popularity. But religious leadership was not a popularity contest, Sybrandy told himself, and he forged on. When the robe had been delivered, the ordination sustained, everything eventually fell into place.

Bishop Sybrandy was good at his role. He made the rounds of churches painstakingly, traveling hours, sometimes, on any given Sunday, to thrill the congregations of crucifix-bearing churches as far away as Carbondale and the San Luis Valley. He cut ribbons at the openings of parochial schools in Louisville and Durango. He gave the Easter sermon live via satellite to four media markets in Wyoming, Colorado, and Kansas.

It had been he, Bishop Sybrandy, who had urged the populace of the state to stand firm in their faith when the great economic bust of the late '80s had rolled around and the oil market had hit the skids. It had been Sybrandy, resplendent in his robe and still easily combing over his receding hairline, who stood firm as the housing market plummeted and unemployment rose. It was Sybrandy himself who had gone along with then Governor Matlin to meet with technological giants such as Ripon and DZI, to convince them to move their corporate headquarters to the city nestled on the eastern side of the Rocky Mountains. Slowly, the economy started to bounce back.

What had seemed like a gift from the Lord himself had occurred in the fall of 1990: A call from the Vatican, announcing the upcoming visit of Pope John Paul II to Denver, as part of the Pontiff's worldwide tour. It had all gone downhill from there.

While the economy improved and the population of the city of Denver and indeed all of Colorado soared, the visit of Pope John Paul II so exceeded the hopes of the powers-that-be in New York that suddenly nothing Sybrandy did was enough.

It had been the crowds, the overwhelming crowds of young and old, well-dressed and natty, serious and jubilant that had done it.

Sybrandy, for years—more than a dozen years now—had tried to explain to New York that the thousands, no millions, that they had seen overflowing the streets and spilling into the thoroughfares of Denver were not all churchgoing, dues-paying Catholics. They were not all confessing their sins, saying their Hail Mary's, reciting the rosary. Sybrandy had argued, loud and long; the bulk of the worshipers of the Pope had either been tourists, the curious, or gangly teens who considered field trips wonderful alternatives to the drudgery of class work. But New York hadn't been convinced.

"You clearly have the faithful there," Borden had told him in that low tone he usually reserved for excommunication. "Get them into church, and teach them the discipline of their faith."

The pressure had started. Membership and collections, collections and membership. For fourteen years now, Sybrandy had been fighting the battle, and losing, it seemed. Because nothing was going to wipe out, dim, the image that Borden and the others had in their heads of the pontifical crowds.

And then, last night, the final blow had come.

"We're sending someone out there, someone to help you," said Borden, who was now an archbishop, made two annual trips to Rome, and served on the High Council of Discipline.

A Father Henry Hamilton was on his way. Sybrandy was in a panic—sure of the pattern that was playing out before him. A replacement was coming, someone to observe, report back, and ultimately be on hand to take Sybrandy's own place as Denver's Bishop.

Sybrandy had been praying his rosary intermittently since the phone call of the night before. Sixty-four rounds had already been said. Fasting had occurred to him, but he presided over a breakfast meeting of the Lions that morning, and the danish had been too good to pass up. Of course, there had been some jesting over coffee about the antics of this misguided child, but nothing serious. Sybrandy told the gathering that the Church was not at all impressed by Peter Banks or his behavior, and had no comment on the situation.

This was a direct order from Borden, actually, and Sybrandy wasn't about to disobey a direct order. He had briefed Borden after seeing the story in the paper, and was relieved when the "hands off" directive came down from New York. There was enough to worry about in Denver without taking on the sins of the flesh.

The spectacle that Peter Banks had become was nowhere in Bishop Sybrandy's thoughts Thursday evening as the strains of Channel 7's evening news intro emanated from the tiny TV.

Even as the top news story began with the small boy's face peering at the reporters and cameras, his eyes glazed over, his mouth moving mechanically, Bishop Sybrandy did not look up. He was busy with his prayer, his pleas for forgiveness, for the faults of his faith, his lack of humility, the temptations leadership brought with it.

"But please, please don't bring Father Henry Hamilton here to replace me," he prayed, and above his head, the screen cut back to Reverend William Werthall, who was saying that he was unafraid to support a mere child, unafraid to follow the word of God, no matter what previously held opinions he had. "Think of the Gospel and the Lord's directive to Abraham to kill his own son. Surely, the devout don't stop and consider if they agree with the Lord, they are to follow. He is our Shepherd, we are the flock," the Reverend Werthall said.

And that is when Bishop Sybrandy raised his head from his prayer and stared at the dusty screen. Sybrandy knew Werthall, not only from Colorado Faith Against Abortion meetings (in which the two were on the same side) but also from a more negative showdown the two had had a year ago when Werthall was called to task by the media for denying the Holocaust and Bishop Sybrandy, when prompted by his advisers (New York, again) came out with a scathing statement against Werthall's stand. The man could be ugly, Sybrandy knew, and, despite all his talk of the Lord, was as manipulative and plotting as, well, Sybrandy thought now, as Henry Hamilton must be.

Sybrandy crossed himself. Werthall was on his screen, talking about Peter Banks' suspension, supporting him, in fact, regardless of the content of his message.

The bishop had no idea as he looked at Werthall's face on the screen that Peter Banks had announced a second message. Bishop Sybrandy had missed the opening of the story, deep in his own thoughts, and it would take him another four minutes of broadcast, long after Werthall had disappeared from view, to understand that the story had advanced. And so Sybrandy watched as Werthall backed the masturbator and aligned himself with God, no matter what.

It was enough to make the bishop—regardless of his heavy burden—chuckle with delight. "What an ass," Sybrandy thought to himself. "Better him than me."

The next scene Sybrandy witnessed was the view from Werthall's competition: The Mercy Church. The congregation there had put on a protest that afternoon. The scene panned wide on the sizeable crowd, showing signs that read, "Peter's hands are the Devil's Tool," and "Don't Buy in to Temptation" as Mercy's preacher spoke into the microphone about the dangers of lust and the downfall of the young in America.

It was only during the wrap-up, when the anchorwoman, a pert woman with a helmet of black hair and a bright coral-colored suit posed the question: "Do you believe in miracles?" when Sybrandy's stomach lurched as he realized he had missed something important. "Peter Banks insists that one will occur, with Witnesses, no less, in one week's time, and the religious community is split over it."

It was the perfect lead-in to stories of the day's protests over abortion, and soon Sybrandy found himself staring at scenes of the marching faithful interspersed with quieter shots of celebrations at the Planned Parenthood clinics. The bishop grunted and searched for the remote hidden somewhere on his desk. There was no reason to wallow in the hideous abortion issue when he had enough on his plate.

When the remote would not reveal itself, Sybrandy did something he rarely did. He rose from behind his desk and worked his way over to his bookshelf, around piles of books and stacks of reports, to turn off the television by hand. As he got closer, he was thankful for the dust that hung on the screen, blurring the images of dismembered fetuses. He flicked the machine off, received a handful of gray grit for his effort. He cursed the woman the diocese had hired years ago to clean. This would never do with Father Hamilton on his way.

Nor would it do that religious pronouncements were being made across town, and he'd known nothing about them. Sybrandy cursed to himself again. *Holy Mary, Jesus, Mother of God, who were these people who made pronouncements such as these, and who were the media to check in with the likes of Werthall and Honeywell before making the grand pronouncement that the "religious community was split" over the issue? I am the religious community,* Sybrandy thought. *I should've been contacted.*

Sitting back down behind the large mahogany desk—a weak substitute for the soaring offices of New York and their burnished interiors—Sybrandy tried to rationalize. No, it was good that no one had called him yet to get his reaction. Because he had no idea what the masturbator had said, or what it meant. Miracles? Witnesses? Sybrandy hadn't had to participate in a Marian Apparition investigation since his days in New York. It was a small child in New Jersey who claimed to have seen the Blessed Virgin. A toddler really, who didn't understand who the Mother of God was, and who, best as Sybrandy could tell, could've seen Britney Spears in a ring of light and thought it was a godsend. He hadn't had to make a decision at the time; he was merely an assistant to the father in charge of the investigation. But Sybrandy had been relieved at his superior's pronouncement that the vision was merely the product of a runaway imagination. The girl's mother didn't even wear a bra, for God's sake.

The bishop sat for a moment at his desk, reliving the memory of little Racinda Verrezano, until the last vision of her mother's more-than-ample breasts floated through his mind. Then he gripped his rosary with a fierceness that snapped the string holding the glass beads together. As he watched them fall and shatter on the grimy floor, he cursed his luck. Things were out of control. An infiltrator, an infidel—which is how Sybrandy thought of Hamilton—enroute, and people were prophesizing miracles in his own diocese without even giving him notice.

Sybrandy reached for his phone. His secretary answered in her usually subdued voice. "Yes, Bishop."

"Get me Chavez on the phone, and get him quick. And do something about getting rid of that woman who cleans for us. She's useless. I want my office spitspot, do you understand?"

"Yes, Bishop."

Sybrandy replaced the receiver and sat back. If anyone could get him up to speed on Peter Banks and his miracles, it would be Father Gil Chavez. A bookworm, a political animal, and an outspoken civil rights advocate, Chavez was usually a thorn in Sybrandy's side, making trouble that the bishop would later have to deal with. But Chavez was also known for the reams of study he did while in seminary—and continued afterward—on the investigations of miracles. It was said he could recite each instance of Church-approved miracle from Christ's birth to current time.

Sybrandy sat back and waited, letting his feet roll over the remaining glass beads until they were crushed into the floor.

Protestants don't have days like this, he thought.

State Representative Darren Preston, if he had known what Bishop Sybrandy was thinking, would've begged to differ.

Preston had been born a Kansas Protestant. He went every Sunday to the pared-down church on the west side of his hometown to look at the modified cross and listen to the uninspired ramblings of the minister.

When he turned thirty and was eyeing a seat in the legislature, Preston met his wife, a devout born-again. Through her, he met her preacher, the Reverend William Werthall. At that point, everything changed. The thought that Jesus could be so loving as to understand the needs of a man who could not commit to a single woman but who wanted a family nonetheless to raise up and proclaim his name made perfect sense to Preston. It enabled him to marry, to align himself with one of the most popular churches in Colorado Springs, and jettisoned him (with a little help from Werthall at the pulpit every Sunday) into a seat representing the 21st District of the State of Colorado.

Suddenly, people treated him with respect. Lobbyists wanted to talk to him, take him to lunch, ply him with drinks. The hours were long, granted, but that was only during the yearly 120-day session— the rest of the year he collected his paycheck (recently increased by a vote of the same people who received it), sold tires, and visited his district office once a week to ensure that letters were returned promptly.

He bought a sporty car—in which his burgeoning family conveniently failed to fit—and drove it everywhere. It was the life he believed he had been made for. Until Peter Banks had come along.

Now the diminutive legislator sat hunkered down at his usual stool at O'Malley's bar and tried to figure out just what he was going to do. Five hours ago he had stood on the House floor and proclaimed his support of Peter, no matter what the message of God. Now the television above the bar showed scenes of the boy predicting miracles. Preston didn't even want to think of the political implications of miracles. *Gawd.*

As he downed whatever the lobbyists who had also gathered there saw fit to buy him, Preston concentrated on the TV, praying for some indication of whether Werthall was still on board. Eventually Preston was rewarded by seeing Werthall's face, and watching him back the boy who said a miracle was on its way.

"Still, Werthall is a lot less vulnerable than I am," Preston thought to himself. Reverends didn't have to be reelected. The legislator shook his head sadly over the fresh drink that appeared before him, compliments of the trial lawyers' lobbyist.

"Here's to you, Peter Banks. May you rot in hell."

Grounded by his father just seconds after the last word of God had left his mouth, the object of Preston's curse was rotting instead in his bedroom, facing complete and utter boredom indefinitely.

His father, after proclaiming Peter grounded, managed to hold his tongue for the period of time it took Edward, Vivienne, and Peter to push through the crowd of shouting reporters and hissing Pentecostalists into the elevator and then back out through the entrance of the Denver City and County Building to the silence of the Volvo.

That's when Edward Banks had let loose. "You have ruined me, you little bastard!" he shouted as soon as the three seat belts clicked into place. "Just what did you think you were doing up there? Just who gave you the right to bring this on this family? On me?"

If he had had the guts, Peter would've told his father just exactly who had given him the right to bring whatever it was his father thought had been brought upon the family. But the boy's courage was spent, his fortitude nil, as Edward turned the car away from the curb and began the drive home.

"This, this—" Edward searched for the right word, tugging on his pants "—this act of yours makes me look like a complete fool! As if it wasn't bad enough I had to back out of the case, now my son is playing Holy Messenger, for chrissakes. Didn't David Koresh claim he had messages from God? Do you know what that did to his father's business? Think about it, my reputation, my client list, my—"

Vivienne was too tired to even try to interrupt her husband to let him know that Koresh was born to a fifteen-year-old single mother and never knew his father, much less affected his business. She knew because she had read every damn *Time* article there was on the whole Waco disaster, waiting for Peter's well-baby appointments at the pediatrician's office.

Oblivious to his factual inaccuracy, Edward continued. According to him there wasn't a single person in Denver who would take legal advice from a man whose son was obviously some cultist nutcase. "That's what they'll think you are, Peter. Another goddammed David Koresh—"

Vivienne came to life for a brief flash at that moment. "Now, Edward, language please," she said. It was purely a reflexive action, spurred, like a hammer to one's knee, by the expletive that had sprung forth from her husband's mouth.

But it did no good.

Peter took a deep breath from the back seat of the car and asked, although he knew it was precisely the wrong time, the question that weighed most heavily on his mind. "Um, how long am I grounded for?" he squeaked. He wondered if he'd still be able to e-mail Ben.

His father all but exploded. "Keeeryyst!" he yelled, almost plowing into the garbage truck stopped ahead of them at the light. When they finally pulled into the driveway of their home both Peter and Vivienne let out a sigh of relief.

But Edward wasn't finished. He entered the house at a clip, charged immediately up to Peter's bedroom and began stripping it of what he called "mind-mashing shit": video games (he all but wrenched the Nintendo out of the wall), the computer, comic books, the Gameboy, and even the poster of the red Mustang, which Edward tore in half in his rampage. "Life is not a game Peter. Kids today, growing up with all this electronic crap, you're losing grip on reality. For your own sake, Peter, for your own sake, I'm taking these away."

Peter nodded solemnly, hoping his father was done. Wondering if Ben would take him in if he managed to hitchhike to Oregon. But Edward would not be denied his final summation. "And if I ever hear you say you've gotten a message from God, Jesus, an angel or even a fucking aardvark, I'll send you off to military school so fast your head will spin."

Peter received his father's warning silently, praying first to God, and then, as his father's words flew by, to Jesus, an angel and then finally an aardvark, that he live through this moment without wetting his pants. His prayer seemed to work, although whether it was the aardvark who managed it, Peter would never know, because he didn't wet his pants in front of his ranting father. Peter endured, his knees shaking, until his father, his arms full of wires and joysticks and video games, slammed the door behind him.

Alone and full of fear, Peter raced to the bathroom before he burst, and then returned, much more slowly, to sink onto his twin bed and bury his head in its *Harry Potter* comforter and make his apologies to whom he thought really counted in all this. "I'm sorry, God," the boy said into his mattress. "I, I don't think I can help any more." He prayed that his days of talking about God and messages were over. He hoped it was understood that his father was scarier than any Roman tribunal or any Spanish Inquisition. And he wished he was a braver boy, but then God had made him this way.

In a sea of mixed emotions, relief and sorrow, Peter fell asleep, drooling on his *Harry Potter* sheets.

CHAPTER EIGHT

Gail Abernathy had read Jeff Ronald's story—the morning after Peter Bank's prophecy—standing in her kitchenette, still in the T-shirt she'd slept in. She'd had visions that the *Herald* would include whole interviews with each of the Witnesses, and that she'd have to walk into the newsroom and hear the gruff, disappointed voices of editors who had already been chastised by their editors, who had heard from the publisher.

That's how the failure to "get the story" was received on a daily basis. She had seen it, watched colleagues squirm, protest, and come up with excuses that always rang hollow, because there were no excuses. And she had been sure, given her unexplained sluggishness of the night before, that Jeff Ronald would've mopped the floor with her. Beaten her on every aspect of the story.

But it didn't happen. Despite the time she had spent running around the track in her own head and sitting blank-faced in front of the computer screen, Ronald didn't have much more than she did. "Things are okay," she said to herself. "And they're going to get better."

That was before her drive to work, where she'd come close to hitting a stray dog that stood right in the middle of Lincoln Avenue—Gail's panicked swerve forcing her car up onto the curb. The event resulted in three outcomes: the Camry now made a threatening scraping sound whenever it was in motion, she was late to work, and she was no longer alone. She had taken dog with her.

Fraser was not amused. His lead reporter on the top story was late and arrived with some mangy looking mutt following at her heels.

"This is Gus," she'd told him stupidly.

"Fuck Gus," he said, and meant it. "We've got a lot of work to do."

To Fraser, keeping the Peter Banks' "Miracle Story" alive was priority one. It was big, he knew it, because he had already received calls from the affiliates of two of the three major networks and CNN.

Ricardo Shock was already on his way to town and wanted background information. Kitty Casen, with CBS's *Right Now* morning show, was planning a trip. The *New York Times* was sending someone, as was the *Chicago Tribune*. The rest of the world was picking up AP wire or asking for copy from Fraser personally.

The problem with this Miracle story was the news wasn't going to happen, apparently, for another week (six days, Fraser told himself). The public had a remarkably short attention span, one that certainly did not withstand a six-day lull between the action.

It was Fraser's duty, as he saw it, to keep the readers interested during the wait. To do that, he needed something, anything, to say about the subject that would be new and fresh for every day of the next six. Oh sure, there could be a day lapse, maybe, but after more than a decade managing a newsroom, no one knew better than Fraser what it was going to take to keep the public interested until D-DAY. And looking at the spectacle of the smudged reporter who finally made an appearance before him, he doubted she was up to it.

Had she known of Fraser's exact thoughts, Gail would've joined him in his lack of confidence. Surely there was someone else who wasn't that busy on his beat who could take over the stories.

As it turned out, Lindsey Nelson would ensure that neither Fraser nor Gail had the luxury of indulging their doubts. Nelson had decided, after her encounter with the envelope of bloody pictures the night before and the hate call she had received from some Pro-Life advocates that morning, to leave journalism forever. Teaching is what she wanted to do, Lindsey Nelson announced to Fraser just before ten on Friday morning. She was tired of being vilified, personally insulted, and unappreciated in the workplace.

Of course, Martin Overlay could've told Nelson that had she wanted to avoid such an onslaught, teaching should be the last career she should consider. But Nelson would never ask Overlay anything and, in her mind, fuzzy with years of reading British children's novels and reporting on her own blurry image of what the education of young minds was about, teaching was her ticket out. What Nelson's announcement meant to Fraser, early on in day two of the Peter Banks' "Miracle Story," was that there was no one else besides Gail Abernathy to handle it. He would have to work with what he had.

So Fraser called an extra editorial budget meeting for early that afternoon. The editors needed to decide just how to advance the story, and make up a news log for the following week. Today would be easy—an in-depth backgrounder on both the named Witnesses. He had sent Gail out to interview Herron and Sherry as soon as he had recovered from her bizarre entrance with the ridiculous dog. But he wanted her to know where to start for Saturday's story. He was thinking of an "impact" story on how students at Rory felt sitting in the midst (or, more accurately, absence) of a holy spectacle. For Sunday, he was leaning towards an historical issue piece on miracles in general. "Do those interviews and get your butt back here pronto," he commanded. Gail had nodded vaguely at his order.

Jake Herron was less taken aback by the fact that the *Sentinel* reporter had arrived with a spotted dog at her side than Lincoln Fraser had been. Maybe it was because Jake Herron liked dogs, whereas Fraser didn't. Maybe it was because the dog had instantly taken to Miranda Davis' legislative director—nuzzling his snout into the man's hand and laying his head on his lap. Maybe it was because Herron didn't think he had any choice. "This is Gus," the reporter had said, apologetically. "I don't know why I named him Gus, I just did." Jake concentrated on not making a face.

It was Davis who had forced Herron to grant the interviews. They had had a doozy of a fight over it, after Herron had hung up from Jeff Ronald's call, after the evening news had come on and the anchors had started proclaiming his name—mispronounced—over and over from their perches behind their desks. Davis, who could get Denver broadcasts in her office in D.C. via satellite, didn't like hearing that Jake Herron, legislative director for yours truly, was "unavailable for comment." It wasn't good P.R.

"We're public servants, Jake. We never want to be considered unavailable."

"You're the public servant, Miranda," Herron had retorted over the intercom. "Not me. The loonies forgot that today when they picketed my house, and now you're forgetting it."

Miranda Davis took a moment to calm herself, breathe in and out, and let the words fall like rain around her. She had been practicing the technique with a private Yoga instructor for the past six weeks, hoping it would take a little of the edge off. The budget bill was coming, after all. "Jake, I understand that you're upset. And I am fully aware that you didn't run for anything. But when you took the job with me five years ago, you had to have known that some part of my public spotlight was going to fall on you. And that's what your picketing experience this morning was about," she said. Jake only grunted his acquiescence.

"Now, I don't know what this Peter Banks thing is all about, and I don't have anything to do with it. But, fortunately or not, you still work for me. And your behavior in public reflects on me. You need to be available."

It was more than Jake could take. "Oh please, Miranda. Of course it has to do with you. It's an anti-abortion thing. The loonies have just dreamed up a new one."

Davis tried a few mini-breaths. "I don't know, Jake. I didn't get that sense from the reports I watched," she managed.

Jake sighed. "Who knows what these guys are up to? I'm not about to dick around and play their games."

Davis set her jaw and stopped breathing altogether. "You will dick around until we figure out what the game is, because I'm not going to be embarrassed by it, you understand?" She used the tone she had used in the last election when her primary opponent had accused her of shady campaign practices. It was a sound about as sharp as a gutting knife. At the time it caused the seasoned Republican who was debating Davis to lose his train of thought.

It had a lesser effect on Herron, but it still had an effect. "How much dicking around do you think will be sufficient to protect your good name, Miranda?" he asked, not bothering to hide the sarcasm.

Davis sighed on her end, audibly. "Talk to the press, Jake. Be available to them. Tell them you don't know what it's all about. Find out from them, if you can, if the anti-abortionists have any part in this. But don't stay silent, whatever you do. Because then they'll think you have something to hide."

Jake shook his head, staring at the speakerphone over which Davis' voice rang out. She was repeating back to him the same advice he had given her over the years. As if the day hadn't been weird enough, now this, a sort of cosmic trading of places.

It was time to give in. "All right, Miranda. I will talk to them.

Tomorrow, okay? I'll talk to them tomorrow. For now, I've got to call NARAL and explain why I've missed their little fanfare and then go home and probably have to scrape fish guts off my front door because the loonies think they're proving a point. Will tomorrow do, Miranda? Because what I need right now is a good night's sleep."

Davis tried not to smile, at least not so he could hear it in her voice. "That will do just fine, Jake. I think sleep is exactly what's needed here. You go home. And just think, it's a whole 365 days until the next Roe anniversary."

Sleep had, in fact, done Jake Herron some good. By the time he found himself back at the office the next day, the front door still slightly sticky from the previous day's cavorting (he had been wrong about his own front door at home; it had been left unscathed), the vein in his forehead had resumed normal proportions. Interns Mattie and Jennifer, who'd recovered from their ordeal of the bloody pictures the day before, replaced their hysteria with a new sort of energy. Excitement. The phones had been ringing off the hook, they said. Even Ricardo Shock had called from LA. He was flying in and wanted to talk to Herron about this Peter Banks thing. They were less excited about messages from what they called "the usual suspects," the local press. But Jake Herron committed to calling them first. He wasn't interested in getting famous; he was just supposed to be doing damage control until he could figure out what all the fuss was about.

This is why Jake Herron had found himself facing Gail Abernathy and "Gus" just before noon on Friday. He had already talked to Jeff Ronald, whose editors had nixed the "miracle up your ass" comment the night before, much to Herron's relief. Ronald had asked Herron about his life, where he was born, what he did, how he "defined himself." Jake, who had watched Miranda Davis sit through dozens of these sorts of profile interviews, was startled at how hard they were. Recounting basic facts about himself was easy. But he wasn't quite sure what they all meant, and he certainly couldn't "define" himself for anyone. Not for Ronald, not for his parents, not even for himself.

"Give me a break, Jeff," he had said at one point. "If Peter Banks had said your name, would you know why?" That had shut the *Herald* reporter up. And Ronald had left not ten minutes afterward. Jake felt exhausted, watching the rumpled reporter leave. He didn't look forward to having to repeat the feat all over again for Abernathy, and then later, since he had scheduled them successively, for the local news stations, for the wires, and perhaps even for Ricardo Shock himself.

So Jake was somewhat relieved to find himself patting a dog on the head, rumpling the liver-colored ears and chatting about car repairs. Herron had met Abernathy before, sometime, he figured, during the last election. He didn't have any strong reaction to the sound of her name, which would've been his signal if she had burned them in an article. So he figured she was okay, as far as reporters went. He had asked her to sit down in his office, the desk loaded with papers, the day's schedule in Congress still flickering on his computer screen. They sat facing each other in the slightly tattered brown leather chairs, and the dog had drifted amiably over to Jake and had placed his head on the man's lap.

"I'm sorry," Abernathy started, watching the pointer drool a thin line across Herron's Dockers.

Jake couldn't help but smile. Reporters never apologized, not for anything. But the dog didn't bother him at all, and the drool would undoubtedly dry. "Don't worry about it," he said, noticing for the first time that her eyes were bloodshot and red-ringed, as if she had been crying. "I really like dogs."

The reporter immediately brightened. "Really, do you have one?"

It startled Herron. Not because he thought it was an unusual question, but because he realized that while he really did like dogs, and had always done so, he had never considered getting one. "Too busy," he told her, shaking his head in response. "This job is kind of life consuming."

Abernathy nodded. "I know what you mean. I've got the same sort of job. I'm not even sure I have a life outside of this," she said, pointing to her notebook.

Herron smiled carefully. Reporters were supposed to ask questions, not have conversations. He wondered for a moment if this were some sort of trick. But one look at the gray smudge across the front of Abernathy's pants and her exhausted face told him he was probably being paranoid. She didn't look like someone who was up to "tricks," per se.

"So what do you want to know?" he asked, hoping to cut the small talk short and get the whole thing over with.

Abernathy blinked, as though the question had taken her by surprise. It had. *What do I want to know?* she asked. When everything was going to get better, if she'd ever feel normal again, if Dillon would stop asking when she and his dad were going to get back together, whether the Professor would one day, happily, just shrivel up and die. Just where had she came up with the name "Gus." She wanted to know all of these things. But this wasn't the place to discuss them.

"I guess I just want to get a sense for who you are, and why Peter Banks named you as a Witness," she said finally, after a long minute had elapsed.

Herron let the silence drag a little longer. Then he responded with an anger that surprised him. "I'm Jake Herron. I'm the legislative director to Miranda Davis, and I've got no idea why Peter Banks dragged my name into all of this."

Gail felt the statement like a slap, and she blinked hurriedly, praying she wouldn't cry in front of the self-possessed man who sat across from her. *This is ridiculous,* she thought. *Get a hold of yourself. What's wrong with you?* "I see," she managed, trying to write the sentence in her notebook without looking at it. She knew if she bent her head down a tear would escape.

Jake looked on, aghast. He felt panicked, as if it were he who was acting so inappropriately, so out of character. "I mean, I can't imagine why this kid would say I'm going to witness some miracle. I'm not religious at all, haven't attended regular service since I was a kid. If anything, I've seen so much bullshit in the last few years in this job that I've totally been turned off to religion. I mean what it does to people, what it makes people say."

He was talking fast, saying more than he wanted to, but mostly he just wanted to fill the deadly silence and distract the woman who was so clearly falling apart before his eyes.

Gail continued her blinking, but managed to find her voice. "What kind of things? What do people say?" she asked while visions of William Werthall sprang up and she could hear his speech, declaring the Holocaust a "Jewish public relations stunt."

Herron didn't have to think long to come up with an example. "Well, you know we worked on the AIDS bill last year, trying to come up with formulas for funding for states to address the health care needs of people infected with HIV. And we had all these loo—" he caught himself before it was too late, "we had all these people, church people, you know, born-agains, come in and say they didn't want their tax dollars going to treat the disease. They said it was God's punishment and all that, for the sins of homosexuality. They said the suffering was God's will."

Jake Herron was talking softly, but the rising color in his face betrayed his rage at the memory. "I mean, for Christ's sake, have they seen what AIDS does to people? Have they seen it take the life of some guy who's had the same partner for longer than most straight marriages last, or some kid, I mean just some little kid who happened to have been born to a drug user? Do they understand this stuff is literally depopulating parts of Africa!"

Gail nodded, unsure of what to say next. As it turned out, saying nothing was fine.

"I don't know," Herron continued. "I just don't know. I mean, my parents are practicing Jews, they go to temple, they vote for Democrats. They want me to marry a good Jewish girl and settle down, but even that makes me angry. I don't know, it's just everywhere, you wouldn't believe what the anti-abortionists did outside my house yesterday."

Gail just waited, listening.

"They picketed, for God's sake. There were six people standing in my front yard, six people who don't know me from Adam and they were yelling that I was as bad as Hitler. Do they have any concept of what they're saying? Do they realize what kind of accusation that is?

At this point Herron felt his voice rising, and realized he had lost it. Lost it in front of a reporter. "Hey, I'm sorry, I didn't mean to yell," he said. "And, you know, don't write about that."

"About the pro-lifers?" Gail asked, watching as Herron absentmindedly stroked Gus's head.

"No, no, I mean about my parents wanting me to marry a Jewish girl—you don't have to mention that, do you?" He felt like an amateur. How many times had he advised Miranda Davis not to say something to a reporter, even with the magical words "off the record" if she didn't want to be reading about it the next morning?

"Okay, I won't write about the Jewish girl thing, I'm cool with that," Gail said simply.

Herron stared at her for a second. "Thanks," he said awkwardly. "I guess I must be tired. Yesterday really took it out of me."

He was surprised when she smiled at him. "I know that feeling," she said. "I'm sort of jealous of you in a way. I could use a few miracles of my own."

Herron found himself smiling back. "Now what is that? What is a miracle anyway?"

"I don't know," the reporter answered, almost dreamily. "I don't know what qualifies. Maybe it differs from person to person, you know, like what someone would wish for if they rubbed a genie bottle."

Herron laughed in spite of himself. "Like no more loo—I mean pro-lifers? Like a whole day when not one person calls to complain about a bill?"

Gail laughed with him. "Or no one calls to bitch about a story," she said. Then she thought, *or I can actually feel like something, anything, is going the way it's supposed to.* She sobered and said, "You know, I saw Peter Banks make this announcement, and I think he takes it very seriously."

Herron shook his head. "Then I don't know why he would've named me," he said. "I would be the last guy I'd name if I were doling out religious miracles. Truly. I'm like the antithesis of it all. If there were a great holy war or something tomorrow, I'd be the guy on the sidelines, drinking a Pepsi, waiting for it to be over. I don't know if I even believe in God."

Gail was about to nod at the statement when Herron suddenly realized what he had said. "Oh, no, I don't mean that, don't print that," he said, damning himself for the second stupid move of the interview. "I mean, don't put down that I don't believe in God. I mean, I just think with all this shit going on, I don't think he'd like it at all. If he's there." Herron paused, realizing he sounded ridiculous.

"This is really hard," he continued softly, thinking of the votes Miranda Davis would lose if the *Sentinel* printed her legislative director didn't believe in God. "I don't know what this is all about."

He was startled when he heard the reporter start talking. "I don't think any of us knows what this is all about," Gail said. "The people who think they do are the only ones who are totally wrong. Maybe that's why you were named," she said. "Because you at least know enough to say you know nothing."

"Oh God," Herron chuckled weakly. "It sounds like I'm a moron."

Gail smiled at him. "Nah. I know what moron sounds like, and you're not it," she assured him, thinking of Edward Banks. "So what are you going to do until Thursday?"

Herron looked confused.

"When the miracle is supposed to happen," she reminded him.

Herron groaned. "I don't have an answer for that one. Just keep going, I guess."

It sounded to Gail like exactly what she should do, too.

Gail was in the car and clutching her cellphone, desperately trying to get through to Sherry Anderson when she looked at the clock, remembered it was Friday, and dropped her cigarette in her lap. "Shit," she grumbled, "like I have time for this." She managed to pick up the burning item before it could scorch her leg (it had already made a mark on the thigh of her pants). *Shit, shit, shit, shit.*

It was therapy day.

It was always hard to begin the session, there in the tepid comfort of her therapist's office. Gail tried to think of something positive to say. She wanted the counselor to understand that her patient was making progress, however limited. So she started with how it felt to read Jeff Ronald's story that morning, and know she'd been given a reprieve. "You know, I thought I'd totally fucked—sorry—messed up and then there it was, the *Herald* didn't have anything on me."

"So you were relieved?" asked the therapist.

"I kind of felt a little guilty, to be honest with you," Gail admitted, and then looked quickly away from her counselor's shaking head.

"Oh, and I've got a dog now," Gail said quickly, hoping to change the course of the conversation, thinking about Gus down in the car.

"A dog?" Gail's counselor seemed taken aback. "Do you really think that's wise?" she asked.

Gail smiled at her. "It's just temporary, until I find its owner. I didn't have much choice," she told her, "I almost hit it on my way to work today. You wouldn't believe how hard I had to stand on the brakes. He just ran right in front of me!" Gail decided to leave out the part about running the car into the curb and the nasty noise it now made.

Her therapist looked at her, unimpressed. So Gail continued on nervously. "He didn't have a collar or anything, and I didn't think I could leave him there where he'd probably just run in front of the next car. So I decided to take him with me. And I named him Gus, I decided then and there to call him Gus."

Again, no response. Gail thought maybe her therapist hadn't quite understood. "The dog," Gail had answered. "It just seemed to fit."

Still, her therapist was silent.

"I've felt like crying pretty much ever since," Gail said, trying to fill the silence that surrounded them in the shady office. Her therapist had a name, of course, and a boatload of initials after it, but Gail always thought of her as just her "therapist" or her "counselor" and Gail's attendance in that office on a weekly basis as "shrinkdom." When Gail tried to envision the face she had talked to for fifty minutes a week, every week, for the past year-and-a-half, ever since she'd separated from her husband, she could only come up with vague outlines. The only precise images in her head were of the woman's shoes. The sensible but high-priced kind. The kind women who carried Coach bags wore. Women who had a grip on life and made it to every soccer game their kid played. They made Gail feel small, arbitrary.

This woman and her shoes had been there through the whole divorce. And yet, Gail wasn't sure how much help it had really been. She was still trying to figure out what it was that caused her to wake up one morning to the dread realization her marriage was over. Why she now wondered if she'd ever been in love with her ex in the first place. Wasn't this the same thing that was happening with the Professor? At first it was great and then one day, poof, she discovers she can't stand him. What was wrong with her anyway?

Gail pushed the thought aside. "And I'm having some trouble with this drinking thing," Gail said instead, feeling the words float across the room and tangle around her shrink's expensively clad feet.

"We're out of time this week, Gail," her therapist informed her. "We'll start with that next time."

Gail and Gus got back to the paper as quickly as they could. But it wasn't fast enough. She'd missed the editor's budget meeting on the "Miracle Story" and Fraser was busy cursing her to hell and back.

When she re-entered the newsroom, she heard not only the wrath of the balding editor, but also about the decision (hailed by the publisher as "truly inspired") to form a focus group of both young and old men and women from the Denver area to write about their views about watching a miracle unfold (or not) in their midst.

Along with the announcement of the *Sentinel's* "Religious Roundtable," as Fraser liked to call it, imagining it in forty-eight point type, Gail was handed a printout of no less than fifteen possible stories that she was personally responsible for between now and the day after the miracles were supposed to occur.

"You fuck this up, and you won't be able to find a job writing obits in Greeley," Fraser said simply as he watched Abernathy, the stupid dog still by her side, read through the list.

She was too exhausted to fight. With less than three hours to go until deadline, she had interviewed only one of the Witnesses. And she still didn't have a clue as to why he had been named. Of course, she had no idea what would qualify a person as a miracle candidate in the first place, for weren't they supposed to be totally selfless and seemingly impervious to disease and bad smells like Mother Theresa?

Gail made a mental note to give the local Catholic diocese a call. They were the experts when it came to miracles, after all.

CHAPTER NINE

Sherry Anderson had no reason whatsoever to agree to talk with Gail Abernathy. Unlike Jake Herron, she didn't work for a woman who had to convince voters to reinstate her every two years. Nor had Anderson had any practice with the media. When Steven died, Sherry's ex-husband handled the few questions from the press, and the police handled the rest. So on Thursday night, after taking the jarring call from Nancy Hardy at Channel 7, Sherry Anderson went home to her empty condo swearing that she was done with questions and prying. Even Rachel Baum agreed, when Anderson stopped by her office on the way out that night.

"We'll write you up a simple statement that says you don't know why the boy came up with your name and that you do not wish to be interviewed," Baum told her, with the air of someone who could make such a plan and then see that it got done. Sherry took her at her word.

It appealed to Baum to play the role of the protector. She knew what her reputation was among the staff, however undeserved. She was aware of her nickname and had even signed up for a few anger management courses to try to avoid scenes like the one two weeks ago when she had reprimanded a nurse for wearing shoes that scuffed the pristine halls of Clark's Intensive Care Unit. She could use a situation like Anderson's to show the staff she could be on their side, an advocate, a team player. And she was thinking about this when the call from the *Sentinel* was put through on her line.

Baum had been proud of her performance. Hell no, this reporter could not talk to Sherry; Sherry had gone home for the night. And it would be over Rachel's dead body to allow her nurse's dead son to be discussed in a public forum. Sherry had gone through enough at the time of his death. What sort of a person would ask questions like that anyhow, she had vented over the phone.

Rachel Baum had no idea she was providing crucial links to Gail Abernathy on Thursday evening. But it was precisely because of Baum, and the connections she had allowed Abernathy to make, that Sherry Anderson had been compelled to call the *Sentinel* reporter on Friday and leave a message on her voice mail.

"Ms. Abernathy, this is Sherry Anderson. I wondered if you could give me a call back at—" The nurse had left the message after reading the *Sentinel's* article on Friday morning and feeling the dread rush over her as she relived the details of Steven's death: the car in the empty cornfield, the hose duct-taped to the tailpipe and then threaded through the window. This had to stop, Sherry thought, as she sipped slowly on her coffee, the television blaring in the corner as it always did. Surely this journalist would understand that.

Of course, Gail Abernathy wouldn't get the message until half past three on Friday, after it sat for eight hours in voice mail oblivion along with one call from her ex-husband, who wanted to arrange a time Friday night to drop off Dillon for his week with her.

When Gail heard Sherry Anderson's message, still patting the dog who had been following her faithfully since its near-death experience of the morning, she couldn't believe her luck. Here at the moment she needed it was Sherry Anderson's number, and it sounded like the woman was eager to talk.

Gail dialed as if her life depended on it. "Sherry Anderson, please," she told the receptionist who answered the staff line at Clark, "This is Gail Abernathy, returning her call."

The voice that greeted her immediately filled Gail's mind with pictures—did the woman who had a lilt at the end of her sentences, who sounded professional and yet somehow human, have brown hair? Was she graying? Did her eyes betray the tragedy that had taken place three years ago? It was a game Gail played without meaning to, but it was helpful when one had a short period of time to bring someone to life for the printed page.

"Sherry, this is Gail Abernathy. You wanted to speak with me." There was a brief silence on the other end, and then the woman (whose impression in Gail's imagination couldn't have been more wrong) spoke. "Um, yes. I'm calling about what you wrote this morning."

Last night, Gail thought, I wrote it last night, when my brain wasn't working, but she said only, "Yes?"

Sherry took a deep breath. "I wanted to ask you not to write anything like that again. I—I know it was your job to write about Peter Bank's announcement, but now that it's over, I wanted to ask if you could, um, not draw it out."

Gail blinked at the computer screen on her desk. This was not the godsend she had expected. The woman didn't want to talk; she wanted to be left alone. And Gail, watching her own reflection in the black of the computer screen, couldn't help but know why.

"Uh, I, I don't know if that's going to be possible," she said weakly, her eyes flicking over the story log that Fraser had given her minutes before.

"Now look, I didn't ask for this…" Sherry protested.

Gail cut her off. "I know you didn't. I know. It's just that, well, it's not my decision. These things kind of take on lives of their own." How could she explain to this woman about the maniacal inner workings of an editor's meeting, about the twelve or more stories that a group of six people had already decided "will be news" for the next seven days? It was impossible to explain because it didn't make sense. It wasn't rational. Sherry Anderson wanted a compassionate, rational response from a newspaper. It was like asking a rodent with muddy paws to create a Renoir.

"So you intend to drag the whole thing out, all over again," Sherry's voice cracked on the line.

Gail sighed into the phone. "I'm supposed to be writing a profile on you at this very minute," she said. "I'm supposed to give readers some idea of why you are supposed to be the recipient of a miracle in less than a week."

Sherry Anderson sat back in her office chair and stared at the surface of her desk, not knowing what to say.

"What would be a miracle to you?" Gail tried, knowing that it was a long shot.

"If you people would just leave me alone," the voice said slowly. And with that, Sherry Anderson replaced the receiver with a soft click.

Gail sat back in her seat and stared at the dead phone in her hand, silently thanking whomever was out there that she hadn't been named by Peter Banks. Regardless of how much she needed a miracle in her life, she knew the effect the musings of six panicked editors could have on the life of a single private person—and she'd rather eat cockroaches than experience it.

The thought settled into the back of her brain and stayed there, with all the rest. And Gail, who had an hour and forty-five minutes and twenty inches to fill with the profiles of two reluctant Witnesses, ignored her work for the five minutes it took to call her ex-husband and arrange for him to pick up Dillon after work.

She patted Gus as she stumbled through the tense conversation. Only the dog seemed to be in no need of spiritual intervention.

Father Gilbert Chavez was sitting uncomfortably in the outer office of the bishop's chamber, listening through the oak door. Chavez had been called to the diocese for the purpose of discussing the most holy of religious topics, the history of miracles in the Church, but his thoughts were filled at the moment with less than pristine images.

Bastard, he thought. Three things were clear from the voices that came through the door. First, the bishop was angry, angrier than it would seem a dusty television screen and a cluttered bookshelf should make him. Second, the woman to whom he was speaking was an elderly Latina, Chavez thought, somewhere around his own mother's age. And third, from the sound of her whimpering interjecting between the bishop's outbursts, the woman considered her job at the diocese nothing less than her life's calling.

"It's too tall for me, Bishop sir," Lucinda Ortega squeaked at one point while Sybrandy pointed at the dusty bookcases. "I will get ladder and do better next time," she added.

"There will be no next time," Sybrandy told her. He hadn't meant to have this discussion this morning, of all mornings, when the newspapers lay half-read on his desk and there were messages from Borden and two others in New York who undoubtedly wanted to talk about the papers' contents. But the woman had come in to dust, and Sybrandy unleashed his frustration about Peter Banks' prophecy on her.

"Haven't they fired you yet?" he demanded when she had first shuffled in. Ortega, who despite her heavy accent and, in Sybrandy's opinion, reverse syntax, understood English very well and had been shocked at the statement.

"No, sir, Father, Bishop sir," she had barely managed to respond.

The bishop had assumed the situation had been taken care of last night, and now felt put upon to deliver the message himself. He thought it would be a quick task. Unpleasant, but almost instantaneous. And he was getting angrier the longer it took, the more the frail-looking Hispanic woman argued with him.

"I clean this church since my children were this big, Bishop sir," she was telling him now. "They like *you* now, big. Really big. My son, he's in seminary."

Sybrandy grunted at her rolled r's and tried to wave the woman off. How many times did one have to fire someone before they left? "That's all now," he said. "You can go now."

She wouldn't have moved one inch had not Sybrandy himself opened the door. It was then, as he stood to one side to let the tiny woman out, that Sybrandy saw who was waiting in the outer office.

"Father Chavez, how nice to see you," he muttered, embarrassed at the discussion his colleague had undoubtedly overheard.

"Good morning, Bishop," Chavez said, his eyes on the woman who now came into view. He had been right; she was a Latina, maybe a bit older than his own mother. And she was on the verge of tears.

"*Buenos dias, Senora*," he said to her gently, nodding at her and ignoring the bishop's disapproving stare. She came closer to him at the greeting and he reached to take her hand.

"*If you need work, come to my church tomorrow, at the corner of 32nd and Zuni. We'll see what we can find. There's no need to take this abuse.*"

Of course, Chavez had said it all in Spanish, tripping lightly over his native language and keeping his gestures to a minimum. Still, the bishop shot him a glance.

"I'm just telling her to pray, Bishop," Chavez pretended to translate.

"*Oh Padre*," Lucinda Ortega responded to the man who now gently held her hand, "*I am afraid of him, he is so angry. And he is the bishop*," she told him in Spanish.

"*He may be the bishop, my dear, but he's forgotten the Christ child*," Chavez said quickly. He knew he was on thin ice. There was too much similarity between the Latin all of his brethren had learned and the Spanish he was clipping out as fast as he could.

To cover himself, he pretended to translate again. "I told her to pray to Christ," he said, hoping that he was covering the words the bishop could make out.

Chavez needn't have worried about Sybrandy catching the true meaning of his words to Ortega. The bishop had never excelled in Latin; he had hated it. His joy was in numbers, and the only number he could think of at the moment was zero. He had zero time left to deal with this woman. "It's good of you to comfort her, Father, but we have much to discuss."

Chavez nodded at the clear admonition and turned back for an instant to the tiny woman before him. He locked eyes with her and squeezed her hand. *"God bless you,"* he said in closing. *"Go in peace."* She smiled finally, and nodded at Chavez. *"A mañana,"* she said.

Sybrandy nodded at the parting. "Ah, very good, very good," he said, adding, *"Dios te bendiga"* as they watched the woman disappear down the hall. That one he had learned in New York.

"Very nice, Father," Sybrandy said. "Let's get down to business."

So Gil Chavez sat down to discuss one of his favorite topics.

"God himself wants us to believe in miracles," Chavez said, feeling the same adrenaline rush he always felt when he discussed the topic, regardless of his distaste for the man sitting across from him.

"They're everywhere in the Bible, sir, everywhere. In Matthew, in Corinthians; Acts is all miracles, that's all it is. Jesus' very life is a miracle considering the immaculate conception."

Sybrandy grunted at the other man's enthusiasm. It seemed silly really, for the priest to be reciting the Bible, for God's sake. Sybrandy knew what was in the Bible! It was the rest he was curious about. The fakers and the cheats and the way the Church handled them.

But Chavez seemed to want to talk about fairy tales. "Even after Biblical times, there were no shortages of miracles, Bishop," he went on excitedly. "There's St. Paul the Simple who exorcised demons in the fourth century, St. Sulpice the Pious drove the devil out of the river Vierzon three hundred years later. St. Paul, a bishop, like yourself, drove a dragon out of Leon—"

Sybrandy repressed the urge to chuckle. He envisioned Henry Hamilton as a scaly reptile and himself with a sword. "Take that, you ingrate," he would say.

But Chavez was pushing on. "There's the levitation of Joseph of Copertino, Teresa of Avila, Alfonso Liguori—" he was listing breathlessly. "Visions of our Mother Mary in Fatima, Lourdes, Guadalupe, and even as recently as 1981 in Medjugorje."

"Yugoslavia is a long way away," Sybrandy said tiredly to the priest, thinking it had been a bad idea to call him in.

"No, no, this is even more interesting." Chavez was really caught up in it now. "From what I've read and seen on TV, this young boy seems to be experiencing inner locution. Except this time a mortal seems to be hearing directly from God himself, Bishop. Directly, it is, it is—" Chavez's dark eyes shone as his sentence went unfinished.

"What it is, is a pain in my ass," the bishop said sharply. He noted the ferocious gaze Chavez couldn't suppress. "Well, consider the source, man," Sybrandy continued. "By God, I would love to think it's on the level. But from this child—who isn't on our rolls, who apparently made his first contact around the question of, of, *masturbation*! And now he's naming Witnesses, one of whom is a Jew, to some absolute proof of God. And he has given an exact date. As if our Father can keep to a schedule like the *TV Guide*. This is not faith. It's a circus!"

Chavez gritted his teeth. "There is precedent, my lord, for the prophesizing of dates. The Mother Mary appeared in Fatima and told the people there that a miracle would occur on October 13th of that year. That day, before seventy thousand witnesses, the sun jumped and flew erratically overhead. The Holy Mother again appeared in Guadalupe, and spoke to a young boy who believed instantly, but needed her help to convince the bishop of the province of her presence. She told him to go to the hilltop at the center of town the next day, and when he did he discovered thousands of fresh flowers in the dead of winter—"

Sybrandy cut him off. "Hogwash!" he bellowed. "Flying saucers and dandelions—next you're going to tell me that Peter Banks' body will remain incorrupt after his death and the room will smell like roses! Didn't anyone teach you the role of symbolism in the Bible, the use of exaggeration to teach a lesson, to garner faith?"

Chavez took his own turn at interrupting. "Sir, both the events at Fatima and at Guadalupe have been investigated and approved by the Church," he said.

"Well la-dee-dah!" Sybrandy snapped back, then colored at his own childishness. It was just so goddamn frustrating, this wallowing in fairy tales while Henry Hamilton was on his way. Peter Banks was making a fool of him, Sybrandy thought. The masturbator is a great manipulator, he mused darkly.

"Father Chavez," Sybrandy said after a long silence. "Father Chavez, we must be rational about this," he paused to straighten his mantle and took a moment to phrase the question appealingly. "If a miracle is happening in our midst, we must know about it, and sing it out to the world in all of its beauty and joy." Sybrandy drew a deep breath for effect. "But if a pretender is among us, we must not dawdle in dreams. Remember the words of Mark: 'Do not trust every spirit but test the spirits to see whether they belong to God, because many false prophets have gone out into the world...' Remember that, my son, and help me." Sybrandy suppressed a smile when he finished, gazing at the shocked look of the priest in front of him.

Chavez, for his part, was not gazing in horror on the face of the bishop before him because he had never heard of the passage just quoted. The words, Chavez knew, could actually be found in the book of John, not Mark, as Sybrandy seemed to think. But the young priest finally realized why he'd been called to the diocese that morning.

Sybrandy already had his mind made up and wanted guidance about how to silence the young boy and bury the miracle he foretold.

Chavez lowered his head to his arms and in the darkness of his inner elbows, he considered his options. He could storm out, refuse to have anything to do with the railroading the bishop seemed to have in mind. That's what Chavez felt like doing, but he knew that it would mean he would forever remain on the outside of whatever the Church chose to do with Peter Banks. Chavez didn't want to be on the outside of the only miracle he might get a chance to witness in his lifetime. So he concluded in the ten seconds he spent with his forehead on his arms that the only real option was to play along with the bishop. To kow-tow, and join sides in this mockery.

"Bishop, I understand you completely. I'm here to help you in any way I can with the investigation of Peter Banks. I can prepare some questions for the interviews if you would like."

Sybrandy felt a wave of relief rush over him. Finally, finally the little spic was getting it, he thought. Interview questions, yes, they would be helpful. There had to be some standard for interrogation. The Witnesses, the boy himself. He'd uncover something to prove that the boy and his message were a complete charade. Sybrandy knew that Borden and the others in New York would probably already have a complete plan for how to proceed. But he didn't want their help. If anyone was going to prove Peter Banks a sham, it would be Sybrandy himself. Alone against the false prophet, he would make his stand.

They couldn't possibly replace him then. Could they?

Gil Chavez watched the man in front of him, marveling at the range of expressions that crossed his pasty face.

In the end, Gail Abernathy wrote the profiles the only way she knew how, mixing hard-won facts with whatever personal observations about the Witnesses she had been able to garner in their brief contact. Then she went a step further.

The facts were the easiest. Jake Herron handed her a brief resume when she'd left his office, so summarizing his accomplishments at the University of Colorado in political science, as an organizer for the Sierra Club in Colorado and then as field director for Miranda Davis' first campaign was a piece of cake. If she'd had the time, Gail would have called the institutions listed on the résumé and checked on each assertion. But considering Herron's public position on Miranda Davis' staff, Gail figured she could rely on the man not to try a cheap trick like resume padding. Besides, deadline was approaching.

On Sherry Anderson, records at the State Department of Health gave the woman's professional history—her bachelor's in nursing at a small college back East, her Master's at Denver University, her spotless license. Gail considered it a piece of luck that the nurse had been both married and divorced in the County of Denver, and City Hall had records of both events, the first taking place in 1975, the second in 1980. Sherry had retained custody of her son, Steven.

"Nothing like raising a five-year-old on your own," Gail muttered as she took notes. She wondered if Sherry's son had begged her, the way Dillon was doing now, to "move back in with Daddy" and "make us a family again." Gail shuddered. She wondered if Sherry Anderson drank heavily, if she picked up stray animals off the street.

"Stop it," Gail said to herself out loud. A glance at the clock overhead told her she had less than an hour until deadline.

Gail was already aware of the details of Anderson's son's suicide.

In journalism school, her professors lambasted the practice of reporting news using old articles (that's how sloppy reporting is perpetu-
ated, they'd say) but in real life and on deadline, Gail knew it was
common practice. Maybe if Peter Banks had said the miracles would
happen next August, or if Denver were a one-newspaper town and
not the home of one of the hottest newspaper wars in the nation,
Gail would have had the time and the luxury to call the small college town in Iowa and ask questions about a suicide three years ago.
But that would've meant missing deadline and incurring the wrath
of Lincoln Fraser who was already jumping around the far end of
the newsroom, yelling about uncommitted journalists who couldn't
take the heat and turned to teaching "nose-picking brats."

So Gail used the facts she had, painting a rough picture of what
was known publicly about both Witnesses. But to leave the profiles as
nothing but a recitation of education and jobs, marriage and divorce,
would never do. Such profiles read like obituaries and didn't answer
the question that readers who were following the Peter Banks story
would undoubtedly have: Why them? Gail tried her hardest to
breathe some sort of life into the stiff factual history.

At least she had laid eyes on Jake Herron. She could describe him
as tall, slender, and dark-eyed. That his hair, unruly with waves that
weren't tamed at all by his constant habit of drawing a hand over his
bangs, fell into his face. She could detail his cluttered desk, the blinking
of the congressional schedule on the computer screen. And she had a
few choice quotes that conveyed the deep sense of betrayal he felt after
years of watching religion used as the excuse to perpetuate hate. Keeping her word, she didn't mention that his parents pressured the twen-
ty-eight-year-old to marry a Jewish girl. But she did make it a point to
include that he was raised in the Judaic faith but was not religious now.
(And Jake would pay for that sentence, when his mother read it on the
Internet in White Plains and immediately phoned him to convey her
disappointment.) Jake Herron was someone Gail could make human
for the readers.

Sherry Anderson, Gail sighed, looking again at the clock and noting the twenty minutes she had to go, was another thing altogether.

A single mother who raised a son for twenty years, only to hear
that he had committed suicide in a cornfield. A divorced woman
who had never remarried, a psychiatric nurse who spent her time

consoling those who suffered tragedies similar to hers. A woman who surrounded herself with pain and suffering, and who only wanted to be left alone.

In silence, Gail wrote by the "seat of her pants." It was a phrase an old *Associated Press* reporter used when he worked in the statehouse and critiqued articles of the rest of the corps. It meant that the reporter was assuming things, attributing feeling to a situation that had not been proven with a quote or a fact. For Bob Hughes, the AP veteran, the only sin committed by writing by the seat of one's pants was if it were done with the intent to twist a story, distort it somehow, to make a legislator or whomever the principle was look stupid. Gail knew she was not guilty of this sin.

In journalism school, where old articles were not relied on and resumes were checked and double-checked, "writing by the seat of your pants" was heresy. It was fiction. It had no place in the black-and-white world of newsprint. Gail Abernathy, on the Friday night that followed Peter Banks announcement, committed that heresy. She sat with the little she knew about Sherry Anderson and wrote as if it had been Gail herself who had raised that son only to lose him. That the loss was something Sherry Anderson had never gotten over, something that haunted her as she walked through the halls of Clark. That it played in the corner of her eyes and had made the world a threatening, painful place to be.

"For Sherry Anderson," Gail wrote, the words flying out from her fingers, "any miracle Peter Banks may have knowledge of would only be three years and a million tears too late. And whatever proof of God that may be offered a week from Thursday will have to be balanced against a cold morning in a gray cornfield when a crueler proof of His nonexistence came to light. If anything, being named as a Witness makes life that much more painful for Anderson. 'I didn't ask for this,' she said in a telephone interview. 'Leave me alone.'"

Gail stopped typing and reread the paragraph. The quote was accurate, at least. The rest was pure conjecture. For a moment Gail considered the delete button before her. But Lincoln Fraser had bounced his way back toward her end of the newsroom and at that moment bellowed from behind her, unwittingly ensuring that the words would remain. "Are you done yet, Abernathy?"

"Just filed," Gail responded, hitting the button that dumped the copy into the editor's computer "in-box."

For the next hour, as the "Profile of the Witnesses" story made its way through editor and copy editor, only small changes were made. Lincoln Fraser added the words "Regalia, Iowa" to the description of the cornfield, a copy editor threw a "he said" into the section concerning Jake Herron's repugnance for religious hatred. But nothing at all was altered in Gail's prose describing Anderson and the suicide.

"It really flows," Fraser said to Gail before she and the dog left for the evening, a phrase that made her more nervous.

Despite Gail's second thoughts, the story would run, complete with the copyright that was now de rigueur on all Peter Banks stories. Picked up by the wire, it would grace breakfast tables as far away as Florida and Vermont the next morning. Gail Abernathy was left with the exhaustion of the day and a sinking feeling that she had lost her last shred of integrity.

It wasn't the kind of mood that lent itself to the smooth parenting of a traumatized eight-year-old and dinner at McDonald's. "You're late," Dillon announced as soon as his mother appeared at the door of the Tacoma Community Center, out of breath. "And you smell like cigarettes," he added.

Gail sighed and paid the grumpy center director who had stayed behind with Dillon as he had watched the rest of the "good" parents arrive to pick up their kids before the center's closing at six. Late parents, or "bad parents," as Gail reminded herself as she felt the moniker spear her somewhere beneath her right breast, were charged a dollar per minute after six.

She handed a twenty to the center director. "Keep the change," she told the woman, taking Dillon by the hand.

At least Gus had given them something to talk about. Dillon took to the liver-spotted dog immediately, asking his mother if they could keep him, despite the apartment lease's regulation against it. Her answer was no, but Dillon appeared not to register it. Dillon wanted to name the dog. "Chester," he said. "That's better than Gus." And Gail surprised herself by not allowing him even this one thing when it came to the oh-so-temporary stray dog.

"No," she said firmly. "His name is Gus, and that's final."

She gave in when Dillon insisted they get her chicken sandwich and his Happy Meal at the drive-thru so they wouldn't have to leave Gus in the car alone, and then Dillon fed every one of his fries to the dog on their way home.

It wasn't until they were inside the cluttered two-bedroom unit and had shed jackets and poured a bowl of water for Gus, that Dillon let the zinger fly. "So you're just going to get rid of Gus like you did Daddy?" he asked, petting the dog's head with one hand and holding the other out in the general direction he figured his dad was in.

It was then that Gail rose to fish the bottle of scotch out of the garbage where she had thrown it two days before. She poured herself a stiff one.

"Sweetie, I didn't 'get rid' of your father. We both decided to get a divorce," she said, knocking back three fingers of amber liquid and pouring herself another.

"He said it was your idea," Dillon's tone made Gail think he'd be a good reporter. Certainly a better reporter than she was.

"It doesn't matter whose idea it was, honey. We both decided it would be for the best. The important thing for you to remember," she took another gulp here, "is that we're not divorcing you. We love you, and you will always be our son." It sounded hollow and ridiculous to her, and she wondered how it sounded to Dillon. Draining the glass and refilling it, she wondered what had possessed her to ever think she was capable of being a mother. *Can't use fiction here, can you?* she chided herself.

Dillon eventually got bored with the topic and watched a Disney video for what Gail estimated to be the sixty-seventh time until it was bedtime and the small, sandy-haired boy climbed into his neat twin bed and picked out a book for their nightly read-aloud. It was only then that Gail realized the trouble she was in.

"If I had half a giraffe," she started, hoping her memory would carry her through the Shel Silverstein book.

"It's a giraffe and a half," Dillon corrected her, looking cross.

"Okay, okay, I was just trying to liven it up a bit," she told him, feeling the pit in her stomach grow. She tried placing one hand over her left eye, to keep the words on the page from crossing.

"What's wrong? Why are you covering your eyes?"

"Mommy has a headache, Dillon," Gail said, trying not to tear up. She really hadn't thought about the scotch as it had disappeared. She had just refilled the glass every time it emptied. She read on as best she could, switching eyes to stop the lines from veering off the page or mixing together. Then, after kissing her son good night and pulling the door until it was open just a crack, Gail sunk into her own bed and let the tears come for the fifth time that day.

I'm never going to make it, she thought, looking at the bare walls. The creak from her bedroom door opening panicked her at first; she wouldn't want to be caught in a total meltdown by Dillon. But it was only Gus, who for whatever reason, had come looking for her.

Now he sunk his drooly jaw down on Gail's lap and looked up with his soulful brown eyes. "I'm not going to make it, Gus," Gail said softly to him, tracing a line down his straight snout. "I'm just not going to make it." The dog raised his head and looked at the woman before him, with an expression of calm and hope.

Gail Abernathy, feeling she needed whatever warmth she could get, fell asleep with her arms around the fifty pound dog, his warm head on her chest, and dreamed that Darren Preston and the Professor were lovers.

CHAPTER TEN

Saturdays had become fairly stress-free in Lisa Marretti's part of the world. The baby often slept through the night now, so Lisa could wake up rested and start the day by making pancakes with Ed. They occasionally had time to eat every last dollop of syrup before the baby woke up. Sometimes Lisa had time to read the paper, to see what was happening in the rest of the world while she dealt with the challenges that new motherhood, January, and Indiana presented her with at home.

But the Saturday Gail's story on the Witnesses was published, stress became the order of the day. Headlined by the *Indiana Daily News* as "Denver Braces for a Miracle," Lisa started reading the story and wondered if Coloradoans were expecting a bizarre weather change or a two-headed infant (she'd had such nightmares herself). Instead, she found herself reading about Peter Banks, his question about masturbation (seemed reasonable to Lisa), and his recent prophecies. Cool, she thought after the first couple paragraphs.

As she read further, she felt her heart sink into her stomach.

"You okay, honey?" Ed asked, looking at her as if she'd said something.

"What?" Lisa looked up, putting on what she hoped would be a normal face.

"You just groaned. I thought you smacked your elbow or something," Ed said, still watching her curiously.

"Oh, yeah, ugh, hit my knee on the table," Lisa said quickly. "No biggie." Ed settled back in his seat. Lisa took a breath and returned to the article. "Peter Banks named two witnesses to the upcoming events meant to establish proof of God," Lisa read to herself from the article. "Denverites Jake Herron and Sherry Setliffe Anderson."

"Oh man," was out of her mouth before she could stop it.

"What?" Ed asked, interested. Lisa had to think quickly.

"I think the Pacers lost again," she managed.

"As usual," her husband replied.

Lisa smiled tightly against the hard set of her jaw. Suddenly nothing was usual.

Back in Denver, news continued to develop through the weekend, however forced it may have been. The *Sentinel's* competition, the *Herald*, was having its own issues with the story, how to keep readers interested, what constituted thorough "Miracle" coverage, how they were going to avoid getting scooped by the *Sentinel* again.

"His Excellency is unhappy," the *Herald's* managing editor, Truman Newhouse, told his editors at a rare Saturday morning meeting. Our beloved publisher doesn't think there will be enough momentum in the story to carry it through another five days."

"Jesus Christ, Newhouse," mused John Carter, the city desk editor "What does he want us to do, hold a few human sacrifices to keep everyone in the mood?"

"If you could arrange it, that certainly would be helpful," Newhouse deadpanned. "Any other suggestions?"

It was that female editor, Sue whatever—Newhouse could never remember her name—who answered his question with another that was foremost in all their minds.

"Has anybody thought about what we do if there is no miracle?" she asked in a low voice.

Newhouse shifted uncomfortably in his seat. "We've built up to things that were flops before, haven't we?" he answered.

"Sports does it nearly every week," Carter said.

"Aren't we supposed to be reporting the news, not making it here?" said Byron Diggs, in his annoying way. They ignored him.

"I understand that Sybrandy and the Catholic Diocese in Denver are starting an investigation," Carter tried to be helpful. "That should be good for a story or two."

"Or it could kill us altogether," Newhouse considered. "Suppose they declare Peter Banks a sham and we still have three days to go?"

"Surely they'll wait to draw any conclusions until D-DAY," Sue-something said.

"Oh right. Since when do the Catholics wait for anything?" John Carter couldn't help himself.

"I beg your pardon," she shot back with a near-hiss, her long fingernails playing with the cross at her throat.

"Gentlemen, ladies, I'm sure we can do a story about the undertaking of the investigation, and hope they hold off on conclusions until after D-DAY," Newhouse had inadvertently picked up her word for it. "But we really need something to draw it all together, something to banner every story with. Some moniker that can run over the story, no matter what it says. Something that says to readers, 'Okay, here's the newest in the Banks' saga.'"

"Like 'Countdown to the Millennium,'" Carter muttered.

"That's it!" Newhouse said. "We can do 'Countdown to a Miracle.' Too bad we've got five days, not ten, to go."

"Of course, the millennium was the perfect example of us leading up to—with great ardor—an absolute flop," John Carter said, not disguising the edge in his tone.

"It wasn't our fault nothing happened," Newhouse shot back, his face red, thinking of the generator and forty gallons of water that were gathering dust, five years later, in his garage.

"More relevant," Sue Something said, "is that readers didn't care that nothing happened. They read the paper for the thirty days we did 'Countdown to the Millennium,' they read every day when we counted down to the Final Four in basketball, and they'll read the paper for the five we do the 'Countdown to a Miracle.'"

"Will His Excellency make us add a question mark to that, like the *Sentinel* did on their masturbation headline?" Carter asked quietly.

Newhouse glared at him.

"There will be no question marks at this paper," he said with finality. "No one ever won a Pulitzer for a question mark."

"No one won it for great millennium coverage either," Carter said, and the meeting was over.

Ricardo Shock arrived at Denver International Airport at the same time the *Herald* editorial staff was reviewing the disappointment the Millennial New Year had been. If he had been in the room with Newhouse and Young and the others, Shock would have been able to tell them that no one was more disappointed than he himself when the lights failed to go out at midnight and the crowd steadfastly refused to riot in Times Square.

But this was different, Shock would've reminded the *Herald* editors. Peter Banks' prophecy would have a newsworthy ending either way. Because either the miracle would occur and could be reported, or Peter Banks would turn out to be a liar and a cheat and he could be figuratively hung out to dry by the best executioner in television journalism: Shock himself.

For Shock, it was Peter Banks who was the story, and Peter Banks whom he needed to focus on. With Peter Banks in his sights, Shock had landed at DIA with camera crew and luggage in tow and decided to waste no time. "We're going directly to the Banks' residence," he shouted into his cell phone, talking to his producer, Morty, back in L.A.

"You going to have something for tonight?" Morty wanted to know, "Do I carve out four minutes on the nightly news?"

"More," Shock responded, as he always did to questions about air time.

"Ricardo, these people may not even want to talk to you. They haven't agreed to an interview or anything, right? What are you going to do if they say no—talk about the neighborhood?"

Shock felt his spine tingle. "Of course they'll talk to me!" he said. "Everyone talks to me, sooner or later."

"That's my point, Ricardo. What if it's later?" Morty asked. The short man, who had dealt more successfully than any other with the turbulent ego of Ricardo Shock, was nervous. It was a very fine line to tread, between upsetting the prima donna of "talk news" shows and having to air four minutes of finely trimmed front lawns because Shock couldn't fulfill his end of the bargain.

"It'll be sooner," Shock answered, as Morty had known he would.

"It better," Morty told him, and hung up. In the end, he would reserve three minutes for his star reporter, and then have to fill with some feel-good dog story.

Shock listened to the click on his end of the line and snapped his cell phone shut. "Find me a cab," he barked to the nearest cameraman. "We're heading to Sultan Lane."

It made sense to Sherry Anderson to go shopping on Sunday. It was a way to get away from the phone, for one thing, which hadn't stopped ringing since the *Sentinel* ran Gail Abernathy's story on Saturday morning. Not wanting to tempt fate by going out, Sherry had spent the entire day inside her apartment, wincing every time the phone rang. When Sunday dawned, she was determined not to waste another day doing the same thing. Sherry needed to buy a gift for a wedding shower she had agreed to attend for one of the pediatric nurses at Clark. The shower was the following Saturday, two days after Peter Banks' miracles were supposed to materialize, but the woman getting married would not be thinking of it that way. The bride-to-be's life had not been turned upside down by the pronouncements of a twelve-year-old boy.

For Sherry, it felt like she was suddenly caught beneath a giant overturned glass tumbler. It wasn't Peter Banks' announcement that had done it; she had nothing against the boy. But Gail Abernathy had stripped Sherry naked, she thought, and put her on display. And now Sherry was trying to shake that feeling, the sense of being stared at, by walking anonymously around the Cherry Creek Mall.

Here under the cavernous ceiling, on the polished tile walkway, a woman who looked like Doris Day could go unnoticed. Here, no one could connect her with the woman Gail Abernathy had written about for Saturday's paper, no one knew that the woman was the Sherry who was haunted by the death of her son, the sound of the police officer's voice over the phone, the specter of death all around.

Here, she was just Doris Day, in search of a nice pewter platter. Sherry had decided on pewter because it was one of the few things she had left from her own wedding, twenty-six years ago. Most of the china was broken, the glasses gone, the appliances fizzled out or sold at garage sales. But the pewter serving platter remained intact. Though she couldn't remember just who had bestowed the wedding gift, it was important to her, the things that lasted, as if the platter served as proof that one day she had been like other people. A wife and a mother, although she had evidence of neither anymore.

It was in housewares at Macy's, while she had been dismissing the crystal jellybean bowls and the porcelain vases as being too temporary, too fragile, where Sherry saw him. It had happened before, of course, these glimpses. And at the very least, she was thinking to herself when she was finally able to catch her breath and listen to her pounding heart slow to a normal rate, Gail Abernathy hadn't written about it. But it was there that Sherry saw the curve of the blond hairline on the back of a young man's neck as he had disappeared around the corner of the cutlery section.

"Steven?" She said it out loud, her steps quickening. "Steven," she called again, louder this time, because she could see the faded cotton T-shirt and the jeans and note the tan—even in January—on the arms. But when the young man turned to face her, she saw that his eyes were all wrong, and his nose jutted out far past where her son's had, and of course it wasn't Steven, because Steven was dead.

Silly, silly woman, she chided herself, and then let the streams of psychiatric training on grieving take over. It was part of the process, this mistaken identity. It was common, especially among those who had lost loved ones suddenly, in the cases of accident and homicide (or suicide). Dead husbands would be recognized at bus stops, brothers at construction sites, mothers in the supermarket. On second glance, it was never them, just people who had one or two characteristics in common with the deceased. The incidents were signs of the brain seeking the familiar for the familiar, and still adjusting to the shock.

Sherry had just explained the phenomenon to a bereaved mother that past week, a woman who had lost her four-year-old to leukemia and kept mistaking the soft mewing of her cat for a child's cries in the night. "It'll pass," the Triple D had told her.

Of course, it hadn't passed for Sherry. This kind of scene, her calling her son's name and chasing strangers around corners, occurred as often as twice a week. If she had been in therapy still, Sherry knew, the psychiatrist would've told her it was a sign she was still holding on, she was still working through the death. A sign, he would say, of lingering guilt.

Don't think about it, she told herself, then turned her concentration back on the shiny, fragile offerings of the department store. It was futile. Here was the stemware, so translucent and soaring it was hard not to pick it up, and finger the smooth, cold globes. Here was the china, thin and milky, like the skin of a baby, but much, much cooler. And now Sherry was inside the reverie that kept her so occupied, that had taken over like a vigorous vine and stunted all other growth.

What had she done? When Steven was a baby she had held him, against the advice of her own mother, every time he cried. She had felt so powerful then, so in control. In the fifth grade Steven had been selected for a part in *A Midsummer's Night's Dream*, so Sherry took a week off so she could make costumes for the entire cast.

There was the divorce, early on, before the play and before Steven's obsession with music and soccer and all the other things that made him who he was, who he was before he stopped being who he was. It didn't make sense to her, no matter how many times she went over the past. It hadn't been the divorce. She knew when it had happened that Steven was as relieved as she was. No, not the divorce. So what had it been?

When Steven entered high school, she remembered, there had been terrible fights. She was standing in front of the cookware now, and in the reflection of the Teflon-coated frying pan she could see a piece of her face looking back, gray and mottled. He had been an adolescent, for God's sake, she told herself. It was normal to have struggles. And yet, there was the reflection of her face, that part just around the lips, staring back at her, just as it had stared back at her in Steven's face. They were so much alike, especially around the mouth. When he got angry, as he often had in those days, she could see the edges of that mouth twitch, the edges of the mouth that was hers but was reflected back when she saw her son.

For a while, it had all seemed to calm down. Steven's surly attitude was gone, his interest in all things relating to plants was born, and he had begun to date. A stint working at a large greenhouse just south of Denver sealed his fate. Steven decided to major in horticulture, with a dream of owning his own greenhouse, of spending hours in humid, airy plastic tunnels, watering and pinching and clucking over this herb or that flowering bush.

And that is why he had chosen Iowa. The university there teemed with both cutting-edge horticultural studies and the more practical agricultural curricula. Sherry had balked at him going so far away— should she have stopped him? The burnished metal of a copper double boiler made her face glow. If she had put her foot down, made him go to Denver University, would he be alive today?

Of course, she reminded herself, even DU has spring break. It always came down to this. To spring break, to the Ides of March and the week that Steven had come home to announce that he wanted to quit school. How could she have known back then, when she had been on-call three of the five nights he had been home, that he would soon be gone? At the time it seemed like the worst thing that could ever happen was to watch her only son drop out of school halfway through because he had failed some biology class, because the professor had been an asshole. Because he was just fed up.

"Over my dead body will you be quitting school," she had informed him, watching that mouth that she knew so well twitch in anger.

"You can't stop me," he'd said defiantly.

She remembered how she'd shaken, how she'd wanted that control, to be able to sweep him up in her arms and put him in a baby sling and carry him around until the wild notion of quitting college had left him and he could return to his full-size, adult body and go back to Iowa with a renewed spirit.

But he refused to regress to babyhood. Looking up into his face and feeling shock once again at how tall he had grown, how much he looked like an adult, she knew she had lost. "I can't stop you, but I can tell you you'll be making the biggest mistake of your life."

How could she have known, the psychiatrist would later ask. It was a normal, parental response. She had been called to Clark that night and the argument had ended. When she came home at four in the morning, Steven was passed out, the smell of marijuana pervading the house.

The five days had been nothing more than a repetition of their first conversation. The fight, the admonishments, the anger, her getting called away, him getting high. When he left that Friday, to drive back to school—stalwart in his determination to pack up his dorm room and head out to find a gig playing electric guitar somewhere in New York—she refused even then to give him the go-ahead for his plan.

"Maybe the drive will help you think," she had said to him, giving him a quick, unexpressive hug. And then turned, the back of his neck with its year round sunburn and the sweep of his hairline all that was visible. He drove away, not bothering to wave. It was the last time she saw him alive.

Guilt, she thought, staring at the placemats, linen napkins and yards of tablecloths. It was the one thing Gail Abernathy hadn't written about in her article. And yet, it was in the story. It stared up at her in the phrase that described how Sherry's eyes looked, how she was "haunted."

"Fuck it," she said to an oven mitt. She didn't want to talk about the guilt, about whether she should or shouldn't have it. It was the reason why she had left therapy, why she had decided to "major in death." It was hers and hers alone. It was what made her a mother, the only thing besides a pewter platter that proved what she had been. Her secret.

Until, of course, Saturday's damn article. She hadn't even read it when the first call came. She could barely remember the mornings when she used to sit down and smooth the front page at the crease, looking into other people's lives. Now she showered immediately, drank coffee, ignored the blaring television, and went about her day. Except on Saturday, when she had picked up the ringing phone and tried to place the voice she heard at the other end.

"Sherry, I just wanted to call and see if there's anything you need."

"Ray?" A wild guess, really. The voice seemed totally out of place, like it belonged to some other time. Why would her ex-husband be calling now?

"Yeah, hi," he said. "I don't mean to intrude, it's just that I read the article this morning and I thought maybe you'd want to talk or something. You know, about Steven." There was a long pause now, as if Ray were trying to ascertain whether it was allowable to even breathe the name over the phone.

"The article?" Sherry felt rather lightheaded at the sound of Ray's voice.

"In the *Sentinel*, this morning. I'm sorry, babe, I guess I didn't realize that you were still, still you know, stuck—over Steven."

"Stuck?" Sherry felt like she was going to throw up, only there was something blocking everything, her thoughts, her stomach contents, her ability to breathe. What did he mean, stuck? What was in the paper?

"Have you read the story?" Ray finally asked, tiring of the one-word responses he was getting from his ex-wife.

Sherry couldn't find the words to answer him for a while. "Not yet," she had said finally, hoping it didn't sound as bad as she thought it did. No, she wished she had said, *I don't read the paper now, I don't need it.* But people always looked at her as if her head had fallen off when she said things like that. As if they had never had a son die and watched their world shrink.

It hadn't been a long conversation, that one. And after she had bid Ray goodbye, it didn't take her long to find a pair of boots and head down the elevator to the newspaper box that stood on the corner outside of the condo. Of course, it hadn't been the right newspaper, and she hadn't realized it until she had fit a quarter in the slot.

She stared at the *Herald* within the machine for a full minute before slamming the door shut and walking another block to a convenience store where she purchased the *Sentinel*.

She couldn't resist reading on the walk back home—the article started on the front page, after all. At first, it was rather interesting, the background on Peter Banks, the naming of the Witnesses, the details on Jake Herron, whom Sherry couldn't help but like. She could remember being his age, being frustrated with the limits life was revealing.

Then Sherry Anderson started reading about herself. It made her dizzy, as she approached the steps to the condominium complex, to see the recitation of her nursing degree, the date of her divorce. There was a brief description of her role at Clark, something she could have never described in such a succinct manner. It was in the elevator that she reached the part about Steven's suicide, about the cornfield in Iowa, the hose that lead from the tailpipe of the car to the front window. Sherry didn't even notice when the elevator door opened; she stood leaning against the wall, holding onto the railing that ran around the six-foot-square opening.

"Are you going up or down?" a woman's voice asked her politely.

Sherry looked up from the paper, her face ashen. "I'm sorry, I'm getting off here," she said, noting the floor number. Safely inside her own unit, Sherry read the rest of the article through blurring tears. Here was the woman haunted, who held her grief in the edges of her eyes, the woman for whom no miracle could be enough.

There were four calls for her after she had finished. Two from women at Clark, professionals who wanted to let her know they were there for her if she needed them. One was from her former psychiatrist, who wanted to know if she was seeing someone, getting help, even if it wasn't him. After the last call, she had disconnected the phone and retreated to bed, studying the smooth plaster ceiling and light fixture over her head. It filled the day.

Hence the necessity to get out and do something on Sunday. Sherry finally found what she was looking for at Macy's, after her encounter with the Steven look-alike, after the memories relived in crystal vases and copper pots, after swearing aloud at an oven mitt, she came to the pewter. And there was a tray. It was bigger than the one she and Ray had been given all those years ago. And it didn't have the same sort of handles. But it would do. Smooth and solid, impervious to the rough handling of divorce and death, of the flight of years, and of the blind alleys that started appearing when she was a young wife and seemed to close in a little more each year.

The perfect gift. And she had it wrapped as she waited, paying by credit card and asking the cashier to make sure to wipe the fingerprints from the shiny, mirror-like surface so that it would emerge from the box pristine.

Mission accomplished, Sherry Anderson returned home to the television set and carefully made bed with the light fixture overhead. As she made coffee, her pager went off. Relieved, Sherry viewed the display and dialed the phone.

It was really about time, she was thinking as she waited for the duty nurse to pick up on the other end. It was highly unusual for her to get a full morning, and even part of the afternoon, without a call from Clark. Death was a constant, either the danger of it, or its immediate impact. There were mothers and fathers and sisters and brothers and husbands and wives to talk to. And for some reason, during the entire time she had stared at housewares at Macy's, there hadn't been anyone who had wanted to talk about it.

When the voice answered at the duty station, Anderson identified herself and told the nurse she had been paged. "Oh Sherry, it's Tanya," the woman said sunnily, making Sherry smile.

"Hey Tanya, I was just shopping for you. I hope the pager was working. I didn't get a signal until just now."

The woman laughed. "Oh, it's working. I just paged you to let you know that Clark has a new record. The girls and I just figured it out, and we thought we'd call you. In the last sixty hours, we haven't had a stiff. None. Not a single death. We think it's some sort of world record. Pia Mendelson says she can't remember a time like it, and she's been here forever."

Sherry was quiet, holding the phone close to her ear, trying to keep her breathing under control. Pia Mendelson hadn't been at Clark forever, but her twenty-seven years of service did make her a source of institutional memory. It was an oddity. People were brought to hospitals because they were near death, so the presence of its ultimate consequence was evident. Always. Transfers to hospices notwithstanding, Clark saw its share of death. It was a thought that finally prompted Sherry to respond.

"What about Hospice?" she asked, hoping somehow, that Clark had just stepped up its cooperation with those freestanding facilities that existed to ease the transition between this world and the next.

"None, Sherry. None," Tanya told her triumphantly. "Not a god-damn one, can you believe it? I thought of that too, and we checked. Not one in just over forty-nine hours. It's as if everyone just decided to hang on. Pretty cool, huh?"

Sherry felt her hand start to tingle and so loosened her grip on the receiver. "Yeah, really cool," she managed.

"I mean, if this keeps up, you're totally out of business," Tanya said, laughing, and when silence greeted her at the other end, she added, "You know I'm joking, right?"

Sherry shook her head in the privacy of her kitchen to clear the buzzing. "Of course I know you're kidding, honey," she told the bride-to-be. "But it's really weird." There was some sort of bustle on the other end of the line and it took Tanya a few seconds to return to the conversation. "Sorry about that, Sherry, we thought there was going to be a code in 212, but it was a mechanical glitch; Mr. Corey is doing fine."

Sherry felt her heart sink but she forced herself to sound cheery, "Well, that's good," she managed.

"Hey, I'll call you as soon as someone kicks," Tanya said breezily. "But I just wanted to let you know we still love you, even if we are kind of in a holding pattern over here."

Sherry mumbled something in response and bid the young nurse goodbye. Tanya's choice of words, her reference to a "holding pattern," was stuck in her mind. As if Clark were an airport and no one had taken off in a while. Sixty hours, she thought tiredly; no one had died since Mrs. Collins, the mother who had delivered a healthy baby boy in the midst of a massive cardiac arrest. Weird.

In the days to come, there would be plenty of time to speculate on the curious lapse at Clark—to wonder why death chose to be absent suddenly, without any apparent scientific reason. But for now, on a Sunday afternoon (Day Five according to the *Herald* editors) Sherry Anderson was content to dwell on a single thought.

It can't last.

CHAPTER ELEVEN

Jake was late for work Monday. He let the interns think it was because of all this Peter Banks' fury. But it wasn't.

Sure, Peter Banks *had* complicated the weekend. Herron read Abernathy's story on Saturday morning and was relieved. But his boss, Davis, thought it made him, and thus her, sound totally non-religious—not something that would go over well with the voters. "I don't have to be that secular," she told him Saturday night. "I'm a Republican, remember?"

"A moderate Republican, Miranda," he told her, the only reason he had agreed to work for her in the first place. "Most moderates don't feel that having God on the political agenda is appropriate."

"Well, try to sound a little more like a believer, for my sake okay?" she had said. "Atheists aren't that popular around here."

Atheist. This word bothered Herron more than he could say. He *wasn't* an atheist; he was just tired of the whole thing. And he thought Abernathy had done a good job getting that across.

Sunday's papers weren't as gratifying. The *Sentinel* ran a feature by a Lifestyles reporter on the history of miracles, and the *Herald* had chosen to focus on prophets, psychics really, in and around Denver, from the list of sources of those who'd predicted the millennium would be the end of the world.

Herron had hoped to learn more about Peter Banks, get some background. Despite having been so sure the boy had been sent by the pro-lifers, discussions with the local reporters on Friday convinced Herron otherwise. He also hoped Monday's papers would have some details on who Peter Banks was and just how he'd come up with the Witnesses' names.

So Jake collected both the *Sentinel* and the *Herald* from his front lawn Monday morning and treated himself to reading both of them before he got dressed. He'd woken up early, figuring he had plenty of time. He figured wrong. He wasn't even halfway through the *Herald's* local news section when the phone rang. It was probably another relative, calling to remark on Saturday's profile, Jake thought, or (and he was excited about this) Ricardo Shock, calling to confirm the interview on Tuesday they had arranged. But it was neither.

No, this was some Catholic priest, a Father Gilbert Chavez, calling to ask if he and Bishop John Sybrandy and another man, Hamilton, could arrange a time to speak with him.

"Why?" Herron had asked stupidly. Of course he knew why, but despite the news stories, it still didn't seem quite real.

"We're doing a routine inquiry into the prophecy," Chavez told him, trying to sound nonchalant.

"I'm Jewish," Herron had responded. "I don't know anything about the prophecy that wasn't already in the papers."

Chavez tried to sound comforting. "We just want to find out more about who you are, since you were named," Chavez assured him. What the young priest really wanted to say is, "You are part of the witch hunt that will begin today and not end until Peter Banks is crucified," but he didn't. Sybrandy and Hamilton were in the room, listening. It had been their idea that he call the Witnesses and arrange interviews.

Herron just sighed. "Why don't you call me at the office, when I have my schedule in front of me?" he had said. He'd talk to Miranda later about whether he needed to deal with the Catholic investigation on this. Annoyed, he went back to his paper. But his concentration was shot. The loonies were everywhere and he couldn't escape them. Even the woman he'd met last night—the one who kept popping into his head this morning—turned out to be one of them. He only had to remember her face to feel his stomach drop.

He'd been out for a beer—hoping to relax a little, feel like himself again—not some "named witness" the papers kept referring to. He was sitting at the little corner pub on one of Northwest Denver's most commercially successful blocks, and the woman started a conversation.

"I've never been to Denver before. It seems really nice," she'd said, out of the blue, as she slid onto the bar stool next to him.

She was attractive. Tallish and slender—with glossy dark-blonde hair and deep green eyes. She took a sip of her white wine.

For a moment, Jake wondered if his luck were changing.

"Uh, yeah, it's a great town, I've lived here for years," he responded, immediately regretting how stupid he sounded, wishing he had some sort of smooth reply. She must've liked what she'd seen, he tried to reassure himself. She'd started the conversation, after all.

But her next sentence dashed any hopes Herron may have held that it was his good looks, his "Jesus-like" countenance, as Mattie would've said, that was making the woman approach him.

"I had to come, as soon as I heard about Peter Banks," she said.

Herron was silent, picking up the pieces of his shattered ego.

"You're Jake Herron, aren't you?" she continued, softly.

"Yep, that's me," Herron admitted.

"I'm sorry," she said then, unexpectedly. "You must feel like there's no place you can go to get away from it. I didn't plan on this, you know, I was here, getting a hamburger and saw you come in. Your picture was in the paper. I was sitting over there." She pointed to a table in the corner, set for one, and then, as if to confirm her story, a waiter appeared and they both watched for a moment as he hesitantly put down a plate with hamburger and coleslaw at the empty place. "I'll be right back,"she said, hopping off the stool.

He watched numbly as she retrieved her supper and brought it back to the bar. "Anyway, I'm Leslie Brimhall. It's nice to meet you," she said, taking a bite out of the burger.

Jake watched her chew for a second. He couldn't think of a single thing to say.

She smiled. "Okay, now it's your turn. You're supposed to say, 'Hey Leslie, nice to meet you. Where do you hail from?'"

Jake shrugged, trying to hide his smile. She seemed so at ease with herself, and he wished he had that sort of confidence. "I'm sorry. Where are you from, Leslie?"

She grinned. "I wish I could say somewhere exotic. But I'm from Akron, Ohio, about thirty minutes south of Cleveland."

Jake nodded. He didn't know anything about Ohio, except that they elected conservative Republicans and their state motto was "With God, all things are possible." He remembered that because the ACLU had made a big case out of it a couple years ago. Leslie was cute, but he couldn't deal with any closet conservatives. "What sort of things do you like to do in Ohio?" he asked, wondering if anyone would ever answer that sort of question with "picket abortion centers" or "throw lamb chops."

She tilted her head slightly and beamed. "I'm a sailing nut," she responded. "You guys have the mountains, but we've got the lakes! You mountain climb?"

Jake couldn't remember the last time he'd gone hiking. Probably before he started working for Miranda, three years ago. There hadn't been time. He shrugged and shook his head. *I look like such a loser.*

"I'm dying to meet Peter Banks," she said after she had let the silence hang between them. Looking directly at Jake, she asked, "What's he like?"

Herron smiled. Now they were on familiar territory. She was trying to trick him, and he was too good to be tricked. *She must be a reporter,* he thought, *a fucking reporter.* If he had anything to hide, he might have felt slightly apprehensive. As it was, he felt nothing. "I don't know. I've never laid eyes on the kid."

To his surprise, the woman smiled. "Really?" she asked, excited, like a child.

"Really," Jake said, now confused. Usually when you told a reporter something that didn't jibe with their theory of conspiracy or wrongdoing, they looked disappointed, not excited.

"That's cool, that's really cool," she said to him, still looking pleased. There was a small smudge of ketchup on the edge of her lips, and Jake found he had to make an effort not to wipe it off with the side of his thumb.

"I'm probably not the person to talk to," he told her finally, watching her chew, noting her supple neck each time she swallowed. "I don't have a clue what's going on."

Again, Leslie smiled. "You know, I was really excited when I heard about all this, and I had to make all sorts of emergency arrangements so I could be here. I wanted to know if it was real. And the fact that you're confused, that you have doubts, makes it all that much more authentic."

Herron narrowed his eyes in question. "Huh?"

"You know. The miracle."

Jake snorted. "Oh, the miracle, yeah. Well, I don't know. So far it hasn't done anything good for me, except maybe spur every relative I have to call me over the weekend."

Leslie nodded. "Yeah, I can see how that would happen."

"And maybe, just maybe," Jake went on, "help my social life."

He regretted it the minute he said it. It made him sound desperate, which he wasn't, he reminded himself. And he certainly didn't want some woman—the first really good-looking woman he'd run across in a while—to think he was. "Uh," he started, but Leslie Brimhall was already laughing.

"I thought it was only in Akron that social lives had become scarce. Could it be a nationwide phenomenon?" She went back to her burger and left Jake Herron submerged in thought.

She was nothing like the last woman he'd dated, a staffer for Harrison Rheinhold from New York. They met in D.C. during a committee hearing on the war on drugs. Unlike the Rheinhold staffer—Jake strained to remember her name—Leslie didn't pick at her food or talk about caloric intake or the presence of sugar everywhere. He had already observed that she wore very little face paint, something he appreciated in a woman. She was dressed simply, in slacks and a blouse. And she didn't even seem to care that there was a piece of pickle on her lap.

They sat there at the bar, she with her glass of wine, he with his warm beer and later a glass of iced tea, and talked about everything. Where they grew up, how weird it felt to meet adults born in the '80s, why they would never return to a high school reunion no matter what.

While the hours passed (two-and-a-half, to be precise), Jake would find himself often surfacing from the conversation to note the strange intimacy that had sprung up so suddenly. He ate some of her coleslaw, and then bought an order of fries, which they both devoured. He gave her his phone number. Just in case she needed anything.

For a moment there—well, more than a moment, Jake would have to admit as he looked back on it Monday, he had felt himself falling in love. Here was a girl—okay, a woman, he chided himself—who could think and talk and eat as if, well, as if she hadn't been programmed by twenty years of *Cosmo*.

Jake talked about his job, his simultaneous respect for Miranda Davis and his disappointment in her. The compromises politicians made, the "go-along to get-along" mentality. "I mean, isn't there something to the theory that if you lead, they will follow?" Jake said, telling Leslie about the recent vote his boss cast on a bill that would've allowed clean needles to be distributed free to heroin addicts to stop the spread of AIDS.

"It's just not politically smart to help addicts kill themselves, Jake," Rep. Miranda Davis had said, despite scientific evidence that such needle exchange programs really did cut the spread of AIDS. "You can't tell me that a heroin addict is concerned about his or her health."

Leslie shook her head. "So they made it about fault, not about suffering. Humans have a long history of doing that."

Jake was taken aback. She'd really gotten it. Really saw through it all the way to the core. He was delighted. Not even the Rheingold staffer had supported needle exchange. He looked at Leslie Brimhall more closely. She wasn't a classic beauty in any sense: her upper lip could've been fuller, her nose had a tiny twist in it, her cheekbones weren't all that pronounced. But there was something about the way it all mixed together that made her so alluring. That and the way she smiled sideways and laughed with her gut, not her throat.

A group of teenagers got rowdy in the back corner of the pub, and the manager asked them to leave. "I can't imagine what it's like to be in high school these days," Jake said, offhandedly. "I mean, with the drugs and the violence and the gang shit."

"Columbine wasn't the result of gang violence, Jake, you know that. Those kids would've been safer in an inner-city school."

Jake thought about it for a moment. Leslie was right, of course. Columbine High School was in a well-to-do, predominantly white suburb. The teenagers who killed thirteen people and then turned the guns on themselves had affluent parents and nonviolent, drug-free homes. No one wore colors. "So it's just crazy kids who should've been stopped by the police long ago?"

She shook her head. "Ah, now who's making it about fault? I think it's more about feeling disconnected, alienated," she paused for a moment. "Soul-less."

"Soul-less?" Jake felt the bile rise in the back of his throat. "Like a 'moment of silence' in schools would've made all the difference?"

Leslie looked surprised. "Well, it certainly couldn't have hurt. I think prayer can do a lot of good."

And then he knew. She was a loony. Jake felt his back stiffen against the wooden back of the bar stool. "You're big into prayer, huh?" he asked, trying to sound like his life wasn't depending on her answer.

Leslie laughed then, almost spitting out a gulp of wine. "I'm a minister," she said easily. "I have a congregation in East Akron. I drafted someone to cover for me on Sunday—and will have to make up a bunch of meetings when I go home next week. But no one was going to stop me from coming."

"You're a—" he couldn't seem to get his arms around it, "religious person?" he finally finished.

The smile faded from Leslie's face. "Why do you say it like that?" she asked him. "Like I've got the plague or something?"

Jake felt his rage rise. Why this one, why did this one have to be a loony too? But instead of lashing out, he shook his head. "Just a bad day at work," he said. "A really bad day."

"Your work? What would that have to do with my calling?" she wanted to know.

Calling, Jake thought. She thinks she was called. She had *dedicated* her life to the same stupid book that had provoked two thousand years of the bloodiest wars and human oppression in history. She was one of *them*. His hands felt clammy.

"Oh, nothing. Hey—look at the time, I'm going to have to run. Nice meeting you," he stumbled over that last part. He paid his bill hastily and left the bar. Her face had been full of confusion and sadness while his, he was certain, had been nothing but twisted fury.

On Monday morning, if he was going to be honest, it had been the call after the one from Father Chavez that made Jake Herron so late for work. Because it had been from *her*, from Leslie Brimhall, and it had left him in a daze that eventually sent him back to the bathroom for a second shower in an attempt to function normally.

"Jake, this is Leslie. I'm sorry to bother you so early," she had said as soon as he picked up the phone.

"Uh, yeah," he had managed, trying to suppress both the feeling of dread and the leap of joy his heart made at the sound of her voice.

"I just wanted to, I don't know, tell you how bad I feel about how things ended last night. And, um, I wanted to tell you I really enjoyed our conversation. Well, at least most of it."

"Yeah." Jake desperately tried to regain his composure as he stood in the living room with the clock ticking away on the mantle.

"I wondered if you'd be willing to meet for coffee sometime, maybe Tuesday?" she asked, despite his monosyllabic responses.

"Tuesday," Jake said hollowly. *Why would he want to have coffee with a Bible thumper*, he thought. *Fuck her*. So it was a surprise when he heard himself say, "Tuesday would be fine."

He heard the smile in her voice. "Good, thanks. That really makes me feel better." They said goodbye and Jake hung up, then sat down on the couch for what seemed just a moment or two to collect his thoughts. But it lasted a lot longer than that, and when he finally raised his head, the clock on the mantel was chiming nine. He headed back to the shower for another go at waking up.

Ricardo Shock took his first shower at the same time Jake Herron was taking his second. It had not been a good night for Shock, either. During the same wee hours in which Herron had been ruminating over the state of his dating life and what seemed to him had come to a single choice between *Cosmo* girls and born-agains, Shock had been tossing and turning over the tongue-lashing he had received from Morty when the producer was told, with four minutes to air time, that there would be no feed from Denver because Edward Banks would not allow his son to be interviewed on Sunday.

"We're not taking interviews," Edward Banks had told Shock brusquely after the television personality fought his way through the crowd outside the stately home on Sultan Lane. "I'm not exposing my child to this circus."

Shock looked into his adversary's bulging eyes and smirking mouth and had summed up the situation in an instant. *Here was a man as insecure as a pro wrestler*, Shock thought, if it were possible. A man who blustered and scoffed as a sort of defense mechanism; who thought (mistakenly!) that if he intimidated, he'd win. Well, Shock had interviewed pro wrestlers. And now he'd interview Edward Banks too.

"Mr. Banks," Shock tried again, his foot firmly on the weather stripping to the man's front door. "Think about it. We're talking national news here. It is watched avidly by tens of millions of people across the country. Have you nothing you want them to know?"

Edward Banks wasn't in the mood listen. The crowd outside his home, which had gathered there in increasing numbers since his son had let fly with this prophecy, had severed what was left of his nerves. Plus, they were ruining the grass. "No," Edward said stubbornly. "Not even if you were the president."

Shock smiled. What Shock was thinking, but didn't say, was that he himself had a higher approval rating then the president, and the gap was increasing. What Shock did say, leaving Edward miraculously silent for a few moments, was, "I understand, Mr. Banks. Except I keep thinking that people will want to know just who Peter Banks' parents are, and how they came to raise a prophet. You know. Like Mary and Joseph."

It was perhaps the only biblical story that Edward Banks knew by rote. Others he was half sure of, when God had asked that guy—was it Isaac or Abraham?—to kill his only son, when he starved that bunch of people in the desert, when—oh, who really had time to study these things?—one bride was substituted for another. But Mary and Joseph, now these were two people he knew of, two characters whose roles in the whole thing were made abundantly clear, year after year, in those cheesy manger scenes, on Christmas cards. And the idea that admiration, as opposed to humiliation, could be the result of Peter's "Act" was enough to make Edward reconsider.

"Well," he said to Shock, who had his foot in the door. "Well."

Vivienne had crept up behind her husband, curious about why he insisted on holding the door open when all those maniacs were still out on her lawn. She had redone her hair for maybe the fifth time that day, but even after sessions with both the curling iron and hot rollers, she didn't feel any better. She was no closer to Jackie O (whom she couldn't imagine in hair rollers). And the crowd outside seemed to get louder as the hours passed.

"We don't need no Proof!" the Mercy Church group was howling (the double negative bothered Vivienne more than the message did) and "Death to the blasphemer!"—this from the Pentecostalists, who seemed to have a sort of group lisp that made them sound anything but serious.

"Edward, Edward, close the door now," she said to him in a sharp whisper as she looked over her shoulder.

"Vivienne, this is Ricardo Shock," Edward said.

Vivienne's hand flew to her hair. "Oh, Mr. Shock, yes, of course." She did recognize the man, which was more than Edward had done.

Ricardo Shock smiled at her, noting that her hair seemed to defy gravity in the usual suburban way. He knew he was inches away from an interview because he had managed to garner an introduction.

He pushed his previous analogy a little further. "Mrs. Banks, it's an honor to meet this millennium's Mary," he said.

Edward beamed, but didn't look at his wife. This was lucky, because it took Vivienne a few breaths to figure out just whom he meant. Mary Queen of Scots, she was thinking quickly, Mary Kay, no no, oh, that Mary!

But it was here that Shock made his fatal error, the one that cost him a slot on the Sunday night broadcast and so upset Morty, his long-suffering producer. Because Shock assumed that this warm and fuzzy scene at the front door meant that he would gain entry then and there, into the house and away from the crowd behind him, so he said, "Now, this won't take long, Mr. Banks," and waved a hand at the cameraman behind him to start hauling his equipment and electrical wires in, which provoked that all-too-familiar burn up Edward's butt and face.

"I said not today, Mr. Shock." Edward bristled to the smooth but startled face before him. "And I meant not today. I won't be pushed around. If you want to come talk to my wife and me—and Peter"— Edward Banks said the boy's name as an afterthought. "We can make an appointment for tomorrow. I'm a very busy man, Mr. Shock. Very busy."

Shock sighed. It was his mistake. He hadn't given Banks any reason why the interview had to be then, had to be on Sunday (although later, back at his hotel room at the downtown Radisson, Shock thought of plenty reasons that he could have listed for the necessity of a Sunday interview). He met defeat the best he could.

"Very well, Mr. Banks," Shock replied, thinking that he'd tell the makeup artist to skip the powder on this one so that when Edward would finally appear on *The Shock Report*, he'd look suspiciously like Richard Nixon, with about as much to hide. "Shall we say ten a.m. tomorrow?" Shock asked.

"Make it eleven," Banks said, not wanting to seem too agreeable. Shock nodded, then began the arduous task of turning the cameraman around and heading back to the rented van.

Edward watched the men go until the multitude remaining on the lawn realized his door was open, and now there was a clear path between them and a real live blasphemer.

"Repent!" screamed one particularly vocal man who wore suspenders over a Colorado Avalanche T-shirt.

"Not in a million years," Edward Banks shot back glaring at the hockey fan with a face that was nothing less than a physical challenge. The man approached the door, his handmade sign wielded like a spear. For a moment Edward didn't move, too startled by the rush of activity. And then he heard Vivienne give a slight "eep" at the sight of the man running toward them, pole vault style. So Edward slammed the door.

"Joseph never had to put up with that," he commented to his wife, who was nervously playing with a lock of her hair.

"Oh Edward," Vivienne scolded him weakly. "Don't let anybody hear you." With that she left her husband in the front foyer, who was making faces through the small windowpane at the now-frothing Pentecostalists, and went to tell Peter that he would be talking to Ricardo Shock on Monday.

CHAPTER TWELVE

Peter Banks never intended to become a religious spokesperson. In his mind, he had merely asked a question and received an answer, and then, sort of as a payback, he was asked to deliver the message: name the Witnesses and give the date. After he'd delivered the message, he figured he was through. While he still had the two tapes to play back in his mind, while he still could feel the warmth of the voice and the flood of calm that came over him whenever he heard it, his task, as he saw it, was at an end.

So he was quite puzzled by the fanfare that had raged all around him and his home since he had named the Witnesses. It never occurred to him that he wouldn't be able to venture outside the house. That if Ben still lived in the neighborhood, he wouldn't have been able to go to his house, or to even catch a ray of sunlight on his face. The yard had filled up steadily since the first evening news broadcast following his pronouncement in the Mayoral Conference Room. He watched them sometimes, out of his bedroom window, the faces, the signs, the odd assortment of humanity who felt it was their duty to come to his front yard and yell expletives at his father whenever the front door opened.

The phone had been disconnected after Edward had realized that the media—and the non-media—were not going to back off as easily as his clients did at work. Reporters were insisting on audiences, the curious wanted to know why Peter had been chosen, the angry wanted to weigh in with their rage, the skeptical with their protests, the devout with their blessings. There seemed no escape.

There was no question that Peter would not be able to return to school anytime soon. If the phone had been connected, Edward would've received a call from Mr. Overlay asking that the boy not disrupt the "learning atmosphere" with his presence. It didn't matter. Neither parent was going to let the boy out of the house to face the Pentecostalists who were hissing on the front lawn—it was too dangerous.

Not that it bothered Peter to stay home. It wouldn't have bothered Peter if he were sent to the moon. Not when he had the replaying tape of God's voice in his head, reverberating through his body. He didn't really listen to the words anymore; it was just the tone, the calming, comforting tone. It was fine to be Peter. Just Peter.

He still didn't know what was wrong lately with his mother. But he understood that no matter what, she'd be all right. In the end, anyhow. And he continued to miss Ben; wishing his best friend were around to talk to. But Peter knew that Ben had gone where he had to go, and he was grateful for the friendship that was, and any new friendship that might hover on the horizon.

In the midst of all this—well, bliss—Peter was still a twelve-year-old boy. Since God had said it was all right, he regularly jacked off and was thankful. He still loved blowing the heads off of aliens in his video games, reading about magic (he wished he had a stairway that changed directions) and watching mindless cartoons. He still didn't quite understand chemistry, or the electoral college, or girls. But he wasn't upset about his lack of clarity on these issues. When he should know, he figured, he would.

Vivienne had convinced Edward to return the Nintendo to their son, not wanting him to be bored, or depressed, or use his free time to hear more voices. And so, since the glorious moment he had recovered the Nintendo, Peter set out to beat Zelda and rule the world. And it was quite an unwelcome interruption on Monday morning when Vivienne had come into his room and announced he had a mere thirty minutes before the Ricardo Shock would be arriving to speak with him and he needed to get ready.

"I was thinking maybe your blue blazer and a white dress shirt," Vivienne said, standing in front of Peter's closet, her hair tied in some sort of white pieces of cloth. He could see the tiny pink lines all over her head, where her scalp showed through. It looked like it hurt.

"What's wrong with your hair, Mom?" he asked, hoping she didn't have have some illness women got when their front lawns were besieged.

Vivienne's hand flew to her head. "Oh this," she laughed nervously. "These are rag curls, honey. I haven't done this since I was your age."

Peter looked skeptical. "It looks like it hurts."

"Oh no, no, not at all," she said, flicking the hangers across their wooden rack. "Now, where are those khaki pants of yours?"

Peter stood up from his place on the bed, to emphasize his protest. "Mom, I don't have anything to say to this guy," he said with as much finality as he could muster.

"He's not a 'guy' Peter. He's Ricardo Shock."

Peter shook his head. "Dad told me never to talk about it again," he complained. "Now you're telling me to go ahead and say anything."

Vivienne turned her attention from the closet to look at her son. For a moment she was quiet, letting Peter's words sink in. A flicker of doubt played in the corner of her mind, causing an unnamed panic to rise in her abdomen. She dismissed it quickly.

"We don't want you to just say anything, Peter," she told him. "Just tell the truth."

Peter sighed and knit his brows together. He was trying to think of the things grown-ups said to each other when they were discussing what they would and wouldn't let their children do.

"But Mom," Peter finally said, "I don't think it's good for me to have this kind of exposure." It was a concept he had heard a teacher mention during a class debate over kiddie beauty pageants. But he couldn't quite get the word to come out of his mouth right.

Vivienne balked at the admonition. Two days ago, she would've agreed with him. But that was before Ricardo Shock, with his sleek black hair and broad shoulders, had showed up on her front stoop and compared her with that Mary. Mary, she had decided Monday morning, would have waves of curls and a sort of natural beauty. That's when she had decided on the rag rolls.

"Peter, we've already got more exposure than is good for any of us. Mr. Shock is allowing us to set the record straight," she said.

Peter, of course, knew when he had lost. He hadn't heard Shock bowl his parents over with his biblical analogy, so the boy would never know precisely when it was that he had lost, but lost he had. He was going to have to talk to the guy. And, if he could read his mother's face right, he was also going to have to wear a white button-down shirt, khakis, and a blazer to do it.

There was a brief flurry of activity at the Bank's house before Shock's arrival. For the past five days, the three inhabitants of the house on Sultan Lane had done little but drift about in their socks, Edward sometimes challenging one of the inhabitants of his front yard, Vivienne trying new hairdos, Peter playing Nintendo. But in the fifteen minutes before Shock and his crew entered and began to mill about, there was nothing but frantic movement. Peter was scrubbed and dressed, Vivienne took the rags out of her hair, and Edward paced and cleared his throat. The parlor was cleaned up, sticky glasses from Edward's numerous gin and tonics were hidden in the dishwasher, the odd curler was banished to the master bedroom, the trash was put in the back mudroom (no one had the nerve to take it out into the backyard and across to the alley—it was crowded with reporters even back there.)

In the heat of all the activity, Peter had taken off the blue woolen blazer, and when they heard the long-expected knock on the front door, he forgot to put it back on. He hadn't intended to disobey his mother, appearing on national television in a white shirt that set off his pale and plain face in an aura of brilliant glare. Later, after it was over, truth-in-television consultants would remark that the wardrobe selection for the Shock interview had been planned, a clear ploy to make the boy look younger and more innocent. Others would point to the light reading the cameraman used as having been the manipulated factor. Arguments and reports would ensue, and the issue would be debated in at least one broadcast journalism class as far into the future as 2025. But only Peter would know precisely that his singular shirt, like so much of what had happened to him, had been nothing but an accident.

Shock arrived at the Banks' home at eleven o'clock and proceeded to fight his way through the crowds up to the red front door. To make his journey across the now thoroughly trampled trough of mud, Shock stopped and talked to a few of the protesters, pretending the camera was on and making a big show of telling those before him to talk into the microphone, whose cord was tucked neatly into his pocket, attached to nothing). Shock usually didn't go to such extremes to keep a crowd happy, but he had just spent a good forty-five minutes getting his hair into "viewing form," and didn't want to have to repeat the feat because of rough handling.

The strategy worked. His hair still smooth, his suit unmussed, Shock knocked. He had to blink for a few seconds to recognize Vivienne Banks when she opened the door, because where yesterday there had been largish waves and careful teasing, now stood a tumble of corkscrew curls, barely brushed, framing her face like a sink full of suds.

"Mrs. Banks," Shock said, "how nice to see you."

Thrilled at the generic greeting, Vivienne escorted Shock and his entourage in and settled them into the parlor, offering to get them all coffee.

They would sip coffee, adjust lighting, and come to know the make-up artist's powder puff intimately in the next three hours. Edward blustered about the importance of raising children, and gave Peter several pinches on his cheek as if to demonstrate their closeness. Later, media analysts would voice their horror at the amount of blush used on the boy—another example of manipulation, they would say—but no blush had even come close to the young prophet. The flush of his face was due entirely to his father's pinches.

Shock spent time interviewing both Edward and Vivienne, before moving to Peter. His strategy was to both exhaust the parents and give them their own words to worry about before moving to their son. He didn't want them to pay too close attention to Peter, interrupt during the questioning, or have time to prep him further. The cameraman, a seasoned vet named Bob Frances, had already been instructed to operate "on pause" with the parents. Frances—who had been given just those instructions during the state dinner in Japan when the then-U.S. president had thrown up on his dining companions—was so proficient at the procedure, he had filmed the exorcist-like vomiting in its entirety, not wasting a bit of film on the president's prepared speech.

He did an equally good job at the Banks' house. For instance, Bob Frances filmed Edward Banks' awkward struggle to answer a simple question about what "religion" he practiced, but managed to shut off the camera in time to let a long diatribe about the importance of the practice of law go by. Frances got Vivienne Banks in an odd, misty moment about how confusing the world had become since she was young, but managed to avoid her sticky sweet summation of how important it was to her to be a mother.

By the time Ricardo got to Peter, Edward had already excused himself to the kitchen to make a gin and tonic in privacy and Vivienne was disappearing every ten minutes to push another corkscrew out of her face. Peter was a sitting duck. In his white shirt, powder on his nose, and his cheeks still smarting from their earlier brutalization, Peter sat in a stiff red chair that his mother usually never allowed people to sit in and answered Ricardo Shock's questions the best he could.

At first, it was easy. "Tell us about the first time you talked to God, Peter," Shock prompted. And Peter, once again, patiently explained that he hadn't talked to God, he had prayed and then woken up with an answer.

"God said in the message that it was all right to masturbate. That he was busy and that as long as I was doing something that didn't hurt anyone else, it was all right," Peter finished. Shock smiled, thinking he would re-tape his first question so that he used the word "message from God" and wouldn't have to include Peter Banks' admonition about wording. Then he said, "Tell me about the second message."

The second message, Peter patiently explained, had come unexpectedly; he hadn't prayed for it. But it was like "a favor," he said, for God, and he explained about his part in naming the Witnesses and telling them the date of their proof.

Shock nodded, his face frozen in an expectant gaze, which was his trademark (he listens so carefully, one reviewer had commented when analyzing Shock's rise to fame). When Peter was done, the cameraman paused to change the film canister and Peter sat back with a sigh of relief. It was over. He had told the news guy both messages, and he hadn't screwed it up.

But Shock wasn't finished. Not even close. And when the cameraman gave the thumbs-up sign, Shock's questions were fired more rapidly, and all the boy could do was answer the best he could.

"So you said God is busy," Shock said. "What is He busy doing?"

Peter was shocked. "He didn't say, exactly," he said, but when Shock refused to go on to the next question, when the man just sat there and let the camera run and watched Peter, the boy continued. "I think He's probably just trying to take care of all of us," Peter said carefully, trying to feel the warmth of the voice again, trying to be calm. "We're a lot to handle, I'm sure."

"So you see Him as a loving God?" Shock asked as a follow-up. "A sort of father figure?"

Peter fidgeted in the red chair. "His voice sounds nice, real warm and low. And aren't we supposed to call him Father?"

But Shock wasn't answering any questions. "So you prayed, and got an answer. Do you think that everyone who prays gets an answer, or is it only you?" the coiffed man asked him.

"Oh no, it's not only me." The idea embarrassed Peter; he had no idea what happened to everyone else, but he couldn't imagine that God would reserve such special treatment for him alone. "I mean, I don't know if people get these kind of messages in their heads, but I think God answers everyone in one way or another."

Shock didn't give the boy a chance to think about his answer. He fired away with another question. "And what about the really devout, the churchgoers, do they get more answers than everyone else?"

Peter sat for a moment in silence. Part of his problem was that he had no idea what the word "devout" meant; it sounded like some sort of eating word, like devoured. And he had never gone much to church. He couldn't even remember the name of the one Vivienne dragged them to on the occasional Christmas.

"I don't think you need to go to church to pray," Peter said. "I don't think you need to go to church to get God's attention, you know." He was struggling here, trying to find something in his two messages that would help. Finally, he hit on it. "I mean, God said as long as we don't hurt one another, it's okay, right? So I think if you don't hurt people and you pray, he listens."

Shock tried to suppress a grin. This kid was fantastic. Wait until the public hears they don't have to go to church; the ratings will skyrocket. "So, you can pray anywhere? Where did you pray when you got your answer, Peter?"

"In my bed, on my knees, under the covers," Peter told him. "Of course the other message just came while I was playing Nintendo."

"Do you think you could pray on a bus?" Shock asked.

Peter fidgeted some more, a sort of avoidance technique. This guy was really going crackers, he thought.

"Yeah, sure, I think you can pray anywhere. Just don't hurt anyone," he repeated, hoping Shock would just stop.

But the nation's preeminent newsmagazine host wasn't about to stop. Here he had a kid who could make nearly everyone in the country feel better about his or her religious habits, feel empowered with a personal slice of heaven or own phone line to the "Big Guy," and he wasn't going to let Peter go without more milking. "Peter, what does God think of the war in Iraq?"

"Where's Iraq, again?" Peter asked, feeling panic rise.

"It's in the Middle East," Shock answered.

"Are people hurting people?" Peter finally asked, desperate for some sort of hint of how to answer.

"Well yes," Shock answered him, surprised, "Thousands have died since it started."

"Then I don't think God would like it," Peter offered, silently praying that if he were answering wrong, God should let him know. No voice came into his head.

"And what about homosexuality?" Shock asked, gleeful that he thought of it.

Peter didn't have to ask what that meant. When you're twelve and the object of Billy Frye's and Chris Paulo's revenge, you got accused of being gay about every twenty minutes. "Does homo…does being gay hurt anyone?" Peter asked, never having considered the morality of the thing. To him, being gay was just the worst thing anyone could say about someone else at Rory Middle School.

Shock felt the heat rise in his face. "I don't think so, not if the person you're with is also gay," he said, reassuring himself that if it sounded stupid, he could tape over it.

"Then what's the problem?" Peter asked, baffled.

"How about abortion?" Shock pressed, wanting to get the question out before the boy's mother re-entered the room; she'd been playing with her hair for a long time now.

"Abortion?" the boy asked.

"Abortion. Stopping a pregnancy before it can come to full term, before the baby is born," Shock said.

Peter shrugged. "Is the baby, before it's born, a person?" he asked.

It was Shock's turn to look puzzled. "I don't know, that's something people don't agree on."

"Then I don't know," Peter said, and then looked terribly relieved because Vivienne had walked back into the living room. "I guess the mother always knows best," he said then, more to please Vivienne than to answer the question.

Shock felt the hairs on his head stand up. This kid was going to generate some ratings, there was no doubt about it.

"So Peter, what do you think the miracles will be?" Shock asked, finally getting back to the subject at hand.

"I don't know," Peter replied. "He didn't tell me. I was just supposed to deliver the message."

"But you said God told you that these people would get proof of His existence, right? So, what would be proof for you? What would make you believe in God?"

Peter felt funny at the question. "I already believe in God," he told Shock. "So He doesn't have to show me anything."

"But the Witnesses, Peter, the Witnesses, what will He show them?" Shock pressed, nervously now, because Edward Banks had also come back into the parlor, and was looking a little miffed at how long this was going on.

Peter sighed. "I guess that depends on them," he said.

The interview was over.

Because it would take a couple hours for Shock and his film crew to gather their belongings and review the tape at a local affiliate before sending it via satellite to L.A., the Banks family had a little lag time before what was left of their world was blown to pieces.

Peter, exhausted from his interview, had promptly fallen asleep again on the *Harry Potter* coverlet on his twin bed. Vivienne indulged herself in a bath, but only after she had spent a good twenty minutes with a fistful of hairpins to ensure that her curls were not in any way compromised. Edward, having been thoroughly irritated that his role as Joseph was not at all played up during his interview, decided to head for the office to see what sort of vicious legal maneuvers he may be able to make in some of his pending cases.

Gail Abernathy would end up being their savior. And it was guilt that drove her. The weekend had been a long one for Gail, the hangover Saturday was deadly—but that wasn't something she could explain to the highly charged Dillon, who seemed to want to do everything loud, in bright spaces, and all at the same time. Lincoln Fraser called incessantly to check up on the stream of events for background for the Sunday piece a Lifestyles reporter was doing. And the Professor, who always went home to see his lovely wife on the weekends, called once from the small-town newspaper office where he wrote a weekly column to tell Gail he loved her but that he couldn't stop thinking how she walked like a horse.

"It was one of the things that drew me to you," he said, and Gail felt like ripping the phone cord out of the wall.

Her only comfort had been Gus, who seemed oblivious to Dillon's enthusiastic crashing. The dog had essentially glued himself to Gail's hip as she moved around the house. Gail called a few dog pounds to see if anyone had reported a missing pointer since Friday, and was surprised at how happy she had been to hear that no such reports had come in. "You can just stay with me a while," she had said to his big liver-colored face. Gus had drooled his reply onto the knee of her jeans.

It pained her to leave Gus at home Monday morning, after she made sure that there was a full water bowl. But despite having to separate from the silent, eager-to-please dog, going back to work seemed almost a relief. Dropping Dillon off at before-school day care, she felt the weight of total responsibility drop—at least temporarily—from her shoulders. For ten whole hours, maybe eleven, she wouldn't have to ensure the small boy wasn't about to be hit by a car, fall from a stair, or bathe with an electric cord.

Instead, all Gail had to do was write the next story on the editor's log (a continuing saga of the events of the Religious Roundtable, one day old and floundering already), and keep up with whatever was breaking in "real life" on the Peter Banks story.

It was one of those "breaking events" which made her the Banks' savior. She had been sitting at her desk, sorting through the tapes of last night's Roundtable discussion and despairing at the monotonous, often shockingly ignorant discussion of some of Denver's most "normal" and "celebrated" personages when the phone rang.

"Gail, it's Joan at Nine," the voice said. An image of the woman flashed into Gail's mind. Joan was a writer at Channel 9, a reporter who gathered the news, wrote it, and then watched it butchered by the anchors every night. She and Gail had met on a presidential tour years ago, and had often spent time in dingy bars together, drinking and comparing notes on the frustrations of their professions. Gail remembered, with a smile, that Joan had related how she wasn't allowed to use words that were more than three syllables when a certain male anchor was presiding over the desk. "They trip him up," she half-sobbed and half-laughed into her margarita. "Try doing a story on the dangers of electricity without using the word itself, or electrocution for that matter."

Gail greeted her friend, wondering what today's horror was. "Hey, who's anchoring today?" she asked.

But Joan was already whispering. "I don't have much time," the woman was saying softly. "You gotta get over here. Ricardo Shock just brought in a tape of an interview with that Banks kid and they're cueing it up. If you just happened to show up, they may let you in on the thing if you fawn over Ricardo enough."

Gail suppressed a gag. Joan was right. It would be great to have the story in the paper the morning after *The Shock Report* aired the interview. And the *Herald* wouldn't have it. But the thought of pretending to be impressed by a man she had once seen at an execution exhort his fellow reporters to "be silent" so they could hear the "last breath" of the doomed was going to be a challenge.

"I'll be right there," she whispered back to Joan.

It took less than a minute to fill in Lincoln Fraser before Gail was out the door. The Channel 9 studio was downtown, just six blocks from the *Sentinel's* office, and Gail ran the whole stretch. It wasn't an easy feat with a head full of Sunday night's scotch and lungs that were more accustomed to breathing in Marlboro Lights than air.

When she arrived, she was panting, which—she thought cynically—would probably help her case with Shock. It did.

The national personality had been at the station offices for twenty minutes and he was already frustrated. No one was giving him the attention that he deserved. An editing room had to be cleared for him, and it was taking some time. As if anything that had happened anywhere else could've been as important as the words of a child prophet, drawn forth by the expert questioning of the world's most preeminent newsman. Shock was standing in the hallway outside of one of the soundproof editing room, waiting for it to empty, tapping his foot, when Gail arrived.

He felt better when he saw her flushed face, noting her heavy breathing and the pleading tone she used when she asked if she could have the honor of viewing the film so that the *Sentinel* could tell its readers of the huge implications of such an interview. "We won't be able to carry the story if you make us wait for the real-time airing of *the Shock Report*," Abernathy was careful to note. "It's way after deadline. The paper will be printing already."

And so it was decided. And in the small editing room, a tiny cubicle full of electronic devices able to record, cut, voice-over, and repaste, Gail huddled in the back, barely able to view the square screen as Shock, his cameraman, and one or two of the station's news editors watched the proceedings.

Shock didn't bother with the footage of Peter's parents. It made Gail queasy to watch the greasy face of Edward Banks smear by on fast-forward. Then there was Vivienne, her hand in her hair, then on her lap, then flying back and forth like some confused, injured bird. Finally, the production assistant at the controls slowed the video and Peter's pale face and square brows slid into view.

"Okay, here we go," Shock said triumphantly.

Gail watched, stunned, as Shock pressed and prodded Peter through his perceptions of God, the Church, and some of the most divisive issues of the day. She bit her lip, hard, when the young boy innocently answered questions about homosexuality and abortion. She tried to ignore Shock's comments in the background, but it was impossible.

"Look, look," Shock was saying, "see his eyes, see how they shine? It's like he's seeing something."

A station news editor who was watching commented that part of the glare they were picking up could have to do with the white shirt the boy was wearing. "We can adjust the lighting, which should dim the reflection a little," he said helpfully.

"No fucking way," Shock barked. "Jim," he said to the man at the control panel, "see if you can turn up the light, make it brighter. I want those eyes to pop off the screen."

Gail watched as they manipulated the controls on Peter Banks' frozen face until he looked, in her opinion, like a cross between an alien and one of those overly cute teardrop children that summer artists like to paint. It wasn't the only trick Shock pulled.

By editing out most of the questions, the prodding, and editing in a length of footage where Shock was sitting in the Banks' living room nodding that he and the cameraman had filmed when the Banks were being powdered. It looked like Peter had simply started talking, making pronouncements without being prompted.

The abortion discussion was cut the most, with Peter simply stating "mothers always know best." There was no equivocation, no pondering left in the final cut. Gail couldn't help but feel frightened for the boy when she saw the final run. Peter, calm and knowing, his eyes shining with what she knew to be artificial light, was preaching a forgiving, understandable doctrine of theology. Suddenly, religion was easy and accessible.

Gail rubbed her chilled arms. "He's fucking doomed," she whispered.

When Shock and his merry men were through with Peter, ninety minutes had passed. They turned their attention to his parents, debating whether to turn down the glare on Edward Banks' sweaty face. Gail imagined a similar conversation about the pros and cons of editing out Vivienne's flying arm, but she didn't stick around to hear it.

Shock was about to make a twelve-year-old boy—a plain, clearspoken innocent—into the next pop icon. And it was all her fault. Gail didn't even wait until she was outside the studio to light her cigarette. She ignored the glare of the receptionist as she walked through the outer waiting area, the tendrils of smoke leaving a long and telling trail. "I got him into this," Gail muttered, thinking about the discussion she and Peter had had in his backyard, thinking about the story she had broken (on his back, she told herself) about the masturbation incident. In her mind she could see his face, first as it had appeared to her in Banks' backyard, then as she had seen it on the stage in the Mayoral Conference Room, and last, electronically manipulated so that his pupils shone with white light.

He wasn't even five feet tall.

"He's doomed," she said again as she walked back to the paper. She didn't bother returning to the newsroom. Instead, she took the steps two at a time down to the underground garage and found her car. Thirty seconds later, she was on her way to Sultan Lane.

Vivienne had no intention of opening the front door to anyone. Ricardo Shock had exhausted her with his long stay and entourage. What she had imagined was going to be an enjoyable family chat with a superstar had turned into two brief individual interviews with her and Edward and then what seemed like a lifetime with Peter.

There were times that morning she hadn't even been able to see her son. Not with Shock leaning forward, the cameraman and his contraption closing in on the Peter's left, and another assistant holding a sort of spotlight on the right. It was as if she had been cut off totally from them. Like Peter didn't need her at all. Just like Edward didn't need her. Not as a woman, anyhow. She felt the familiar wave of doubt roll over her. What had she done? What had she lost? The line of questioning brought her to the master bathroom, where she could take a long look at herself, yet again, in the mirror.

She grimaced at what she saw and decided to take a bath.

That's where she'd been when the pounding had started on the front door. At first it was just annoying. Really, as if she hadn't noticed them all out there already, as if they needed to add volume to their presence. But the pounding continued. And soon it was irritating the rest of the crowd as much as it was irritating Vivienne. They weren't so silent about it.

"Give it a rest!" someone yelled.

"What makes you so special?" shouted another.

There was snickering and booing and then—it must have been a Pentecostalist, Vivienne thought, the shout "Liberal Media Whore!" rose and reverberated. It was more than Vivienne could take. She grabbed a robe and rushed downstairs.

"Please come in." Vivienne told Gail as soon as she wrenched the door open, "Maybe they'll quiet down."

Gail, rubbing her hand to try to get some feeling back in it, stepped into the neat foyer and looked sadly at the living room beyond it. There was the red chair where Peter Banks had sat as he answered questions, and there was the couch Ricardo Shock had occupied during the interrogation.

"Look, there's going to be trouble," Gail said, without thinking of how to frame it more gently.

"Trouble?" Vivienne asked, looking dazed. She was still dripping. But the woman reporter in front of her was insistent.

"Trouble," Gail repeated. "They are going to make quite a deal out of Peter's interview today, and I'm afraid that a lot of people are going to be affected by it."

"A deal?" Vivienne asked, and then thought she should stop repeating everything the reporter said. Weren't they already making a deal? Wasn't life already falling apart? She studied her bare feet instead of looking at the reporter's face in front of her. She'd never had very nice feet.

Gail tried again. "Peter's interview. You saw it, right?"

"Most of it," Vivienne said, feeling another wave of guilt roll over her. Had Ricardo Shock touched her son in some way? How could she have let that happen? She held her breath. "He didn't touch Peter, did he?" she demanded, feeling the weight bare down on her.

Gail was stunned by the question. When she finally spoke, she did so carefully, knowing that Vivienne was crumbling before Gail's very eyes. "Listen, they talked about abortion and gays and a lot more. It's, it's hard to explain. It's not so much what they talked about, but how Peter looks, how he sounds. Shock is trying to make him out to be the next Christ or something. Someone to be looked on as a leader, as a spiritual guide."

Vivienne looked at her blankly. "Peter's twelve," she said finally, wondering if she and this woman were talking about the same person.

"I know he's twelve," Gail told her impatiently. "And I also know that *The Shock Report* is going to make him look like a supernatural occurrence at nine o'clock tonight. Which means that tens of millions of people are going to want a piece of him. Can you understand what I'm saying?"

Vivienne shook her head and a pin fell out, clattering to the floor between their feet. "No, I'm sorry."

Gail took a deep breath. "Look, how many people do you think are outside on your lawn right now?" she asked.

Vivienne laughed half-heartedly. "There are about seventy-five, give or take a few of the kids. I counted them," she said.

"Well," said Gail, "try to imagine if there were two thousand."

Vivienne's smile disappeared. "Two thousand?"

"Maybe more," Gail told her. "Remember when the Pope came to Denver?" Vivienne shrugged. "This will be worse, much worse," Gail said, and looked around the house. There were just too many windows, too many doors. "You can't stay here," she said finally. "You need to go check in at a hotel, under some other name. They'll have security, and you'll be up off the ground. It really makes sense."

Vivienne looked startled. "Leave my home?" she said softly, as if she had never considered it before. Shouldn't she talk to Edward about this? But Edward had left just after Peter's interview, to put in a couple hours at the office. And besides—Vivienne stopped herself. She wasn't going to think about it.

Before Gail could think of anything persuasive to say, Peter appeared on the stairway. "I'm ready to go," he said quietly.

Gail looked at the pinched, pale face with surprise. He seemed so calm. He still wore the same white shirt they had filmed him in. But now there was a smudge across the left collar.

Vivienne looked at him slowly. "You want to go to a hotel, Peter?" she asked, desperate for advice from someone familiar.

"Yeah," Peter said, "I think so."

"We'll have to call your father," Vivienne sighed, as if too tired to even think about how to accomplish the feat.

Peter nodded at his mother and crossed the living room toward her. As he came close, Gail noticed the dirt under one of his fingernails. *He's just a kid,* she thought.

"We must call Edward," Vivienne repeated. "I'm not sure he'll agree this is a good thing." But Vivienne underestimated the toll two hours at the office—near the smirking Darcy and the exasperated and embarrassed glances of his other colleagues—had taken on her husband.

Edward needed an excuse, any excuse, to get the hell out of the office. He had already eaten three rolls of Rolaids. "Of course we must take precautions," Edward said to his wife over the phone. "Immediately," he added, "I was just going to call you to tell you that. I'll meet you at the Clay Hotel in half an hour."

Vivienne was taken aback. This was Edward's idea? And how had he decided on the Clay, she wondered. Wouldn't the Westin be a better idea? It was much more modern—and modernity soothed Vivienne's nerves. Still, she didn't want to argue. "A half hour," she said to her husband. "At the Clay Hotel. Okay."

Gail stared as Vivienne hung up the phone and then stood lost in thought. That's when Peter spoke.

"Mom?" he said, "I guess we should pack now, huh?"

Vivienne blinked, then nodded. "You're right Peter, we don't have much time." Then she was gone, flitting off to the master bedroom and leaving her son and this reporter alone in the living room.

Gail rolled her eyes. Once again, Vivienne had left her son alone with a reporter—didn't she get it? Immediately, that "Itty-Bitty Shit Committee" that ruled her head these days turned the tables.

"You're really something, judging Vivienne," the committee said.

"At least she's still married, not drinking all the time, and not having an affair that could endanger her job." Gail shook her head, trying to shut them up.

Peter spoke. She'd almost forgotten he was standing there. "Your name's Gail, right?" Peter said, as he approached her slowly.

"Yes, that's right, Peter," Abernathy said. "We talked before."

Peter nodded. "I remember. I'm glad you came."

Gail felt a shiver rise up her back. The committee was silent, their recriminations banished. And even though there was no lighting to speak of in the foyer, and certainly, no production engineer could fiddle with any knobs that could affect what she was seeing now, there it was.

Peter Banks' eyes did have a sort of shine.

PART III

THE PROOF

CHAPTER THIRTEEN

Sherry Anderson had used Monday to catch up on paperwork, clean off her desk, and return phone calls. But the lack of any death, any impending death, even any vestiges of recent death, meant her day moved slowly, too slowly.

It was almost a relief to return to her condo, place the pager on "high" with the hope it would go off, and then sit down to be hypnotized by the rumble of television. Sherry was interrupted once, during the local news, by the sound of the phone.

It was a priest, a rather nice one named Father Chavez. He wanted an appointment—just to talk—because the Church was looking into the Peter Banks matter. Sherry, who had been raised Catholic, who had spoken to what seemed like a million priests after Steven died, was amazed by the use of the words "the Church" to describe Catholic hierarchy. As if there were no other alternative, as if anywhere else people gathered to pray was a total sham—like sitting in front of a no-parking sign to wait for a bus.

"I'm sort of busy at work right now," she lied easily.

"I understand, Ms. Anderson," Father Chavez said gently, hating his role in the whole thing. "We won't take up much of your time," he let the statement sit there, waiting for her reply.

Sherry sighed. "All right, as long as it doesn't take too long. I can talk to you tomorrow afternoon. Say, about two?"

Chavez agreed immediately, wishing the two other men who sat across from him would suddenly burst into flame and incinerate their own plans.

Sherry made a note for herself in her appointment book, which was curiously smooth and white with its upcoming week sitting empty before her. Then she went back to watching television, muting out on the commercials, the constant flickering promise of new life and instant happiness. It was the teaser that brought her out of her reverie. She hadn't been paying attention, but suddenly, there it was, a brief, ten-second blurb about the upcoming "volume" of the newsmagazine *The Shock Report* and the "revelations" of a child who "many say" is the mouthpiece of God Himself.

There was Peter Banks' face, which was pale and glowing, his eyes shining with an intensity Sherry Anderson had only seen before in death vigils. The boy was talking on the screen, but the sound had been muted out so that the announcement about the upcoming show could be made. Peter Banks' eyes were looking straight out. To Sherry, it felt like they bored straight into her soul, seeing all there was to see there and understanding it without judgment.

"Oh my God," she said.

Jake Herron hadn't planned to watch television at all. His tapes had done their duty, recording local news so he wouldn't be caught off guard in the event that a national issue would be raised and Miranda Davis would be asked to comment on it. He would watch them tomorrow, he figured, before work, fast-forwarding through the drivel to make sure he didn't miss anything. But Monday night he had no other plans besides Chinese takeout and a good long sleep. It had been too much of a day to do anything else.

He was concentrating on stoking his fury over Leslie Brimhall. "Miss Calling" as he referred to her privately. She'd tricked him into talking to her, pretended to be normal, and then just kinda let it fly that she's a minister? Holy shit! What, did he have some kind of a sign taped to his back: "All religious fanatics apply here?"

She should've introduced herself as a loony in the first place. Wasn't she supposed to wear a robe or something? There was a time in that bar that he'd been imagining her with that blouse off. Holy shit. His stomach flipped.

As he waited for his beef and snow peas to be delivered, he tried to think of all the reasons—besides the obvious—that she wouldn't be right for him. "This is stupid," he said. "There wasn't anything special about her."

But the clock on the mantle refused to agree with him. And when the beef and snow peas came, he found himself trying to imagine what she would've ordered (he decided she'd probably go for Kung

Pao chicken) and he realized at that point he was in deeper than he would've liked.

The phone rang. It was his boss, and he felt his heart drop in disappointment. "You figure everything out with the Catholics?" Miranda Davis wanted to know.

Jake sighed. "Yes, yes, I'm meeting with the Holinesses Tuesday, early," he said.

He could almost hear Davis smile. "Good, hey, I wanted to tell you that *The Shock Report* has something on tonight about the Peter Banks' thing. We got a heads-up call from Channel 9," Davis went on.

Jake's head felt heavy. Great. Just what he needed. He had enough to think about without watching Peter Banks talk to the damnable Ricardo Shock. "Okay, Miranda," he said to her, because he couldn't think of anything else to say.

Right before Peter Banks appeared on the screen, Jake Herron was struck with the thought that the Ricardo thing was probably good luck. At least it would make coffee with Leslie that much easier. They'd have something to discuss.

Of course, all thoughts of Leslie Brimhall would slide to the back of his mind when the interview started. Peter Banks' eyes glared into Jake's, as if the boy knew, somehow knew, that Jake Herron was lonely and tired and sick of beef and snow peas and interns and endless discussions of policy and dreamed of a woman who could eat a cheeseburger with gusto.

Father Gilbert Chavez was enjoying the peace of the dim interior of his own church, Our Lady of Guadalupe Cathedral on Zuni Street in northwest Denver. It was empty in the evening on Monday, except for one of the small basement rooms where a regular meeting of Narcotics Anonymous met. Chavez grinned as he waved to a few of the regulars, faces he'd much rather see than those he had stared at for the past day and a half.

Now his job was done, as Chavez figured it. He had done the dirty work and assembled the victims whom he knew the bishop and this new honcho from New York were planning to tear apart. Chavez hadn't liked Henry Hamilton when he met him. A tall, smooth man with perfect teeth and thinning hair, he spoke with a New York accent and had managed to fit the words "your people" into his first conversation with his Hispanic colleague. Chavez had watched as he and Sybrandy danced carefully around the Peter Banks issue until they had both concluded that the other felt likewise about the boy, and then they had joined forces in the endeavor.

And I am the Judas who has sent them to their peril, Chavez grieved, as he moved around the empty altar, straightening a cloth here, a candlestick there. He used his thumbnail to scrape a bit of wax off the sacrament table.

Still, they would have gone ahead without him, and then he wouldn't have been able to see for himself, this miracle, this foretelling, he would've had to hear it all through their mouths. "Please, forgive me, Father," Chavez mumbled, walking through the pews and replacing the kneelers.

Despite his guilt, Chavez couldn't help but be excited about the interviews scheduled for Tuesday and Wednesday, and the program that was supposed to air that evening on *The Shock Report.* He found out about it by chance, when he'd called the Banks' residence (probably for the fiftieth time), and Vivienne picked up the phone.

"We're leaving," she announced before Chavez could even introduce himself and tell the poor woman what it was he wanted from her son. "We're leaving because Peter is going to be on television," she said.

"I'm sorry," Chavez started, because it seemed like something one should be sorry for, and because the woman sounded as if she would like nothing better than to erase the past week. "Mrs. Banks?"

Vivienne could barely understand the man was saying her name.

"Yes, this is Mrs. Banks," she said, after she thought about it.

"Mrs. Banks, this is Father Gilbert Chavez. I'm calling to try to arrange an interview with Peter, just a little talk so the Church can be informed about the events that are happening here," Chavez swallowed hard at the last line, barely choking it out.

"Oh," Vivienne replied, her hand going right to her hair. The Mary coif had suffered greatly through the bath, despite all her efforts at pinning. She tried to think fast. "But we're leaving now, because Peter will be on *The Shock Report* and then there will be no escape." She was just telling Chavez what Gail Abernathy had told her. "There will be two thousand people in the yard," she added, remembering the statement.

"I see, Mrs. Banks. Well, then, if you are not traveling far, would it be possible for us to see Peter on Wednesday?"

"Wednesday?" Vivienne tried to think ahead an entire day. "Can the Fathers speak to Peter on Wednesday?" Chavez heard her ask someone in the background. There was a voice responding, although he couldn't hear what it said. A woman's voice, he thought. Definitely a woman's voice.

"Um, yes, yes, that will be all right," Vivienne said. Chavez heard the voice in the background speak again, and after a pause Vivienne answered, "Around noon, I should say. You'll have to come to us. We'll let you know where we are when we get there."

Chavez scribbled the words "noon" and "Wednesday" on the paper in front of him—and then as an afterthought, added *The Shock Report.* The addition made Bishop Sybrandy's eyebrow shoot skyward and his face look even more disgruntled than usual. Chavez ignored him. "Thank you, Mrs. Banks," he said, feeling as if he were talking into a void, "and—uh, one more thing," he added, hoping he wouldn't lose her before he had a chance to ask. "What time will Peter be on tonight?"

"Nine o'clock." Vivienne had looked up the program in the *TV Guide* that morning, when she was still excited about playing Mary, when the curls were still intact.

Father Chavez thanked her and wished her luck on her escape. Then he replaced the receiver and answered the barrage of questions Sybrandy threw at him while Henry Hamilton looked on.

To Sybrandy, Chavez thought now as he returned a hymnal in the pocket on the back of one of the pews, the fact that Peter would be addressing the nation was a devious blow.

"We haven't even decided whether the boy is credible or not and they're giving him the audience of a pope!" Sybrandy wailed after Chavez had explained about the Ricardo Shock interview. Chavez bit his tongue so he wouldn't point out that Sybrandy had indeed already decided about the boy's credibility.

Henry Hamilton remained silent through Sybrandy's outburst. Chavez noted with some distaste that the man had longish fingernails, carefully filed, and as he watched Sybrandy react, he tapped these nails together. "There is nothing we can do to stop it," Father Hamilton finally declared, halting his finger motion momentarily and then resuming once the words were out of his mouth.

"No, there isn't, Father," Chavez said softly. He was enjoying a kind of excitement at the thought, that despite all the best efforts of the men at the table with him, Peter Banks would go on, say what needed to be said. Chavez left them shortly thereafter, not daring to look over his shoulder as he exited Sybrandy's office, the two of them undoubtedly head-to-head in discussion.

And now, it was almost time.

Chavez made his way through the rest of the cathedral quickly, not stopping to pick up mail or the typed copy of his sermon for Sunday's Mass. He left hurriedly, taking the steps in front of the soaring, aging building two at a time. From there, it was only a matter of sixteen strides until he was in the yard of the modest house the congregation kept for the resident priest.

Inside, Chavez flicked on the television and took off his shoes, feeling the ache of his toes. He was thinking that he might have to check in with a doctor soon, find out if he had the beginnings of arthritis, get a prescription for all the new aches that seemed to appear faster than the line at the confessional. But then Peter Banks' face filled the screen. The boy started to speak, and Gil Chavez forgot his toes and the events of the afternoon and stared in delight at the plain-faced boy with square eyebrows who seemed to speak the truth of the Lord without the need for a robe, a book, or even a staff.

Lisa Marretti was a fan of Ricardo Shock, one of the millions who gave the television personality his great approval rating. She liked the way he moved on screen, the clothes he wore, his big wide mouth, and the way he could shape it and twist it to show that he either totally believed someone or could immediately detect a fake.

So it wasn't odd that Lisa Marretti would be glued to the set when *The Shock Report* was scheduled to air. It *was* odd that she was this nervous. She had already sent Ed out, told him to go have a beer with the boys, told him that she needed some time while the baby was sleeping to enjoy her show on her own.

Ed left because that's the way he was. Easy-going. Easy to please.

There was nothing dark or brooding about him. *So different from the last man in her life*, Lisa Marretti thought many times. Just one of the millions of ways Ed was different.

Marretti tried to calm herself by walking up and down the stairs, checking on the sleeping baby, picking up the stray sock or toy, and talking to herself. "There's nothing you can do," she kept saying. "Don't be silly. It's really out of your hands."

But she didn't believe her own words for a minute.

She had already seen the previews. She knew that Peter Banks would be on tonight. And while she was a thousand miles away from Denver, the thought made her heart race.

He was the one who had picked the Witnesses. He was the one who had picked the Witness whom Lisa Marretti knew. Well, sort of knew. *You never even met!* she chided herself. *You don't know these people!* It was the same way she had felt three years ago, when she heard the body had been flown back to Denver. Her housemates kept telling her to go, but how could she? No one in Denver knew anything about her.

"Nothing needs to be said," she said to herself, just as Peter Banks' face filled the screen.

In the course of the ten-minute interview, Lisa Marretti would hear the baby cry, then settle, then cry again. But it wasn't until the program was over that the young mother would go check on the infant, but Lisa still wasn't quite all there.

It would take Ed another two hours to venture home from the local pub, to stumble up the stairs and brush his teeth, to look in quickly on his son and then head off to bed. That had been his plan. But there in the middle of their king-size Serta, Lisa was sitting up, stock straight, staring out into the night. It wasn't until Ed pulled at one of the sheets, trying to get himself tucked into the jumble of covers when she'd said, "Ed, I'm going to Denver."

It took Gail Abernathy more time than she expected to check the Banks family into a suite of rooms at the Clay Hotel. Actually, it was getting them to the Clay that took so very much time; the checking in part was relatively easy. Still, it didn't matter which part was hard, what mattered was that Lincoln Fraser had not been in a forgiving mood.

"Where the fucking hell have you been?" he raged when Gail arrived in the newsroom with only seconds to deadline.

Gail didn't have time to argue with him. "Look, Lincoln, I'm the only reporter in this fucking country who has previewed the Peter Banks interview with Ricardo Shock, the dick. I am also the only reporter who knows where the fuck Peter Banks is now, and that he and his family have gone into hiding. And I'm the only reporter who can get to them for you. So, do you want me to write about the interview that will have everyone talking in the morning, or do you want me to quit now?"

Fraser looked startled, then angry, and then scared, in that order. Finally, he waved a hand at her dismissively. "Just write, goddammit. Just write." So that's what Gail Abernathy did.

In the end, it really wasn't that hard. She knew what she had seen: the shining eyes, the pale face. And she knew what she had heard, a clear message of a loving God who wishes only that humans stop hurting one another. She tried to use as little fiction as possible, but she had to be creative with a few paragraphs on the response the program would bring. "The interview, some observers forecast, will strike a note with the public that will reverberate for some time," she finally managed. *Some observers*, she laughed to herself. *Me.* She mentioned that the Banks family had retreated to a secluded location because of the response the interview was expected to elicit, and then she filed the story, thirty-five minutes after she began, and left the newsroom without a backward glance.

It took some time to pick up Dillon, pay the "overtime" on the day care, collect Gus, and hit the grocery store for a few supplies. Dillon wanted fried chicken; Gus needed dog food. And Gail, although she would not permit herself to form the full thought consciously, needed a drink and knew she'd be stopping at the liquor store after their grocery run.

"Where are we going?" Dillon wanted to know, his eyes wide with anticipation.

"We're going to meet some very special people who are staying at a big, pretty hotel," she told him, hoping that Dillon would not think it boring to spend a few hours with a rather bizarre family and watch the interview in its final form when it aired in an hour or so.

But Dillon seemed content to chew on fried chicken in the car, feeding pieces of it to the serenely waiting Gus who sat at his side. Gail parked the car in the lot outside Raven Liquors and instructed Dillon to wait, feeling better about leaving him because of the presence of the dog.

Inside, she avoided the eyes of the cashier, an older, tired-looking woman who had often struck up a conversation. Gail was a regular, after all. The bottle of scotch, single malt tonight, because it was a special occasion, weighed heavily in Gail's hand. She wrote the check quickly, because looking at it made her heart sink.

Back in the car, Gail halfway filled a not-so-clean coffee cup and talked to Dillon about what was new in fourth grade, after-school day care, and the importance of not feeding Gus any chicken bones, no matter how much he might look like he wanted one. "Chicken bones can kill dogs, you know, sweetie," she said.

Dillon nodded solemnly and proceeded to carefully peel chunks of meat off the bone and hand them over to the pointer. Gail wondered how much her son had eaten off the three bones she could see stripped, in the bottom of the bag. She pushed the thought aside, then started the car.

The Clay Hotel is one of Denver's finest—an historical site full of arched ceilings and stained glass that had been renovated over the years to provide modern service and accommodations while still serving tea in the fashion of the early 1800s. When Gail had checked Vivienne and Peter in earlier, she was astounded at the price of the suite, and silently thanked God it was Vivienne's credit card she was handing the clerk, not her own.

Two-and-half-hours later, with a small boy whose greasy hands held a bag of Albertson's fried chicken, a bottle of scotch in a brown paper bag, and a dog that she was sure was forbidden inside the carefully appointed interior of the hotel, Gail held her breath. "Follow me, Dillon. Just walk like we know where we're going."

It seemed impossible to Gail, with all the red-coated staff rushing here and there to assist with luggage, deliver messages, and show guests to their rooms, that she and her entourage would pass unharrassed. But pass they did.

In the elevator she pushed the "close-door" button down hard, and miraculously—she hesitated even *thinking* that word—the door closed without admitting another guest. The Banks' suite was on the

eleventh floor, and Gail, Dillon, and Gus stood outside the door looking both ways over their shoulders to make sure the coast was clear.

It was Peter who answered their knock.

"Hi," he said simply, standing back to let them in. Gail stopped herself before she could reach out and muss up the hair on his head. She
closed the door behind the three of them, making sure that Gus's tail
was clear. She started the introductions.

"Peter, this is my son Dillon and uh, our dog, at least for now, Gus.
Dillon, this is Peter," Gail said.

Peter smiled at Dillon, and Gail felt some relief that the boy prophet hadn't had the response of snarling at someone younger than himself. She imagined that Chris Paulo would not be as welcoming of a
new, younger kid. But then, Chris Paulo hadn't talked to God.

"You play Nintendo?" Peter asked Dillon, delighted. And before
Gail could say a word, the two disappeared off the foyer of the suite.

Gail stood with Gus and surveyed the room. Not bad, she thought,
noting a big-screen television, a green upholstered couch, and the
easy chairs. Vivienne and Edward Banks were nowhere to be seen.

"Hello," Gail called out, trying to hide her aggravation at parents
who were supposed to be protecting their son but didn't seem to
even notice his existence.

It took several minutes for Vivienne to appear, but when she did,
Gail understood her absence. Peter's mother looked completely different. Her corkscrews were gone, and in their place, a carefully
brushed and pinned chignon. It made her look more together, more
confident, but one look into her eyes and Gail knew that the woman
was still spaced out.

"Oh, I didn't hear the door," Vivienne told her. "Edward just got
back from the office. I've been trying to gather myself."

Gail nodded, not knowing what to say. "Gathering" was an interesting word for it.

"It shouldn't be long now until it's on," she said finally to Vivienne,
hoping the woman hadn't noticed the bottle Gail was still holding.

"Yes, yes of course," Vivienne said, but only because it was expected of her. She'd rather have just gone to bed.

Gail finally decided that Peter's mother was never going to play
hostess. "I'll just turn on the tube, if you don't mind," Gail said,
walking past Vivienne and placing her bottle on the bar in the cor-

ner of the room before heading to the huge television set. Vivienne squeaked her acknowledgment, as if she had suddenly remembered what they were all there for.

The screen filled with white and then Peter Banks' face appeared and for a moment Gail thought they had missed part of it. But no, it was only a preview. "Coming up, he's just a boy, but he's spoken to God and he has a message for all of us: Peter Banks talks to Ricardo Shock, exclusively on *The Shock Report,*" the announcer said.

Then the screen cut to a commercial for a feminine hygiene product and Gail turned to Vivienne. "Do you want to get Mr. Banks?" she asked. Vivienne rushed out of the room, her hand on her head.

Gail was grateful for the moment alone. She went to the bar and poured herself a tumbler of scotch, wondering if she should call the Professor, check in. She dismissed the thought. There wasn't time to sit and chat about his weekend home with the wife, whether he missed Gail or not, or worse, the similarities between her gait and that of an Appaloosa.

She took a seat in one of the overstuffed chairs that, flanked by an enormous couch, surrounded the television, and watched the advertisements fly by. She hadn't even heard the boy enter the room, but suddenly, Gail was aware that Peter Banks was standing next to her, waiting expectantly.

"Hi," he said to her when she turned to him, startled.

"Peter, you're just about to be on. Are you excited?" she asked, searching his face for some sign of the stress of the past days' events. But he looked calm, his expression much like that of Gus, who lay at her feet.

"Oh no, I don't care," he told her, his eyes locked with hers. "I came out because I need to tell you something," he said.

Gail felt her heart sink. Maybe in the short time the two had played Nintendo, this prescient boy had discovered the truth of how much she had hurt Dillon with the divorce. She waited, her heart pounding.

"I couldn't tell you before, because this one wasn't supposed to be public," he said. Gail felt panic rise all over again, another wave. The affair with the Professor? The fact that she couldn't stop drinking? Could he have known these things, this messenger of God, were matters that shouldn't be discussed in public?

She tried not to wince. "What is it Peter? I'm listening." She took a quick gulp from the tumbler and felt shame flushing her cheeks.

"You're one," he said. "You're the third."

For a moment she didn't understand what he was trying to say. One of what, the third what? Her mind raced, and she didn't realize her hand was shaking until she felt the cold of the liquor splash on her fingers. Then she understood at the same time he spoke.

"You're a Witness, Gail," Peter Banks said simply. "He wanted you to know that, but only you."

Gail felt a thousand questions leap to her mouth. If she had had a chance, she would've asked, "What exactly did He say?" and "Why me?" and "What's going to happen?" and "How come I wasn't named in public?" But there wasn't time. Vivienne and Edward had come out of the room to the left of the seating area and had arranged themselves on the green upholstered couch.

Edward Banks grunted to her, a greeting, Gail assumed. It was clear that Vivienne had been trying to convince her husband that it was all right that Gail was there, that a reporter was joining them. Vivienne didn't quite know why, but she needed someone else there. Things were too much for her. Everything was too much. She needed Gail as backup.

Edward looked like he was trying to act confident and in control, but failed miserably. His hair was mussed, his glasses smudged, and his tic of constantly pulling at his pant cuffs was in full force.

"All right, let's get this over with," Edward muttered as ads rolled by.

Gail tried to find her voice, but failed. Peter had arranged himself on the floor with Gus, paying more attention to the dog than the screen. Gail figured Dillon was still immersed in Nintendo.

Suddenly, Ricardo Shock's face filled the spot where a Cheer commercial had once been. "Since September 11," Shock began, "we as a people have been searching harder than ever for meaning in our life. Was our tragedy as a country a sign from God? Is that God angry?, Are we being punished? Is this evidence that God doesn't exist, that there are no such things as miracles?"

Gail grimaced, taking it in. Shock was standing in a studio somewhere while the screen behind him flashed pictures of the crumbling World Trade Center towers. The TV star managed to look grave and sincere at the same time, flashing the teeth that had made him famous.

"But something happened a few days ago in the unlikely place of Denver, Colorado, the heartland of this great nation, and suddenly, for many, the idea that a miracle could actually happen has been reawakened." The scene projected behind Shock now changed from footage of mass destruction to a still photo of Peter Banks with a caption under it that read: "God's boy?"

Gail tried to ignore the man's blunder at calling Denver the heartland. She was trying hard to concentrate, to see how the whole thing was going to come off in its edited form, whether it would have the impact it had had when she had seen it uncut, in the editing room earlier in the day. But Peter's earlier pronouncement about Gail had thrown her off. She didn't have the concentration it took to watch Shock wax eloquent in setting the scene for the interview. Reality felt like it was slipping away, along with everything else she had once thought was forever in her life.

Without being totally aware, Gail noticed that Peter's face had appeared on the screen, and that the boy was talking, his eyes shining even more, if it were possible, than they had when she had seen them on the small screen in the editing room at the station. She couldn't quite hear what he was saying because of the roar in her head.

But she needn't have worried.

The Peter Banks interview would go down in television history as one of the most talked about "news" events since the Walters-Lewinsky interview. Gail, still unable to hear, to comprehend what was coming out of the television speakers, bent down and put a hand on the head of the dog at her feet.

It was the only thing that made her feel better.

CHAPTER FOURTEEN

According to the *Herald's* "Countdown to the Miracle," it was Day Two, Tuesday (Wednesday was one, and Thursday was D-DAY or "G-" day as some of the editors were calling it.) And it was early, about nine in the morning when the odd trinity showed their faces at Rep. Miranda Davis' office on Denver's Capitol Hill.

Herron was in a panic when they arrived. Not so much because three holy fathers wanted to find out who he was and what he believed, but because, according to the scribbling in his own calendar, he had double booked the appointment. He had already agreed to meet with Ricardo Shock at 9 a.m. on Tuesday, and the thought of the television personality showing up at the same time as the holy men made his mind reel.

He couldn't believe that the mistake hadn't occurred to him last night, when he was watching the incredible Peter Banks interview and Shock's own face was on the screen in full view. The interview had completely taken Jake. The way Peter spoke, the calm and logical things he'd said. Jake sat for the full ten minutes without speaking, not even cheering when the little boy came out with what would surely be the pro-choice activists' next "Don't Leave this Private Decision Up to Uncle Sam" slogan: Mothers know best. (He was unaware that the pro-lifers were at that very moment supervising the painting of huge banners with a slight variation: Mothers know best, and they don't kill their children.)

After Peter Banks was finished and *The Shock Report* had turned to other issues—a new fad diet that was already suspected of killing two teens in Illinois—Jake had sat in the darkness for a long time, trying to pinpoint exactly what it was that was so earth-shattering about the boy's glowing countenance. Jake couldn't put a finger on it. And suddenly he felt exhausted, as if the adrenaline that had been keeping him going had melted away. He went to bed thinking about

Leslie Brimhall, and for the life of him, couldn't remember what the big problem was.

But in the bright light of day, it came rushing back to him. And on top of the pit in his gut caused by his apprehension over his afternoon coffee date, Jake Herron now had to deal with the scheduling conflict from hell. Ricardo Shock and the "Men in Black." It was a disaster, a stress factor just off the charts. He pressed the heel of his hand to his forehead. Jennifer stuck her head in his office and he scowled at it, knowing she was going to tell him that the Men in Black were waiting outside.

"I know they're here. Just let me think," he said, wiping his hands on the sides of his pants.

The intern made a face and then came into the office and shut the door behind her. "You had a call. Some guy from *The Shock Report* to tell you that Ricardo Shock had to cancel the interview. He's on his way to Iowa somewhere," she said.

It took a moment for Herron to register it. "Shock's not coming?"

"That's what I mean, Mr. Jesus Man," she said. "Now, do you want me to let the Catholic guys in?"

Jake smiled at her. "You mean the Men in Black? Yes, yes, by all means, show them in."

Bishop Sybrandy was the first to enter, followed closely by Chavez and Hamilton. The three stood and shook hands with Herron, who Sybrandy could've sworn he met somewhere before but couldn't place. Then the four of them sat down in chairs in front of the overflowing desk, and Sybrandy took a moment to gather his thoughts.

The bishop had gotten very little sleep after the Peter Banks interview. New York had called before the boy's face had even faded from the television screen, and they were screaming.

"This is a disaster, Sybrandy. You know that, don't you?" Borden had all but yelled over the phone.

"Well, sir—"

"There's no well about it!" Borden interrupted. "That boy has made a mockery of the Catholic Church: attendance is not required, abortion is up to the mother, and homosexuality is fine. What kind of abomination are we dealing with here?"

Sybrandy let the man talk.

"You need to put an end to this," Borden directed, ignoring the other man's silence. "Have those interviews started yet? Do you have anything you can use?"

Sybrandy sighed. "They start tomorrow, sir. The Witnesses tomorrow and then Peter Banks on Wednesday."

He could almost hear the other man's blood pressure rise two thousand miles away.

"You get on it, Sybrandy. We can't let this thing go any further, do you understand me?" The archbishop paused only long enough to take a breath, he didn't expect an answer. "Now put Father Hamilton on," he said.

Sybrandy watched, suspicious and disillusioned, as Henry Hamilton spoke to Borden. Hamilton was careful to use short, often cryptic answers, Sybrandy noted with disgust. It was impossible to determine what Borden was saying, and Sybrandy had wondered about it ever since.

Suddenly, a sound in the room made Sybrandy snap back to reality, and he took a moment to realize he was sitting in one of the Witnesses' offices.

Jake Herron cleared his throat, trying to remember the last time he had three people in his office and there had been complete silence. He was pretty sure it had never happened before.

Finally, Sybrandy spoke. "First, I want to thank you for allowing us to come here to ask you a few questions. Please know from the beginning that we are here merely as a precaution. False prophets, in the history of mankind, have been a regular and dangerous phenomenon," Sybrandy said.

Jake nodded, then instantly regretted it. He didn't want these guys to think he agreed with them. Jake supposed that false prophecy was indeed a regular occurrence. But he wasn't quite sure that these were the people who should be evaluating it. These were officials of a church, after all, that had followed the likes of Cardinal Richelieu and, for a great deal of history, saw nothing wrong with drawing and quartering those who did not agree with them. Still, there was no way to take back a nod.

Sybrandy noted the silence and decided to get on with it. "So, Mr. Herron, you are of the Judaic faith, are you not?"

"I was raised that way, yes," Jake answered.

"So you still practice that faith?"

Jake concentrated on not squirming in his seat. "Not religiously," he answered, then felt the flush rise in his cheeks.

"And what is it that has come between you and the Jewish religion?" Father Hamilton jumped in. "Could it be that you are finding Christ?"

The vein in Jake's forehead did a backflip. *Finding Christ? Holy shit,* he thought. *Try finding loonies, dealing with the gory pictures, lamb chops in baby socks, chum on the office door.* He tried to think of something to say. "I don't think that's the reason, no," Jake answered carefully. He noted that the Hispanic priest, the one who had yet to speak a word, smiled at him.

Hamilton's face was unreadable. Sybrandy, on the other hand, looked like he had just caught a piece of chicken in his throat.

"I see," Hamilton said after a long silence. The tall priest made a few scratches on the pad of paper he balanced in his lap. Jake could just imagine the note: "Not finding Christ. Strike One."

Hamilton tried again. "So how would you describe your current spiritual state, Mr. Herron?"

Jake's mind went blank, the vision of Hamilton's writing wiped out by the question. "I wouldn't," was the first answer that came to his mind, but he suppressed it as too flippant; Miranda would be furious if she heard about it. Instead he said, "I guess I'm still searching."

Hamilton made more marks on his paper; Sybrandy refolded his hands in his lap in an attempt to keep them from shaking. But Chavez again only smiled.

"And Peter Banks, Mr. Herron. Do you know him?" Hamilton continued.

"Only what I've seen on television," Herron answered him, pleased to get off the subject of religion and on more familiar ground.

Hamilton nodded, but wrote nothing. "Has he asked you for any money?"

"Money?" Jake asked, and then laughed weakly. "No, no one has asked me for money—I'd be the wrong guy to pick if money was your angle," he added. Really now, Herron was thinking, did they know how little he got paid? Absurd.

"Is there anything else this Peter Banks might want?" Hamilton asked him, without looking up from his paper. "A political favor, perhaps?"

Jake tried not to look as startled as he was. "He's twelve years old, I think," he managed with a straight face.

"As I asked before, Mr. Herron, is there anything else Peter Banks might want?"

Jake couldn't help himself. "What in the hell would a little boy want from a sole staff member of a single representative in the u.s. Congress? I can try to help people find their way through the maze of the Social Security administration," he said quickly, "but what good would that do for a twelve-year-old boy?"

Hamilton raised his head from his paper and locked eyes with Herron. "Perhaps his father could be better served?" he said ominously.

Jake shook his head, "His father?" he asked.

"Edward Banks, the attorney, I am told he is a Republican like yourself," Hamilton answered.

Jake shook his head. "His father hasn't asked this office for anything," he said, getting fairly miffed at the line of questioning.

"Yet." Hamilton responded.

Jake didn't get it. "What was that?" he asked.

"His father hasn't asked you for anything, *yet*," Hamilton repeated.

And Jake exploded. "This is bullshit!" he shouted at them. "Edward Banks would have better luck handing out miracles at City Hall. At least they can fix a ticket," he said. "What do you think we do here? Give people discounts on their taxes or something?"

Hamilton seemed unruffled at the outburst. "Do you have reason to think Edward Banks has some trouble with the irs?" he asked.

"This is ridiculous!" said Jake, now standing. "I have reason to think nothing about Edward Banks. As for Peter Banks, the only facts I have seem to point to a little boy who wanted nothing more than to jack off without going to hell. He didn't ask me for anything!"

Hamilton stood in turn. "I'm sorry if we've upset you, Mr. Herron, but I think that Shakespeare would be instructive in this instance. *Thou doth protest too much.*"

"Oh for Christ's sake," Jake blurted, taking three steps and opening the office door. "I will not participate in this—this—" he couldn't think of the word for it, and then it hit him, "this *inquisition* any longer. I have better things to do!"

Sybrandy, swallowing hard, stood and followed Hamilton out past

Herron. Gil Chavez hesitated, then rose to his feet. But he stopped at the door where Herron waited, and leaned in a little.

"They do not speak for us all," Chavez whispered to the man who looked disturbingly like the popular image of Jesus. Jake just looked at the priest, not knowing what to say. Chavez continued, watching the backs of Sybrandy and Hamilton disappear out the front door. "They haven't asked you what's important," Chavez whispered.

Jake stared at him, waiting for him to leave.

"What would be a miracle to you?" Chavez asked after a pause, looking into Jake's eyes. Again, the man who looked like Jesus held position, staring. "Think about it; it's important," Chavez said. Then he turned and left the office to join his superiors outside.

Jake stood for a second longer, feeling the rhythm in his forehead and knowing that if he didn't get an ice pack soon he would have to meet Leslie Brimhall looking like Frankenstein.

The interns—who had witnessed the scene at the door and watched the Men in Black be banished from Miranda Davis' office— were twittering in the background. Finally, Jennifer said, "Jake, um, do you want me to get Miranda on the line so you can fill her in?"

Herron didn't have to think long to answer. "Absofuckinglutely not." Then he stepped back inside his office and closed the door behind him.

Ricardo Shock had made the decision to go to Iowa before the Peter Banks interview aired on Monday night. Morty had been ecstatic with the footage, sure they had a blockbuster, and had pressed Shock to think of ways to keep the momentum going. Three days, he kept saying to his star, three days is forever in television.

"I was going to interview the Witnesses," Shock had told him, when he sent the feed from Denver. "That would be a logical next step."

But Morty scoffed at the idea, rolling his eyes in the privacy of his own office in Los Angeles. "Logic, my dear Ricardo, doesn't sell ads," he said. "Now that we've got Peter Banks all but glowing on the screen, how fascinating do you think some Jane and John Doe Schmoe are going to look? What are they going to say that can top the boy?"

Shock started making a humming noise. So Morty continued.

"Nothing, I tell you, there's nothing they can say that won't be a let-down after tonight. Now think about it."

Ricardo had to agree his producer was right.

"What we need is to build some excitement right now," Morty continued. "We've got the prophet, now what about the miracles?"

Ricardo shrugged, forgetting he was on the phone. "I don't know about the fucking miracles, Morty. No one knows."

"Exactly," Morty said the word hard, biting off the end of Shock's sentence. "No one knows, but we can speculate, can't we?"

Shock couldn't figure out what his producer was talking about. "What do you mean speculate? It could be anything."

"No, no, miracles are pretty predictable," Morty said. "Just think about it. Fish multiply, illnesses are cured, people are brought back from the dead," he said the last phrase with emphasis.

Shock still didn't get it. The silence over the telephone was deafening.

Morty sighed. Really, it should've been him who had been blessed with those great teeth. "Look, Ricardo, think about the Bible. You remember the Bible, right?"

"Uh, not much," the star said quickly.

"Well, I do," said Morty, "There aren't many surprises."

"You want me to go on national television and predict what the miracle will be?" Shock asked, thinking not about journalistic responsibility, but about how much of an ass Liz Smith would make of him if he were wrong.

"No, no, now calm down," Morty told him. "I don't want you to predict, I just want you to speculate."

"Oh right," Shock had said, perturbed at being lectured at after he'd brought back the best interview his network had had since Monica Lewinsky wore that hideous pink suit. 'Hello, ladies and gentlemen, I think that Thursday a bunch of water will be turned into wine.' Not very convincing, Morty."

The producer shook his head and tried not to think of just how much money they were paying this good-looking moron.

"Now think, Shock. Think. Is there anything interesting about either one of the Witnesses?"

"One's a nurse," Shock said, "and the other one's an ass-kisser to someone in Congress—." He stopped. "You think the miracle will be something political?" he asked, getting excited all of a sudden. "Maybe a comeback by Carter—or even—" and here Shock could barely contain his glee: "Jesse Jackson actually gets elected to something?"

"Jesus Christ, no!" Morty couldn't imagine how the man on the other end of the line managed to dress himself every morning. "No one wants to hear about politics. Politics is boring. Why do you think no one ever votes? Now think. That nursey woman, does she have family?" The producer was trying to prompt his television star, trying to get him to realize it for himself. Morty had been in Los Angeles too long not to know that stars preferred to think of everything as their own idea.

"The nurse, no, she doesn't have a family. She had a son once, but he offed himself," Shock recited it from memory, proud at the background research he had done, which had amounted to reading the profiles of the Witnesses in his briefing packet.

"Yes, and what does that mean to you?" Morty asked.

"She's going to have another baby?" Shock asked, excited again.

Morty slapped his own forehead with the palm of his hand. Then he took a deep breath and tried to keep his voice low.

"Biblical miracles include bringing people back from the dead."

Shock blinked. "You mean—?"

Morty smiled. "It would certainly be a reasonable suggestion, don't you think?"

Shock pressed his famous teeth together, as if doing so helped him to get a handle on it all. "So how do we do this?"

Morty grinned and signaled his assistant with a thumbs up gesture. He'd finally won the moron over, a victory regardless of the time it had taken. "We'll get you a segment on tomorrow's evening news," Morty said. "You get your ass to the scene of the crime, as they say. Just talk about the suicide. Then talk about Peter Banks and what he said, and then just stand there, with pictures of the dead kid flashing behind you, and wonder for the audience just what the miracle could be," Morty said.

"You think they'll get it?" Shock asked him.

Morty sighed. "I think they'll get it, Ricardo."

Ricardo Shock had instructed one of the studio interns to let his appointments know he'd be in Iowa instead of interviewing them and hopped the next plane.

He was in the air when Peter Banks addressed a nation.

» «

Gail Abernathy had been listening to a buzzing in her head ever since Peter Banks told her Monday night that she was a Witness. It wasn't the roar that it had been directly after his statement. That roar had dulled a little. But the sound was still there, and it seemed to rise and fall of its own accord. Like when she saw the Professor.

It was Tuesday morning, after she had dropped Dillon at day care, and after she had reluctantly said goodbye to Gus, leaving him at home. She had gone to work full of plans to talk Lincoln Fraser out of what the editors had logged in as the Peter Banks story of the day— another wordy diatribe from the Religious Roundtable and a rundown of what Peter Banks would do on "Miracle Day," as the *Sentinel* was calling it. Much more relevant was the nationwide reaction to the Peter Banks' interview. She was willing to bet that the bookings on United at Denver International Airport had skyrocketed after the broadcast, and she already knew of one death threat—because she had still been at the hotel room when Vivienne had called the Banks' voice mail number and heard the raspy voice detail how he was planning to dismember her one and only son.

This was news, Gail planned to tell her managing editor. In addition, there was also the fact that Darren Preston, who had been keeping his head pretty low since vowing to stick with his original backing of Peter Banks, would be in a very embarrassing position now that the interview had aired, and his reaction would make for several inches of newsprint guaranteed to affect the next election. She thought about Reverend Werthall as well, but discarded the idea of interviewing him. He didn't have an electorate to deal with. There was no way he was going to reverse himself.

She had mentally outlined her argument—and it had to be an airtight one to get Lincoln Fraser to sway from the damnable list— when she ran into the Professor at the elevator bank.

"Hello there," he said, with that same "I'm gonna drill you" smile she noticed the first time they had met.

"Hello yourself," she responded, wondering why the smile hadn't changed even though his ability to drill clearly had.

"I thought I might run into you here," he said, and then more softly, "seeing how you're neglecting the legislature these days."

Gail threw him a look. "It's not by choice. I got assigned this story, you know," she whispered to him. The elevator arrived and the Professor waved a waiting teen on board.

"We'll take the next one," he said jauntily.

He moved back into the recesses of the hallway, a hand firmly on Gail's arm, pulling her with him. The *Sentinel's* offices took up three full floors of the mammoth building, but there were seventeen other floors of accountants and lawyers and even a Ticketmaster outlet, so the elevator bank was a busy place.

"When am I going to see you?" he asked, when he was certain no one was looking.

The buzzing in her head swelled again. Like an ocean tide coming in, she could feel its force. "I don't know," she managed to say. "I'm really busy with this Banks story, and, uh, I have Dillon this week."

The Professor only smiled. Gail knew that he was proud to still have all of his own teeth. "I'm sure you can make some time for me, though," he said. It wasn't a question. "Maybe a few pops at Monet's this afternoon?"

Monet's was the restaurant inside the Denver Museum of Art. Just two blocks from the statehouse, it wasn't exactly what Gail called discreet. The buzzing increased. "I'm not going to be able to get away for lunch," she said, hoping to be heard over the din in her head.

"I was thinking more of a happy hour," the Professor noted, his smile sliding once again into the "drill you" mode.

Gail was surprised at her irritation. "I'm really trying not to drink as much these days," she said with some conviction.

The Professor laughed. "Oh yeah, I forgot," he said through his chuckle. "I mean, the last time we were together you kept telling me that all evening and then, boom, there's an empty scotch bottle next to you when I wake up in the morning."

Gail felt her face flush. "Yeah, well, I'm still trying," she said, and then wondered just what the hell that meant, since she had managed to drink every night since the one the Professor referred to.

"Hey, it's all the same by me," the Professor told her, still looking amused. "I just want to see you."

"Maybe this weekend," she couldn't help but say, knowing what his answer would be.

"Don't be stupid," he retorted, annoyed. "You know I have to go home on the weekends. Legislative duty and all that."

Gail pressed her lips together. "Look, I've got to get to work or Lincoln Fraser will have my hide," she told him. "If I can get away—" but the Professor cut her off.

"Monet's at two. A drink or two. You can have iced tea if you want."

"I —" she tried to repeat her doubts.

"Don't worry," the Professor interrupted. "You'll be there." The buzzing subsided as soon as the Professor left her standing at the elevator bank. She watched him go with a pit in her stomach. At one time, she reminded herself, the thought of meeting him, of spending just an hour or two with a man who stared so intently into her eyes, who caressed her face, it had made her heart pump wildly. Now she felt slightly nauseated.

Four levels up, she confronted Lincoln Fraser by telling him the Religious Roundtable tapes of the night before were nothing but hooey. "Now really, Lincoln, just how many column inches do you want me to write about one forty-five-year-old male participant who's decided that God resides in the mountains and that's why he moved to Colorado?"

Fraser smirked. "God moved to Colorado?" he asked, and then, acting just like the Professor, wouldn't let her reply. "Be aware that if you can't speak the English language, you can't write it, either," he said irritably.

Gail flinched, but she stood her ground. "I hear that Kitty Casen is arriving in town today," she told her boss, hoping the sound of yet another national personality, the star of the morning show, *Right Now*, would convince him that the reaction story was warranted.

But Fraser was nonplussed. "I don't give a shit if the Pope himself came to Denver. We're sticking with the Roundtable because we said we would. You can do the reaction story on top of it."

Gail opened her mouth to speak but didn't have time.

"End of discussion," Fraser added quickly. "You can do the "Lead in to Miracle Day" story tomorrow. Okay?"

She didn't bother to protest. With two stories due, one involving the review of two hours of tape full of rambling discussion, there was no time to argue.

About the time that Jake Herron was ushering the Men in Black unceremoniously out of his office, Gail Abernathy was half-heartedly taking notes from the Religious Roundtable's tapes. At the point when Herron was nervously raking his hands through his hair, anticipating meeting with Leslie Brimhall, hours later, Gail had finished the story on the Roundtable and had moved on to the reaction story.

It turned out to be harder than she thought. Not because there wasn't a reaction. There was. United Airlines had reported an increase in ticket sales following the Peter Banks interview (Lisa Marretti's was one of them, but Gail wouldn't have known to ask.) Vivienne Banks told Gail that she had reported the death threat to the police and that they were currently investigating it. Kitty Casen's producers confirmed that the star was indeed in Denver on Tuesday and would broadcast Wednesday's show from there (but they didn't let on that Kitty would be standing next to the urinals in Rory Middle School's gym bathroom). And State Representative Darren Preston, although squeamish about answering the phone, did admit to being "somewhat put off" by the Peter Banks' recent statements on *The Shock Report* and "didn't know what to do."

But Gail couldn't seem to get her thoughts to slow down enough to put the pieces into a coherent report. The lead formed and then disintegrated before she could type it into a sentence. "Two days until the miracles are expected in Denver and—" She could get only that far.

And what? And she had been named as a Witness. And Darren Preston was trying to squirm out of a tight situation. And Peter Banks continued to act like a normal twelve-year-old boy despite his messages from God and a death threat. And it was after one and Gail Abernathy could not think of a thing in the world she wanted more than a nice cool glass of Chardonnay. It made her feel terribly guilty.

"You're one," Peter Banks had said to her. "You're one of them." And so she was to expect a miracle too. But, as she cleared her desk for lunch, she couldn't for the life of her think what it might be.

Maybe Peter made a mistake, she thought, as she jammed a thumb on the elevator call button. Maybe he was just trying to make her feel better. She really wasn't thinking about what she was doing until the maitre d' seated her opposite the Professor and handed her a menu.

When the Professor leaned over and took her hand in clear view of the rest of the restaurant patrons and said, "I knew you'd be here," the feeling of full defeat struck her across the face.

Gail took her hand back and put it in her lap. "Funny, I didn't know I'd be here," she said, wishing he'd wipe the smile off his face. She waited for a reply, but the Professor was too busy ordering drinks. "I think a nicely chilled chardonnay would do for starters," he told the waiter.

Gail tried to fight down the buzzing that had again swelled. Hadn't she told him she didn't want to drink? But hadn't she just been thinking how nice some chardonnay would taste right about now? She rolled her eyes at the internal discussion. *Really,* she thought, *normal people don't have these kinds of thoughts.*

Finally, she felt she had to say something. "I wasn't planning on drinking with lunch," she managed.

The Professor smiled. "You weren't even planning on coming to lunch today," he said. "I know you better than you know yourself."

Gail felt her heart sink with the answer. It seemed that he did. This over-sexed, under-performing adulterer seemed to have the perfect picture of her in his mind. And it wasn't one she liked. For a moment she thought of telling him that she too was a Witness. She tried to imagine what he'd say, just how predictable he would think that was.

Instead, she offered him another piece of news. "I found a dog," she told him, taking the wine glass that the waiter proffered and immediately tasting it. It was cool and crisp and almost made up for the smirk that traveled across the Professor's face as soon as she had swallowed.

"A dog," the man across from her laughed. "That's all you need right now, a dog." He seemed to find the news terribly funny. Gail took another gulp of wine, then put the glass down.

"I don't see what's so funny about it. He was in the middle of the street—I almost hit him. I couldn't let him just go to the pound. So I took him home, and I named him. And I'm just keeping him until I find his real owner."

"Right," the Professor said, trying to stifle his laugh because of the look on her face.

"Craig," she said, using his real name to get his attention, "this just isn't working for me." She could feel her hand shaking at the words, and she could barely believe they were coming out of her mouth. But she felt better. She took another few sips of wine to steady her nerves, then refilled her glass.

The Professor watched as she poured. Then he laughed again.

"Now, now, you don't even know what you want," he said to her. "See, didn't want lunch and here you are. You didn't want wine and just look at you. I think you're just thinking you don't want exactly what you do want, which means I'm in great standing." He seemed to find it irresistibly funny.

Gail blinked back the tears. It wouldn't do to let him see her cry, which would only give credence to his argument. "I'm a Witness, goddammit," she wanted to yell at him. "You can't treat me this way." But she knew she'd never say it aloud to him.

"What way?" he'd answer, and then point out that all he had ever done is take her to nice restaurants and then have, or try to have, sex with her. "You knew I was married," he would say. He'd said it before. "I never lied to you," he'd also say, because he'd said it before. "I'm just a transition man." His definition for himself. A package she had purchased. Caveat emptor, he would say, murdering the Latin and then laughing at it.

"I'm really confused right now," she said.

"So what's new?" he said dismissively. "Listen, let's not talk about this anymore." He watched her eyes fill. "Why don't you just take the afternoon off? I don't have any committee meetings, and I know a nice place where we can take all our clothes off."

Gail drained her glass and shook her head no. "I've got another story to write before deadline," she answered, refilling the glass.

It was only after she had topped it off that he spoke. "After three glasses of wine? Surely you need to take a little rest before anything coherent can be written. Come now, we can ask the waiter for the food to go."

The buzzing seemed to rise each time he spoke. Or maybe it was amplified with every sip of wine. It was hard to tell. All she knew was that something in her head was roaring, threatening to drown out all other sounds. "I need to get back to the paper," she said softly, hoping for all the world that no one else could hear the din she could. Carefully, because she felt she had to balance her head on her neck or the weight of it would be too much and roll off, she stood.

The Professor was not pleased. "What the hell do you think you're doing?" he asked, for once the smile disappearing.

"I'm going back to the paper," she said, again, softly, hoping her mouth was making the words audible because she couldn't hear them.

The Professor stood with her. "You're being unreasonable," he said, throwing some money on the table and walking with her to the door. "You get this way sometimes, and then you come back, I've seen it before." His statement, however true, made her furious, and she walked faster, trying not to feel the effects of three fast glasses of wine in the mid-afternoon sun.

And then the old Victorian house that stood just two blocks from the statehouse caught her eye, and she stopped.

"I hope this means you're coming to your senses," the Professor said, catching up then and breathing a little heavily. Gail ignored him, still looking at the house. On its door was a plain circle engulfing a triangle.

"Isn't that an AA symbol?" she asked, feeling stupid.

The Professor looked irritated. "What?" he asked, looking past her shoulder to where she was pointing. "How the hell should I know?" He put a hand on her arm.

Gail shook it off. "I think it is. I've heard that house is a place they have meetings. Lots of them. Maybe that will work for me," she said, thinking out loud.

The Professor turned purple. "You're really something, you know," he said, raising his voice there on the street. "It's just all a big drama to you, isn't it?" he screeched. "You can't handle it, so you just want to blame something. A few glasses of wine and you're running off to Alcoholics Anonymous. Jesus! You're a piece of work."

Gail felt her face flush with the stares from the passersby. Luke Harding, a lobbyist for the Homebuilders, was one of the people who turned to look at where the shouting was coming from. She could tell by his face he recognized both them.

"You're making a scene," she told the Professor, surprised by the pleading in her own voice.

"I'm not the one who stopped here," he shot back. "You did. This is your scene, not mine. I'll talk to you when you come to your senses." With that, the Professor stalked off in the direction of Luke Harding, to Gail's amazement. She watched him for a while as he greeted the lobbyist with the patented smile, pumping his hand up and down.

Then both men turned to watch Gail, to her horror. She tried to ignore them, looking up at the Victorian, noting the sign again, wishing, praying, that someone would come out of the house and collect her. Take her inside and tell her it would all be over soon. But no one did. The wrap-around porch remained empty. The door, its symbol declaring its purpose to the world, stared back.

Finally, she gave up and walked away. Away from the statehouse, away from the burning eyes of the Professor and Harding. Back to the newspaper, back to reactions to Peter Banks and details about Kitty Casen's broadcast. For the rest of the afternoon, Gail Abernathy fought the effects of a wine headache, excused herself nineteen times to take cigarette breaks, and wished with all her might that she would be struck dead by a freak bolt of lightning.

But the sun insisted on shining.

CHAPTER FIFTEEN

Sherry Anderson almost didn't remember that she was to meet with the Catholic entourage at Clark on Tuesday afternoon. Ever since she had watched Peter Banks on television, Sherry found it hard to concentrate. Something about the way the young boy's eyes had glowed as he talked made it impossible to sit and listen to the report on dead dieting teenagers in Illinois that followed. She turned off the television, and then wondered at the silence of her condo. For a while, she forgot about where she had put her pager. The thought to check it, to make sure it was still working, never even arose.

While the rest of the country was filled in on the health hazards of eating nothing but bananas and orange juice for months at a time (the teens struck ill had four times the normal amount of potassium in their bloodstreams), Sherry Anderson had wandered around the small space of her apartment. She straightened pictures she hadn't before noticed were crooked; she dusted off the figurines on the bookshelf. For a long time she watched the night sky off the balcony, noting that the stars were just where they had always been, even though she hadn't checked them for years.

Maybe it was the calmness of the boy's voice that made her feel suddenly so serene. When she thought about it, which wasn't until she finally bid the stars goodnight and slid under the cool sheets of her bed, she knew there had been a shift, but she couldn't quite put her finger on it. And for the first time in three years, she didn't really care to.

Tuesday morning had been the same. She had no desire to flick on the television and instead had the sudden urge to dig through the storage closet beside the bathroom in search of some of her beading. She never did have a cup of coffee. She was late to work anyway, having lost track of time among the boxes.

If Rachel Baum hadn't been preoccupied with the news that a certain orderly on the cardiac unit had been pilfering morphine, she would've noticed that Clark's beloved Doris Day had arrived more than forty-five minutes after her shift started, and spent another fifteen minutes discussing the virtues of sugar donuts with the cashier in the cafeteria. As it happened, Sherry Anderson's bizarre behavior was overlooked.

While Clark still remained in a "holding pattern," the betting pool about when the streak would break was growing bigger by the day, and it was all the oncology nurse manager could do to hide the cookie tin of money and chart of recorded bets from Baum, Sherry Anderson found her day flying by. After all, there were so many living people to talk with.

Tanya, the nurse who had dubbed Clark's deathless streak as a holding pattern, was in a tizzy over her wedding dress. At the last fitting, she told the Triple D, she noticed for the first time just how ridiculous the giant bow looked poised on the end of her derriere. "I just freaked, you know, looking at this thing. And I kept wondering why anyone would have put it there and why I chose the dress in the first place. I mean, it's too late, you know, to pick anything else. But it's just so, so—big," she finished tearfully.

Sherry had smiled at the consternation. Certainly, this was easier than what she usually dealt with, and still, she could tell, it was so terribly important to the young nurse. "You know, I don't think I've ever seen a wedding dress that didn't have a giant bow on the butt," she told Tanya, putting a hand on the younger nurse's arm. "Maybe that's why you didn't notice it. Because it was on every dress you looked at?"

Tanya was quiet for a moment and then nodded. "You know, I think you're right. The Bianchi had one, and so did the Lauren," she said, the smile returning to her face.

"You could always have them take the bow off, you know," Sherry continued. "I'm sure the back would look fine without it."

Tanya looked startled. "I'm not sure what it would look like without the bow," she answered. "I never thought about it. I assumed I was stuck."

When Sherry left her, to attend to the orderly who had just been informed by The Bomb that he would lose his job if he didn't get help for his drug addiction, Tanya was lost in her thoughts, debating the merits of bow-less dresses and what to do with an extra two yards of silk should the offending article be removed.

It was like that all morning. The orderly was enrolled, tearfully, in a drug-counseling program. Then Sherry spent the better part of an hour with The Bomb herself, assuring her that the anger management program she had been taking was indeed doing some good, despite the administrator's lapse when she had first confronted the morphine thief and threatened to "pump him full of something that would put him out of his misery for good."

"You did the best you could," Sherry said. "These things take time."

It wasn't until after lunch and a brief call from the director of the hospice Clark used most often that Sherry realized she indeed had an appointment that afternoon. The director of the hospice had been nervous, warily checking just why it was that Clark wasn't sending any patients her way. "If we have a problem, Sherry, you need to tell me about it," the director said.

Sherry laughed. "There aren't any problems, Mary. Just no dying people since—" and here she glanced at her calendar and saw her notation about the upcoming interview, "—last Thursday," she said. "Hey, I've got to go. I have an appointment." The director of the Denver Hospice Center hung up reluctantly, not believing for a minute that no one had been near death at Clark in five days.

Sherry had been meaning to talk with the priests in private, in her office. But it proved to be impossible to move them from the front lobby of the hospital and through the busy corridors of Clark without attracting attention. It was Tanya who finally said what all the other Clark professionals were thinking. "Are they here to talk about our holding pattern?" the young nurse asked, stopping Sherry and her odd group just outside the radiology department.

Sherry felt herself blush. "No, no, they're actually here to talk about Peter Banks," she told Tanya. "But I was planning to fill them in on the holding pattern, too," she added.

Tanya nodded, noting the flush in Sherry's cheeks, and giggled a little. "Well, let me know if they want in on the pool," she said mischievously, and then disappeared down the long hall that led to the MRI machines.

Sherry knew she wouldn't be able to get the priests all the way to her office before they started asking questions. "Holding pattern?" It was the tall, thin one who asked first.

Sherry smiled up at him. "Oh, we've been having an unusually long period without—uh—any fatalities, sir," she said as carefully as she could. "It's really quite unheard of for us."

Hamilton was quiet after the response, which she was thankful for, but the Hispanic priest at her left wasn't as discreet.

"How long? When did it start?" Chavez asked eagerly.

Sherry exhaled gratefully as they had arrived at her office door. At least she wouldn't have to answer out in the hallway.

"Last Thursday," she said, without thinking, still relieved she managed to fit all three men into her office. "It's really quite something for us. No one on staff can remember the last time we've had this sort of —uh—lull."

Hamilton, who had looked irked since Chavez had opened his mouth, cut in before anyone else could speak. "Surely, in a modern hospital, five days without a death can't be that unusual," he said, his long nails clicking together in their tent-like formation.

Sherry shook her head at the man. "Actually, it's very unusual. And it has nothing to do with how good the hospital is. People come here only when they are very, very ill. The advent of HMOs has almost made the distinctions between critical care units and others obsolete," she continued quite professionally. "You're not here unless your condition is a life-threatening one."

"Could it be seasonal?" This time it was Sybrandy, trying desperately, although he could not quite figure out why, to follow Hamilton's dismissal of the issue.

Sherry smiled. "No, I don't think it's seasonal," she assured him. "Usually around a holiday, people try to hang on until it's over, but that's, you know, like Christmas. This is late January for—" she stopped herself from blaspheming, "Heaven's sake," she managed.

Sybrandy sat back, defeated. Chavez twitched in his chair, about to say something, then clearly changed his mind.

It was Hamilton who spoke. "Mrs. Anderson, we are here to talk to you about Peter Banks," he said solemnly. "We have grave doubts about him."

His statement seemed to prick Chavez as if with a pin. The younger priest stifled what to Sherry sounded like a yelp.

"Doubts?" Sherry asked, her eyes narrowing. How could one have doubts about the boy she had watched the night before on the television screen, the boy who had put her in this unbelievable mood, whose very existence made the day go faster?

Hamilton shifted in his seat. "Well, ma'am, he made a number of pronouncements last night on national television that are in direct opposition to the tenets of the Church," he said, laying it on the line.

Sherry blinked at him. "Pronouncements?" she asked.

Hamilton could barely hide his irritation. "About abortion, Ms. Anderson—homosexuality," he prompted.

Sherry remained confused. She didn't remember any grand pronouncements on abortion or homosexuality.

"I, I guess I wasn't watching that carefully," she managed to say, embarrassed, because she was sure she had been watching carefully.

"Well," Hamilton was brusque, hoping to get past this idiocy, "in any case, we were watching carefully and we were concerned. You are a Catholic, are you not?" he asked Sherry.

"Uh, yes, I am," Sherry told him. "Although not very active in it," she added. "I'm divorced," she finally said, and suddenly remembered what it was like in the confessional as a young girl.

Hamilton appeared not to have heard her last statement. "So, as a Catholic, you understand, don't you Mrs. Anderson, how seriously we take the prophecy of miracles, don't you?"

She nodded, merely because it was all she could think of to do.

"So then, these 'proof of God' predictions would be worrisome no matter where they came from, don't you agree?" Hamilton continued.

Sherry shrugged; she wasn't willing to go that far.

"And especially since they are coming from a twelve-year-old who has no religious training, no spiritual upbringing, and indeed may never have even opened a Bible in so far as we've seen. It really does make one wonder, don't you think?"

Sherry merely shrugged again.

"To be honest with you," she said. "I don't know what to think." She looked over the three men seated before her and tried to smile at them. Only Chavez returned the effort. "I didn't really think about it, except for the implications of this—this media exposure, until last night. And then, I have to tell you, Fathers, I was really moved last night by Peter Banks. Really moved."

She thought she could detect a slight twitch of a smile in Chavez when she said this. But Hamilton grunted oddly and took to writing notes on the pad on his lap. "Very well, Mrs. Anderson," he said dismissively, "Tell me what you know about Peter Banks."

Sherry looked surprised at the question. Certainly she had just said everything she knew about the boy. "I've never met him, I don't know where he got my name, and I don't know why God has named me as a Witness," she said carefully.

Hamilton made a savage movement in his chair, but he remained seated. "Now, Mrs. Anderson, we really don't know that God has named you as a Witness, we only know that Peter Banks is saying these things."

Sherry smiled at him. "Well, I can't imagine why he'd be saying things like that if they weren't true," she said helpfully.

"Children do lie, Mrs. Anderson. Surely you know that," Hamilton beseeched.

Sherry tried to control the expression on her face. "I don't see that Peter Banks has any reason in the world to lie about this," she told the priest, wondering what it was he wanted her to see.

"That's what we're here to find out," Hamilton said sharply.

Sherry was stumped. "I don't know if I can be of any help to you."

"That," Hamilton answered her, "may well be true."

There was a silence for a while in the room, and then Father Chavez could control himself no longer. "Last Thursday was the date of Peter Banks' prophecy, you know," he said, more loudly than he meant to.

Sherry smiled at him, delighted at the turn of conversation. "I thought of that too," she told him. "Do you think Clark's holding pattern is connected?"

It was Chavez's turn to shrug. "Certainly worth considering, don't you think?"

Hamilton nearly exploded out of his chair. "No, I don't think!" he said, spitting slightly with the last word. "It's purely coincidence and has no part in this discussion," he added.

"Now really, Father, we are here to discuss miracles. I don't think we should be passing things off as coincidence," Chavez retorted.

"Gentlemen!" Sybrandy could not help himself. "I think we need to get the interview back on track," he added, after the two priests had been startled into silence.

Sherry, feeling the tension rise, again tried to be helpful. "Is there anything that I can answer for you, anything that I could clarify?" she ventured.

Father Hamilton looked at her blankly for a moment, the color still high in his face. It was Chavez who finally spoke. "What would it take, Ms. Anderson, to prove the existence of God to you?" he asked, his voice a thread in the air around them.

Sherry, who had expected to answer something simple, maybe her date of birth or when she'd taken her first communion, felt the question dangle. "Father," she finally said after a long moment, thoughts of Steven erupting for the first time that day, "for *that*, I don't have an answer."

Chavez nodded. "Well then," he said, rising and prompting his superiors to follow. "I guess we'll all just have to wait and see."

Jake Herron was nervously waiting at Stella's Coffeehouse at about the same time that Bishop Sybrandy was admonishing his fellow priests to end their public tussle. Herron had spent the rest of the morning and early afternoon with a cool rag to his forehead. Now he was sitting alone with a double-shot-mocha-light no-whip in front of him, wondering why he had acquiesced to this meeting. He pushed the thought away and instead focused on the priests' interrogation that morning.

It had really surprised Herron, the Men in Black's line of questioning, and he was at once angry with them and himself for not seeing it coming. It wasn't like he was naïve, he thought as he played with the foam on the top of his cup. He was in politics, for God's sake. And yet the thought that anyone would think he could be bribed to become the recipient of a miracle was just too much for him.

He was lost in this thought, staring at the coffee, when the table lurched and he watched, as if in slow motion, a wave of foam slide over the side of his cup and hit the surface below with a plop. When he looked up, she was there.

She looked even better than he remembered. The hair gleaming, neatly held back by a barrette. She wore a jade-colored sweater and jeans. Her arms were long and subtly muscled, and one was bedecked with a series of silver bangles. *Are ministers allowed to wear bangles?* Jake wondered. He swallowed and commanded his vein to relax, then he rose and greeted her. He could at least be polite.

"Hi," he said, extending a hand. "Nice to see you."

She laughed then as she had two nights ago in the bar, and he was once again amazed at the white, even row of teeth, and the way her nose wrinkled whenever they were in full view.

"The affairs of the nation must be getting heavy," she said with mock seriousness. "You looked like you just lost your last friend." She sat down in the chair opposite him, stretching her long legs out to one side of the table.

"Can I get you a cup of coffee?" Jake asked.

"Oh no," she answered with the same dazzling smile. "I just want to sit here and talk—if that's okay."

He was struck by it, this willingness to discuss what seemed to him a rather embarrassing moment. His first urge was to go ahead and pretend they had never had a falling out. Maybe discuss sports, or music or whatever it is that normal people discuss.

But then, this wasn't a normal person, this was a goddamn minister sitting across from him. "Okay by me," he said.

Leslie Brimhall leaned across the table. "I studied theology in college," she started, and Jake had to make an effort not to roll his eyes. Of course she studied theology!

"Theology is the study of God—you know, from the Greek, "theo". It's not the study of man's relationship to God, it's the study of God, or what we think we know about Him, or Her, or whatever."

Jake hoped this was going somewhere. He was too old to be in Sunday school. Leslie glanced at his face and knew she wasn't getting through. She couldn't blame him. She'd seen it plenty times before, back in Akron. Some of the congregation had developed a total disgust with all things related to faith because of repeated exposure to extreme fanatics. Still, this wasn't someone she was willing to give up on. Jake Herron was the first intelligent, feeling, good-looking man she'd met in a while. Even if he weren't going to receive a miracle in a couple days (and she was sure he would) she'd be interested. She took a deep, deep breath and forged ahead.

"You've been in politics for years. You know politics is all about competition for power."

At least she got that right, Jake thought, nodding. Except he wouldn't call it a competition. He'd call it a game. A fucking game that uses people as the playing pieces. He was getting tired of all this. "I didn't come here for a sermon, you know," he said nastily.

Leslie nodded. "Of course you didn't. But I needed to tell you that there's a difference between religion and spirituality—and this is the only way I can think to explain it."

"Religion and spirituality," Jake repeated back to her. "All right, I'm listening."

Leslie looked grim. "Religion is what happens when politics meets theology," she said slowly. "Spirituality is what happens when you personally choose to believe in some sort of deity, some kind of omniscient creator in your life."

Jake kneaded his forehead again. "Okay, I get it," he told her. "You're into the personal stuff." A moment passed while he contemplated his half empty cup. "Then what's the big deal with this Peter Banks thing and you? I mean it's a media circus. You can't say it's something personal."

Leslie smiled. "Did you see the interview, Jake. Did you *get* the interview?"

Jake felt Leslie's response hit him. "The interview? You liked the interview?"

Her smile deepened. "It was great," she said. "I just got this great feeling watching him, hearing his voice. If I had any doubts before, I certainly lost them after that."

Jake shook his head, as if movement would cause his thoughts to realign, somehow make sense. "What was personal about it?"

"It was everything I believe. That God is loving and available and doesn't want us to hurt each other, exactly what Peter Banks said."

"I guess," he told her, wishing they could talk about something else. Something that didn't trigger every nervous tic he had. "I wish this Peter Banks thing never happened," he said weakly.

Leslie's face went blank. "Don't say that, Jake, I—"

She never did finish her sentence. He cut her off. "Why shouldn't I say that?" Herron felt his blood pressure rising and ignored it. "I met with three Catholic priests this morning who accused me of bribing Peter Banks to name me, and my boss is all over me because she's afraid I'll sound like an atheist to the voters out there!" Jake paused only long enough to catch his breath. "Who needs this shit anyway? You bet I wish I had never heard of Peter Banks."

Leslie felt her own panic rise. He was right that accusations were insulting, the insistence on "looking religious" for societal reasons was repugnant. Usually she had an easier time reassuring those in crisis. Now she couldn't think of anything to say.

"But what about the miracle?" she asked him, almost pleading. "What about Thursday?"

Jake just shook his head.

"What would be a miracle to you, Jake?" she wanted desperately to know.

Not again. "You know," Jake heard his own voice say, "that's exactly what the one okay priest asked me on the way out. He said it was important. That I know what a miracle would be for me."

He looked at her then, sharply, challenging. "It's an impossible question," he told her. "I mean, do you know what a miracle would be for you?"

Leslie Brimhall studied her hands for a few seconds before answering. And then her voice sounded shaky, for the first time. "I think so," she said, letting the sentence die unfinished. She paused, then added, "But I wasn't named, and you were."

Herron tried to manage a low chuckle, but it came out more like a cough. "I haven't even had a chance to think about it, to be honest with you," he told her, wondering what it was she would want, what would be a miracle for her, but not wanting to ask.

"You only have a couple days left," she told him, leaning forward again, her bangles clattering on the table. You may want to think about it."

Jake felt tired all of a sudden. "What difference will it make," he told her, "what I think about it? Like I've had any say in this whole Peter Banks thing to date."

It wasn't, Jake thought furiously, like God was going to change his mind, alter a little thing here or there, depending on what Jake Herron thought a good miracle would be.

"What if I decided a miracle to me would be tripping over a million dollars just lying in the street? You think that would make a difference?"

"If you thought that way, I don't think Peter Banks would ever have named you." *And I wouldn't be so attracted to you,* she thought.

She moved quickly to change the subject. "So, what are you going to do on Miracle Day?" she asked. "Taking the day off?"

Jake chuckled darkly. "Hell no," he said, knowing it was probably offensive. "I'll be in Miranda Davis' district office with two chatty interns and probably a bunch of press," he said.

"No friends?" she asked.

He snorted. "Not unless you count Jeff Ronald, who's covered my office since I got there. We've never even had a drink together."

"Can I come?"

He looked at her for a moment. "Sure, I mean, it's a public office, anybody can be there."

Leslie made a face. "That isn't what I meant," she said.

For some reason, Jake's heart skipped a couple of beats.

"Yeah, sure, I guess so," he said, after he could breathe again.

CHAPTER SIXTEEN

Lisa Marretti arrived in Denver just about the time that Ricardo Shock was broadcasting from the Iowa cornfield. She happened to catch it—although afterward she wished she hadn't—as she checked into the small motel room just off Hampden Avenue, wondering at the griminess of the city and longing for her own scrubbed kitchen.

She had the baby with her. And Ed had understood. Like he always understood. He told her to do what she had to do. He said he supported her in it. Sometimes she wondered if her husband were an alien or something.

Alex, just five months old, was still in that stage where he put everything he could find in his mouth. She had turned on the TV in the hopes of distracting him, of keeping him from sucking on the floor, the fringe of the lime-green carpet, or putting his mouth around the bottom of the table leg. She was less than successful.

But the TV was on, just the same. And she chatted with Alex, who had discovered the tassel on the end of the bedspread and was slowly moving toward it. "Look at that, Alex," she said. "It's Ricardo Shock, and he's in Iowa."

It was a stark picture that stared back at them. Shock, his hair blowing in the gusty Iowa wind, his suit coat flapping behind him, stood on the edge of a cornfield with nothing but a burned-out Packard in the background. It made Lisa Marretti feel cold, as if she herself could feel the cutting breeze. And it made her lonely, lonelier than she felt when she told Ed she was leaving for a few days, to head to Denver to do what she had to do.

Marretti didn't know that Shock had instructed the cameraman to make the filming dark. The television personality didn't think that the sun beating down, as it was in reality, made for the right backdrop to the scene. "I want it like a film noir—you know, Andy, shoot it as if it were gray and grainy," he'd said.

Andy Beckman hid his annoyance at the star, watching Shock's teeth flash and swearing every time he tried to get a firm plot of ground in which to plant his camera stand. Film noir, he thought. I'll bet Shock never even saw a film noir.

Beckman complied, all the same.

He adjusted the light meter reading to an extreme, as if he were filming on a snowy mountain instead of a dusty cornfield. He narrowed the aperture of the camera and set up the spots so that Shock's face would be half-hidden in deep shadow. He didn't take the time to try to tell the star that film noir was supposed to be about reality—a true depiction of reality—not a manipulation. It wasn't worth it.

Morty would later comment that it was one of the worst segments they had ever aired. "Unappealing to the eye, the mind, and even the dick," he would say. But that didn't stop him from putting it on that night, from letting the nation see it, and hear Ricardo Shock wonder to himself in a cornfield just how would God act, given what had already happened there?

It was because of the dark lighting and the passage of years that Lisa Marretti didn't at first recognize the place. It looked like a moonscape, not a cornfield. The Packard hadn't been there, and the corn was full and leafy the last time she'd seen it. But Shock left no doubt in her mind as to what she was looking at.

"A parent's worst nightmare," he called it. "A fate crueler to the living than the dead," he said. Morty would wince at the wording when he received the footage, the way Shock pronounced "crueler," he sounded like he was talking about the breakfast pastry. But the message was still there. The producer figured accurate pronunciation was by no means a highly held value in his business. Barbara Walters was proof positive of that.

Still, Shock managed to get the message he and Morty had discussed across to the audience. "This is a place that cries out for a miracle," he said, sweeping his hand in the gesture that seemed to include both the burned out car and the short stubby stalks next to him. "But what will that miracle be?" He allowed a pregnant pause to linger—so long, in fact, that Marretti, along with a full third of the viewing audience that night, started fiddling with the remotes, wondering if the sound had been lost.

Which caused his last line to blare into exactly sixteen million living rooms. "If Peter Banks is right, we'll know Thursday," he finished.

Alex was startled by the full volume. His small, pudgy body shuddered under the shock of the sound waves and he started screaming before the statement was finished. Lisa Marretti leaned over to pick up the child, who had crammed a good inch-and-a-half of the chenille bedspread into his mouth and was now screaming around it. She removed the soggy material and swept him up, still staring at the screen now showing a commercial for home loans, and held him close.

She was almost glad for his tears. They covered hers. And made her anonymous for a moment. Not someone who was in a strange town on a mission. She felt around on the spongy bed until she found the remote again and shut off the television. She wasn't quite sure how long she sat there, listening to the cries subside and watching Alex eventually fall asleep, but it must have been a very long time.

Peter Banks wasn't paying attention when Ricardo broadcast his moonscape cornfield to the nation. More precisely, Peter *was* paying attention, but not to the TV. There were too many other things going on. It had been a long day for the twelve-year-old. The night before, he had tried to explore the hotel, but it hadn't gone very well. His mother had been taking yet another bath and his father was busy on the phone in the bedroom when Peter had carefully crept out into the hallway and started making his way along the eleventh floor corridor. He was investigating the laundry chute, thinking how fun it would be to jump through and ride the slick plastic all the way down to a pile of sheets in the basement, when his father's voice filled the hallway.

"Peter! What the hell do you think you're doing?"

That had been the end of his great adventure. He was told in no uncertain terms by his father that he could never, ever leave the hotel room alone again. Not until this was all over.

And so Peter had been a prisoner.

The next morning he tried to sleep in as long as he could—hoping to pass some time. When he finally did wander out to the sitting room, he found the sun full in the sky, a cart of dirty breakfast dishes standing oddly in the middle of the room, and his mother, smoking a long-filtered cigarette and staring at a magazine.

He had never seen Vivienne smoke before.

"What are you doing?" His mother had gazed up at him almost dreamily, her hair swept back in to long tendrils. "Oh Peter, you mustn't get the wrong idea. This is just a stress reducer." Then she handed him a menu and invited him to order anything he wanted.

It was a very long day. He played some Gameboy, then got bored. When his father announced he was heading to the office for a few hours, Peter begged to go with him, but Edward had refused. The elder Banks wasn't about to give Darcy the chance to snicker at his only son.

So Peter waited for news from the outside world. His father returned to the hotel room just as it was getting dark, but he didn't have a lot to say. Edward took the pile of files he was carrying into the bedroom and closed the door.

Even when Gail arrived at 6:45 with Dillon and Gus and a bag of burritos from Taco Bell—Peter's relief was limited. She didn't seem like the same woman who had urged him to tell Vivienne his secret. She didn't seem like the same woman who announced they should all go to a hotel. It wasn't like she was possessed or anything, he reasoned. It was just that she was somewhere else.

He knew this by watching her. The scotch in her left hand trembled slightly. She put it down only to light a cigarette. The burrito in front of her had barely been touched and eventually was fed, along with most of the others, to Gus.

If it weren't for God's voice in his head, Peter would never have survived it. But whenever an adult disappointed him, he'd made a habit to trigger the tape, letting himself feel the words. A few times, Peter caught Gail looking at him as if she had a question, something she was sure he knew the answer to but that she was afraid to ask in front of everyone. If he hadn't been protected in his newfound cocoon, the intensity of her gaze would've frightened him. He had nothing he could offer; his directions had been very specific. As it was, he felt sad and unqualified.

We are two days from the miracles, Peter thought. He suddenly felt the profound need to jack off. He shifted his position to hide the evidence of his desire. Edward came out to join them in front of the television, merely nodding to Gail and his wife as both women

inhaled deeply on their cigarettes. Vivienne, for all intents and pur-
poses, treated Gail as her confidante in all this—a lady-in-waiting to
her queen. It wasn't a conscious decision. Vivienne didn't enjoy conscious decisions. Gail just represented someone to hold on to during
this turbulent time. Vivienne wondered if this were how Anne of
Austria felt when the cardinal was threatening the monarchy. Well,
certainly, she decided, Mary—that Mary—had a friend through it all,
hadn't she? The phone rang.

Peter knew better than to pick up what had now become Edward's
business line. Edward went straight to the wireless phone on the corner of the bar. "Yes?" he said. "Yes, this is Edward Banks."

Vivienne, after looking up from the opening credits to make sure
the call wasn't another death threat, went back to the grainy film.

"This is a place that cries out for a miracle," she heard Shock say.

"That does sound interesting." Edward's voice was suddenly clear.

Vivienne waived her hand at him, irritated at the interruption.

"But what will that miracle be?" Ricardo asked, and Vivienne
watched as the camera spanned the cold, dark field.

"I think that would do fine for an advance, Mr. Harden," Edward
continued. "I can imagine the market is ripe for the real inside story,"
he added.

"Edward!" Vivienne hissed at him, waving her hand again. There
hadn't been a sound from the TV for several moments now, and she
was certain she had missed something Ricardo had said because of
her husband's babbling.

Gail got up to locate the remote and pushed a thumb down hard
on the volume button.

"*If Peter Banks is right, we'll know Thursday.*" Ricardo Shock's voice
shook the room, scaring even Gus back from the Taco Bell bag and
into Gail's lap.

"*Jesus H. Christ!*" bellowed Edward, matching the volume. "Turn
that fucking thing off. I'm talking business here."

Vivienne, Gail and Peter sat stunned. Ricardo Shock had just said
Peter's name to millions of people across the country. What could
happen in a three-minute telephone conversation that would suddenly make Edward forget that?

They didn't have to wait long for an answer.

"Norway and Simmons, the publishing house, wants me to write a book," Edward announced.

No one watched as Ricardo's teeth faded to black.

Father Chavez was on fire when he returned to his small rectory. Part of it was anger. Rage, to be more exact. Rage at the conclusions of his superiors, at the assumptions of these pale and judgmental men who had all but descended on Jake Herron and Sherry Anderson with the express purpose of snatching their glimpse of faith. If they had any to begin with. Of course there was also the fact that he could sense Sybrandy cowering at Hamilton at the same time the bishop couldn't keep his feelings of ethnic superiority to himself. *Chinga su madre*, Chavez muttered under his breath, crossing himself and immediately asking forgiveness for the horrendous curse. *These gringos.*

But the other part of Chavez that was on fire had nothing to do with rage. Something Sherry Anderson had said about Clark. What the other nurse had called "the holding pattern." No one had died in the hospital since Peter Banks had made his announcement. It was unheard of, Anderson had made that clear. There was nothing scientific to explain it. Chavez felt a thrill tingle up his spine. Nothing scientific, no, but there was plenty to explain it.

"Heaven is waiting," Chavez whispered to his small kitchen, running his hands over the Formica as if it were part of an altar. "You are there, my Lord," he said again, thinking about Sherry Anderson's face, the confusion in Jake Herron's eyes. "The questions, they need answers."

Neither Herron nor Anderson had been able to answer those questions: what would be proof of God to them? And Hamilton and Sybrandy never even thought to ask.

"Why is that?" Chavez asked aloud. He squeezed the Formica again and felt power ripple through his hand. The Lord was near, Chavez thought, his heart quickening. For so many years, the priest had prayed in that same kitchen, coming in from Mass or from a visit to the sick, and praying. But always, always, praying to someone, something, that felt very far away. As if long distance, as if one had to shout to get His attention. And, privately, feeling some shame at being so blasphemous of the Almighty, Chavez had often scolded his Lord, the one he had dedicated his life to, as having drifted too far from his flock. But now, He was near.

Chavez clattered around his kitchen, delighting in making noise, and feeling the energy bouncing off the old coffee maker, the dusty toaster, the dim overhead light.

"The questions matter, My Lord," he called out, full volume. "Don't they? Why can't they see it?" As quickly as the statement was out of his mouth, Chavez felt his chest fill with something warm, something soft and forgiving. Something that made the faces of Sybrandy and Hamilton, the hateful fingernails and the bulging belly, melt in his memory. *"Pobre Cabrones,"* Chavez thought without hesitation. "Poor blind *chingas su madre."*

He felt his energy build; he could almost hear it. Singing through the house. He had heard of this incredible sensation of joy, of the complete dispersal of shame and hate and guilt, of the freeing of the heart. The first disciples of Christ experienced it; that was the story, and they shined with it. Chavez had taught that part of the Bible to his congregation many times, and again and again told them to open their hearts and accept the feeling. The high that had nothing to do with drugs, the feeling of love that had nothing to do with sex, the feeling of completeness that had nothing to do with things, the feeling of security that had nothing do to with money. He had urged them to open themselves to it—perhaps every other sermon had a mention. And yet, he, Chavez, had never felt it.

Until now.

Now it was here, the joy, the compassion for those who could not see it. And now, suddenly, the singing. Was it angels?

He had almost done it, dropped to his knees there in the small kitchen, writhed on the floor without having taken off his robe, in the ecstasy that had been promised since he was a small boy in catechism—and then he noticed the phone, its receiver shaking.

The phone's ring was the singing he'd heard. He picked up the receiver, with its cool, heavy plastic, and put it to his ear. His energy drained away.

"For God's sake, Chavez, turn on the blasted television!" Sybrandy barked. Chavez didn't answer. He set the receiver down, crossed the kitchen to the sitting area and flicked on the old black and white. Ricardo's face filled the screen. Chavez could see the burned-out Packard and the flapping of Ricardo Shock's coattail. He felt the cold breeze that cut across the cornfield.

"A parent's worse nightmare," Shock said. "A fate crueler to the living than the dead."

Chavez knew what was happening. *Sherry Anderson*, he thought. *God in Heaven pray that Sherry Anderson is nowhere near a television.*

"This is a place that cries out for a miracle," Ricardo continued, and Chavez felt his heart sink further. "No, anything but this. Fish and wine, yes, talk about that, pander that to the ratings," he muttered, "but not this."

"This is a place that cries out for a miracle," Ricardo repeated, as Chavez sank to his knees. "Please, not a resurrection. Don't make them all expect a resurrection," Chavez prayed, searching for the presence that minutes before had felt so close.

"What will that miracle be?"

Chavez never heard the answer. He reached a robed arm over to the small set and with the flat of his hand, knocked it off its stand. The tube bounced once, and Ricardo's face was on its side, his voice a jumble of static. Then the screen went blank.

Not one prone to violence, Chavez remained there on his knees, on the floor of his sitting room, next to the dead TV. He prayed, silently, without folding his hands.

There were a number of things Father Chavez prayed for on Tuesday night. Some—like the fungus he wished would attack Father Hamilton's long fingernails and cause them to curl and darken—are not worth repeating. Others—the good wishes for his congregational members, especially those who were ill or had adolescent children—were part of his regular repertoire. But he asked for two blessings that were unusual for him, which had nothing to do with his impatience and dislike for his superiors, blessings that related solely to the miracles that were due in two days. Chavez prayed that Sherry Anderson be spared the Ricardo show at the site of her son's suicide, that she not be forced to endure both the painful memory and the empty hope that her son would be brought back to life. Chavez also prayed that he be allowed to witness at least one of the miracles God had in store. "It is not for myself only, my Father," Chavez pleaded. "I'm afraid that if I'm not there, they might miss it all together."

One of Chavez's prayers that night was answered.

CHAPTER SEVENTEEN

Sherry Anderson watched Ricardo Shock Tuesday night in the privacy of her condominium, with the lights dimmed, her dishwasher on, and a pile of beading in her lap. She hoped the boy would be on again. The Banks boy, the one who had made her feel so good just the night before. The interview with the three priests that afternoon had left her feeling more perplexed than anything. They were clearly suspicious of the boy and his intentions, and yet Sherry couldn't see any reason for it. She never considered herself particularly gullible—certainly not naïve. What did the Banks boy have to gain by his announcement? She couldn't figure it. But at least two of the priests had seemed so sure there was some sort of subterfuge going on, some hidden agenda. *Maybe,* Sherry thought as she pulled up her chair to the TV and poured a glass of iced tea, *maybe if Ricardo interviews the boy again, I'll catch on.*

The credits came up and the voiceover began. For the first few moments, Sherry felt some excitement and anticipation. Yes, they were going to stick with the story, the "miracle story" as they put it. Here it was. Soon, she'd have answers.

Ricardo Shock stood in the middle of a cornfield in the dark, his coat whipping around him. He was yelling, yes yelling, to be heard over the wind. Sherry could barely make out what he was saying.

"A parent's worse nightmare," the words were spitting into the microphone from between those large, square teeth. And suddenly, Sherry knew what she was looking at. The scene she had pictured in her dreams, in her hours of sleeplessness, in her long sessions with the therapist. The cornfield. The one where it all happened. If she'd had the strength, Sherry Anderson would've turned the television off. But she didn't. She was frozen, aside from her shaking left hand. Her mind was in freefall.

There was nothing in the police report about an abandoned Packard, she thought. Would it have been that cold when Steven was out there? How had this awful man found the spot, and just what did he think he could accomplish by putting it on television for everyone to see, for everyone to know? He stood there, explaining she was a Witness, explaining the death of her son, explaining the prophecy of Peter Banks. Now what was he saying? She held perfectly still.

"What will that miracle be?" Ricardo said.

For a moment, Sherry Anderson stopped breathing. It was there, clearly, what he meant. The implication was plain. She allowed herself one small sip of air. Could Steven come back? After three years and the funeral and the cocooning and the layers and layers and layers of protection, could he come back to her with his blond hair and quick smile and the lilt on the hairline at the back of his neck?

She could hug him then, oh, and feel the way her arms barely fit around him, he had gotten so big. She would laugh, of course, because she could still remember when he was so tiny that she could tuck his head under her chin and his toes would barely reach her bellybutton. He had grown so. How many times over the last three years had she imagined just hugging him again, feeling his heat, the smell of cotton and cigarettes (and okay, every now and then, pot) and just knowing that he lived again? She could imagine tilting her head back and taking his face in her hands so she could see it clearly, every inch of it. What would he have said?

Long after Ricardo's face had faded from the screen, Sherry Anderson was still glued to her chair, her eyes open but seeing nothing, her mind working first fast, then slow, through the options.

"I was so mad at you, I killed myself." Would he say that?

"How could you have made me kill myself?" She could hear it in his voice, each word, where the pauses would come.

"It was your fault, you know," he would say it with that rasp that she had always loved so much. "All that pressure, I was never good enough."

He would come back and tell her everything she already knew. There hadn't been a note. Nothing. As if he wasn't about to help her out, that he knew what she would think, that she'd know it was her fault. "Over your dead body, you said," he could say. "I made it over my dead body."

She would have an opportunity to apologize. But would he accept it? Would he ever accept an apology from the mother he hated so much that he did the unthinkable? She doubted it. She worked it forward and backward in her mind, trying to imagine her son forgiving her. Trying to imagine him returning her hug, a pat on the head, like he always did as a sort of cute reminder that he was so much taller than her now. But it didn't work, in any version.

Sherry Anderson eventually fell asleep in front of the television that was tuned to Channel 9. The very prospect of Steven coming back, a resurrection, as Ricardo had implied, would be a miracle that would take so much courage to face. More courage, she wearily decided just before she slipped into sleep, than she had left.

Kitty Casen had been all for her producer's decision to send her to Denver the day before the miracles were scheduled to happen until she found out that the plan was to film from the urinals inside Rory Middle School, where it had all started. "You want me to stand next to some nasty toilet?" she asked incredulously, her nose twitching at the thought.

"Kitty, honey, it'll be perfect," Michael, her producer, said. "What people seem to be forgetting is that this all started with a little boy jacking off. You need to be the one who reminds them of that."

"I don't approve of that, you know," Kitty told her producer.

Michael Lasky didn't have to clarify what it was his high-strung star didn't approve of. He knew. In fact, that's why it made Kitty the perfect person to do the story. Lasky's network bigwigs had been tearing their hair out ever since Ricardo had stolen the story out from virtually everyone by doing the first Peter Banks interview. Since then, the country had been tuned into Ricardo, following it all as if there were going to be miracles, and as if there really were a true prophecy.

Any attempt by the other networks to jump on the bandwagon fell flat. Banks wasn't giving any more interviews, and ABC had already put on every talking head known to have a thimble's full of information on theology. Enough was enough. Lasky needed either the Pope or a new angle. The Vatican had flatly turned him down.

So the urinal was his new angle.

"Look, Kitty honey," Lasky said, trying to move a little closer to her, get her attention away from the fleck of lint that seemed to be bothering her so much on the front of her skirt. "You need to tell the truth about what's going on. It's Wednesday. According to that kid, the miracles happen tomorrow. You need to tell people that they may not want to hold their breath."

She nodded miserably and boarded the plane. Three hours later, she whipped through DIA unnoticed behind black sunglasses and an Adrienne Vitadini scarf. Not that being noticed had been a big problem in the past months. She hadn't been in any of the magazines in months. Getting too old, she worried to herself. And now she was on her way for a date with a urinal.

On Wednesday morning, Gail Abernathy was back at the paper, trying to keep her shaking hands from being noticed by Lincoln Fraser. She didn't generally spend enough time in his presence to expose herself to intense scrutiny, but today it was important. The "budget" of stories the editors had come up with for Thursday was out of hand. The Religious Roundtable was expected to make its prediction of miracles, and there was supposed to be an hour-by-hour schedule of the Witnesses' agenda for Thursday. "We want to know where they'll be when the miracle happens, Gail," Fraser said. There was a "react" article slated, to reveal how people felt about Ricardo Shock's latest story, the one dubbed "x-Files" by the editorial staff, and there was supposed to be an interview with Denver's own Bishop Sybrandy as to the status of the investigation on the miracles. The paper also wanted a feature on how the Witnesses were holding up under the stress of it all, and a sidebar on the number of "religious" people currently living in Denver.

"Fraser, what were you guys smoking in the editorial meeting this morning?" Gail asked, nervously petting Gus. She had decided that morning she needed the dog's calm presence to get through the day ahead.

"I'll take that as your ill-advised stab at humor, Abernathy. Otherwise it'll seem like you're getting a bit insubordinate. What the hell is that dog doing here again?"

"Who's going to write all this, even if the stories were out there?" Gail continued, ignoring the mention of Gus.

"You do as many as you can, and we'll hammer out the rest, honey," Fraser said, attempting to be calming.

"Okay, Fraser, look, let me just give you a rundown on the list. The Religious Roundtable has already made predictions ad nauseam. They usually amount to invasions by aliens or that Cher will dress with taste. Two: the Witnesses, of which there are a total of two, are both going to work tomorrow. They do not have an hour-by-hour schedule they're planning to release to the newspapers. Peter Banks said four o'clock, and at four o'clock I would imagine that everyone will kind of stand around and wonder and wait and if nothing earth-shattering happens, we're going to have a lot of space to fill; and three—"

Fraser cut her off. "What do you mean if nothing earth shattering happens? No matter what happens, it's earth shattering—either a miracle will happen or it won't. That's a story. Story one, the prediction was right. Story two, the prediction was wrong. What's the problem?" Gail tried to keep her temper. "Story two is a bit shorter, don't you think?"

Fraser gave his reporter a look of disappointment. "Maybe I should get someone who can handle this. You can go take your dog for a walk."

Gail ignored the remark. "A react story to Shock's visit to the cornfield is totally unjustified. He was pulling at straws and speculating in what was really an irresponsible and certainly unethical way about what the miracle would be. The fact that he manipulated the filming of an Iowa cornfield in broad daylight to make it look like it was the surface of the moon only adds to the indecency of the whole thing. I won't be part of furthering that sort of—"

Again, she was cut off. "Oh fuck you and your high horse. I'll find someone else to pick up the story. You just stick to Banks, all right, and that's only because you've established some rapport with the family. If you hadn't, I'd fire your ass now, you hear me, you, you—" Fraser reached for a word and for a moment Gail cringed, waiting to hear "drunk, or alchy." But what came out was "baby."

"That's what you are, you know. A baby. Grow up, Gail. Grow up and get with it. Nobody cares about you and all your ethics. And get that goddamn dog out of here this minute. He's a distraction—and a big, smelly, health department violation to boot. Just write the news,

Gail. That's what we care about, now—"

She didn't wait to hear the rest. Fraser had let loose on her in the middle of the newsroom, just around the corner from the same bank of elevators she and the Professor had argued at just a day ago, although it seemed like a million years ago.

One of the elevators was just closing when she hit it, stuck her arm into the narrow space and prayed that the door would reverse direction. It did. And she was out, Gus right behind her.

She knew exactly where she was heading, although she had no idea what to do when she got there.

Lincoln Fraser stood in the middle of the newsroom watching Gail and the damned dog exit. He couldn't figure out what it was with that woman lately. She seemed to be getting further away from the kind of reporter he had thought she was: tough, reliable. Maybe it was only because she was out of her element. Maybe she needed to deal in politics, where the sharks were ever-present and the sides constantly shifting. Maybe it was this foray into religion that made her uneasy. Something so clear-cut that she just couldn't handle it.

Gail got to the three-story brick building across from the statehouse in record time. But she had no memory of the walk. Somewhere along the way, she'd lit a cigarette. And somewhere along the way, she'd twisted her ankle and was now walking with a bit of a limp. Gus seemed to think everything was going well, however, trotting along right next to her. Gail absentmindedly stroked his head as she climbed the stairs to the place. "Great," was all she could think to herself, "Great, they'll think I'm some street person, just limping in from outside, coming in to get warm or something—" and then she caught herself because really, what would it matter what these people thought? This was an AA meeting house, right?

The Victorian on the corner of Logan and 14th Street had been left to the area Alcoholics Anonymous organization more than forty years ago upon the death of a grateful member. Since then, meetings ran round the clock for age groups from teens to retirees. There was no sign outside the house, given the concerns over anonymity—only a triangle in a circle was painted unobtrusively on the front-door window. Still, most in the city knew what the house was, what it meant. Walking in the front door, looking over her shoulder to make sure no one was watching, was almost more than Gail could take.

She hesitated on the threshold. But Gus rushed past her into the hallway, committing her. "Welcome," a voice said, high and crackly—the kind of voice that would come from a fairy tale witch. The face didn't quite match, however.

"You're in the right place," the woman continued. She didn't seem to be at all upset by the presence of the dog. Gus had walked halfway into the large foyer, turned around and sat, as if waiting for Gail to catch up. The woman had reddish hair, combed back neatly into a ponytail, and she was wearing one of those sweatshirts Gail always wondered who bought at the mall, the ones with the mirrored chips glued on into abstract designs.

Gail tried to think of something to say.

"There's a meeting just started, right over there," the woman said, apparently unconcerned that Gail hadn't spoken.

"There, sit right down and I'll get you a cup of coffee." The woman led Gail into one of the large meeting rooms off the foyer, but Gus showed no signs of coming along.

It had happened so fast. Going from the newsroom to this place— it all seemed a blur. There were voices talking now, but she couldn't quite make them out. Gail kept her eyes on the carpet, a bluish sculpted affair, once popular in the 1970s.

"Here you go, honey," someone whispered to her.

Gail looked up to find the mirror-clad woman handing her a Styrofoam cup of watery looking coffee. It made the mud the *Sentinel* put out look gourmet.

Gail managed a weak smile as a thank you.

"I'm Vicki, and I'm an Alcoholic," a woman across the room was saying now. "I just wanted to say how grateful I am to be an alcoholic, to have been led to these rooms by my disease, and to have had a chance to meet all of you and make these kinds of friendships. I know that my Higher Power has been keeping a close eye on me."

Gail shut the woman out. Grateful? She tried to keep both hands around the bottom of her cup. When she held it with only one hand, the coffee sloshed around.

What would Dillon think? "Hey honey, your mother is a drunk and she has to go to these meetings where the carpet is in really bad shape and the coffee is this weird tan color and the people wear little mirrors on their shirts—"

And what would she say to Dillon's father? The thought made her heart squeeze so tight she suddenly stopped breathing. When she finally managed to inhale, she made a sharp wheezing sound that caused the current speaker, a man with puffs of white hair shooting from the back of his baseball hat, pause and stare at her.

Then he continued. "I'm having a hard day today, lots of triggers."

"Triggers," Gail's mind picked up. "How about one to squeeze and end all this?" she thought. "If this is supposed to help, I'm in the completely wrong place."

Carefully, she raised her head from its gaze on the carpet and peered around the room. She wasn't very far from an exit. Not far at all. She put the cup down carefully on the carpet. It tilted menacingly in one of the sculpted grooves, but didn't spill. There, there was a door that clearly led back into the main hallway where Gus was waiting, where the front door was. Gail picked up the strap of her purse and silently slung it over her shoulder. Head down, she tiptoed as best she could with her twisted ankle back out toward the hallway.

When she shut the door behind her, she let out a long sigh of relief. No one had followed her out. The escape was clean.

"Gus, c'mon Gus," she whispered to the dog, who had now decided that the foyer of the AA building was a great place to take a nap. "Gus," she raised her voice a little. The dog sat up, his head in the air, and he beat his tail on the hardwood floor.

"Come on, Gus," Gail said again. "Now."

She couldn't figure out what was making him so ornery. Usually he wouldn't leave her side. Finally, the dog raised himself on to all four legs, stretched, and trotted up to her.

"We're going," Gail whispered to him, glaring her dismay.

She had just turned toward the front door when the voice called out after her. "Don't leave before the miracle," it said.

Gail turned, and then swore inwardly. If she had just kept going, it would've been a clean escape. But now here she was. Face-to-face with the redhead who had just said something about miracles and leaving that was clearly intended to try to make her stay.

Gail tried to be polite. "I'm afraid I wouldn't know a miracle if it hit me over my head," she said lightly, taking a backward step toward the door.

"Oh, sure you would," the redhead said, stepping forward.

Gail froze. Surely, this woman would get the hint that she wanted to leave. Gail wondered for a crazy moment whether anyone had ever been kidnapped by AA before, and if there was something sinister about the whole thing. Would she be taken, abducted, and then returned without her brain, wearing only a mirror-studded sweatshirt?

Gail jumped when the redhead put a hand on her arm. "A miracle," she said, "you'll know right away. You can feel it. It's when something happens that you never believed could have. It's when you find out you knew something you couldn't have known, or you're suddenly relieved of a great burden, or when something you've always wished for suddenly happens in a way you never imagined."

Gail shifted uncomfortably under the redhead's intense gaze. *Really*, she thought, *as if with Peter Banks around I need lectures about what miracles look like.* She tried to sound lighthearted. "Really. Sounds wonderful."

"It is," the woman agreed, apparently missing Gail's dismissive tone. "It will feel like a reminder that you know more than you think you do. That you really are connected to the fabric here, that the world really does make sense, to someone, somewhere, and every once in a while you're allowed to see just a little bit of that sense."

The woman has a screw loose, Gail thought. Maybe that's what giving up drinking does to you. Makes you rant and rave like a Bible-pounding lunatic. Externally, Gail smiled brightly. "Well, it sounds like you've seen a lot of miracles," she said evenly, taking another step toward the door, pulling her arm away until the redhead's hand dropped.

The other woman smiled, almost sadly. "I see them every day, honey," she said to Gail. "But it's the ones that come so close and yet don't happen, *those* are the ones that break my heart."

"I can imagine," Gail muttered, taking another step toward the door, praying that no one would come in and block her way.

"I hope you come back, honey." Gail felt the doorknob under her hand—one quick turn and she'd be out.

"Oh, I will," Gail said, crossing her fingers on the knob, an old childhood habit. Gus moaned in a way she hadn't heard before. "I think he has to go out," she called out to the woman.

Whatever the woman replied, Gail didn't hear. The sunlight

caught her full in the face, and Gus, his tail between his legs and his head down, followed her.

"Hurry up,'" she told him, crossing the street quickly. "We've got stories to write."

While Gail Abernathy returned to the *Sentinel*, trailing the liver-colored pointer behind her, Father Gilbert Chavez was preparing for what he was considering the most trying hour of his life: the interview with Peter Banks.

Chavez knew that Sybrandy and Hamilton were on the warpath. Shock's broadcast from the cornfield, the mere suggestion that another resurrection was in the wings, had the Vatican screaming from across the ocean.

"This is over," Hamilton had informed Chavez when he walked into the bishop's office that morning. "This is over today. Do you understand?"

Chavez could only nod.

Maybe it was all for the best. Maybe the world just wasn't ready for it. He had spent a sleepless night after picking up the broken pieces of the rectory's television set. How he would explain it? It seemed to him what had started out as a magnanimous offering from above was being twisted and perverted by everything that touched it. Maybe modern-day society made it impossible to witness the glory of God. They may have burned Joan of Arc at the stake back in 1431, but certainly, they were doing as bad, if not worse, things today.

If Hamilton had decided to ignore the miracles that were going to happen here, the ones that Chavez was convinced were for real, then maybe it was for the best. If the Vatican ignored them, maybe the media would ignore them. Then the miracles could happen, unimpeded by camera and Ricardo.

This hope is what kept Gilbert Chavez from telling Henry Hamilton what he really thought of him and his long nails, or from grabbing Bishop Sybrandy by his own vestments and shouting into his face. This, Chavez thought as the three men approached the Clay Hotel, must have been what it was like for Christ to carry his cross up that long and bloody hill.

"Help me, Father," Chavez prayed silently.

The men traveled without speaking, their long black robes beating in unison on their calves, each man with his hands linked behind his back, his head bowed. The doorman at the Clay Hotel opened the heavy brass and glass door, wondering if someone inside were dying, and if this was the entourage come to perform the last rites. Chavez bit his mustache when he saw the expression on the man's face—fear mixed with dread—and wondered bitterly for how many years the common man had viewed a group of clergy with such emotion, and if it would ever change?

Vivienne had called Chavez that morning to let them know where the interview would take place, but she'd done so under duress. It had been Edward's idea. He called it "wonderful material" for the book. Despite more than a fair warning, she was shocked to hear the rather severe knock Hamilton delivered on the hotel room door, which she opened tentatively.

The gust of smoke that escaped nearly bowled Sybrandy over. Hamilton, standing slightly to the left and behind Sybrandy, pushed past the bishop and strode into the room, ignoring Vivienne's attempt at a handshake. "How good of you to come," she managed, after they had arranged themselves around the coffee table. Sybrandy started to exchange pleasantries, but Hamilton stopped him with an abrupt wave.

"Where's the boy?" Hamilton asked, the edge on the inquiry obvious. Chavez bit his lower lip and said nothing. *Think of the cross*, he berated himself. *It is heavy, ¿no?*

Peter was glad he had hid in the bedroom when he'd heard Hamilton's sharp knock. Peering out at the odd scene—the three men in black robes, the tall one with long fingernails, the fat one who was still breathing heavily, the dark-skinned one biting his lip—he wondered what would happen if he refused to come out to answer their questions.

"Peter!" he could hear Vivienne call. "Peter!"

Debating his position, Peter was surprised to see his father emerge from the bedroom on the other side of the suite. Vivienne turned, just as startled as Peter, a hand flying to her hair (she had braided it now, with the ends carefully coiled around her ears, making her look something like a heavy-coated mountain ram). "Oh Edward! You startled me. Is Peter in with you? These are the men from the Church who want to talk to him."

Edward Banks grunted at the clergymen and took a seat opposite them. "I'll just be taking notes here," he told them importantly.

Vivienne colored with embarrassment. "Edward's writing a book for Norway and Simmons—" she began, as if to excuse her husband's statement. But Edward stopped her.

"It's none of their business, Vivienne. Don't you understand the book industry? This is top secret. We certainly don't need the church in on this!"

Chavez tried to keep his mustache from twitching. Not that the cross he bore felt any lighter, but the look on Hamilton's face, the tic in his eye, made it clear that the announcement that a major publisher intended to spread the story the Vatican wanted so much to staunch was not going over well.

Turning from his investigation of his superior's face, Chavez saw Peter standing in front of the door behind which he'd been hiding. Peter was smiling. "Hello," the boy said simply. "I'm Peter."

If Chavez had been watching, he would've seen Hamilton's lip twitch slightly, and Sybrandy break out in a sweat. The boy, so small and plain, so unassuming, filled Chavez with hope. *There are miracles,* he thought. *With or without the Catholic Church, God forgive me.*

Vivienne fluttered over toward her son. "Come sit down, Peter," she said, as if she was glad of some support in the room full of clergy. "These men want to talk to you." Peter took a seat on the couch next to Hamilton, nodding to Edward across the coffee table.

"Well, you've been a very busy young man," Hamilton started in, lowering his gaze so that it was level with the boy's own. "You've caused quite a stir." Peter nodded. "Talking to God must make someone very popular," Hamilton continued.

"I don't know," Peter answered. "I have never talked to God."

Hamilton's lips narrowed. For a moment, Edward turned pale.

"You told the principal at your school that you talked to God," Hamilton said. "Are you telling me now that you didn't?"

"No sir, I mean, yes, sir, I—" Peter hesitated, confused. "I told the principal that God had left me a message. And that was the truth. God has left me two messages. I prayed to Him and asked a question. Then there was one message, an answer. Then there was another, a kind of, well, announcement. It wasn't a conversation. I didn't *talk* to Him. That's all."

Peter sunk lower into the couch, trying to catch his breath. The explanation always left him somewhat winded. Color had returned to his father's face.

"I see," said Hamilton, hissing. "So God's been leaving you messages." He paused, reaching for a question, something, anything to expose the boy for what he was. Then his face lit up. "Can I see one of these messages?" he asked.

Peter knit his brows together. "See them? Oh, no, they aren't written, sir. I just hear them—you know, up here," Peter pointed to his head, just behind his ear. "I hear the voice, *His* voice."

"So you are hearing voices—" Hamilton started, but Chavez couldn't help himself.

"It's called inner locution, Your Grace," he blurted out. "In Medjugorje, it was the chief means by which the Marian is said to—"

Hamilton's arm darted out within an inch of Chavez's face, the long-nailed index finger held up as a warning. "Father Chavez, no one asked for your opinion in this matter."

Chavez felt his blood begin to boil. Surely they were not going to brand this young child as insane. He could see the necessity of bearing a cross on his own, the lesson to be learned, the strength to be garnered—but to saddle a child, an innocent, with an accusation such as "hears voices?" This was too much.

"As a matter of fact, my opinion, my expert opinion, was requested in this matter, Father Hamilton," Chavez said curtly, "by Bishop Sybrandy here."

Hearing his name caused Sybrandy to sit bolt upright. "Hmmm, well, uh," the plump bishop began.

"Silence!" Hamilton commanded. Both men froze in their seats. Peter felt his back teeth begin to ache from having been clenched together so hard for so long.

"Now, boy, answer me," Hamilton started again, turning back to Peter. "You've been hearing voices, yes?"

"Well, actually, just one voice, sir. *His.*"

"One voice," Hamilton repeated, his voice barely a whisper.

"Yes sir, *His* voice," Peter said.

"His voice," Hamilton repeated, as though hypnotized. For a moment, Chavez thought he was watching a conversion. That the skeptic would suddenly gain faith. But it was a mirage.

"How do you know it's His voice?" Hamilton asked quietly, still holding Peter's eyes with his own.

"He told me," Peter said, "and I just knew. You know when it's Him," the boy went on, staring right back into Hamilton's eyes. "It's a real warm voice, you know, and kind of familiar. And He told me not to be afraid, and I wasn't."

Chavez squeezed his eyes shut in an attempt to block the tears. "And the angel said unto them, 'Be not afraid, for behold, I bring you good news of great joy, which will be to all people.'"

"Silence!" Hamilton exploded. "So the voice in your head told you that he was God," Hamilton said, and watched Peter nod. "And if I told you I was the Devil, would you believe me?"

Peter, glancing quickly at the long fingernails and then back into the sky-blue eyes, just shrugged. "I guess," he said uncertainly.

"I see," said Hamilton. "And if I spoke to you in your head and told you to do things, would you do them?" he asked.

Peter squirmed in his seat, and Chavez tried to think of some way to stop this folly.

"I don't think so," Peter said.

"Why not?" Hamilton asked, his voice barely a whisper.

"Because the Devil's not very nice," Peter said simply.

"Ah, and you don't want to be bad, do you, Peter?"

"No sir, I don't."

"But the Devil lies, doesn't he?" asked Hamilton.

Peter shrugged, "I don't know anything about the Devil, sir."

"That's right Peter, you don't," Hamilton continued, winding up now, for this was where it was going to count. "And you don't know that he sometimes can get inside little boys' heads and lie to them. You didn't know he did that, did you?" Hamilton asked.

Peter looked genuinely surprised and Chavez felt his heart sink, his cross becoming heavier and heavier.

"So then, Peter, isn't it good that I came along to tell you—warn you, really—that we can't be sure whether it was God in your head or the Devil?"

Peter made a move as if to speak and Hamilton held up one of his hands to the boy's mouth.

"In fact, since this voice told you to go ahead and well—masturbate—" Hamilton said the word slowly and with distaste. "Then it's pretty certain that it was the Devil after all, and you've been follow-ing the wrong instructions, my son."

Chavez felt the weight of the world slowly release onto his own shoulders, and couldn't bring himself to look at the boy. If he had, he would've felt better.

Peter was standing now, standing in front of the couch where Ham-ilton sat, blocking his father's view of the priest and causing Edward to lean severely to his right to follow the action. Peter reached out and carefully took the long-nailed hand that had been held up in front of his face and pulled it down just a few inches so that he could see Hamilton unobstructed. And then he spoke.

"That wasn't the Devil in my head, mister," he said, forgetting his mother's instructions to call all these men dressed in black pajamas 'sir.' "You don't have to worry about that at all."

Chavez, his bent head now upright, stared first at Peter, whose face was as clear and untroubled as a child at recess, and then at Hamil-ton, who looked stunned, then, as the moments of silence passed, increasingly angry.

Abruptly, Hamilton stood up. "Bishop Sybrandy," he announced, looking down on the fat man struggling to get off the low couch, "our business here is done." Chavez got to his feet, aware and glad he was being ignored.

"Mrs. Banks," Hamilton barked at Vivienne, who looked very con-fused over by the bar at the far end of the suite, "thank you for your time. We will write up our report in the next day or so and release it to the public." He took a step toward the door.

"Just a minute here," Edward boomed, standing, throwing his note-book down on the chair. "What about the miracles? What has your investigation—if you want to call it that—revealed?"

Hamilton didn't like the man's tone, nor his expression. He leaned in towards the boy's father. "There are no miracles here. I would sug-gest you get your boy some medical attention."

"Medical attention," Edward spat out the words. "This is my son you're talking about!"

"His story is a fantasy," Sybrandy tried to explain from slightly behind Father Hamilton. "He's hearing things," he said, but then Hamilton cut him off.

"We're done here, Bishop," he said curtly, and with that, Hamilton walked past Peter and opened the suite's door himself, showing Sybrandy out and then following him into the hallway.

Vivienne gripped the side of the bar for balance. Here it was, her worse nightmare.

Edward flipped the departing men his middle finger, then returned to the bedroom and his typewriter without a word to wife or his son. Hamilton had left the door to the suite open, a clear indication that Chavez was expected to follow. But he hesitated.

Leaning forward, he held his hands out to Peter.

The boy needed no coaxing, and put his small hands in Chavez's palms. "My son, how do you know you hear God's voice?"

Peter was silent, then smiled. "Because of how I feel," Peter said, thinking of the calm the voice gave him.

"Like masturbation?" Chavez continued, wincing at the question, not wanting to hear the answer.

Peter laughed. "No, no," he said, "like how his voice sounds, and, well, little hints I get."

"Hints?" Chavez asked. "Can you tell me about them?"

Peter shook his head. "I'm only supposed to announce the Witnesses," he said. He scratched his jaw for a moment, he'd just had a thought—not a thought, really, but a whisper. The boy nodded to himself. "But you can watch TV with me if you need to," Peter said finally, his voice soft.

It took Chavez a moment to understand just what the offer meant. Somehow, Peter knew about the small TV that still lay broken in the middle of Chavez's sitting room.

Vivienne never heard her son's conversation with the priest. Irritated by her husband's quick exit, she had followed him back to their bedroom as soon as Hamilton and Sybrandy left. She wanted to ask him how they could stop these Catholics from going public with their pronouncements. Edward merely waved a hand at her, interrupting his typing only for a few seconds, "We're not stopping anything," he told her over his shoulder. When she returned to the living room, she stopped dead in the doorway, staring at the scene in front of her.

Chavez was on his knees, his arms around Peter, sobbing.

CHAPTER EIGHTEEN

Truman Newhouse, editor of the *Herald*, did a jig in the middle of his office when he received word the Catholic Church had issued its proclamation that Peter Banks had been reviewed by the clergy and was found to be a "mentally ill little boy" who needed treatment. "The Church," the release went on to say, "is not expecting any miracles to happen tomorrow at four o'clock and is saddened by the state of affairs that has distracted mankind from other true works of God."

It mattered not to Newhouse if the Catholics had decided Peter Banks was all bunk. Either way, their decision made a great story. And their decision to the negative actually made a bigger story than it would have if they had decided the young boy was for real. After all, if Peter Banks were for real, the miracles would be the story, and they weren't due until Thursday afternoon. Being that Newhouse had a paper to put out and it was Wednesday afternoon, the Catholic Church's pronouncement made big news.

"We'll just have a miracle front page," he informed his publisher.

There were a number of stories for the day, all having to do with the Peter Banks prophecy and not one of them that made the boy look good. Kitty Casen, after all, had come to town and broadcast her morning talk show, or at least part of it, from the urinal in Rory Middle School. Her upturned nose nearly folded in half as she spoke, Ms. Casen was out to remind all real Christian folk that this story started, after all, in such a rank and smelly place and concerned—yes, she said the word, "masturbation" at its outset. Newhouse figured he could pair that story with a reaction piece about Shock's latest segment and then use the two as bookends for the Catholic Church announcement. It would take up all of page one, above the fold, but he had no ethical problems with putting yet another Iraqi suicide bomber and the dreadful state of health care in the u.s. down in the left-hand corner of the page, with a two-inch toehold. The president's speech on the economy could go inside. Way inside.

Back at the *Sentinel*, no one had even yet read the faxed statement from the Vatican. Lincoln Fraser was busy with his own problems. One of the *Sentinel's* biggest advertisers, Urban Lighting Fixtures, wanted to, as the owner put it, "Take part in that miracle business" with its Thursday ad.

Specifically, Raymond Carr wanted the *Sentinel* to artfully airbrush a cross into the blades of a ceiling fan it was featuring in its full-page ad in the Style section. "You know, subliminal suggestion," the light magnate explained, pronouncing the word better than any newscaster ever had.

"Subliminal advertising is illegal, Ray," Fraser had said gently. But he knew that he was going to be outvoted by Delp, the *Sentinel's* publisher.

"It isn't subliminal unless we say it's subliminal," the short, somewhat out-of-breath publisher admonished. "I don't see the problem with a slash this way and a slash that way, which just happens to make a cross, do you, Ray?"

"No sir!" smiled the bleached-blond millionaire who had a penchant for starring in his own commercials.

"In fact, I would say that if someone tried to come along and say we couldn't put a cross into your Western Wind Mover, that that person would probably be violating the First Amendment. Right, Fraser?"

Lincoln Fraser bit down hard on his back teeth and hoped Delp would let the question go without a reply. He wasn't so lucky.

"Fraser?"

"Yes, sir," he answered.

"Well good. I'm glad that's all cleared up." Delp was a man who didn't like to spend a long time thinking about anything.

Lincoln Fraser tried to keep his hands at his sides. Last night his wife noticed his scalp had begun to bleed in certain places, and scabs were springing up where hair used to be. She was worried that if he kept it up, he could scar back there.

Gail Abernathy got the fax from the Vatican a good two hours after it had been sent and just an hour and thirty-five minutes before her normal deadline. It wouldn't have been that bad, had she not also been three sheets to the wind following the two glasses of red wine and three scotches she just finished at the pub that sat conveniently at the foot of the elevators in the *Sentinel's* building.

She tried to tell herself, and Gus, who was still at her side, moaning a little, that it had been time well spent. She had managed to tell the Professor a thing or two. A thing or two that she would've never had the guts to say had she not been drinking. For instance, she had told the Professor that she didn't think they should see each other again, that she wasn't getting anything out of the relationship, and that the relationship was endangering her career.

"Now that was a score on my part," she muttered to the dog, holding onto the railing to keep her balance as the elevator headed upward. Gus moaned.

Of course, the Professor had been as dismissive as ever. "You've told me this before, Gail, and yet we've gone on seeing each other. You must get something out of the relationship. No one's fired you yet, so I can't imagine it can be that bad for your career."

"My career is very important to me," Gail had told him, she remembered now, as the doors opened to the newsroom and she made sure to look down, keep her eyes on the dog, so no one would get a clear view of her face.

"Of course it is, dear," the Professor had said, in *that* tone, the one that meant that he knew she thought it was but everyone else in the world knew that it was a joke.

"I went to an AA meeting today," she told him.

"I can tell," he chuckled, and she had felt her cheeks getting red.

"The woman there told me I'd be able to recognize a miracle," Gail continued, afraid that if she stopped, she'd have to acknowledge what he'd said.

"Now that sort of goes along with the theme, don't you think?" the Professor said lightly, signaling the waitress for another round.

It had gone on like that for an hour or so. Maybe more. It astounded Gail just how much time could be spent on a conversation that went nowhere with a man that she had grown to hate in a pub where she had no business being in the first place.

"I'm going back to that AA meeting tomorrow," Gail told the Professor, after her tongue had gotten so thick that she had trouble with the word "tomorrow."

"Yes, I think that's a good thing," the Professor responded, smiling. Then he invited her back to his loft, because of course that's what he always did. But when she looked at her watch she realized that she had less than two hours until deadline and, according to what the log had said that morning, something like four or five stories to write, some of which had no content to them at all.

"I'm completely fucked," she said to him.

"What's new?" the Professor had said, and left.

Gail knew he would go back to the loft and nap—he'd had as much to drink as she had, after all. And then, in a few hours, he would call again. Because he would get lonely, and the weekend was still two days away, and his wife was safely ensconced upstate.

Gail felt the pit in her belly grow as she took her seat in front of her computer. Gus whined one final time as he walked in a circle under the desk before finally lying down, his head on her foot.

That's when she saw the Vatican fax.

"Omigod," Gail said, reading just the first paragraph, and then starting over and reading the whole thing. "Oh my God." And then she lost it. Totally.

Crying in a newsroom is not altogether a rarity. Emotions run almost as high as egos at most major papers. But Gail wasn't known for her timidity, and the sobs, however much she tried to stifle them, drew attention. "Hey, hey, you okay?" Gail almost didn't recognize the voice, soft as it was, which came from Paul Hull. His head was bent around the computer screen that separated his desk from hers. And when he didn't get an answer, he did what a good reporter would do and repeated the question. "Are you okay?"

Gail finally raised her head off her desk and looked back at him. "No," she said through a sniffle. "I'm not. I have six stupid stories to write—none of which I'm prepared for—and now the Vatican has decided that this nice innocent little boy, who *I* exposed to the world, is certifiable, and now I have to write about that, too." She stopped long enough to hiccup. It gave Hull a chance to cut her off.

"Hang on there a minute. I think you've missed a few things around here. Some of those 'Miracle Stories' on the budget have already been written, my dear. And I should know, because I wrote one of them."

Gail sat up a little straighter, unsure of whether to be happy or afraid that somehow someone else had written her stories.

Hull continued. "Fraser figured you were at the Banks boy's hideaway, getting some scoops for tomorrow—" Hull rolled his eyes to indicate just how naïve he considered Fraser's thinking—"so he got one of those do-nothings in 'Living, Loving, and Cooking' to write a review of the Shock interview. Then Kitty Casen did a kind of show from the urinals at Rory Middle School"—Hull stopped long enough to let the look of surprise, then disgust, register on Gail's face—"so Fraser called me in to handle that one."

Gail didn't know whether to smile or cry. *Look how expendable you are,* sang the committee in her head. "So what's left?" she asked, turning toward the computer to summon up the *Sentinel's* budget of stories due the following morning.

Hull continued his omniscient narration. "Well, you can forget the sidebar on the religious in Denver. We don't have the room now that Kitty Casen's staked out the urinals. They spiked that one."

"So I've still got the interview with the bishop, which I haven't done, a schedule for the Witnesses, and a story about how they are holding up?" Gail asked, peering at the screen.

Hull checked his own computer. "Looks that way." He was silent for a moment. "How drunk are you?"

Gail grimaced. "I'm getting straight real fast, Paul. Real fast."

Hull nodded. "No judgments here. I've seen worse. But you've got something like ninety minutes and between the Witnesses, the bishop, and the Vatican, there are fifty to sixty inches of copy due."

"They don't even know about the Vatican yet," Gail told him, nodding toward the copy desk. "They may not have space for it. Maybe one of these other stories will just drop out."

Hull shook his head. "Don't count on it. Old Delp has been walking around here all day whistling. Rumor has it he's agreed to airbrush some sort of religious icons into the pork roast ads in the food section and tomorrow's paper is going to be as profitable as they come. He wants these miracle stories, and he wants 'em bad."

Gail sighed into her computer screen. "How many days do we have to go with this?"

Hull smiled. "Just one, honey. Just one. After tomorrow, all there'll be is cleanup. Remember the millennium?"

Gail groaned. "Can anyone forget?" And with that, she picked up her phone and punched Fraser's intercom button. "Hey, Fraser," she yelled into the receiver, "you're going to need a new layout on the front page—the Vatican has just decided that Peter Banks is a nutcase," and then, because she knew what was coming, Gail Abernathy held the phone a good foot from her ear to let the profanity spill over her. "Thanks, Fraser; I knew you'd say that." And she hung up.

Clearing space on the front page for the Vatican's pronouncement was much easier, of course, than actually writing about it. It wasn't just that Gail Abernathy didn't believe Peter Banks was schizophrenic and hearing voices, as the Vatican's fax suggested. It was that Gail didn't believe the Vatican believed it. And to write it, to write it and put it out there—"report the news," as was her mandate—somehow seemed both patently unfair and, well, wrong. Like she would be perpetuating the lie.

Hull saw her hesitation and tried to coach her through it. "C'mon now, you're not supposed to care about what you report. You're supposed to be impartial. Tell the readers what the Vatican said," he whispered each time there was a lull in her typing.

The problem with doing what Hull suggested is it left out facts. Facts like Peter's actual mental health, facts like what agenda the Church had for making such a finding, facts like the context in which all of this was happening. This is what she kept saying to Hull every time she picked up the phone and dialed yet another number, seeking another viewpoint, looking for more information, information that she didn't have time to get, even if she knew where to find it.

"I'm looking for background, Paul, to make it understandable," she kept saying.

"My ass," he would throw back, good-naturedly.

As it turned out, the other stories were eventually forced to meld into one, or one with two sidebars, because the Witnesses were called for their reactions to the Vatican's pronouncement, as well as to get a handle on how they were holding up. Surprisingly, the Vatican's pronouncement had little effect on either of them.

"Oh gee, like I've ever lived my life according to what the Pope had to say," Jake Herron instantly reacted to her news, and then asked her to let him respond again, on the record this time, in some way that would be slightly less offensive to some of Miranda Davis' constituents.

In terms of how he was holding up, Herron told Abernathy that he was just glad it would all be over by four the next day. "I have a life I need to get back to, I really do," he said, repeating it as if to convince himself. "I'll be glad—no offense, Gail—when I don't have to talk to you every day." He was actually smiling when he said it.

Gail had a much shorter conversation with Sherry Anderson. The psychiatric nurse who was so accustomed to dealing with death seemed even more distant than she had in their first conversation. It didn't take long for Gail to figure out why.

"How am I holding up? How should I be holding up? After watching what people like you have put on television—what people like you have decided to dredge up and throw in my face? The very place where Steven committed suicide? I've already talked about this with that other reporter, that horrible Carmen Riddle. She works at your paper. Don't you people talk to each other? What's wrong with you?"

Gail's brain was slow to catch on, still having to slog its way through the oxygen-deprived cells compliments of the scotch. Carmen Riddle? It finally hit her—Riddle was a Lifestyles reporter, the one who must've done the review on Shock's "film noir"—of course she had called Anderson. And of course seeing the Shock piece would've been more heart wrenching for Sherry Anderson than anything else Gail could imagine. No wonder Sherry Anderson wanted this all to be over.

"Sherry, I'm sorry. I'm so sorry," Gail tried to respond, but Anderson was having none of it.

"You are not, none of you are. You're writing a story, right? Nothing's going to stop that. Not how I feel, not how anyone feels. You're going to write your story no matter what it does to anybody."

Gail sighed. The woman was right. There was no point in arguing. "Sherry, the Vatican announced today that they've decided Peter is a fraud, that he's mentally ill, and that he's hearing voices. They don't think there will be any miracles tomorrow," Gail talked as fast as she could, hoping she could get it all in, get a reaction from Anderson before the woman hung up on her. "What do you think?"

For a while, there was a gaping silence, as if Sherry Anderson had stopped breathing (which she had). Gail held her breath too, hoping Anderson would say something, anything—no not *anything*. Something supportive of Peter so he wouldn't be hanging out there in the wind all by himself, a twelve-year-old boy, alone, against the Catholic Church and every fucking media outlet in town. Gail heard what sounded like a sob. A short, high-pitched exhale of breath immediately followed by a sharp intake. "Sherry?"

Sherry Anderson wanted more than anything to tell Gail Abernathy to shove the entire miracle story up her ass and take the whole of the media industry with her to hell. But something stopped her. Perhaps it was her psychiatric training, the years of working in the professional field of mental health and its automatic aversion to the "labeling" by anyone, especially the untrained, of a young boy. Perhaps it was her professional integrity that was insulted by the Vatican's off-the-cuff assessment that Peter Banks was a schizophrenic.

Or it could've had something to do with Sherry Anderson's maternal instinct. She'd raised a son up to twenty years, and she had experienced the protective nature, the mother-bear instinct that can cause women to double and even triple their strength in order to rip would-be attackers limb from limb. It could've been that.

Or it may have had something to do with the way that just watching Peter Banks on the television—that first coast-to-coast interview in which Peter had explained how loving he thought God was, how God would want people to get along, how Peter's eyes had shone and his skin glowed, how Peter looked so, so, serene. Perhaps that's what had an influence on Sherry Anderson. Whatever the reason, and maybe it was a combination of all three, Sherry Anderson's rage at the media industry was interrupted, paused, as if between waves of indignation. A new feeling crept in. "They've decided Peter is a fraud," Gail had said. It hit Sherry in the stomach like a brick. It took a few moments to get herself into some state in which she could speak. But when she did, Sherry was certain of her words, and they came out as if blown from a cannon.

"Fuck the Vatican," Doris Day said, and she hung up.

With ten minutes to go until deadline, Gail Abernathy did something she'd sworn she'd never do—call her ex-husband for a favor. "Hi, it's me," she said shyly, instantly wishing she had used her name and not assumed he would know who she was.

His answer was silence, indicating that he recognized her voice.

"I'm really running late at work and I wondered if you could pick up Dillon from day care, just for an hour or two, and then I'll pick him up from your...place." She'd almost said *home*. Keep it together, she prayed.

"Have a hot date or something?" he asked. "Too drunk to pick up your own son?" he sneered. "When are you going to get your priorities straight?" he demanded. Actually, he said none of these things, Dillon's father. After a long sigh, into which Gail read all of these horrors and more, he merely agreed and said he would expect her by nine. Then he hung up. When Gail replaced the receiver, she was surprised to see her hands were shaking.

"Booze or fear?" Hull asked from behind his computer, as if he didn't have the balls to show his face with such a question.

"It's the same thing, isn't it?" Gail answered. Then she looked back into the screen of her own computer.

It was going to be a bloodbath. She had everything she technically needed for the story. The bishop had refused to comment, other than to refer to the statement he'd already faxed on Vatican letterhead, so she had his response. Both Witnesses had weighed in. Vivienne wasn't answering her phone, and Gail had managed to get the meanderings of a professor of theology from the University of Colorado, who'd indicated that the Church had always been loath to endorse or condone claims of miracles in modern days. But no matter how many times she had rewritten the thing, no matter how many times she had cut out the more damaging quotes from the Vatican's fax, pushed them further and further down, pumped up the quotes from the theologian, from the Witnesses, pull them further and further up, there was no fixing it.

Peter Banks was doomed. She put her head in her hands.

"Abernathy! Where the hell is your piece!" Fraser's voice rattled the computers, most of them now empty, halfway across the room.

"Not done yet," she yelled back.

Hull gave her a cross look. "It looks done to me, baby," he said in a hoarse whisper. "Just because you don't like what it says doesn't mean it isn't done."

Gail stuck out her tongue, then smiled weakly. "Look, you've been great. But you just haven't been there, Paul. This kid, this kid is anything but crazy. He could be full of shit, I'll grant you that, but he isn't crazy. And to say he is, it's just...I don't know. Someone must know what's really going on. Someone must. I just haven't been able to find them. And I haven't been able to find them because I've been drinking myself under the table with—" She'd almost done it. She'd almost said she was with the Professor. That would've been death. "With a damn dog," she finished, and then quickly stuck her hand under her desk to pat Gus on the head in apology.

Paul Hull shook his head. "Don't be stupid," he said, looking like he was losing his patience. "It has nothing to do with what you were doing this afternoon and everything to do with the fact that you are anything but objective about this story. No one else would even be looking for another angle on this. They'd just write it. Now stop fucking around and—"

Lincoln Fraser's bellow interrupted him.

"Abernathy, what the hell is holding you up?"

Gail held her breath, praying for something, anything to happen, and then, hoping to hold her editor off, yelled back,

"I'm trying to figure out how to paraphrase, 'Fuck the Vatican.'"

Then her phone rang.

Chavez would never call himself the answer to anyone's prayers. And the decision he made Wednesday night, after returning to his empty living room and sitting silently in contemplation of the pieces of his television, had been a hard one. The Church, the one with the capital "C," had been his life. His congregation, his cathedral, his "beat," as he liked to call it, had been hard won in a life struggle of prayer and church politics. To throw it away now, as he was sure he was doing, was a sacrifice he had never even considered making. That is, until Peter Banks had tendered his innocent invitation to share his hotel television.

Until that moment, Father Gilbert Chavez, a known expert on the history of miracles in the Catholic Church, a strong and compassionate religious leader in a community of faithful and overwhelmingly Latino Denverites, hadn't realized the difference between a comfortable faith and a fervent belief. In the past, the path had been one of traditional sacrifice in order to gain traditional benefits. Now Chavez, as he rubbed his mustache and felt the ache in his chest, faced the fear of singular sacrifice, of personal risk, for no other benefit but the truth, the fact that a messenger of God, a true messenger of God, needed his help to be heard.

When he picked up the phone to call the reporter at the *Sentinel*, Gilbert felt a rush of joy flow through him that he would have trouble describing for the rest of his life.

And that is why it almost sounded as if he were laughing when he told Gail Abernathy that he was one of the three-member tribunal who had considered the case of Peter Banks.

"I, for one, think he's for real," Chavez said.

CHAPTER NINETEEN

The dissenting opinion, the split in the Church, and the fact that Peter Banks was either God's messenger or completely insane was the lead story in the *Sentinel* on "Miracle Day."

The *Herald*—which hadn't had the call from Chavez, and which would've missed it anyway since their reporter, being completely sober and in control of his life, had finished his piece by five that night and left work early—went with the official Vatican statement faxed from Sybrandy's office that deemed Peter Banks in need of immediate psychiatric treatment. Truman Newhouse had paired that story with Kitty Casen's visit to the Rory urinals and ran both across the top of the *Herald's* front page. Thursday morning Newhouse was snorting with laughter right up until the time he unfolded the *Sentinel* and read its headline: "Banks prophecy prompts split in Church," at which point he choked on his toast and began to frantically page Randy Young, his lead editor, cursing as he dialed.

Bishop John Sybrandy had had a similar—if more excruciating—experience. He had seen the *Herald* first, buying it on the way to his office, feeling the smoothness of its newsprint, the coolness of its sheets. "Now we can get back to normalcy," he thought, hoping against hope that Henry Hamilton would soon take himself and his long nails back to New York where they belonged and leave him in peace.

The first order of business, Sybrandy thought as he read the headline in the *Herald* that trounced Peter Banks as a mentally disturbed child, was to hire a new cleaning lady, something he hadn't gotten around to with the likes of Hamilton and Peter Banks taking up so much of his time. But his delightful morning was to end abruptly as he entered his office—what used to be a sanctuary in the very meaning of the word, he would think to himself later—and found Hamilton inside, scowling in a dreadful manner.

"Good morning, Bishop," Hamilton said in a tone that implied anything but.

"Good morning." What was vexing Hamilton now, Sybrandy wondered crossly. Surely they were done with Peter Banks. All that had to transpire was to wait until four o'clock and soon the name Peter Banks would be nothing but an unpleasant memory. Sybrandy walked slowly across the office, trying to ignore the sound of stray rosary beads as they cracked under his shoe. He would wait until Hamilton revealed the source of his ill humor. It didn't take long.

"We should be hearing from Rome soon," Hamilton said, working his long fingers into parallel planes and then collapsing them again into fists. He stared straight ahead as he said the words, not looking at Sybrandy.

The Denver bishop tried to sound less confused than he was. "Rome?"

Hamilton still didn't turn to look at him. "Both Rome and New York, I would think. I've taken the liberty of asking your secretary to fax the article to Borden; I thought he should see for himself. We will have to decide quickly our response to Chavez."

Sybrandy rubbed his eyes in frustration. The man was making no sense at all. The article was beautiful; he had read it himself. What in heaven's name did all this have to do with Rome and New York responding to Chavez? "Father Chavez?" Sybrandy muttered.

Hamilton exploded. "Do you know nothing? Could it be you are that stupid? The only miracle here in Denver is that the Church has managed to exist at all under your tutelage, Bishop Sybrandy, and that, if I have anything to say about it, is at its end!"

Sybrandy felt his stomach turn at the onslaught, his face go red. In a defensive reflex, he brought his hands together to his chest and realized he was still holding the *Herald*. Triumphant, he held it out for the other man to see.

"You're faxing this to New York? You're calling me stupid because of this? What in our holy God's name are you talking about?" Sybrandy's voice rose as he gained confidence. But instead of seeing Hamilton's face collapse into a look of contrition, which was what Sybrandy was fully expecting, the scowl only deepened. And the tall thin man started shaking his head.

"No, *Father*,' Hamilton said, enunciating Sybrandy's title. "It's this article I faxed to New York." Here he held up the front page of the

Sentinel, its seventy-eight point headline clearly visible across the room.

Jake Herron woke up Thursday morning and knew he needed some help. It wasn't just that the vein in his forehead seemed to be on overdrive the minute he opened his eyes or the fact that he hadn't been intimate with a woman in about eight months now. It was that he felt completely unprepared for the day that lay ahead.

As he shaved, he wondered how he'd gotten to this point.

He used to be the answer man.

He, Jake Herron, used to feel confident as he got ready for work. He knew how to answer almost anything. That's what he got paid for. Miranda Davis would be faced with a policy decision, one day on a child welfare issue, the next on a tricky foreign trade debate, and he would be able to dissect the various agendas, the pros and cons, and tell her which way to come down on the issue or whether to hold off on making a decision until a later date.

He could do it without breaking a sweat, sitting back in his office chair, usually chewing on a pencil or fiddling with the computer. He liked doing it. It defined him, this role.

And now he couldn't even bring himself to choose a shirt.

He was finally dressed and halfway to the car when he saw the papers. And it wasn't until Jake read through the entire *Sentinel* article that he finally figured out whom he'd call.

Not just because Chavez was the sole dissenter who had come forward in the *Sentinel* article. In fact, that wasn't the reason at all. It was just that the *Sentinel* article reminded Herron of the intense Hispanic priest who'd lingered behind while the others had left his office in a huff, who had asked him with such earnestness what a miracle would be in Jake Herron's eyes. The same question Leslie had asked yesterday. The question Herron still couldn't answer.

He needed help, all right. Jake started dialing Our Lady of Guadalupe Church before he was halfway out of the driveway. Thank God for cell phones.

Lisa Marretti didn't need any answers Thursday morning. As she moved around the small motel room—diapering Alex, repacking their things into the duffle bag—she had more information than she'd ever wanted. What she needed and what she prayed for as she bunched, rather than folded, clothes together was courage. The courage to do what she knew she had to do today.

The stories in the morning papers didn't bother Marretti, because she hadn't read them. She did hear about what the television news called the "Vatican Split" from the *Today Show*, but the conflict barely penetrated her whirl of thoughts. At first she envisioned some sort of architectural problem in Rome, some large crack in a marble building—that's what it sounded like, anyway—but then they mentioned Peter Banks' name, and suddenly the announcer had her full attention.

Still, it hadn't fazed her. "So, some people think he's nuts," she said to Alex. She was used to talking to the baby as if he were an adult. All the magazines said it was a good idea to communicate with an infant that way. It was supposed to help them develop their speech skills sooner. Lord knows she needed someone to talk to.

I should've told Ed, she kept telling herself. He would've understood. But she had never really been clear enough about what happened back then. An old boyfriend, just there, then gone. It was so long ago, she should've just let go of it. What would she say to Ed, anyway? Lisa Marretti felt a surge of anxiety pulse through her. What would she say to the Witness?

"You always run that risk. Remember that, Alex," she told the baby, as the newscaster continued on to the day's weather. "Any time you stand up and tell someone something they may not be really happy to hear, you run the risk of someone telling you you're crazy."

She paused a moment and rifled through her purse to make sure she still had the Ziploc bag she had carefully stuffed inside. "Your mother may be called crazy before this day is out, Alex." Her voice was shaking by the end of the sentence, so she sat down on the bed and reached for the baby on the floor. Clutching him to her, she put her chin over his soft, warm head and closed her eyes.

Gail couldn't believe it when she got to the parking garage on Miracle Day and found her parking space—the one she paid seventy-five bucks a month for—filled by an ungodly lime green Hummer.

"You've got to be fucking kidding me," she said to Gus, who wagged in reply. "This is my space!"

For about ten minutes she drove around in squealing circles in the garage trying to find a spot and coming up empty. Parking had always been a mess in downtown Denver, which was the reason Gail had finally broken down and bought a monthly space in the garage. Her effort, she thought darkly, hadn't changed a thing.

Irritated, she left the garage and turned left, the only way she could on Lincoln Avenue, and finally found a space at a two-hour meter next to one of the new downtown bars, Cielo's. "Just great," she snapped to no one in particular as she dug the last three quarters she had from her purse. "Five blocks from work and I'm going to get a ticket anyway." Again, Gus looked nothing but cheerful.

By the time Gail made it to work on Miracle Day, trailing Gus behind her, the editorial meeting had already taken place and the assignments had been posted. Paul Hull was to cover Sherry Anderson at Clark Hospital; Carmen Riddle—the Lifestyles reporter—was taking Jake Herron at Miranda Davis' office. Gail was to be "cleanup," installed at her desk at the *Sentinel* to write the story that the others would call in.

"You've got to be kidding," Gail stared at the morning log with amazement.

"Why would I be kidding?" Fraser humored her, still in a good mood from the slam-dunk of the morning's lead story. "It's your story. You're writing it. Nobody's taking anything away from you."

"It would be nice to witness a miracle, Fraser," Gail said to him, turning to look him in the eye.

The man laughed in her face. "Yeah, well, it will all be on camera. It's not like you're going to miss anything, honey," he said.

"And Carmen Riddle? Is there anyone more uninspired for this?"

Fraser gave her a glance that indicated he would just let that one pass. Gail went on to fresh ground. "What about Peter Banks? Aren't we covering him?"

"Holed up in some hotel room somewhere? What are we supposed to be covering? You'll get his reaction after whatever does or doesn't happen. It's not like he's going anywhere."

"But Peter Banks is the key to this whole story!"

Fraser smirked. "Gail, I think you're getting a little carried away now. Sure, we got that one priest saying the kid's for real. It was a great steal on a story. You were all over it. Good for you. Now don't take it too seriously. Jesus. Get a grip."

Gail looked a little past her managing editor, feeling uncomfortable under his gaze.

"So, I guess that means you're not expecting any miracles in a couple hours," she said softly, hoping the smile on her face would take away the earnestness in her voice.

Fraser snorted. "The only miracle here, honey, would be if your hands stopped shaking long enough to write this story." And then he was gone, the scabs on the back of his head dwindling, smaller and smaller, as he moved to the far end of the newsroom.

Gail stood for a moment, trying to absorb the blow. Cautiously, she checked her peripheral vision to figure out who had heard that last comment. Possibly Sydney Fielding, the intern, who was sitting at a computer just a yard away, filling in a graphic. And maybe the newest city desk editor. Gail felt the color creep into her face. "Oh God," she thought, wondering if she were going to lose it then and there.

But something wet and cold was nudging at her hand, interrupting her panic. "Gus," Gail breathed slowly. In a daze, she followed him back to her desk, sitting down slowly, and then watching him make three circles in the "leg-space" area to finally collapse at her feet.

Gilbert Chavez almost didn't get Jake Herron's desperate phone call. There were so many people trying to call him that morning, his secretary could barely keep up. She did seem to be enjoying it all. "It's Ricardo Shock," she breathed to him, wide-eyed, around seven-fifteen in the morning.

Minerva Mendez usually didn't start her duty at the church until ten a.m. But Chavez, having seen the article at 5:45 when the papers were first delivered, called her at six and asked her to come in early. He hadn't slept at all after his conversation with Gail Abernathy, but remained in his living room, staring at his broken television and praying to God he'd done the right thing. He thought he might feel better when he saw the paper. But the headline, the one that screamed at him from the damp lawn in front of his bungalow, only made him that much more nervous.

"What do you want me to tell him?" Minerva asked.

Chavez placed his hand over the receiver in exasperation. "What you've told everyone—I'm occupied for the moment and will call back as soon as possible."

Her carefully made-up brows shot skyward. "But Father, this is Ricardo," she cooed, then stopped, stricken by the look on his face.

"Father Chavez is out at the moment," she said into the receiver, her mouth pulled into a pout. "Can I take a number where he can call you back?" Chavez sighed and massaged his temples. Would it never end? As if in answer, the phone rang shrilly again. "Our Lady of Guadalupe," Minerva said brightly. "No, Mr. Herron, the Father is out right now. May I take a number where he can call you back?"

Chavez bolted up out of his reverie. "Wait," he said. "Jake Herron?"

Minerva looked perturbed. "You don't want to talk to Ricardo Shock but you do want to talk to Jake Herron?"

Chavez bit his tongue and reminded himself of the pain of unchristian thoughts. "Yes, Minerva, I do want to talk to Jake Herron. Please transfer the call to my office."

The Village Inn wouldn't have been either man's first choice for a meeting place, but it was situated between Herron's office and Chavez's church, and they served breakfast quickly, so it would have to do. Jake Herron had a glass of ice water pressed against his forehead when Chavez sat down in the seat across from him. Hurriedly, the political aide put his glass down and stood up to greet the priest. "Father, it was good of you to come."

Chavez waved him down. "Please, sit down. You don't look well."

Jake stared at the man before him and then burst out laughing. "I don't look well? Father, I hate to say this, but you look like hell."

For a moment, Chavez was silent and Jake felt like kicking himself. And then the dark mustache lifted and the priest began to chuckle—first softly, then within seconds his whole body was involved: shoulders pumping, feet stamping. When they were done laughing and Father Chavez was busy wiping his eyes on his napkin while Jake Herron poured coffee for his guest, the table became awkwardly silent as each struggled with his thoughts.

Finally, Jake spoke. "I really need your help with something. I mean, I don't know if you'll be able to help me, but I hope you can. I hope someone can, because I just don't think I'm up for it."

Chavez took a grateful gulp of coffee and considered for a moment. "Up for what?"

Herron smiled. "A miracle," he said, wincing slightly at the word. "I mean, you kept asking me what a miracle would be to me, and then this woman asked the same thing. I thought it would be an easy question to answer, but it's not. It's just not."

Chavez felt a sudden release, a bit of tension ebbing away. But he was too taken with Jake's question to wonder at the feeling.

"What makes it hard?" he asked, biting the words "My son" off the end of the sentence before they had the chance to escape his lips. Herron wouldn't appreciate confessional manners at a time like this.

Jake shrugged. "It's the mixture of reality and miracle that makes it hard," he said after a few minutes. "I thought at first it would be easy, you know, like okay, it would be a miracle if all these damn pro-lifers went away," Jake broke off and looked up at Chavez suddenly. "Father, I'm sorry, I don't mean to be disrespect—"

"Stop, Jake, I get it. It's okay. Tell me what you mean. What's wrong with thinking the miracle might be all the pro-lifers going away?"

"I—I don't know exactly. Except that there are too many variables involved, people who may be, well, like Mother Teresa, you know. I don't want to do away with her—I mean, I know she's dead and all. I—God, this isn't making any sense, is it?"

Chavez smiled. "Actually, it's making complete sense. The world is very gray, very complicated. The human animal is not a wholly good or evil sort of enterprise. So winning one political issue doesn't really constitute a miracle for you?"

"Well, winning would be a miracle. But winning by making all the people who disagree with you disappear, now that's sort of fascist, isn't it?"

"Yes, yes it is," Chavez said, thinking more about Henry Hamilton than Mussolini at the moment.

"So what is a miracle?" Jake asked.

Chavez felt himself sag in his seat. All of the exhaustion of the night before came flowing back into him. This is what he had been called for, wasn't it? "Miracles are things, at least traditionally, that inspire people to believe," he told Herron. "We aren't supposed to require them in order to have faith, but they are perks, sort of bonuses, along the way. Call them spiritual experiences, if you like, when you enter into a place where you feel God near you, where it seems for a moment that, yes, believing seems to make sense."

"But what is a miracle?" Jake pressed the point.

Chavez shook his head. "In the Bible, there were a number of miracles: changing substances—water to wine—healing, multiplying foodstuffs, that sort of thing. In those days, when people died of hunger and the most basic of illnesses, feeding people and making them well were miracles."

"And now we have Denny's and HMOs to do that," Jake interjected.

"Arguably," Chavez said, his mustache twitching.

"So what would be a miracle today?" Jake asked.

"What would it take for you to believe in God?" Chavez asked the man across the table, then instantly regretted it. Chavez had seen much sorrow in his time. As a priest, he attended funerals and comforted those who had lost loved ones, and he had seen grief attach itself slowly to some people like a fungus and spread. For others, it whipsawed around and choked the life out of them. In Father Chavez's expert opinion, the man before him, the one who looked for all the world like Jesus, had suddenly succumbed to the acute sort of grief.

"You know, Father, the sun could eclipse and birds begin to talk, and I'd still be so damn lonely it wouldn't matter. I think God picked the wrong guy for this miracle thing."

Chavez reached across the table, took Jake's pale hand in his own brown one, and squeezed it.

"No, my son. He's got the right person. You just watch."

The betting pool on Clark's "holding pattern" had grown so large that it no longer fit into Tanya's coffee tin and had to be moved to a pillowcase—all $1,244.63 in cash. It made Tanya nervous to have it there, locked in the pharmacy cabinet with the narcotics. Too many people had keys to that cabinet, she thought. And she'd be damned if someone went and stole that money before she had a chance to win it. The cash would really add some style to her honeymoon—and that thought alone was enough to make her dig a five out of her pocket and put herself down for a few more slots on the pool chart.

"Colleen, I want 4:03 this afternoon, okay? I'm putting my money in now." But Colleen Morrey, the shift nurse, shook her head at the command. "Sorry. Doris Day has money down on every minute between four and four-fifteen, honey. You'll have to go earlier or later."

Tanya scowled. "Sherry? Since when did Sherry get into this kind of thing?"

Colleen smiled. "Don't ask me. She came over after those priests left yesterday and plunked her cash right down. First come, first served, remember."

"I'll take four-sixteen, then," Tanya told her, stuffing her bill into the case and getting change. "God, I want that money."

"You and the rest of us, honey. You and the rest of us."

Sherry Anderson would've liked to have been down at the nursing station, putting money down on 4:15-4:20, but from the moment she walked in that morning—willing herself not to read the paper with the news she already knew about the Church's decision about Peter Banks—Rachel Baum had cornered her.

"We need to talk in my office, Sherry. Now."

Doris Day tried to smile at the stern face before her, but couldn't muster it. Instead, she followed the slender woman to her office and sat there among the mauve decor, preparing herself for an onslaught of anxiety. She would've made a good boy scout.

"I've already had a call from the *Sentinel*, Sherry," Rachel started in as soon as her door shut. "They're sending a reporter over."

"Gail Abernathy or Carmen Riddle?" Sherry asked.

"Neither," Rachel shot back. "Some guy, Paul Hull. He's coming to 'observe.' In case of a miracle—" At this Rachel rolled her eyes. "I can't see how this is going to do Clark any good in the public's eye."

Sherry shook her head in confusion. "I'm sorry, I don't understand, Rachel. A miracle at Clark wouldn't be good P.R.?"

Baum grimaced. "Look, I know how it sounds, but think it out. This is a medical facility." She said the last two words slowly, separating each syllable. "That means we're scientifically based, academically trained. We are inspected by the Joint Commission on Hospital Accreditation. We are not a spiritual healing sort of place. If a miracle happens here, we're doomed."

Sherry was silent, biting the inside of her lip.

"And if a miracle doesn't happen here, we're also doomed," Rachel added quickly, sitting back in her high-backed chair with a flourish.

"How's that?"

Baum exhaled dramatically, as though having to explain something basic to a first-grader. "God has a place in medicine, just not on the front lines. If a kid says we're going to have a miracle here and we don't, it'll look like we've been forsaken or something."

Sherry felt her cheeks burn. "Maybe I should just take the day off then," she said, trying to keep the sharpness out of her voice.

Rachel seemed oblivious to the tone. "I thought of that too, but it won't work. It would make it seem like you don't feel comfortable bringing a miracle here, or that we don't feel comfortable having it here, which makes us seem Godless."

"But that's the truth, right?" Sherry couldn't help but say.

Rachel leaned forward in her chair. "The truth and public perception have nothing to do with each other, Sherry," she said. "I just wanted you to know the kind of situation you've put the hospital in. I want you to keep it in mind as the day progresses. Thank you. That's all." With that, Rachel Baum rose, walked to the door.

Sherry Anderson faced Miracle Day with a growing feeling of dread.

CHAPTER TWENTY

When he was grown and had kids of his own, Peter Banks would often wonder what his life would have been like if he'd never asked God's opinion of masturbation. It was the kind of wonder that led in circles, because, being the precise man he would grow into, Peter would also have to wonder whether things would've been substantially different if he hadn't insisted on telling the truth, punching Chris Paulo in the nose, or doing any one of a number of things that ultimately led him to Miracle Day at the Clay Hotel.

This sort of musing would leave a middle-aged Peter Banks feeling exhausted. But then one of his daughters would bound into the house begging for a snack, a toy, a favorite game, and he'd remember that changing anything would mean changing everything. And *that*, he'd be unwilling to do.

Miracle Day had started slowly for Peter. It had been too long since he'd been visited by anyone in the outside world. His mother was increasingly distant, his father increasingly loud. The morning newspapers had come—both of them, as is the practice of the Clay Hotel—and Peter had watched Vivienne weep over the Vatican assembly's pronouncement that her son was a mental case. It hadn't disturbed Peter in the slightest. He still had the tape in his head, the calm voice, the gentle reverberation. It was merely a matter of playing it back, which he did whenever his mother took a particularly sharp intake of breath.

Edward Banks had bellowed over each of the headlines, snorted at the contents of the articles, and then snatched the papers—before his wife had a chance to finish the *Sentinel's* piece about the dissenting priest—to take into the bedroom where he was writing his book.

"This is perfect, more than perfect," the elder Banks chortled. "A split in the Church only adds depth to the plot!"

Peter looked sadly at his mother and saw the pain on her face, the confusion in the fine lines around her eyes.

He hadn't received any other messages from God. Not the kind where he could hear a voice or play the tape back or experience the calm and the warmth that the first two allowed. Yet Peter had started *to know* things. Little things that didn't seem very important on their surfaces. Like the priest's television being broken, or the surety that one more stressful event and his mother would require some serious psychiatric treatment. Peter shut his eyes and tried to focus. No, the fact that his mother was so close to the edge anyone could see. It was patently obvious. What Peter knew, in his precise way, was that the single stressor was coming, and wasn't far off.

"Maybe you should lie down, Mom," he said in a voice he hoped was somehow as calm and warm as the one he carried in his head.

Vivienne smiled wanly.

"Yes, Peter, I think that might be a good idea," she said. "Maybe your room would be best, since Edward is so busy in ours," she added apologetically. "You can watch TV out here."

Peter nodded and tried not to look too surprised that his mother was *encouraging* him to watch TV.

Lisa Marretti arrived at Clark Hospital just as the wave of television vans flooded the main driveway into the parking lot. It didn't help matters that three ambulances also arrived with the vans, each carrying accident victims from a stretch limo rollover. As the vans continued to block the main driveway, vying for the one parking space that remained near the double doors, the ambulance drivers leaned on their horns and shouted obscenities out their windows.

Clark had always been a busy urban hospital. And since the so-called holding pattern, the four-hundred-bed facility had become even more busy. Beds were full; the emergency room was working overtime to get people on their feet and transferred elsewhere. Tempers were short. At three-thirty on Thursday afternoon, when the melee from the parking lot had become almost unbearable, an exhausted resident dressed in spattered blue scrubs came out to try to explain to the ambulance drivers that they should take their occupants across town, to St. John's.

Lisa had covered Alex's tiny ears with her hands, hoping to forestall a major crying fit. It hadn't worked. Neither had the resident's plea. "St. John's sent 'em here," one ambulance driver said. When the

TV vans finally unblocked the entrance, all three ambulances pulled up in front of the emergency doors and began to unload.

The resident didn't waste any time. "Someone call Rachel Baum and tell her to send me every nurse we've got working in an administrative capacity," he said to an orderly. "Tell her they don't have to do anything special. It'll be IVs and basic wound care from what I see in the ambulances. And don't take any shit from her either."

The orderly, who later would tell a convention of psychic healers that he had seen a strange blue light in the resident's eyes when this direction was given, called Baum right away.

Lisa Marretti had already figured out that the emergency room was the last place she needed to be. Heading in the main front entrance to the hospital, she waited her turn behind the television reporters, who were refusing to take "no comment" for an answer. She sighed and hitched Alex up further on her hip. She hadn't expected it would be hard, once she got this far, to deliver the message she had come to deliver.

"I need to speak with Sherry Anderson," Marretti said when her turn came.

"You and everyone else, honey," the receptionist told her apologetically. "I'll put you on the list, but it's a long one."

Marretti tried to smile and failed. "C'mon Alex," she said softly to her son, and headed toward a long row of plastic-covered chairs—a waiting area that was clearly set up for long waits. There were piles of dog-eared magazines on the end tables and an old cardboard box full of grimy toys in the corner. She set him on the floor, just in front of her chair, and handed him one of the Lincoln logs from the box. It wasn't really age appropriate and it certainly wasn't clean, but Lord, she prayed, let it do for now. She felt his diaper with a sinking heart. It was time for a change.

Jake was all business when he finally got to the office. "Has Miranda called yet?" he asked the interns, without exchanging so much as a "good morning." He was relieved when they took the hint.

"She's on the floor this morning, with some roll call votes. Then committees in the afternoon. She says she wants you to call her. She wants to talk to you about this Peter Banks stuff."

Jake nodded. Of course she did. He already knew what she would say. This Peter Banks stuff was a mess, that's what she would say. She wanted nothing to do with a theological dispute that had the Vatican in disagreement and a young boy's sanity under scrutiny. Politics, she would say, meant choosing your battles carefully. And this battle, she would say, had no winners.

Jake kneaded his forehead with the heel of his hand. There was nothing like listening to an entire conversation in your head first before having to hear it live. Then he picked up the telephone and dialed his boss. "Miranda," he said, when he heard her pick up the phone, "It's Jake."

"It's about time," she said, with more terseness than usual. "I couldn't believe the papers this morning. What a blood bath."

Jake silently cursed the advent of the Internet. "I know," he agreed. "Any suggestions?"

"I take it the media has already arranged to be over there this afternoon?"

"Oh yeah," Jake twirled a pencil absently in the air before him. "I've got all three television stations and both newspapers scheduled to be here this afternoon at four," he told her.

Jake heard the long sigh travel the two thousand miles at lightning speed. "What's your game plan?" she asked him finally.

This was the question he hoped wouldn't come. "I don't know, Miranda. I just don't know."

That opened the floodgates. "This is what happens when you don't pick your battles carefully."

"I didn't pick this battle, Miranda—"Jake tried to stop her.

"This is the last position we want to be in," she continued, undaunted, "between a warring church and a potentially committable young boy. We don't even have any deniability here."

Jakes mind reeled. "Deniability?"

"We don't know enough about everyone's agendas to know who to side with, have an excuse for our involvement."

Jake clenched his teeth. "Miranda, I don't need an excuse for my involvement. It was totally involuntary. I was named. I don't know why. Peter Banks, from what I can see, has no agenda. The Men In Bl—the Church, at least the guys who are calling him crazy—their agenda is clear. They don't like people coming in and saying it's possible to talk directly to God without help from the Church. That's obvious. So if we're going to side with someone, it oughta be Peter Banks."

"You're not going to side with anybody, is that clear, Jake?" It was a statement, not a question. "Involuntariness is the worst position a politician can ever get themselves into. It's another way of saying 'I couldn't help myself,' for Christ's sake!"

"Okay, Miranda, okay. I promise, I won't side with anyone."

"Damn right you won't. Now, buckle down and pretend it's just any other day. And if we're lucky, it will be." She let a few seconds tick by before adding. "Oh, and I need a statement for this afternoon's committee meeting. Federal highway funding. Okay?"

Jake was still trying to figure out how to respond when the phone went dead in his hand.

Sherry Anderson had tried to explain to Rachel Baum that it had been a good twenty years since she had done any sort of real medical nursing, but the other woman had refused to listen.

"Look, they need people in the ER, and they need 'em now," Baum responded, barely looking at her. So Sherry Anderson found herself standing over a clearly befuddled businessman with a gash across his forehead.

"I'm suing that bastard!" the gentleman managed, as Sherry carefully wiped blood from his face and asked the orderly to apply pressure to the wound.

"I see," Sherry replied, trying not to get involved in the discussion. She suspected the man had a concussion and might have been hallucinating.

It took her two tries to get the bleeding stopped, the bandages and gauze neatly wound around his head. "I'm going to give you some antibiotic by I.V.," Sherry told him, ignoring his next outburst, something about raccoons being better drivers.

"I think he's going to need some stitches," Sherry told the orderly after she'd hooked up the I.V. She was surprised how quickly all the basic nursing techniques were coming back to her.

It was easy to forget about the significance of the approaching hour. "You're going to be fine, Mr. Johnson." She patted the man's shoulder calmly. "The resident will be right with you." She felt relief wash over her—but only for a second, because she looked up and saw a young brown-haired woman carrying a struggling, slightly bluish infant in the front of the emergency room.

"Help him, please! He's choking!" the woman pleaded.

Doris Day never hesitated. "Oh my God, get a trach kit!" she yelled, and then jogged toward the woman.

"Help!" the young mother sobbed.

"It's all right, honey," Sherry said as she approached, arms out. "How long has she been like this?"

"He," the woman said automatically, trembling. "Alex—I—he stopped breathing—over there," the woman pointed toward the waiting room. "I—ran—"

"It's okay, it's okay, this happens. It isn't your fault," Sherry gently took the baby in her arms, something the mother allowed her to do with reluctance. *Lord, let's hope this is a swallowed object, and not an electrocution of some sort,* Sherry thought. There were too many outlets around the waiting area in the main lobby. "Where's my trach kit?" she yelled again.

"Right here," the orderly was standing next to her.

"First things first," Sherry said, more to herself than anyone. But the young mother standing next to her nodded as if at attention. "Let's make sure that we can't get it out the easy way." Sherry laid the infant on his back and carefully pried open his mouth. Nothing. Then she gently turned the child over on her arm and sharply hit his upper back with the heel of her hand. Again, nothing.

"What's your name, honey?" she asked the mother as she righted the child after this last procedure.

"Lisa," the woman said to her through her tears. "Lisa Marretti."

"Where are you from, Lisa?" Sherry asked as she prepped the baby's skin with Betadine and a clean surgical cloth from the trach kit.

"Indiana now. Iowa originally."

Sherry smiled sadly. "I know Iowa some. It's pretty there," she lied. "Now, Lisa, my name is Sherry, and I'm going to do a simple procedure called a tracheotomy," she told the mother. "I'm just going to make a little cut right here and put a tube in so Alex can breathe. Then we'll have lots more time to clear his airway and get him breathing normally. Okay? Do you understand?"

"Yes, I—I, go ahead," the mother said, her face ashen.

Sherry Anderson felt her fingers work through memory. Finding the exact spot, making the incision, feeling the rush of air, inserting the tube. By her count, they had maybe ninety seconds left by the time she had restored oxygen to the baby before any brain damage would occur. It was only then that she asked the orderly to get the resident.

"And get him fast," she told him.

Alex was returning to his normal color. And so was his mother.

"Omigod, you're Sherry Anderson," Lisa Marretti had suddenly noticed the name tag on the woman who had just saved her son.

Doris Day smiled at her. "That's me," she said, and then wondered why the mother started crying all over again. "I have something for you," the woman said finally. "I—I was dating Steven when he, when he—" was all she could manage.

Jake Herron had never had a harder time writing a committee statement. Federal highway funding isn't all that complicated. The Feds had money they allocated for interstate highways every year; it was no mystery. The only thing up for grabs was deciding which state got how much of the pie, and how many strings the Feds were going to tie to that pie. Usually the strings were matters of highway safety: speed limits, drunk driving laws, things of that sort. Herron, on a normal day, could write a highway funding committee statement with his eyes closed and his hands tied behind his back.

But today was anything but a normal day. For starters, the interns just wouldn't leave him alone. "Don't you think you should put on some makeup, Jake?" one of them asked.

"I'm really trying to keep the makeup to a minimum these days," he shot back, trying sound upbeat, trying to regain a sense of humor. "You know, only when I wear the black pumps and sequins."

They hadn't thought it was funny. "You're going to be on camera, Jake. You don't want to look like Nixon."

"Give me a break," he had said, pulling at his cowlick. "I don't have anything to hide like Nixon, either."

"At the time of the Kennedy-Nixon debate, even Nixon didn't have anything to hide, Jake," Jennifer said, sniffing like she had caught him in some historical inaccuracy.

"No makeup," he bellowed, more loudly than he had intended.

Later, it was more of the same.

"I think we should clean off your desk," Mattie suggested after lunch, after they thought he had forgotten about the makeup debate. "I don't think it reflects well on the office that it looks like it does."

Jake looked down at the piles of papers, mounds of calendars and committee reports, GAO and CRS studies and census bureau data, old cups of coffee and last week's front pages.

"The desk looks fine, Mattie. Now I have a statement to write."

"We could just put everything in a box, Jake, and after the news crew is gone, we could put everything back where it was. It's not like you have to organize or anything—"

"No, Mattie,"

"I could do it, Jake, you wouldn't have to touch any—"

"No!" Again, his voice was louder than he had intended. Mattie actually jumped at the sound of it.

"Okay, okay."

He hadn't even reached the halfway point in the statement when Jeff Ronald from the *Herald* had shown up.

"Hey, Jake," the reporter called from the office door. The interns hadn't even announced him, apparently still cowering, so his arrival took Jake by surprise.

"Jeff, what time is it?"

"Don't worry, we've got some time yet. I just thought I'd come early and see how it feels to be in the midst of a miracle."

Jake made a face. "It sucks," he said. "And that's off the record."

Ronald smirked. "Of course."

"Hey, do you mind if I finish some work up here real fast?"

Jake was surprised by the look on the reporter's face.

"You're really working today?" Ronald asked.

"What would you have me do?" Jake answered.

Ronald grinned. "I don't know, what did all those other miracle watchers do? I just don't remember reading about those kids in Medjugorje brushing their teeth."

"They probably have a lot of cavities by now?" Jake retorted.

Jeff Ronald settled himself into one of Herron's four office chairs. "You just go on with what you have to do, I'll just sit here basking in your aura." Jake gritted his teeth, wondering if he had brushed them this morning. "Hey, has anyone ever told you you look a little like Jesus, man?"

Jake sighed—federal highways had never been like this.

They just kept coming after that. First Channel 4, then 9, then 7, then some woman named Carmen, from the *Sentinel*.

Jake was e-mailing the statement, perhaps the worst he had ever written, back to Washington, when Leslie showed up, out of breath and wearing a long, crinkly, blue silk skirt and a white knitted top. Jake noted just how far Jeff Ronald's eyes popped out of his head at the sight of her and felt his own heart stop for a moment.

"Hey," he said, then wanted to kick himself.

She smiled, showing all those teeth. "I thought I was going to be late. You've got quite the crowd here."

She wasn't overstating it. The room was filled with reporters and cameras. The floor was snaked with heavy electrical cords and duct tape. Jennifer and Mattie had taken up residence on the edge of Jake's desk, hoping he wouldn't notice their breech of protocol long enough to make them move.

"It's a circus."

Leslie patted his hand tentatively. "It won't be long now."

There was nowhere to offer her a seat. Jake tried to signal Jeff Ronald to offer her his, but the reporter didn't get the hint. He gave up in exasperation.

"That's just the trouble," he said finally, hating the silence between them, in the midst of the din. "Won't be long until what? What are we waiting for?"

There were a million answers he expected her to give. Pat ones like, "A miracle." Or irritating ones like, "Have you decided what the miracle will be yet?" or hollow ones like, "I don't know," but he didn't expect what she actually said, which was, "It doesn't really matter now, does it?" And then she took his hand.

For Jake, it was the most comfortable moment he'd had all day. The feeling of her warm fingers in his, the rush, for a few seconds, of carelessness, as if whatever came *didn't* matter. As if all these people in his office, all these cameras and microphones and cords didn't exist and, even if they did, couldn't harm him. Where it came from, this feeling, he didn't know. But he wished it would last forever.

But, of course, it didn't.

"It's time, Jake. Where are you going to sit?" asked the newscaster from Channel 4 as he flicked on the Klieg.

"I wish I were somewhere else," Jake whispered."

"We can go anywhere you'd like," Leslie whispered back.

"And miss the miracle?" Jake was astonished, wasn't that the whole reason she had come?

Leslie laughed. "The miracle happens to you, Jake. It doesn't have anything to do with all this," she waved her arm at the bustle in the room.

Without waiting for him to answer, she picked up her purse and headed for the door. "C'mon," she said, ignoring the stunned looks from the reporters in the room. "I could really go for some Kung Pao chicken."

Jake didn't hesitate, even for a moment.

Gail didn't know how long she had been asleep when the phone next to her ear jarred her awake. Its long, insistent ring shattered a dream about being trapped in an elevator shaft with the Professor—sliding down a shaft that seemed to have no bottom.

"You know you like it like this," the Professor was saying.

"You're crazy," Gail was trying to say, but nothing came out of her mouth but bubbles.

The phone rang again. Gus nuzzled Gail's hand.

With a start, Gail raised her head from her desk and blinked a few times. A wave of embarrassment rushed over her. Just how many people had seen her passed out cold at her workstation—she wiped at her desktop furiously—and what comments had been exchanged over her head?

She didn't have time to think about it. The phone rang again. "This is Gail," she answered.

"Oh, thank God," the voice was breathy, clearly in a panic.

"Vivienne?"

"Yes, thank God you're there, Gail, I don't know what to do. They could be here any minute."

"Vivienne, slow down, what are you talking about?"

"We've had another death threat, Gail. He called here; he called and said he would put an end to this miracle stuff once and for all. That's what he called it. 'Miracle stuff.'"

Gail grinned in spite of herself. It couldn't be a reporter, she was thinking. A reporter would've said, 'miracle shit.'

"Vivienne, now, calm down. We've been through this before, remember? Nothing happened. It's just a prank."

"No, Gail, this was different. This man, he said, he told me—" Vivienne broke off.

Gail wondered for a brief moment just why Vivienne hadn't turned to her husband for moral support in such a frantic situation. But then she knew. She'd met Edward Banks.

"Vivienne," Gail tried to keep the panic out of her own voice. "Vivienne, tell me, how was this different?"

"He—he knew our room number, Gail," Vivienne breathed. "He said it to me, said he was coming to get us."

"Oh Jesus," Gail couldn't stop the comment. "Vivienne, grab Peter and go down to the lobby. Get out of there now. I'll meet you in the lobby."

"Okay—" Vivienne barely choked out her answer.

"And Vivienne," Gail added, "don't stop for anything. I mean it, I don't care what your hair looks like." But the phone was dead.

Gail replaced the receiver with a shaking hand. "Fraser!" she yelled even before she had turned around. "Fraser!"

But her managing editor was nowhere to be found. Instead, Gail spied an intern working on the calendar in the corner.

"Hey, hey you—" she couldn't remember his name.

"Yeah?" said the youth, looking up, surprised at being called on.

"I need you to tell the managing editor when he gets back that I went to the Clay Hotel. There's been another death threat to Peter Banks, and this one looks like the real thing. He can call me there. I'll be in the lobby."

"Okay," said the intern, turning back to his computer screen.

"Write it down!" Gail heard the screech in her voice but didn't have time to apologize. Calling Gus, she made her way to the elevator bank. The intern watched her go, unaware that he'd have to repeat her message not only to Fraser, but to two other people who would phone, frantically looking for Gail. He didn't see any reason he shouldn't tell them where she was—it's not like the bitch said it was a secret.

The Clay Hotel was only a block-and-a-half from the *Sentinel* building. It made sense to walk, unless, as Gail figured, you were going to need a car to take a boy somewhere safe while the cops kept a look-out for some wacko. "C'mon, Gus," Gail commanded as they entered the parking garage under the building and headed for her car.

Time was of the essence, and Gail was trying to figure out the fastest way from the garage exit to the Clay Hotel's parking. The problem was that the exit emptied out into a one-way street, one that ran in the opposite direction of her destination. To make up for that inconvenience, she'd be forced to make no less than three left turns. She was thinking about the best way to double back when she stopped short at the sight of the lime-green Hummer.

"Fuck!" The word echoed around the concrete walls. She couldn't believe she'd forgotten, after what a pain in the ass it had been that morning. What she really wanted to do was cry. Running was her second choice. Gail decided that running made more sense.

"C'mon Gus," she said, and they both took off, woman and dog, pounding across cement walkways and dashing through traffic on Lincoln. They were only a block from Cielo's when Gail caught the heel of her shoe in a street grate on 12th and hit the pavement face first, her ankle twisting into a position she'd never seen before, the sound of tearing cartilage audible above the traffic.

For a moment the pain was all she could think of. And then the rage took over. "Oh for Christ's sake," she swore loudly. "Why does this happen to me? To me. At a time like this." She could just picture Peter and Vivienne trying to blend in with the ornate wallpaper in the lobby of the Clay Hotel, wondering what had happened to her, why she was taking so long. "Fuck," she swore again. "Miracle Day, huh? Where is God when things like this happen? Where is he when people beat their kids to death? Where is he when a ten-year-old picks up a crack pipe, huh? Jesus, Peter, of all the questions you could've asked him, why did you have to ask him about jacking off, huh?"

She hadn't realized she was shouting all this until she caught the expression of a couple men in suits crossing Lincoln with their brief-cases. The humiliation only made her angrier.

"This is just great, just great. Peter will be dead. I'll be a fucking failure, and a drunk, and an adulterer." She was picking herself up now, testing the ankle to see if she could put any weight on it. "No," was the answer. She stopped for a second. "Are you an adulterer if you aren't married, but the person you're sleeping with is? Does it matter if he can't get it up?" Gail started to hop now, the only thing she could think of to do, heading toward her car and counting the telephone poles that she slowly passed. "One." tShe gave up fighting the tears, it was a losing battle. "What did that woman say, what did she say, Gus, don't leave before the miracle? What happens if you bust up your ankle on the way? Two—" she counted another telephone pole. "What happens if you've just been forsaken? Huh? What does it mean then, Gus?"

Gus, silently walking beside her, had no answer.

"I'll tell you what it means. It means there is no God, that's what it means. He's not there. He isn't. Three. He isn't there. He—" And she stopped. Because there, there on the third telephone pole was a notice. A handmade sign really. The kind of easy flyer people make with their computers. A dog was missing. That was all. It really wasn't anything startling. Except that there was a picture on the sign, and the picture looked a hell of a lot like Gus. In fact, the picture looked exactly like Gus.

But it wasn't the picture that was mesmerizing Gail. It was the words on the sign. So few of them really.

"Dog Missing," it said. "Reward." And then it had a phone number. And under the phone number was one of those scanned in photos, and under the photo, were three words. Three words that made Gail close her eyes for a moment, as if she had read the sign wrong. But no, when she opened them, the sign still said the same thing.

"How—?" Gail was confused. She remembered the voice of the red-haired woman in the mirrored shirt: "It will feel like a reminder that you know more than you think you do. That you really are connected to the fabric here, that the world really does make sense to someone somewhere, and every once in a while you're allowed to see just a little bit of that sense."

Gail steadied herself by placing a hand on the pole. The words under the photo were right at eye level. Seventy-eight point type, she'd have to guess. Carefully she touched them with her fingertips. She knew it wouldn't matter to anyone but her. But for her, it changed everything. Just three words changed everything.

Under the picture the three words said: THIS IS GUS.

CHAPTER TWENTY-ONE

For the first time in his life, Hull was beginning to understand his managing editor's scabby head. The relentless pressure, the sudden crises, the unbelievable mishaps.

At first, Hull had figured luck was on his side. He'd had to sneak into a major metropolitan hospital—flitting past the receptionist and the line of television morons and then jumping into a "Doctors Only" elevator that happened to open at just the right time. He had found out from Carmen Riddle which office belonged to this Anderson woman—but he wasn't halfway down that hallway before he heard the announcement that all administrative-duty nurses were to report to the ER. He managed to get down there just in time to watch Sherry perform a tracheotomy on a choking infant.

This was the stuff dreams were made of. "Here she is supposed to receive a miracle in her life, and she performs one—now that's a story," Hull all but sang to himself, scribbling furiously into his notebook.

Then the day had gone into the crapper.

Because the really big story—the one he was here for in the first place—seemed to have passed him by. Not that it didn't happen, just that he didn't see it. And he was standing right there.

"Well, it's just about time," Hull had said to Sherry Anderson as he glanced at his watch and then up at her blood-spattered scrubs. He noticed she was busy folding a piece of dog-eared paper and putting it back in a Ziploc. When he spoke, she turned and looked at him as if she had never seen him before.

"Paul Hull," he said, "The *Sentinel*."

The nurse's eyes seemed to be shining, something that Hull took for the emotional spillage following the baby's rescue.

"I thought maybe you'd be getting ready," Hull checked his watch, and then tapped it again. "The miracle should be right here, or it's a little late or something."

Sherry Anderson put a hand on the brown-haired woman's arm and smiled at her. Then she looked back at the reporter and shook her head. "I think it's over now," she said to him.

Hull felt his throat tighten. "What? It's over? It happened? What was it? Can you describe it?"

The nurse before him was shaking her head. "I don't know what a miracle is," she said to him softly, "but everything is different now."

Hull fumbled with his notebook, trying to get the sentence down. "What, what is different? Why?"

The silence that followed made Hull look up quickly. And he was surprised to see how stern the nurse's face looked all of a sudden.

"That," Sherry Anderson said to him when his eyes met hers, "is really quite private."

"Private?" the sound of Lincoln Fraser's scream echoed through the newsroom. "What the fuck does she mean—private?"

"Private?" Morty bellowed from the studios in Los Angeles. "Are you sure the baby isn't a reincarnation of her son? Or an undiscovered grandson? Or something?"

"No relation," Shock assured him from his end.

"It's a non-story!" shrieked Kitty Casen from the lawn of the Banks' home. No one had told her they had gone into seclusion since Monday, and Kitty didn't read the papers. "Do you mean that I went into those urinals for nothing?"

"What does Riddle say? Any word from Davis' office?" Fraser bellowed.

"What about the politician guy?" Morty yelled from L.A., "Did you send someone over to what's-her-face's office?"

"Jeff, tell me something happened over there," Truman Newhouse demanded over the phone.

"I wish I could, boss, but at the last minute the Herron guy just left with some blonde from Ohio. Seems they had a hankering for Chinese food."

"They left?"

"Chinese food!" Morty felt his ulcer returning.

"I stood in the boy's locker room for this?" Kitty Casen whined to her producer.

"The story is," proclaimed Newhouse around five o'clock on Miracle Day, "this whole thing was a hoax."

"We can't say it was a hoax," announced Morty at the afternoon meeting, "because we broadcast Peter, and—" he swallowed a little at this, "that goddamn cornfield. So we go with 'mysterious.' Miracles are mysterious. We get Shock up there in front of Clark hospital, and we talk about mysteriousness."

"Michael," Kitty barked into her cell phone, "get me the next flight out of this godforsaken place."

"Where in the fuck is Gail?" Lincoln Fraser screamed, and pulled out three more hairs.

Father Gilbert Chavez took his seat rather gingerly in the Hunan Garden so as not to knock over any of the already full teacups. He smiled broadly for a long moment at the couple across from him, and announced his news as if it were a good thing.

"They are already saying that the whole thing was a hoax, I just caught the tail end of the news on KOA," he told them.

Jake Herron grimaced and shook his head. "Maybe it was me who failed," he told the priest. "Maybe it was because I couldn't think of what would be a miracle to me." He slid his hand over Leslie's, slowly tracing the outline of her fingers.

Chavez couldn't help but notice the couple's eyes meet, their faces soften. Jake held both hands up. "Hey, it's no biggie. I feel great, really. Best I've felt in a long time. But I didn't see any miracle and I figure if something was supposed to happen but didn't because I didn't do something I was supposed to do."

Chavez chuckled. "Do you really think, my son, that you could stop a miracle if God meant it to happen?"

"So how do you explain it?" Jake said easily, leaning back in the booth. "Do you think that Peter Banks was lying all this time?"

Chavez sighed and looked Jake in the eye. "No, Jake, I don't."

"Excuse me," Leslie said, "I'm off to the ladies room. Jake, maybe you can introduce me to this 'religious person' when I get back." There was a twinkle in her eye.

"Oops," Herron said as he watched her walk away. "I guess I'm not only a miracle-spoiler, but rude, too."

Chavez smiled. "Just slow on the uptake," he said.

"Slow, huh?"

"I think so, yes," the priest answered with a smile.

"So you don't think it was a hoax?"

"No, I don't."

"And yet, the nurse won't talk about what happened to her, and no one saw a thing. And I can't talk about what happened to me, because, frankly, not a goddammed thing happened to me," Jake saw the priest wince at the blasphemy and felt instantly sorry. "Excuse me, Father, it's been a long day."

"Jake, do you remember our conversation this morning?"

Jake studied the priest's mustache for a moment and nodded. "Yeah, and I'm no further along than I was then."

"Oh really?" asked the priest, and then, with his voice lowered and his eyes on the figure now walking back to the table he added, "you don't look so lonely anymore."

Jake Herron felt all the blood drain out of his face.

"Mysterious ways, Jake. He works in mysterious ways." Chavez, picked up his chopsticks and practiced with them. "It's a pleasure to meet you," he said, turning to Leslie Brimhall. "My name is Father Gilbert Chavez."

Peter and Vivienne huddled in the corner of the lobby at the Clay Hotel, sitting on a damask love seat, hoping Gail Abernathy would show up and take them somewhere safe.

At first, Peter thought it was sort of exciting. He hadn't left the hotel room in three days, so the feeling of simply walking out into the hallway and then down the elevator was freeing. Vivienne hadn't stopped for anything, not even what was sure to be a fight with Edward to get him to join them. No, she thought, the important thing was to get Peter to safety, and fast. Leaving his father behind made it only that much more of an adventure to Peter.

Vivienne was not nearly as happy about the situation. The man on the phone had frightened her, really frightened her. The voice, with its knowledge of her room number, its promise of violence, had cut through the fog that had dominated her mind and her maternal instinct, for the past week. Gone were thoughts of hair, nicotine, and whatever else had possessed her since Ricardo Shock had made his first fated phone call. Now all she wanted to do was go home, tuck Peter neatly into his bed, and bar all the doors.

But she was forced to sit here in the open, in a vast, vaulted room filled with strangers, and wait. "Peter, I'm sorry," she told her son, pulling him closer with both of her arms.

"Sorry about what, Mom?" Peter had been concentrating on not appearing too pleased about the situation, and now suddenly he shifted that attention to his mother. What could she be apologizing for? He hadn't a clue.

"I'm sorry about not being there for you, during this week. About being so wrapped up in my own thoughts. And now, now all this—I don't know how you're being so brave—"

Peter wrenched his head around so that he could see his mother's face, and then was sorry he had. She was all folded up, her eyes squinting, her mouth at a tilt. It looked painful.

"Really, Mom, I'm fine," he said quickly, hoping her face would return to normal. "Everything's going to be fine."

Vivienne let out a long, steadying breath. "I wish I could believe you, Peter."

Her son smiled. "That seems to be everyone's problem," he said.

Peter Banks would all but disappear from the collective public's mind, as fast as any other less-than-promised news event. Like a delayed execution or millennium bug that wasn't. Only the media would hold grudges for what they saw as not delivered.

In the weeks to come, as Peter turned twelve-and-a-half and then twelve-and-three-quarters, and when Vivienne was released from a long stay at the very private and very expensive psychiatric nursing home where she recuperated from her stressful experience, Peter would get infrequent reminders that there were those who still believed in him or in something they felt he represented.

"Bow to the prophet," a grizzled man would say, sinking to his knees on the sidewalk outside of Peter's new school, six months later.

"Please, please, I have cancer," a middle-aged woman would tell him in the middle of a shopping mall just around Christmas, placing her hands on his head, as if it had curative properties.

If Edward Banks had been around at times like these, Peter was certain, the encounters would've turned violent and loud. But Edward Banks had little to do with his son or his wife, after Norway and Simmons canceled his book contract in the wake of reports of "non-events," "hoaxes," and "recalcitrant witnesses."

The divorce took a matter of years, but the actual split was quite abrupt. It had occurred when Peter and Vivienne left the hotel room. But Vivienne couldn't know any of this yet, sitting as she was on the love seat, clutching her son, trying to figure out what a crazed lunatic would look like. When Edward finally found them in their corner of the lobby, shoving his way over to them, she figured they'd been saved. "Did you get him, Edward? The killer? Did you get him?"

In a perfect world, before he replayed the tape in his head and understood that that was not how it was meant to be, his mother would've been swept into his father's arms, and Edward would've assured them the danger was over. Then the three of them would have gone home, as a family. That's not what happened.

"For God's sake, Vivienne! There is no killer! And if you really thought there was, why did you leave me in the room, knowing he was on the way?"

Vivienne stuttered in reply. "Well, I thought—I thought I should get Peter to safety as soon as poss—"

"And not me, is that it? It doesn't matter what happens to me!" roared Edward Banks, drawing perturbed looks from the desk clerks on the other side of the room.

"Well, Edward, you—you were busy—"

"I was busy, or you just hoped someone would knock me off?"

"Edward, Edward, I wasn't thinking—"

Then Peter asked one of his very precise questions. "How do you know there's no killer, Dad? How did you know about the death threat in the first place? Mom got the call."

Edward stared at his son. Vivienne was silent. Peter barely drew a breath. "It was you?" he asked, confused.

"For the book, son. For the book. It needs a little more action."

Vivienne felt her mind finally fall off the edge of the cliff over which it had been hovering. Her shoulders slumped, her perfect posture lost.

Peter Banks felt his mother's shift and then a feeling of sadness drenched him, as if he had been waiting for a lawn sprinkler to make its rounds, and then it had. He prayed hard that Gail Abernathy would come and take him and his mother away, so they wouldn't have to look at this man before them. It was a prayer that was only half answered, for at that moment, Gail Abernathy was still leaning against a telephone pole on 12th and Lincoln, in front of a "lost dog" flyer. Gus was at her side, calmly panting in the sun.

"Mr. Banks," a voice said and Edward Banks turned around with a flustered look.

"Mr. *Peter* Banks," the clerk continued. And Peter looked up, surprised, because no one called a twelve-year-old "Mister." A desk clerk smiled at him. "Sir, there is a phone call for you." Peter nodded dumbly at the man and followed him to the desk, where he picked up the white courtesy phone.

"This is Peter," he said, hoping it would be Gail. It wasn't.

"Peter, this is Sherry Anderson," and Peter had to blink a few times to figure out that yes, this was one of the names of the Witnesses.

"I want to thank you, Peter," she said.

"How did you know where I was?" Peter asked.

Sherry smiled on her end of the phone. "The *Sentinel* told me where Gail was, some kid there knew. So I just figured she was with you. I wanted so much to thank you—"

"Did the miracle happen?" Peter asked, interrupting.

Sherry leaned back in her office chair, fingering the note. "I think it did," she started, unfolding the paper before her and looking at the writing there, Steven's writing. The note the police had never known existed. The one he had left for his girlfriend at the time. The note Sherry had imagined to have been all about her.

"That's what counts," Peter said, interrupting a third time.

"Don't you want to know what it was?" Sherry asked, slightly exasperated.

"Oh no," the little boy said evenly. Then he hung up.

Jake, for his part, felt much like the renowned Triple D. He had finally seen it when Father Chavez had pointed it out, but he had been feeling it ever since Leslie Brimhall told him she wanted Kung Pao chicken. It was both complicated and simple. And he was so grateful that it had happened to him.

But none of it was making the media happy.

Lincoln Fraser stood in the middle of the newsroom and tried to find someone he hadn't shouted at yet. Carmen Riddle was busy sobbing over her computer keyboard, trying to write a fifteen-inch story about what hadn't happened at Miranda Davis' office that afternoon. The only problem was, when she finally reached Jake Herron on his cell phone at ten minutes to six, the man had insisted a miracle had occurred after all, but it turned out to be something he wasn't inclined to discuss.

"I was the Witness. So it registered for me," he said.

"So you saw something that no one else did?" Carmen tried to keep her voice somewhat civil and failed totally.

"Call it a feeling," Herron said.

"A feeling," Carmen echoed back. "What do you mean, a feeling?" Herron hung up.

At the other end of the newsroom, Paul Hull was hunched over his own keyboard, trying to piece together his story about the nurse who had saved an infant and then refused to talk about her own experience with a miracle, but also refused to say it didn't happen.

"Either it did happen or it didn't," Fraser finally screamed into the general vicinity of the city desk, spraying at least three reporters with spit. "You can't have it both ways. And," Fraser added, "someone find me that goddamn sorry excuse for a reporter Abernathy so I can fire her to her face!"

The sun was setting when Gail finally stroked the sign on the telephone pole one last time. Looking down at Gus, she smiled at his eager face. *It is such a small thing,* she thought. And yet, just the small sign that maybe she wasn't totally wrong about everything after all—this, this was big. Not *news,* but big.

"Jesus, Gus, what time is it?" she asked her companion in the fading light. The pointer wagged silently. She checked her watch. Either Peter was dead by now or still alive and out of danger. There was nothing she could do. She reached into her bag with her breath held and let it out slowly as she retrieved her cell phone. She dialed with stiff fingers. A woman's voice, somewhat elderly, answered, "Hello?"

"I'm Gail Abernathy," Gail said. "And I've got Gus."

Printed in the United States
95062LV00002BA/450/A

9 780978 945695